Blade of the Betrayer

Shadow of the Betrayer, Volume 1

Michael Calloway

Published by Michael Calloway, 2024.

BLADE OF THE BETRAYER

First edition. June 30, 2024.

Copyright © 2024 Michael Calloway.

ISBN: 979-8218452971

Written by Michael Calloway.

Dedicated to my family - Christine and Kristy.

On the Brink of Castelon

Meditation often soothed the soul - before battle. Prayer before righteous battle - gave succor later for men of firm conviction. Prayer. Hymns. Oaths - the rituals of Faith and the holy, true Communion. I was one of many men bearing arms - awaiting a final confession before attending the field with the rest of the cavalry. The air was thick with the scent of oil and steel as the chaplain moved among us, his voice a soothing balm against the clangor of armor being fastened and swords being

sharpened. Each man turned inward, reflecting on his life and the deeds that had led him to this day.

As I knelt there in prayer, my mind drifted back to Strossberg, the barley fields, golden stalks swaying as a storm ravaged the land - upturning fields. It was a memory from mere weeks ago when my father had summoned me. I had stood tall and proud in his study, the shelves lined with ancient tomes and the walls adorned with maps of the Valtorean Empire. Our Empire - that glorious, heady thing which each Valtorean - each Volkian, held close to his heart.

I could smell it now. The scent of pipe smoke had clung to the walls in my father's study. And in those dark days, the smell of despair was hanging in the air. I could remember now - my last parting words to my father.

"Kaelitz," he had said, his voice stern yet not unkind.

My father's face was lined and weathered, his hair more silver than the chestnut brown of my youth. He stood by the window, gazing at the sprawling estate - the deserted villages and the thunder outside.

"My son," he began, turning to face me fully. He clasped his hands behind his back, straightening his shoulders with visible effort. "There are matters we must discuss, unpleasant though they may be."

I nodded solemnly, steeling myself for ill tidings. "Of course, Father. What troubles you?"

A sigh escaped him, and he sank into the high-backed chair behind his desk, gesturing for me to sit as well. "Our family has held these lands for generations, Kaelitz. Tended them, nurtured them. But I'm afraid... I have not been as diligent a steward as my forebears." He grimaced, his gaze turning northward. My father's fingers drummed a slow rhythm on the polished mahogany of his desk. "The war effort demands much from us all. Grain, horses, men... Our stores dwindle, and our fields lay fallow."

"We've not the hands to work the earth as we ought. I'm sure you know." His voice was heavy, weighed down by an unseen burden, before he paused, seeming to gather his resolve. "So - I took loans. Loans from the Duke of Saxonia-Pomerdania." He pushed a letter in front of me - and I looked.

"The treasure fleet I invested in, - sent across the Citalantic Ocean to Valcaz-Cruz was lost." He grunted.

I stared at the letter, the Duke's seal staring at me accusingly. A sense of dread settled in my gut as I read the words, each striking like a physical blow. The Duke was calling in the loans, demanding payment in full. But it was clear from my father's ashen face that we did not have the means to satisfy the debt.

"What will happen, Father?" I asked, my voice sounding distant to my ears. "If we cannot pay?"

He closed his eyes, his shoulders sagging as if under a great weight. "The Duke has the right to seize our lands and holdings as recompense. The estate, the fields, the villages...all of it will pass into his hands."

I shook my head in disbelief, rage, and despair. Our ancestral home was lost, and our people were abandoned to an uncertain fate. It was unthinkable. "There must be something we can do to forestall this!"

My father looked at me then, a deep sorrow etched into the lines of his face. "I fear there is only one path left to us, my son. To you." He pushed another document across the desk, the parchment adorned with the Duke's crest. "In lieu of payment, the Duke has offered to forgive a portion of the debt...if you enter into his service. Into the Imperial Army."

My heart seized in my chest as understanding dawned, and I looked up at my father, my eyes widening in shock as the implication of his words sunk in. The Duke of Saxonia-Pomerdania... Even the mere thought of the man sent a shiver down my spine. I had heard tales of him since I was a child, whispered stories passed down through generations of my family.

The Duke was a formidable figure, a man whose cruelty was matched only by his cunning. He was considered ancient, his white hair and weathered face bearing the marks of countless battles and intrigues. But his eyes haunted the stories - one a piercing blue, the other hidden beneath a black eye patch, a testament to some long-forgotten war.

I had seen him once, years ago, when he had deigned to visit our estate. I remembered how he had looked at my father, a sneer twisting his thin lips as if he had found our family's existence distasteful. His one good eye had roamed over our lands with a calculating gaze as if he were already plotting how to wrest them from our grasp.

And now, he had found his chance. The weight of my father's revelation settled heavily on my shoulders as I stared at the parchment before me. To enter into the Duke's service, to march under his banner in the Imperial Army...

"Father, there must be another way," I said, my voice tight with barely suppressed anger. "The Reichskammergericht, the Imperial Court - surely they could overturn this, force the Duke to grant us more time to pay."

My father sighed heavily, shaking his head. "You know as well as I do that the courts move slowly, Kaelitz. By the time they reached a decision... It would have been too late. The lands already seized - there would be nothing left for you, even in the unlikely chance you succeed, my son." He stated before he looked at me, standing up.

"Your grandfather served. It is a chance to make a fortune - frankly, less risky than heading to the New World."

My father stood up and walked around the desk beside me, placing a weathered hand on my shoulder. "Kaelitz, my son, I know this is not the path you would have chosen. But we must think of our family and our legacy. The Duke's offer, while distasteful, maybe our only chance to save what we have left."

I shook my head vehemently, shrugging off his hand as I faced him. "No, father. I cannot - I will not - serve under that man. The mere thought of it sickens me. Have you forgotten the stories? The whispers of his cruelty, his treachery? I would sooner die than march under his banner!"

My father's face hardened, his eyes flashing with anger and desperation. "You speak of honor, young Kaelitz, but where is the honor in letting our family fall to ruin? In seeing our lands, our very name, stripped away and forgotten? Is your pride worth more than that?"

I met his gaze unflinchingly, my jaw set with stubborn resolve. "It is not pride, father. It is the principle. I am a Von Ardent, and we do not bow to such a man, no matter the cost. If I must serve, let it be in the Imperial Army proper!"

My father's brow furrowed, eyes narrowing as he considered my words. The silence hung heavy between us, broken only by the crackling of the fire in the hearth. Finally, he spoke, his voice low and measured.

"The Imperial Army proper, you say? And how do you propose to secure such a position? With what influence? With what connections?" He said. "You would leave our lands barren - our property seized."

I paused, considering his words. He was right, of course. But there had to be another path that did not lead to servitude under a cruel and dishonorable lord.

I turned to face my father fully, my voice steady with conviction. "Father, there is more to life than lands and titles. More even than the Von Ardent name. There is honor, tradition, and glory. The very principles upon which the Holy Empire was founded."

I gestured to the portraits lining the study's walls, the stern faces of our ancestors seeming to watch us from across the centuries. "These men, our forefathers, did not measure their worth in acres and crowns. They stood for something greater. They fought and bled and died for the Empire, for the ideals it represents. How can I do any less?"

My father's expression softened, and there was a glimmer of understanding in his eyes. "You speak of the old ways, of a time when a man's word was his bond, and honor was valued above gold. But those days are fading. The world is changing, and we must change with it or be left behind."

I shook my head, unwilling to accept defeat. I turned around, anger in my voice.

"I will go to the capital," I said, my voice steady despite the fear churning in my gut. "I will petition the Emperor himself if I must. Surely, he will see the injustice of the Duke's actions, the unfairness of his demands."

My father let out a humorless chuckle, shaking his head. "The Emperor, Kaelitz? Do you think he will concern himself with the plight of one minor noble family? He has an empire to run and wars to wage. Our troubles are beneath his notice."

I clenched my fists, frustration boiling up inside me. "Then I will make him notice! I will not let our family, our legacy, be destroyed by the machinations of one cruel man. I will find a way, Father. I swear it."

My father looked at me for a long moment, his expression unreadable. Then he sighed.

"You have heart, son," he said, his voice tinged with pride and resignation. "But heart alone will not save our family. Von Löwe is a powerful man with deep connections in the capital. To defy him is to court ruin."

I stepped forward, my gaze intense. "Then let ruin come if that is the price of honor. I will not bend the knee to a tyrant no matter how high he sits. The Von Ardents have served the Empire faithfully for generations. Surely, that must count for something."

My father's face reddened, his temper flaring. "It counts for nothing in the face of raw power! Do you think the Duke cares for our history and our loyalty? He sees only what he can take, what he can control."

He slammed his fist on the heavy mahogany desk, rattling the ink pot and quills. "Damn it, Kaelitz, I am trying to protect you! To protect our family! Why can you not see that? You are my only heir - my only son."

I could see the desperation in my father's eyes, the weight of generations pressing down upon him. But I could not yield, not on this. My honor, my very soul, demanded that I stand firm.

My father's shoulders slumped, the fight draining out of him as he realized the futility of his arguments. He looked older in that moment, the lines of care and worry etched deep into his face.

"Very well," he said, his voice heavy with resignation. "If you are determined to walk this path, I will not stand in your way. But know that you go with a heavy heart and that the consequences will be yours."

I nodded, a lump forming in my throat. "I understand, father. And I am prepared to accept those consequences, whatever they may be."

My father turned away, gazing out the window at the rolling hills of our estate. The golden light of late afternoon bathed the landscape in a warm glow, but there was no warmth in my father's eyes.

"Your mother's gardens," he said softly, almost to himself. "She loved them so. She tended them with her own hands, coaxing life and beauty from the soil. And now..."

His voice trailed off, and I saw his shoulders tremble slightly. I stepped forward, placing a hand on his arm in a gesture of comfort.

"What will you do, father?" I asked gently. "When the Duke's men come. When the estate is seized."

My father laughed, a harsh, bitter sound. "What can I do? I am an old man, Kaelitz. My fighting days are long behind me. Perhaps I will go to Vien." I felt a pang of guilt at leaving my father to face this alone. But I knew in my heart that I had to forge my path.

"I will write to you," I promised, my voice thick with emotion. "As often as I can. And I will find a way to restore our family's standing, to make the Von Ardent name one that is spoken with respect once more."

My father nodded, still not meeting my gaze. "I know you will, son. You have a fire in you, a determination that reminds me of your grandfather. He was a stubborn old goat, too."

Despite the moment's gravity, I felt a smile tug at the corners of my mouth. "I will take that as a compliment."

My father finally turned to face me, his eyes glistening with unshed tears. "It is. The highest compliment I can give." He clasped my shoulder, his grip firm. "So - you will join the Imperial Army?"

I nodded, not trusting myself to speak. Then, with a final squeeze of my father's shoulder, he looked at me.

"...Are you sure?" He asked - this time, not mentioning the estate. He gazed at me - with worry. "You are a smart man. I can write to a counting house - or perhaps, the Reichskammergericht, to take you as a-"

"I'm sure, Father."

My father sighed heavily, the lines on his face seeming to deepen. "Kaelitz, my son, I know your heart is set on this path. But I fear you do not fully grasp the challenges ahead."

He turned slowly to his desk, running a hand along the polished mahogany. "As junior nobility, our family's position is... Precarious. We have our title, yes, but little else. No great wealth, no powerful connections. In the Imperial Army, that will matter more than you realize."

Picking up a framed portrait of my grandfather in his military uniform, my father continued. "Your grandfather fought hard to earn his commission. He has won accolades in the Zephyran campaigns and the Crusades. But even with his accomplishments, he never rose above Colonel. The high command, the generalships - those are reserved for the old aristocracy. The Von Mühlenburgs, the Schwarzenfelds. The Von Löwe family."

He set the portrait down and fixed me with a sad gaze. "I do not say this to discourage you, Kaelitz. But I want you to have clear eyes about the road ahead. As a junior officer from a minor noble house, you must be twice as clever, twice as bold, twice as ruthless as your peers to even have a chance of advancement."

My father walked to the window, the fading sun casting his face in shadow. "The Imperial Army is not like the storybooks. There is no glory, no shining path." He said. "But so be it. Ride to Strossberg - and head straight to the recruitment grounds. Only speak to Commandant Barlow - he's a supervisor from the Imperial Army. He'll set you in the right way - perhaps, even get you a commission."

I nodded solemnly, my resolve hardening like tempered steel. "I understand, Father. I'll write. Soon."

He stood up - and, without another word, hugged me.

I blinked back to the present - to the makeshift church I was at - I hardly realized tears on my face were beginning to form. A craving for vengeance - for revenge. For glory.

Unlike home, we didn't have the luxury of confessional booths or ornate altars adorned with gilded icons of old saints where one could kneel and feel the comforting shadow of divinity. Here, our chapel was the open sky, our altar a makeshift crate of supplies, and our confessional the quiet corner behind the tents where whispers could be exchanged with the slight assurance of privacy.

The chaplain made his way down the line of soldiers, offering absolution and final blessings. When he came to me, I bowed my head and closed my eyes, trying to steady my nerves.

"Do you repent of your sins and ask for the Steel Lord's guidance?" the chaplain asked gently.

"I do," I replied, my voice barely above a whisper.

The chaplain clasped my shoulder. "Then - go with His blessing, and be unafraid," he said solemnly. It brought peace - despite having been told to me a thousand times. Today - I needed it more than ever. Today was the day history would be made in the fields of Castelon.

A man has little way of knowing if the battle he was heading into was a skirmish - or one of those battles written about centuries later. Castelon - Castelon was its own monster. As with war - Castelon Fields is many things to many men. What would occur there would scar men for the rest of their lives. It would change men - and perhaps, it was in this moment that the Savior decided the fate of our beloved Empire. But - what the Savior decided - was not for the hearts of men to know. We were obligated to our Emperor to be present on the battlefield - and to have faith that the Savior deemed our mission just. We had a force beyond measure with an army of fifty thousand troops from the Holy Valtorean Empire. It may have been the most significant military host gathered by the Empire in over forty years.

As the chaplain's words faded into the cold morning air, the handful of men around me began to mount their steeds. The beasts snorted and stamped, as restless as their riders, sensing the impending chaos that was to come. From our position, the view of the entire army was staggering—a sea of armored men, flags fluttering in the wind. The sound of metal clanking, horses neighing, and distant orders shouted in commanding tones created a terrifying and exhilarating cacophony.

Around me - were the faces of friends - comrades from the same town I hailed from. Among these comrades were a few fellow young nobles, fresh-faced and filled with the fiery zeal of youth; they were friends who shared the same untested dreams of glory and honor. Alaric, a young baron with eyes like storm clouds, rode beside me. His family crest—a rampant lion—was emblazoned proudly on his breastplate. Alaric's laughter often cut through the tension of our more sad moments, and now, as we prepared for what may be our defining fight, his joy seemed a vital shield against the growing dread.

"Kaelitz, good Lord. You look like you didn't sleep at all!" He grinned at me, his teeth flashing white against his tanned face. "Ready to carve our names into the annals of history?"

I managed a strained smile, tightening my grip on the reins of my steed. "As ready as one can be for such things," I stated. "You kept your powder dry, right?"

"Of course!" He grinned - checking his bandolier - half-a-dozen wheel-lock pistols of satisfactory quality. "And what about you?" Alaric's question hung in the air momentarily as I adjusted my gear, ensuring each piece was secure. My saber was sheathed at my side, the edge honed to a razor's edge, and my pistols loaded and ready within easy reach. "All set," I responded with a nod, pushing aside the gnawing fear that tried to seep into my bones.

The sound of horns suddenly pierced the morning haze, deep and resonant, signaling the time had come. Our conversation ended abruptly as duty called us to focus. We fell into formation, our horses lining up shoulder to shoulder as the army slowly marched toward the battleground.

My eyes gazed forward - towards the halberdier columns marching grimly ahead of us. One could tell each regiment's sheer expertise - the veterans from the chaff, simply by the way they held formation and their step. The dirt - that hushed fatalism they spoke in. Few men assigned to halberdier duty lived long - a constant, dimmed youth was the trademark of an Imperial halberdier in these days, the continual weariness in their eyes as they trundled past. Drums and fluttering flags marked their steady advance, the banners emblazoned with the Imperial Eagle, soaring above all - and then, the second banner - the just-as-sacred regimental banner that a man would die to protect.

Those lovely regimental and provincial banners are fluttering. The heraldic wolf of Volkia fluttered next to the stoic bear of Stadtenmark. Each of those smaller banners, a symbol of pride for those men, stitched into the fabric with the care of a mother's love for her child - sent off away to the front. No small wonder these men would die for such symbols, for they were not merely dyed cloth - they were something far more in the hearts of men.

Our Empire's pride was in the halberdiers as they marched onward in those columns, followed by arquebusiers and demi-cannons. Each of these regiments was a combination formed in the style of the Castelorians - a mixture of halberds, cannoneers, and arquebusiers. A formation widely adopted throughout Aurisca for nearly fifty years, that of a Terjico - a wonderous thing to behold, each column holding its unique character and discipline - though, too often, they all died the same bloody way.

Then - there was us. Those lesser nobles - adorned in simple plate and equipped with pistols and cavalry swords, were assembled at the front, alongside plate-armored knights towards our flanks. My comrades were nervous but energetic as I checked my sides. The knights accompanying us were grim, clad in thick, bullet-resistant plate armor, their visors down and expressions unreadable, yet their posture spoke of unyielding resolve. They sat astride massive warhorses, bred for battle and towering over our lighter mounts. This was a cavalry that could break an enemy line with sheer force, provided they reached the right point at the right time.

Then - the horn called out - our steady trot, turning into a steady run; as we moved closer to the fields of Castelon, the terrain began to reveal its challenges—the ground became undulating with shallow dips and rises, perfect for maneuvering but treacherous for those unfamiliar with its subtle tricks. Perhaps - this should have been the first clue to what lay ahead, as it was just enough to disrupt our momentum - but the first sight of the enemy drove away our thoughts as we saw our foe; they were arrayed across the opposite ridge, a dark mass bristling with pikes and banners of their own, an ominous mirror to our forces.

"There they are - the bastards!" Alaric said - having caught up beside me. "Eclairean dogs." He spat out, and his eyes narrowed, scanning their formation as if trying to decipher a challenging puzzle. "Look at how they stand, brazen, as if the very soil of Castelon belongs to them." His hand instinctively went to one of his pistols, fingers brushing against the cold metal in anticipation.

"We'll teach them otherwise," I shouted back, feeling the weight of my sword at my side. The echo of clashing wills and steel seemed inevitable - an adrenaline building up, with drumbeats - a symphony that rose in intensity as we rode forward.

"At the double-quick!" shouted an officer just ahead of us, a few cheers rising from the throats of soldiers, a ripple of determination spreading through our ranks. The sound of hundreds of hooves thundering across the earth was like the roar of an oncoming storm as we parted away from the infantry columns, rushing ahead and screening them.

My doubts were steady. Mounting perhaps - as I saw our foe closing in - our first opponent was the famed Eclairean cavalry, steeped in equestrian traditions, perhaps more so than our own. They faced us from across the fields in their great masses. They had sent out a light cavalry regiment to prevent us - the duty of us demi-lancers would typically be to avoid them as well - so the main body of the cavalry could continue, unhindered - but, rather than that we surged towards them - impetuous, focused on the kill - both the heavy cavalry and light cavalry, mixing in as one significant charge.

Today, it was dictated that one grandiose charge in a sweeping maneuver would drive our foe from the field, like in so many battles before.

The Eclairean breastplates and tall, helmeted plumes gleamed in the morning sun, and their lances were held at the ready. I knew their reputation - fierce, nimble riders who could strike fast and then melt away before a counterattack could be mustered. We were armored like tanks in comparison; our horses were bred for power and stamina to withstand the crush of a massed charge.

"Stay steady, Kaelitz!" Alaric's voice cut through the chaos, his eyes glinting fiercely beneath his plumed helmet from ages past as he drew his pistol. I pulled mine - as we eyed them charging towards us, their formation a stark, disciplined line, the tips of their lances aimed with lethal precision. The ground beneath us seemed to tremble with the collective thunder of our charging steeds, heralding the collision that would soon unfold - were it not for the fact they broke away - splitting in two.

On our left - a few whizzing bullets smashing into the dirt as they discharged a handful of carbines - a skirmishing force, while another body of Eclairean cavalry circled to the right side - sunlight glinting off their lances.

While - fundamentally, even a novice could see them preparing for a hammer-and-anvil, preparing to dictate the momentum of the entire battle... It was simply too late to maneuver for our bulky force - and our ranks had no cohesion in command. It was there that the Eclaireans had us beat.

So - here, the youth of Valtor charged headfirst - perhaps, one would have heard the old knights slowing down and wheeling back - but we were drawn in, swept up in the enthusiasm of battle. Our horses' hooves kicked up clods of earth as we pressed toward the enemy.

"Remember the Emperor!" We bellowed, hefting the familiar banner high above our regiment - a cry from many others shouting out in our charge - as the Eclairean's skirmishers split away - doubling back at a gallop, though a few of them were too slow to stop our reckless charge - the sheer momentum catching them.

Our two formations crashed into one another like two unstoppable forces of nature, the world exploding into a cacophony of steel on steel for those too slow. Horses screaming as they trampled across the bloody field, lances shattering, and men falling from their steeds—to be trampled underfoot or skewered—while pistoleers fired into the chaos. Gunpowder smoke filled the air, mixing with the dust kicked up by the horses, creating a gray mist that obscured vision and made breathing difficult.

My blade missed its mark as the Eclairean I had aimed for deftly guided his horse aside, dodging narrowly as he bucked his horse to go even faster - and we passed each other in a thunderous blur, and I struggled to bring my mount back under control. All around me, the charge had met in a vortex of violence. Cavalrymen on both sides traded crushing blows, lances piercing armor, or glancing off steel plate. Pistols and sabers rang out as riders closed to the grand melee - the light cavalry we smashed into having been practically eviscerated in a single, bloody moment - blood seeping into the ground of horse and man alike, a cascade of gore that marked the field.

Here - in the chaos of melee, I was trapped. I wheeled my horse about, - occasionally trading blows with a few overwhelmed stragglers. It was only a few seconds into this chaos that I glanced out past the smoke and the dirt clouds hanging low to the ground - that flanking regiment of cavalry of Eclaireans coming in - circling us to smash us from our rear - as cannons rung out from the Eclairean's side.

Cannonballs ripped through our ranks, sending men and horses flying in eruptions of blood and gore. Screams of the dying filled the air as our melee faltered in the face of the bombardment. Just ahead of me - the outstanding Graf Heinrich bellowing orders, trying to rally us, even as his black armor was splattered with crimson. The thunderous barrage threw the charge into chaos as we frantically tried to reform and meet this new threat - but then, out of the smoke, the Eclairean cavalry appeared, fresh and eager for battle compared to our disorganized troops - and a horrific melee occurred - with us on the receiving end.

The Eclairean cavalry smashed into our disjointed ranks with terrifying speed, their lighter horses far nimbler than our destriers. All around me, the battle dissolved into utter chaos as men screamed and died. Lancers found themselves shot point-blank by these light cavalrymen or slaughtered by round shot. All around me, the proud men of the Empire were being cut down and trampled into the bloody mud. The Eclairean tactics had shattered our vaunted charge, and now - it was little more than butcher's work, as I fought - and fought.

My thoughts in this disorienting melee were frenzied, and I was scrambling for survival more than victory. Thoughts of strategy or command had dissolved into a primal urge to live through the onslaught. I parried a thrust from an Eclairean saber, feeling the shock run up my arm as our blades met with an almost lost clang amidst the tremendous tumult.

In this dire moment, my mind flickered back to the old barracks tales of old wars and the legendary heroes who turned the tide single-handedly. But here, surrounded by the blood-soaked earth and dying cries, such tales seemed distant fantasies. Thoughts ran through me - would we die here, in this forsaken field? What had happened to the great knights who rode behind us?

When such thoughts run through your head - the battle is already over. Casting a glimpse from behind - the Valtorean knights stood in reserve, having refused to be drawn in - the sole knight among us was the Graf - clad in bulky, black plate armor - the odd bullet pinging off his enchanted armor as if swatted by an invisible hand. Yet even magical armor has its limits, and I saw him falter under a particularly fierce assault by two Eclairean riders. Their lances had been discarded, now relying on swords that flashed faster than the eye could follow.

Graf Heinrich managed to unhorse one with a mighty blow of his broadsword, but the other's blade found a chink beneath his arm. The great knight grunted a rare display of pain before retaliating with a savage cut that sent the Eclairean sprawling into the mud. In a rare realization, I noticed where I was in this chaos. Perhaps through Providence and sheer fate - I was lucky enough to find myself on the flank, on the opposite end of Eclairean's bloody momentum - yet, it provided hardly any relief - cannonballs ripped through horse and man alike, the only thought coming to my mind was a glance back over at our lines - what could we do here?

And worst of all - the steady drums of the Eclairean foot marched steadily closer, their royal banner raised high, perhaps higher than our

Imperial Eagle that lay on the ground, trampled with blood and lost in the chaos.

Then - a voice cut through the chaos. "Retreat! Fall back - damn you all!"

I didn't need more encouragement - I turned, with what others remained on the flank - and I bucked my horse onward, fleeing the horrific slaughter. I felt the gaze of each man ahead of me - each halberdier and officer watching what would have been a glorious charge to break the back of the skirmishers - fail catastrophically. We left our standard in the mud and blood there - and as we fled - we were slowly followed by those skirmishers - ensuring our retreat back as the odd bullet whizzed past us - the bizarre horse keeling over as we rode for safety.

We filed back - behind our lines, seeking safety, as the battle raged onward. Out of the six hundred demi-lancers, perhaps only a hundred remained as we reassembled ourselves. Shame filled our hearts as we watched the battle unfold - and then, I looked around.

Alaric - was nowhere to be seen, still stuck in the fray or worse. My heart hammered as I scanned the chaotic landscape, desperately hoping for a sign of him amid the carnage of the battlefield. He was not only my comrade but my closest friend since childhood, his family crest almost as familiar to me as my own - and then...

"You did well today." A voice rang out. That of Graf Heinrich - my commander, as I turned back. The scarred visage of him glancing over at me, blood that coated that black plate armor belonging to someone. His helm was lifted upward - a middle-aged man with a blond beard and a tired, worn-looking face. "Though - I suppose the same cannot be said for the rose of Valtorean nobility." He scowled. "Had the knights simply followed our orders - we would have smashed through."

Heavy with fatigue and frustration, his eyes shifted from my face back to the battlefield, where the sounds of fighting still raged fiercely. "But what's done is done. We must regroup and prepare for what comes next..."

"What about us?" I asked. "The demi-lancers?"

The Graf sighed, his gaze drifting over the remnants of our once proud unit. "Exhausted, broken men will not win the battle." He shifted his weight, the armor creaking slightly as he moved. "We will take stock of who remains, rearm, and wait for a chance to counterattack or reinforce another line. But likely - there will be no more."

"I... I see." I stated. A feeling of cravenness overwhelmed me despite how I tried to push it down. Somewhere out there - on the field was Alaric - and I had left him.

Fresh troops were marching up to plug the gap our retreat had opened in the line. Halberdiers and pikemen, led under the command of Lord Commander Duclaire, were interspersed with companies of arquebusiers. They marched forward, coming up to where we had been slaughtered, their faces set in grim determination. They were still out of range, but it was a matter of time before they entered the range of the Eclairean guns.

And yet - I still stood there, watching, alongside a dozen other boys who couldn't stop but to watch other men do their task for them. The Graf - noticing our spirits rising, came up beside us.

"You will have your chance again before this war is through," he declared. "Let the failure temper you like fine steel. The next time - we will triumph. We will have vengeance - for our Emperor. But - pray, do not do anything foolish in despair. It is not just your lives at stake, but the very fate of the Empire." His words, meant to steel our spirits, hung heavy in the air as we watched lines of troops march toward imminent danger. The men's armor glinted under the wan sunlight that struggled through the smoke-filled sky, a silent testament to hope and impending doom.

Other men - perhaps, would have been satisfied with being in the rear, having already bloodied themselves. But I wasn't - I had run, simply waiting for the moment to present itself in our first action. A call in my blood - as I looked over the fields of men marching forward. I was unharmed - miraculously. But - how could I go back - knowing full well I hadn't even drawn blood? I would be labeled a coward - a craven, coming back home.

Lord, protect me if I must tell Alaric's family I ran and left him there.

There was only one thing left I could do - the honorable thing, the foolish thing. I grabbed my horse's bridle - forcing the weary beast towards the front.

"Boy! Stop!" The Graf shouted - trying to stop me, as I ran forward. I didn't dare look back - for fear of what I might see in his eyes—disappointment or anger, perhaps both. But my mind was set; the fire of redemption burned too fiercely within me.

I made my way to the front - where a halberdier regiment was crossing a bridge stream, stoically marching under the fire of distant cannonballs as I rode up. The steady beat of drums - the Valtorean eagle fluttering as these men marched - the aged sergeant looked up at me - as I winced from the sound of cannonballs and bullets whizzing past us.

"Aw' come on lad. Ain't nothin' to be afraid of." He said. I stared at the sergeant - now noticing his eyepatch, feeling my face flush with embarrassment. "I'm not afraid," I lied unconvincingly.

The old soldier gave me a knowing look. "First battle, eh? There is no shame in it. We've all pissed ourselves the first time shot and shell flew around us." The crude words made me bristle, but I held my tongue. I was here to prove my courage, not argue with a grizzled veteran.

"Now, boy - you have orders for us?"

I shook my head. The sergeant - marching forward, glared at me.

"Then get off that damned horse, fore' someone gets you."

As if to punctuate his warning, a cannonball collided with the bridge ahead, sending stone and timbers flying. Men cried out as they were tossed like ragdolls. The column staggered, then continued its advance - despite the gore and death surrounding us. I quickly clamored off my horse - joining them in their regiment. My feet found uneasy footing among the cobblestones slick with rain and blood, the rhythmic marching of the regiment my only guide as I tried to keep pace. The air was thick with gun smoke and the harsh cries of men giving orders, their voices barely carrying over the sounds of explosions around us as I made my way to the front.

The sergeant glanced over at me - my saber drawn as I marched forward.

"You ever been with us halberdiers before? Tis' bloody work - not for a noble sop like you." He grinned - and I met his gaze with determination; today, I would prove my worth or die trying. "I may be a noble," I replied, my voice steady despite the cacophony around us, "but I am a man, first and foremost."

"That's the spirit, lad!" He clapped me on the back with a force that nearly sent me stumbling forward into the mud. But I steadied myself, gritted my teeth, and kept moving. The ground beneath our feet became increasingly treacherous, a mire of blood-soaked earth and dislodged stones that threatened to send us to our knees with every step.

The drums of the halberdiers kept beating as we kept a steady pace forward. I couldn't help but be amazed by the stoicism that presented itself around me. The odd man fell from a stray bullet or a slice of shrapnel, but the ranks closed up quick as anything, barely pausing in their relentless advance. The stench of black powder and blood mingled in the air, a foul perfume that seemed to define this hellscape, as the sergeant gazed over at me.

"Well, lad." The sergeant said. "Here it is in a nut'shell. You see those bastards?" He gestured to the enemy awaiting us - at the top of a slight hill. "It's your job to impale 'em before they impale you." The grizzled veteran laughed, his remaining eye twinkling with mirth at my expense. We were closing in for perhaps the bloodiest work for a man - spear wall against spear wall.

The drums stopped abruptly as we reached the base of the hill. Everything seemed to pause—a stillness before the storm. Then, a shout emerged from our front, "E're we go lads! Remember yer' oaths!" It rippled through our ranks like wildfire, and with it, we surged forward.

I gripped my saber firmly alongside the other men around me. The air was thick with gun smoke—a volley cutting down the first rank ahead of us as we climbed over their bodies, the screams of the wounded mingling with the battle cries of the living. My heart pounded in my chest, a drumbeat synchronous with the fervor of war that enveloped us. Each step up the muddy slope felt like wading through a nightmarish swamp, and each inch gained a small victory in itself.

Then - with a great roar - we lunged forward. The clash of steel - halberd against halberd, arquebusiers were firing - desperate screams - horrific noises. All around me, the battle raged at close quarters. Men cursed and spat and cried out as they killed and died. The din was deafening - steel rang against steel, firearms cracked, and officers bellowed commands. Underfoot the ground turned to sucking mud mixed with blood and worse.

The Eclaireans we faced - were formed similarly to us in formation. While tacticians and strategists could have argued over ratios - on that battlefield, as we closed in to kill each other - the simple fact came down to training.

The Eclaireans lacked Valtorean zeal - they were a medieval, backward people, relying more on their flashy cavalry - their infantry lacked the fire of conviction that bound ours together so well. But regardless - they held the high ground, backed by cannons. Bloody work was in abundance - as we scaled the hillside - slick with blood, men tripping - and dying, suffocating in the mud beneath us as we marched forward. I couldn't help but feel myself outarmed - a cavalry saber did little against a pike or halberd in the thick of such a melee. Yet, it was all I had, and I was determined to wield it with all the fury and resolve a desperate man could muster.

As we pushed them back - a colossal boom announced our front row's obliteration under the impact of a cannonade of grapeshot. Shrapnel hissed through the air like demonic whispers, finding flesh to tear and bone to shatter - narrowly missing me as I ducked, a sharp fragment grazing the side of my cheek. The metallic taste of blood filled my mouth; it mingled with the grit and gunpowder that hung in the air. For a moment, the world seemed to slow down, and every noise intensified—my heart pounding in my ears, the rasping breaths of dying men around me, as I stuck down for a second - glancing over.

To my side - was a fallen comrade, a young man like me, his lifeblood draining into the churned earth - his arm missing from the elbow down, a grotesque testament to the brutality of grapeshot. He tried to speak, his lips moving feebly, but no sound emerged save for a harsh gurgle. His eyes met mine, filled with pain and pleading. I knew I could do nothing for him but offer a silent prayer to the Savior, who I hoped might be watching over this forsaken field.

From seeing him, I knew it could have been me, and it might still be me - if we didn't take the hillside and silence those guns. Pushing forward - killing, was our only option. There was no retreat - no fallback - it was do or die.

The sergeant's screaming and cursing brought me back to the terrifying present. "Push, you sons of whores! Push!" he roared, his voice rising above the din of battle. I found strength I didn't know I possessed, trudging uphill.

The Eclaireans fought with desperate courage, their polearms jabbing and thrusting to hold us off. But we were an unstoppable tide, driven by fury and fueled by the need to survive as we moved uphill. Their wall of pikes broke, fleeing back and routing as we drove them from a field. In an instant, we had overrun them, the dead and dying lying around us—and yet, our work was far from over.

Ahead of us - ahead of the fleeing Eclaireans - were their arquebusiers - firing and supporting in volleys - their shots blocked by their retreating men. Our momentum carried us forward with the ferocity of a river bursting its banks, our lines reforming even as we pressed the advantage. The Eclaireans' disciplined volleys began to falter, their shots becoming erratic as panic overtook precision - the arquebusiers fleeing before our charge despite the mud and blood.

As relief filled us - I looked around. The rest of the line was fighting across the plain - few had been as lucky as us. Entire columns - smashed apart by cannon rounds, the dead and dying laying in great piles - the wounded walking back to our lines. Our victory on this flank - while critical, was only one piece in the brutal tapestry of battle - and half of the regiment had perished.

The sergeant—that aged warrior with his eye patch and scars—lay in the dirt and mud, like all the others. His breathing was ragged, and his remaining eye stared up at the smoke-filled sky. "Sergeant!" My voice was lost in the din, but he heard it somehow, his one good eye focusing on me with immense effort.

"Ah... You made it." he rasped, blood bubbling at the corner of his mouth. "S'pose you did well enough in my ranks." Surprisingly steady given the circumstances, his hand reached out to clasp my shoulder, leaving a slick print of red upon my armor.

Then - I heard it. A horn sounded in the distance – a call to fall back. My gaze darted toward where we had come from. And then back to the wounded sergeant. His grip on my shoulder tightened once before slackening completely.

"G'on," he whispered with a bloody grin. "Th' Savior be watchin' o'er me. His good eyes are on me now." He said - a hint of relief in him. As he growled at me, I struggled to break eye contact for a moment. "Move, boy - damn you!" The raspy urgency in his voice spurred me on, a mix of command and desperation that couldn't be ignored.

"Thank you, Sergeant," I murmured, joining the ragged ranks of the retreating regiment as we fell back from the hill we had bled - and killed on. The only thing harder than ascending it - was descending it. Ranks upon ranks of dead and dying lined the path, their anguished faces frozen in time, a ghastly gallery. As we trudged down, each step was haunted by the echoes of those we had left behind. The descent felt endless, each footfall a reminder of the lives extinguished on that blood-soaked hill - a sacred hill that we would all carry with us.

The end of the battle finally approached as I stumbled back with perhaps forty men. My fine, glistening plate turned dented and scarred - my face covered with soot, grime, and splattered blood as we ran.

And then - I saw it. Limp - on a horse, laying down with our old banner - was Alaric, gazing up at the sky. I pushed myself forward up to him - believing him to be dead, his eyes closed and face a mask of peacefulness amidst the chaos. But as I neared, his eyes flickered open, startlingly clear against the dirt that marred his face.

"You're alive," he murmured, his voice barely above a whisper, each word punctuated with pain.

"Thank the Lord," I replied, kneeling beside him - as I gazed back - a cry echoed across the field - the élan of men ignited as a frightful charge of rallying Eclaireans began towards our lines. I nearly fell onto my back - they sought to kill us all.

"The banner," he said urgently, nodding weakly toward the flag beside him. "Don't leave it here - don't you dare." He coughed as I grimaced.

"They'll kill you - the damned banner can wait," I protested, but even as the words left my lips, I knew they were futile. Alaric's eyes hardened, the steel in them sharpening.

"You stupid bastard," he spat, his voice gaining a shard of its old strength. "I'm as good as dead. My legs - they're broken. Take it - and go."

His hands clawed at the mud, trying to pull himself up, but the agony was too much; he collapsed back with a groan that tore at my heart. The sounds of the charging Eclaireans grew louder; their cries mingled with the clattering of steel and thundering hooves. Time was running out.

I grabbed the banner, its fabric heavy with blood and mud, and rose to my feet. Looking down at Alaric, I saw the resignation in his eyes—a warrior accepting his end, he didn't dare look me in the eyes - and I was glad for that, as I turned - and ran.

The odd bullet whizzed past us - but eventually, the Eclairean gave up their pursuit, rallying back to their camp as we made our way to our own. We were the battered remnants of a regiment that had numbered over three hundred at the start of the day. Now - we numbered perhaps fifty.

There were no cheers - when I returned with our standard banner.

Back in camp, I sat staring into the fire, unable to shake the sights and sounds from my mind. A veteran sergeant - another one of the halberdiers sat beside me. Silent understanding surrounded us.

"What's your name, lad?" he asked, his voice a low rumble after a few moments of silence.

"Kael," I replied dully.

The veteran nodded. "Good job."

It was a quiet exchange between us. We didn't say a word afterward - quietly brooding on our luck. Soon enough - I turned in, heading back to the noble quarters I belonged to.

In the coming days, I avoided Heinrich, dreading his reaction to my foolish charge into battle. But when he finally summoned me, his manner was almost fatherly.

"Reckless but brave," he pronounced. "You have potential if you can learn discipline. With proper training, you may make a fine knight." He said to me. But I still remember my answer to this day, facing him.

"...Is it not over?"

Heinrich's expression hardened. "War does not end so easily, boy. There will be other battles, other fields soaked red with blood. The conflict between Valtore and Eclaire will rage on. I give it another few summers before we fight again."

He said that - bitterly, as he turned away before glancing back.

"...I have put a good word or two about you to Lord-Commander Duclaire. He is to be sent to the borderlands - and you, along with it."

Heinrich's words hung heavy in the air, a mix of doom and opportunity bound together like chains. I swallowed hard; moving to the borderlands—a place of desolation and incessant skirmishes—was daunting and oddly thrilling.

"The Borderlands, sir?" I managed to say, my voice steady despite the turmoil inside.

"Yes, Kael. It's a harsh place but one where true warriors are forged. You will learn much under Duclaire's command. He is stern but fair. His leadership has turned many a raw recruit into a battle-hardened veteran."

I nodded, unsure if I was ready for such a drastic change. The fire of battle still burned within me, but our losses clouded my heart with doubt.

"You may leave now. Prepare yourself," Heinrich concluded, his tone final.

I quietly nodded.

"Yes, sir."

Echoes of the Borderlands

Over a week, as we journeyed past the heartland of our Empire and entered the rugged eastern frontier, silence hung heavy amongst us, punctuated only by the occasional clink of armor and the distant calls of wild birds. The lands to the east were fraught with uncertainty and whispers of dissent; it was said that the people there had not sworn allegiance to our Emperor, and their warriors were fierce and unyielding.

One evening, as the sun dipped below the horizon, casting long shadows over the earth, Lord-Commander Duclaire halted our march beside a brook. The men set about making camp with practiced efficiency, their movements almost reverent in the quiet of the twilight. It was here, by that gently murmuring brook, that Lord-Commander Duclaire finally addressed me directly.

Though as deep and commanding as the rolling thunder from a summer storm, his voice carried an unexpected warmth in it. "You've been rather quiet since we left Castelon," he began, his eyes searching mine for a hint of my inner thoughts. I shifted uncomfortably on the balls of my feet, feeling the weight of his gaze like a physical pressure against my chest.

"I am here to serve, my Lord," I replied, keeping my tone respectful and measured. The Lord-Commander nodded slowly as if assessing the sincerity of my words before he continued and sighed.

"Come, sit with me," he said, his voice resonating with a firm but weary timbre. He motioned to a fallen log near the water's edge, and I obeyed, my armor clinking softly as I moved. The Lord-Commander looked out over the water, his gaze distant as if reading the secrets of the ripples.

"You're a young man. You've seen things - haven't you? Terrible things." His words stirred a storm within me, unearthing memories I had buried deep under layers of duty and resolve. "Yes, my Lord," I confessed, the images of battle flashing before my eyes – the clash of steel, the cries of the fallen, the relentless march of death. "I have seen much that I wish I could forget."

Lord-Commander Duclaire turned his head slightly to look at me, his eyes reflecting the twilight as if harboring a sliver of the fading day. "That is the burden of those who serve," he said softly, his voice barely above the whisper of the brook. "Such - is the burden of men. You'll shake it off in time." He patted me on the shoulder, his touch reassuring yet heavy with the gravity of experience. "We march onward to our next campaign, in the east. Have you been to the frontier?"

"No, my Lord. Though, my grandfather told me a few stories of the Crusades." I stated.

"Ah." He stated, the Lord-Commander gazing out towards the forests and sighing. "How much do you know of history?" He said as I shrugged. While I might have been lesser nobility from an unremarkable village outside of Strossberg, I had never put much time into lessons of old. "Not enough, my Lord," I admitted, my eyes downcast.

Lord-Commander Duclaire nodded as if expecting this response. He reached into his cloak and pulled out a small, weathered book. With a thoughtful expression, he handed it to me. "It's a brief history. He was written by monks in the old monastery of Strassu. A great read. I read it when I was on campaign here a decade ago."

I blinked, a bit surprised.

"You fought against the Polanians?"

"Aye." He nodded. "Though, you could hardly call it a campaign. It was a partition. Polania had been a thorn in the Empire's side for generations. A backward land, much like the Kholodians. Yet - they fell easily. Now - we march out there to re-establish order."

"I see," I grumbled. "...When might this campaign be over?" I started - not wanting to voice my reluctance at going on campaigning. I had seen quite enough with the Eclaireans - witnessed sufficient. Home seemed ever sweeter —every day that passed.

Lord-Commander Duclaire gave a small, humorless chuckle, a sound that seemed to carry the weight of years. "That, young Kaelitz, is a question many a soldier asks. The truth is, it ends when it ends. The sand does not bind wars in an hourglass nor adhere to homesick men's desires."

He paused, his gaze turning back to the brook. The water shimmered with the last light of twilight, creating a tapestry of moving shadows and flickering silver.

"These conflicts, they're never truly over. We pacify, govern, and hope to see home again." He stated sorrowfully.

I remained silent, contemplating his insight. The brook babbled beside us, indifferent to the weight of human conflicts.

Duclaire continued, his voice now softer, almost reflective. "When I was about your age, I, too, was thrust into the clamor of war. Though it was so long ago, I hardly remember it. They were the olden days - of fighting with pike and crossbows. Such antiquated times."

He chuckled softly to himself, and then his expression sobered as we silently stared.

"Now, we do the fighting with arquebusies and halberds. Though - I reckon that'll change soon, too. Musketry is the way of the future. So I'm told, at least, by correspondence in the Imperial War Ministry." He chuckled.

"A terrifying thought," I said. "I would dread to fight with each man holding a musket. There would be nowhere safe unless you wore an enchanted plate."

"Very true." He stated, grinning. "I would hate to be in your boots when such a time comes. But meanwhile - I think - you'll do fine as a squire. Keep your head on your shoulders, and you may make it home." He smiled - as he patted me on the back and left me there on the stream.

At that river, the boundary marking the edge of Polania and Valtorea, a realization struck me - it would be a significant period before I would be home again.

Thoughts of my distant homeland tugged at my heart as twilight descended, nudging me back to my tent where the day's burdens lingered heavily, and seeking solace in the dim glow cast by a lone candle, I unearthed parchment, a quill, and an inkwell from within my belongings. The intention to update my father had lingered for too long and was unfulfilled. With a steadying breath, I immersed the quill into the inkwell, its tip hovering over the blank sheet with a slight tremor as I commenced penning down my sentiments.

Only - I simply could not. Instead, as I sat there, the feather quill quivered between my fingers like a leaf in the wind, betraying the turmoil within me. I could not do it - perhaps, once we arrived in Rega, I could bear to write again.

Our journey through Western Polania commenced in the warmth of late autumn, with the sun still high in the sky. As we moved further east, the greenery of the Polanians gradually gave way to the stark, barren landscapes of the borderlands. The change was slow and subtle, but as weeks turned into months, we found ourselves in a land that seemed perpetually locked in winter's cold embrace - the land of Baltiva.

For us just arriving in Baltiva, marching into the old city of Rega, we were put into winter quarters. The local nobility here were descended from old Valtorean nobles—known here as Baltors. Their stone castles, bleak and imposing, were perched atop rocky capes overlooking the harsh, frozen rivers that snaked through the landscape. Our winter quarters in the city of Rega were similarly bleak, constructed from dense, gray stone that seemed to absorb the chill from the air itself.

As we settled in, the stark reality of our situation became increasingly apparent. Though the Baltzers shared blood with us, they were distant and reserved. Their customs and manners were as cold as their climate, and it was clear that our presence was tolerated more out of necessity than welcome. Arguments between the Lord-Commander and the local nobles became a constant as we were settled into the merchant district's many inns - Duclaire buying rooms for us out of his pocket, a gesture that did not go unnoticed by the men. Tensions within the ranks began to surface, influenced by the bleak surroundings and the uneasy relations with our hosts.

"These bastards." One older veteran spat out. "Never grateful, they are. Always havin' us do the dirty work." His voice echoed down the dimly lit corridor of the inn, earning nods and murmurs of agreement from others huddled around a flickering hearth. The fireside provided little comfort against the pervasive cold that seeped through the thick stone walls, and the men's breaths hung visibly in the air, mingling with the smoke from their pipes.

"Aye. These Baltzers - hardly cousins of the Empire, eh?" Mumbled an arquebusier in the early stages of frostbite. His fingers were wrapped tightly around a cloth. "And here we are, marchin' our arses off to keep em' from being lynched."

Duclaire, hearing the grumbles, would stride into these gatherings with his usual commanding presence, attempting to quell the discontent with firm but fair words. "We'll be out of here soon enough, don't you all worry." he would state, standing tall amidst the weathered faces of his men. "We're here for the Empire - not for local politics."

One chilly evening, as the wind howled like a pack of wolves outside the sturdy walls of our inn, Duclaire summoned me to his private quarters — a modest room adorned only with the necessary trappings of military life and a few personal belongings that spoke more of duty than comfort.

He was seated at a small wooden table, over which a single candle flickered, casting long shadows across his weathered face. Maps and dispatches were spread out before him, every edge and corner weighed down with small stones to keep them from curling.

"Sit," he gestured to a stool across from him. As I took my place, I noticed the lines of fatigue etched deeply into his features.

"I've been reviewing these reports from the local scouts," Duclaire began, his finger tracing a line along a map that showed the rugged terrains of Baltiva extending into Lapsid territories. "There's unrest in the outer villages—raids, possibly by dissenters or perhaps even Kholodian infiltrators."

He paused, looking up to gauge my reaction. I remained silent, knowing my role was listening rather than speaking.

"We cannot ignore these threats," he continued, his voice firm yet weary. "It's unfortunate - but we cannot simply sit here in Rega while the Lapsids gather strength over the winter." His eyes narrowed slightly, reflecting the flickering of the candlelight as if mirroring the brewing storm outside and within. "Tomorrow," he said with a decisive tone, "we ride out to these villages at once."

"...Are you sure, sir? Is it truly that urgent?" I stated.

"It is." He mumbled. "The eyes of the Empire are upon us." He stated wearily, as I noticed a dispatch - our Emperor's holy coat of arms on it.

"It's damnable. It's stupid. I ought to have this letter burned; claim it never reached me." The Lord-Commander despaired. "But - there's a point to the Kaiser's... Handling of this. Were spring to come - and the Kholodians notice our... Ill-preparedness on the frontier is very good. They could seize the opportunity to push through and lay waste to both Baltiva and the surrounding regions. We must tighten our defenses and strike preemptively if we must. The Empire cannot afford a weakened frontier this winter."

He leaned back, his hands clasping together.

"You'll be dispatched to Northolt. This - is for the Magistrate there." He fished out a sealed letter. "Northolt is the largest of the villages - loyal to the Kaiser. But - keep your wits about you." He stated. "Take forty men - and keep an eye on the locals." I nodded, understanding the gravity of the task at hand. The room seemed to grow colder as we contemplated the weight of our orders—my mind was already racing with the logistics of the upcoming mission. "Understood, sir," I replied, my voice steady despite the swirling doubts.

Duclaire grimly nodded, his gaze shifting back to the maps before him. He brushed his fingers over one particular area marked with red flags. "I expect little resistance - compared to other fiefdoms. It will be good practice for you." He stated - as he went silent, looking over the map.

"I understand, sir."

"While you're here - finish that damned book already." He added suddenly, his eyes flicking up to meet mine with a hint of dry humor. "A commander should be well-read, after all."

I gave a small smile, acknowledging the jab, as I marched out and promised him - I'd finish by the time we reached Northolt.

Garrisoning Northolt was a simple task, after the grueling winter march, which took about three days. The town was settlers from the League - a mercantile town, that spoke our tongue and shared the Valtorean blood from generations past. The streets, lined with hardy timber and stone buildings, resembled the heartland of old Volkia, so far from home, and they were quite grateful to have our protection.

The magistrate - in particular, seemed relieved.

"Thank the Lord!" He stated - once he read the letter. "The Lithurs, the Lapsids - and the Teutons bandits. They've been nothing but trouble since the snow began. We feared the worst this winter, without the Empire's support." He seemed relieved. "The rest of our brethren - they went back East, to Volkia."

"I see," I stated - a bit more aware of the situation. "So - you're the last Volkian town here?"

"Aye. At least, in southern Lapsia." He replied, his voice carrying a mix of pride and weariness, as he leaned forward, his hands clasped in front of him on the table. "It's a hard place to hold, this close to the wildlands. We've had run-ins before... skirmishes and raids. But never anything we couldn't handle — but with you here..." He smiled. "Perhaps - things won't be so bad anymore. I doubt the Lapsids could stop you and your men."

Unfortunately - he was wrong. There was one thing that could stop us.

The winter.

A few days after we had taken position in the town - a harsh winter blew through the town. It was harsher and more unpredictable than the most ferocious Teuton warrior. The wind screamed night and day, twisting through the cobbled streets like a malevolent spirit. The bitter cold seeped through the very walls of the timber and stone buildings, and despite our ample preparations, morale among my men began to falter. Frostbite claimed the tips of our fingers and toes; the chill invaded our lungs, making every breath a struggle.

I spent those days making rounds, visiting the quarters where my men huddled around meager fires that could barely fight back against the pervasive cold.

During one particularly relentless storm, when visibility was reduced to mere inches beyond our faces, a cry rose from the eastern watchtower — a section particularly exposed to the wildlands. Straining against the howling wind, I made my way there, accompanied by a few of my most trusted soldiers. The watchman, barely discernible behind layers of frost-covered wool, pointed out into the white abyss.

"There! Through the storm!" he shouted, his voice barely carrying over the din of the wind.

Squinting into the snowy assault, I saw them — dark figures, moving as shadows against the blinding whiteness. They were numerous, a dark procession that seemed to merge with the storm itself, a living part of the tempest. "Who the bloody hell are they?!" I yelled, my heart pounding with both dread and resolve. The figures were distant yet unmistakable — the heavy fur cloaks, the small glint of armor...

They were our men.

We rushed them out of the cold into Northolt's sole tavern. Two dozen of our own men, from a border town perhaps a day's march away from ours, had been caught off guard by a Lapsid attack and forced to retreat through the merciless blizzard. Their faces were gaunt, their eyes hollow with the torment of both defeat and the unrelenting cold.

"We held as long as we could," their sergeant, a grizzled veteran named Harlitz, explained through chattering teeth. "But the Lapsids... They got to our granary. Burned it down." He shuddered. "They had us encircled for days, having us starved - hiding in the church..." He muttered under his breath, a haunted look crossing his features. "There's something else out there. We heard... sounds," he shuddered slightly, "not human sounds. Howls. The sounds of the Vuk, no doubt."

"...The... The Vuk?" One man mumbled, his features frozen. "Savior - protect us!" He declared, making a sign of protection. Harlitz nodded solemnly, his frostbitten fingers trembling as he clutched a mug of steaming brew, the warmth barely easing the deep chill of his bones.

I could only blink - the Vuk - a group of wolfmen that ruled over the Kholodian Tzardom. Monstrous men of fur and fang. They were well-known for their bloodlust and how they ruled their barbaric lands - enslaving the humans there into serfdom and their attempts at playing civilized - when, in reality, they were little more than bloodthirsty, oversized wolves.

But - it was odd. The Vuk, as barbaric as they were - practiced a faith with vague similarities to ours, and similarly despised the pagans of Baltiva.

"Are you sure?" I asked, my voice tinged with skepticism and fear. Harlitz met my gaze, his eyes reflecting the flickering firelight and a depth of sincerity that chilled me more than the howling wind outside.

"Yes, commander," he replied firmly. "We all heard them, every night. The chilling howls didn't sound like any wolf we've ever known. And the footprints, too large for any normal beast, encircled our home."

The room fell silent as his words sank in, each man processing the grim possibilities. If Harlitz's account was true, then the threat looming over us was far greater than mere bandits or harsh winters.

"Prepare yourselves," I announced to the room, standing up to assert some semblance of control over the rising panic. "We must fortify our position - I want a double watch throughout the night, just to be sure.

The men nodded grimly, acknowledging the necessity of readiness. I left them to their thoughts, a few sergeants taking over from there, and returned to my quarters to plan. The maps sprawled across my table seemed almost mocking in their depiction of clear lines and orderly towns, so remote from the chaos that swirled outside. Half of them were outdated - the other half simply wrong.

That night, as I pored over strategies and contingencies, a soft knock came at my door. It was Father Johann, the town's priest, his face etched with concern beneath his hood.

"Commander," he greeted me, his voice low. "May I have a word?"

"Of course, Father. Come in." I gestured towards a chair by the fire.

He sat, warming his hands before speaking. "I overheard talk of the Vuk," he started hesitantly. "Working with the Lapsids - correct?"

I nodded, the weight of our situation settling heavily upon my shoulders. "It seems so, Father. If what they say is true..."

The priest sighed, relaxing into his chair, shaking his head.

"Foolish. Simply foolish. The Vuk - they're an honorable sort, and honor the Savior. They would never willingly ally with the godless Lapsids. It must be something else. Something far more dark, and far more sinister." He stated, his voice fraught with worry.

I leaned in - intrigued, yet skeptical. "What do you mean..?"

Father Johann shifted uncomfortably in his chair, his aged hands intertwined tightly as if to draw strength from the gesture. "The Vuk," he began, his voice a blend of reverence and dread, "Are by far, the least of the problems in these lands. For one thing - the cults... Of the Great Foe." Father Johann's words hung heavy in the air, each syllable tinged with an ominous tone that seemed to make the very walls of the room draw closer, as if to listen. I shifted uncomfortably, feeling the weight of his gaze as much as his proclamation.

"The Great Foe," I echoed, sighing. "Out here, in the borderlands?"

"Quite. The furthest away from the scrutiny of the Holy Inquisition. While - their diabolic practice is foolish, misguided... Their blood magic, is quite real." Father Johann's voice took on a grave seriousness, his eyes narrowing with each word. "They've been biding their time, growing in strength and influence in the shadows. They may have swayed some of the Vuk to their cause, or perhaps the Lapsids serve them. These pagans would do anything, to force the Faith - and the Reich, out of their lands."

I let the implications of his words soak in, the gravity of the situation pulling me deeper into my chair.

"Savior..." I mumbled - making the sign of the Holy Icon, while Father Johann nodded solemnly, his eyes reflecting the flickering flames that cast ghostly shadows against the walls of my quarters, and I sighed.

'Father - as much as your tales of devilry excites the mind, and as God-fearing as I am, we need evidence before we act. I cannot rally the men on rumors and fears alone, and scare them into believing they fight the Great Foe."

Father Johann nodded, understanding the weight of military command resting on my shoulders. "Of course, of course. If I were in your boots, I would say the same thing. Anyone would." He said. "But - do me a favor. Surround the village with salt - and put up icons at every entrance. I assure you, these are not mere superstitions but age-old defenses against the darkness that lurks beyond our sight."

As I sighed, I looked at the priest, his earnestness palpable in the dim light of my quarters. Salt was expensive, though the icons were less so. Yet, in his eyes, I saw the sincere concern of a man who truly believed in the threats encroaching upon us from the shadows. "Very well, Father," I conceded reluctantly. I will see to it that your precautions are implemented."

As Father Johann thanked me and departed with a weary bow, my thoughts lingered on his dire warnings. The room suddenly felt colder, more isolated than before.

I longed for a return to Rega - but no such orders would come. Only for a short while.

That winter - hardship passed us by, after we put up the icons, and sprinked salt around the village. It seemed silly - but, reports came in of more and more villages being raided. Yet - we were too few to rally out. More and more report of the Vuk-like things attacking reached us.

The presence of Father Johann's sanctioned precautions seemed to lend a subtle form of protection, or perhaps it was the heightened vigilance of my men, spurred by the tales and fears of supernatural foes. Nevertheless, each night that winter we remained unassailed. Come early spring - we were the sole village left untouched by the chaos that had swept through the region. It was a fact that did not escape the notice of my superiors or the villagers.

As spring unfurled its greenery once more, I was summoned back to Rega - to attend back to Lord Duclaire. To say that the journey there was tense would be an understatement. The roads were fraught with rumors turned all too real, of the ravaged villages we passed—burnt homes and desecrated churches stood as grim sentinels to the devastation wrought upon them. My men, hardened by the winter's trials and the safety our measures had seemingly afforded us, moved with a grim determination.

Once in Rega, I couldn't help but find the contrast between our frontier hardships and the city's opulence was stark. The merchants - and the nobles acted as if the countryside wasn't desolate of life - that there weren't streams of refugees filing out, headed back to Valtorea, seeking refuge from the horrors that had plagued their lands.

I presented myself before Lord-Commander Duclaire, my report ready, detailing not just our survival but how it had been achieved. He seemed aged - in only three months, the old man I knew seemed even more aged. His eyes, once sharp as a falcon's, now carried the burden of countless sleepless nights; they flickered briefly with interest as I recounted our experiences, and he received my report with both skepticism and a touch of awe. He leafed through the pages, his fingers trembling slightly as he absorbed the account of our unusual defenses and the unscathed status of our village amidst widespread destruction.

"You've done well," he said slowly, his voice tinged with a mix of relief and incredulity. "This... approach of yours, Commander, it's unprecedented but seems effective." He paused, looking up at me with a sharp gaze. "We must consider deploying similar measures elsewhere if these... Circumstances continue."

The Lord-Commander leaned back, the creak of old leather a somber melody in the expansive, book-laden study. The walls, lined with the banners and symbols of our forefathers, seemed to hold their breath as Duclaire considered his next words.

"But there is more pressing news," he continued with a heavier tone, picking up a sealed scroll from his desk. "We cannot linger on defense alone. News from our scouts is dire—the Lapsids grow ever more bold, and their raids increasingly audacious."

He broke the seal, unrolling the parchment with deliberate care. The map revealed was detailed, marked with various encampments and paths through the dense woods of Lapsia—a terrain merciless and unforgiving. His finger traced a route deep into the heart of those shadowed lands.

"I am planning an assault," Lord-Commander Duclaire declared, his voice firm, resonating with the weight of command. "No mere counter-raids this time—we shall pierce the heart of the matter, once and for all."

A series of villages were marked on this map, each a bastion of potential Lapsid activity. We were tasked not with reconquest - but to dismantle the infrastructure that fed their insurgence. To sack - to pillage.

"It is imperative," Duclaire continued, his gaze fixed upon the inked routes as if he could foresee the battles that lay ahead. "That we teach them a lesson they will not soon forget. A lesson that shall echo through the hills and valleys of the Lapsids, a stark reminder that the might of our Reich, guided by the Holy Father, cannot be challenged without dire consequences."

I listened intently, my mind weaving through each command, each strategy laid before me. It began to sound more, and more like a punitive expedition. We wouldn't be holding ground - we would burn anything and everything that could aid them in their resistance. Our goal was absolute: to cripple their ability to wage war against us ever again.

I stood there, my body frozen in shock and horror. "And the people, my lord?" I mustered the courage to speak, fearing the answer that would come.

The Lord-Commander's eyes bore into me, his face a mask of cold determination, like a sharpened sword poised for battle.

"Kill them all. Let the Lord sort out his own," he said with a chilling finality.

And so it was decreed, our first real mission in these foreign lands - would of bloodshed and destruction.

The Subjugation Campaign

There was the soft thud of boots on the trail - leaving behind a smoldering village, its ash swirling like dark specters in the early morning air, which was but the fifth village we had come across. The men delighted at first - taking out their frustrations of being cooped up all winter, taking out the fear in their hearts. Yet, as the ash of the fifth village mingled with the crisp spring air, a solemn silence replaced the raucous laughter and shouts that had filled our ranks earlier. The weight of our deeds, the sheer gravity of our actions under the Lord-Commander's directive, began to settle heavily upon their shoulders, as it had already done on mine.

I told myself - it was us or them. These people harbored the monsters that hounded us - the bandits, the brigands that preyed on us; they were complicit, either by action or by silent consent. Yet, as the embers died and the cries of the fallen faded into haunting echoes - I couldn't help but gaze back.

It was a mistake.

"Kaelitz." A voice growled, and I turned to see the Lord-Commander Duclaire, his stoic expression clear on his face, his black plate armor gleaming as we rode on horseback. "Don't look back. You'll sleep better." His advice, stern though it was, churned within me like a storm I could not quell. The path we trod became a blur, the faces of my men mere shadows in my peripheral vision as I grappled with the moral tempest that raged silently in my heart. We were warriors, yes, but had we become mere executioners? The thought haunted me, gnawing at the edges of my conscience with relentless ferocity, threatening to consume me.

It was not of my will - no. I was ordered. What choice did I have in the matter?

As we ventured deeper into enemy territory, the lush verdance of spring seemed to recoil from our approach. Even the air grew heavier as if burdened by the silent screams of those we left behind. The terrain began its ascent into the cragged peaks and deep forests of Lapsia, the path narrowing and winding perilously around cliffs and dense, brooding forests. Here, the Lapsids' knowledge of their land would be their advantage—their final bastion against our ruthless advance.

Preparations for the impending assault consumed our days. Maps were studied under the dim light of oil lamps late into the night; strategies were debated fervently among the officers. The Lord-Commander remained resolute, his orders unyielding as stone, yet I saw the flicker of uncertainty in some of my comrades' eyes—a reflection of my own.

I wished desperately - that this campaign would end. Many others, I suspect, felt the same way. Others, I'm sure - were far less naive.

More than one of my prayers that night - was wishing to have died on the fields of Castleon with Alaric - not to live in dishonor like this.

Lord-Commander Duclaire rode at the front as we marched forward the following evening. His figure was imposing even against the stark white landscape, and his black plate armor bore the scars of numerous battles. A stoic, grim silence followed us—the drums beating—as we marched forward towards the Lapsid's fortress, deep in the forest.

Unknown to us, our doom lurked in the hollow belly of those woods—silent watchers veiled in white were biding their moment to strike.

A coalition of forces. Of Teutons, of Lithurians, of Polanians, of Lapsids. All of them - teeming to get a spill of Imperial blood. But - most of all, what we feared most was with them as they watched us.

As we trudged through a particularly narrow pass choked with snow-laden pines, we heard it—a cacophony of sounds - a volley of arquebus fire, lines of men collapsing, as halberdiers wheeled - only to encounter a sight genuinely terrifying.

Charging out from the woods - was this mighty coalition. What was most terrifying of all - was what we saw armed with bardiches and a musket - their imposing size made them unmistakable. But it was not merely the size of these Streltsy that struck terror into our hearts; their primal, lupine features froze the blood in our veins. Their faces were fearsome tapestries of man and wolf, with eyes glinted sharply under the shadow of their helmets, reflecting a lethal intelligence and untamed ferocity. Their thick and black-hued fur bristled against the cold in stark contrast to the snow.

They were the Vuk.

Immediately—as we processed this horrific fact—they fired a volley in a caracole method, far more disciplined than one would give them credit for. Their first rank fired and stepped out, while their second and then third rank shuffled forward, keeping up a rapid pace of fire that withered our forces in these great volleys.

We returned fire - of course. An odd wolfman or two took a shot - their bodies recoiling, but horrifically - remained standing. Would we need silver to fell them - like the stories told?

And then, with a great roar - they launched into a significant charge - all in a handful of seconds before we could return any organized fire.

Few men from the Holy Empire had the pleasure to fight one of these beasts - even fewer had the chance to survive. A man has yet to feel fear - until a beast twice his size charges him down - and while Valtorean halberdiers were famed - they were not fearless, mainly not the green regiments that the Streltsy no-doubt picked out.

Thus - those poor souls facing the Streltsy charge - ran in terror, breaking before even colliding. Poor souls were leaped upon - pounced, ripped apart, or cut in two by the Streltsy bardiches - a great rout occurring as our flanks began to fold all at once.

Lord-Commander Duclaire - he was an old man, but he sensed what was about to happen, were nobody to take action -

"Rally to me!" His voice thundered above the chaos, piercing through the frightful din of battle, a beacon for the scattering soldiers. I watched as he drew his saber, its blade catching the faint glimmers of the setting sun through the thick canopy of trees, radiating a subtle promise of hope—or perhaps a last stand.

I felt my legs move before my mind fully registered the action, my body responding to his call instinctually. Around me, others did the same; even in their fear, they congregated toward his rallying cry, forming a rough semicircle around our Lord-Commander. But even then, routers fled past us - a great river of men streaming back towards the relative safety of the rear guard.

These poor men were terrified out of their minds. They were the poor, unfortunate levies of the Baltzers—prone to superstition and like this—and they no doubt believed the Vuk were invincible to Imperial steel. So they did the only thing they thought they could do—fleeing a battle they wanted no part in in the first place.

And they were more than glad to leave the men of Valtor there to slow down the Vuk who were nearly upon us now. Their dark forms loomed like specters against the white snow. Their howls mixed with the bloodcurdling sound of a massacre - the air was filled with the smell of black powder and blood. Like the villages we'd been at.

Perhaps - it was a cruel justice. My arms softened, holding my blade - and almost sensing it, Duclaire launched into the melee of the few troops still fighting the Vuk - and almost instantly, their eyes locked on Duclaire.

What choice did I have?

"My lord, we must fall back!" I shouted at him, drawing my saber as I rushed up. Duclaire's eyes turned towards me.

"And forfeit the campaign? Never!" he spat icily, his voice cutting through the chaos like the sharp edge of his enchanted blade - a yellow, holistic glow coming from it. "In the name of the Lord - we must stand here, or we'll be hunted down like dogs from here to Vien!" He shouted - before raising his blade, letting out a defiant warcry - countercharging the Vuk.

It was brave - perhaps foolishly brave - but romanticism has always had a way of creeping into the hearts of men facing certain death. Duclaire's warcry galvanized a handful of the halberdiers whose loyalty or perhaps stubbornness outweighed their terror. They turned on their heels, forming a shaky line alongside the Lord-Commander, as I charged alongside him - into the great mass.

The first thing I remember - was in a single fell swoop - the horse I was riding - had its head slashed right off - and I was flung into the snow within the melee. It was a death sentence - indeed. Yet fate took a strange turn even as my body plummeted towards the frigid embrace of the snow. I slammed into the ground, my breath knocked out, the sky spinning above me, my ears ringing - but before a wolfman could finish me, Duclaire charged past like an avenging wraith, his blade swinging with uncanny precision and speed, severing the heads of two wolfmen as if they were but wheat beneath a scythe.

Chaos reigned around us, men tangled in brutal combat with the ferocious Kholdians. I struggled to my feet, feeling for my saber that had flown from my grasp upon impact. My fingers closed around the hilt just in time - as I saw a wolfman - jumping into the air, an overhead swing that threatened to bisect me, as I jumped to the side.

Moments before, the bardiche cleaved into the snow right where I was, sending up a spray of white powder that veiled my frantic movements. Scrambling away, my saber came up in a desperate arc, tracing a shimmering line of resistance against the horror before me. The Vuk snarled, revealing rows of deadly, sharp teeth, his lupine eyes narrowing with predatory focus.

The battlefield had transformed into a tableau of surreal brutality; men grappled with their fearsome adversaries in a dance of death, the stark landscape painted red with the blood of the fallen. The air was thick with the discordant symphony of metal clashing against metal, cries of agony melded with guttural howls, and the relentless percussion of gunfire thundering throughout the land.

Still winded from my fall, I was forced onto the defensive - battling a beast such as this with only a saber and a breastplate was foolhardy - the duelist style that served me well against Eclaireans and classmates was useless here. A single parry could break my wrist - disarm me, leave me defenseless, and the snow hardly helped matters, providing an unpredictable and treacherous footing. Each sidestep was a gamble; one misstep could mean the end of me. Nevertheless, I had no choice but to dance this macabre waltz as I launched into the one thing drilled into us - counterattack!

As the Vuk was forced onto the defensive, my saber rang out with each swing - each slash. In this desperate ballet, I began to see the patterns of its attacks, the slight twitches of muscle beneath fur that telegraphed its next move. With each passing second, my confidence grew. As the wolfman raised its bardiche for another sweeping strike, I stepped inside its reach, my saber darting like a viper's strike - the haft of the bardiche now being awkward - as he dropped it, a feral grin appearing on his face.

A claw swiped towards me - slashing my head as I was sent spiraling into snow - blood trickled from my face, and the warrior moved on. I laid there for a second, crying out in pain - trying to get up, only to look up.

The rest of the halberdiers that accompanied us - that rallied around us were outclassed. Too many of them had routed - not enough of them having countercharged with us - and now, it was a matter of time. Duclaire was missing - and I was left alone in the snow. My breaths came ragged, the metallic scent of my blood mixing with the pungent odors of battle. I could no longer see out of my right eye - having been blinded. With shaking hands, I slowly propped myself up, using my saber as a crutch. The cold bit into my wound, but it also numbed the pain, offering me a grim reprieve. The chaos had spread out around me; pockets of resistance still fought valiantly while others lay trampled beneath the relentless advance of the wolfmen. Uncertainty filled me - was this the end of our noble stand? The thought was a bitter one, but I pushed it aside. To give into despair here - would be to seal our fate.

With what strength I could muster, I stood tall amidst the carnage, walking slowly towards the melee—I knew that my respite would be brief. Greedily, I gulped down the winter air, each breath forming a mist that veiled my grimace of pain—and then, I saw it.

A small cadre of cavalrymen crested a nearby hillock, their charges frothing at the mouth with exertion. I recognized their banner immediately - the reserve cavalry! Had they been there all along? A glint of hope sparked within me as I watched them thunder down the slope, a lifeline thrown amidst our drowning desperation. Their lances lowered, the standard bearing the Imperial crest billowing in the wind - a horn crying out...

The Vuk tried to wheel around - but even for them - it was too late. The cavalry hit them like a tidal wave, a clash of steel and flesh that sent sprays of crimson arcing through the air. I joined the fray with renewed vigor, lashing out against those flanked by the cavalry's charge. Bones shattered under their mighty charge, and even the fearsome wolfmen found themselves on the back foot - routing and fleeing just as quickly as they arrived - dropping their weapons and fleeing on all-fours, slinking back to the forests where our cavalry could not pursue.

Despite all of our hard work - and our determination, the death toll was staggering. Twelve Vuk dead - for a hundred halberdiers slain.

As for Duclaire - I found him hunched over on his horse, which had been mauled to death. His black enchanted plate armor - ripped off him savagely as he sat there, bleeding on the snowy ground.

"Sir!" I shouted - rushing over. He raised his head slowly, the grime and blood masking his once resolute features, making him appear as some ghastly specter risen from beneath the trampled snow. His lips parted in a labored attempt at speech, a thin stream of blood seeping from the corner of his mouth.

"Leave me," he rasped, the command weak but edged with an iron will that had defined his leadership.

Duclaire's grip tightened on my arm, his gaze piercing. "Listen to me," he said, each word punctuated with a struggle against his injuries. "Don't you dare die here - don't you dare leave a *politician* in charge, or God forbid, one of the Baltizers." His voice waned, the effort draining his remaining vigor. I knelt beside him, trying to assess his wounds through the ruined armor, but it was a futile endeavor.

"Bu-" I said - as I turned, hearing snow crunching behind me. One of the cavalrymen had ridden up - a demilancer, much like I had been in my first campaign.

"Put him on my horse - and quickly. There's not a second to waste." The demilancer's command cut through the icy air, bringing decisive action amidst the horror. With considerable effort, we hoisted Duclaire onto the saddle, his body limp but for the occasional grimace of pain that twisted his features. His bloodstained gauntlets left smears on the white fur of the horse as if marking the creature, and another horseman came up - and I joined him upon his saddle.

And we rode. We rode fast - and hard, other cavalrymen screening the retreating infantry as we beat haste to Rega.

What awaited us at Rega - was the worst welcome a soldier could expect. A gate - barred with annoyed noblemen demanding answers and a comatose superior who can't answer the questions of a dozen functionaries wanting to know why the great Imperial army had collapsed. Words like 'disaster' and 'massacre' were thrown about with reckless abandon, their barbed syllables slicing through the air sharper than any saber. I was swept up in a storm of inquiries and accusations as we demanded entry into the city.

"Stand aside!" I bellowed, pushing forward with Duclaire's limp form still draped across the horse. Only after we forcefully made our presence felt did the gates groan open, begrudgingly admitting us. Inside the stone walls of Rega, the air was thick with the stench of politics and fear.

Duclaire was quickly taken to the infirmary, where the healers' hands moved in hushed urgency, their incantations a soft murmur blending with the clink of medicinal vials. I stood by his side, feeling utterly helpless as they worked to save a man - who, at this point, I didn't even know if he deserved healing.

Finally, after two or three days of retreating troops regathering in the safety of Rega's formidable walls, Duclaire stirred from his lethargy. Any dramatic gesture did not herald his awakening; instead, it was a subtle shift, a faint tightening of his brows as though resisting the encroaching grip of death itself. I was there when his eyes flickered open, revealing the dull fire that still burned within them.

He recognized me immediately and attempted to speak, but his voice shadowed its former command. "Water," he managed to whisper, and I hurriedly poured some into a cup, guiding it to his parched lips. As he drank, I observed the lines of pain etched deep into his face, each one telling a tale of sacrifice and relentless duty.

Once satiated, he motioned for me to lean closer. "The Vuk... did we stop them?" he asked, anxiety lining his voice more than concern for his condition.

"We held them off," I replied solemnly. "But at great cost. The halberdiers suffered heavy losses... We still haven't figured out how many. But it's between a thousand - to two thousand..."

A heavy sigh escaped him, and momentarily, I saw the weight of leadership pressing down upon him. "And the politics?" He sounded resigned now as if fully expecting an onslaught of power plays following our desperate defense.

"Worse than you might imagine," I stated.

"Of course." He closed his eyes briefly, sighing in frustration. "Lord forbid we do anything without a criminal dimwit watching over us." His comment elicited a wry chuckle from me despite the gravity of our situation. The irony was not lost on either of us; here we were, having barely escaped with our lives, only to face battles of a different sort within the supposed safety of the city's walls.

"You better brace yourself." He mumbled. "They'll be looking for a successor. Unfortunately, I only have one recommendation." Though dimmed by pain and fatigue, his eyes held within them a flicker of the strategic mind that had led us through countless skirmishes and unforeseen calamities. "You," he said solemnly, his gaze fixing me with a weight that felt as heavy as the whole armor of a knight. "You must take up the mantle."

The air seemed still around us, chilled and heavy with the unspoken realization of his words. I was taken aback, my mind racing through the implications and dangers of such a position. "Sir," I began hesitantly, my voice barely more than a whisper amidst the quiet bustling of the infirmary. "Are you certain? There are others far more—"

"Experience?" He laughed softly. "Or perhaps born of higher blood? I'm sure the Kaiser's uncle or nephew would love a crack at this." He grinned. "And that's exactly what they'll get. Mark my words. Five more years of this *shithole*, led by the most incapable men the Imperial Court can muster, and you'll wish you had taken the chance to die on that field when it was offered." He paused, his breathing labored from the effort of speech. "Trust me. It'll happen. My days as a commander after this - numbered. Assuming I survive."

He chuckled. Despite his grim prognosis, he seemed in light spirits, a shard of the old warrior's humor glowing through the cracks of his battered exterior. I leaned back slightly, absorbing the full impact of his words, the weight of future command heavy upon my shoulders, as he sighed.

"Bring me some paper and a pen. We must make it official before the other vultures start circling."

Resigned to my unexpected and unasked-for elevation, I fetched the requested items. There was a tangible solemnity in the act as if each step I took towards fulfilling his request were steps taken towards an irreversible fate. When I returned, he took the pen with a shaky hand, his fingers wrapped tightly around it like a lifeline. He began to write with laborious strokes, each letter etched with the certainty of a man who knew this might be his final command.

He finished and handed me the paper. His directive was clear and concise, lacking any flair that often adorned such decrees — it was not a document born of ceremony but of necessity. "Take this," he said, pressing the folded paper into my hand. "Only present it to the Kaiser when he asks for you. And he will."

I nodded, tucking the heavy weight of paper inside my jacket, feeling its presence like a stone against my chest as Duclaire looked at me.

"As of presenting that - you'll be a simple field captain." He stated. "A junior role. But - inevitably, when one of the bastards they put in charge slips up, you'll pick up the pieces. You'll make it." He assured before looking back and resting.

"...Thank you, sir," I stated, getting up - and leaving him to his rest as I wandered outside the infirmary into the cold, dusky evening that enveloped the city. The shadows cast by the setting sun stretched long across the cobblestones - and I took a breath that I didn't realize I was holding back.

Sure enough - the words of the Lord-Commander rung true. Word of his failure filtered back to the Empire, and the ranks of nobility were abuzz with speculation and opportunism. Within weeks, the Emperor arrived at Rega to address the situation personally.

His entrance into the city of Rega - was grand and full of pageantry. The personal guard of the young Emperor Wolfgang was the famed Palatine Guard, mercenaries from the mountains of Aldanaz, renowned as much for their fierce loyalty as for their unmatched combat skills, marching through the streets past the citizenry and even us - the members of the Imperial Army.

One couldn't help but turn dour - seeing them pass us by, with uniforms and armor still gleaming in the waning light. Every steel plate was perfectly polished, a bit-perfect, a stark contrast to our battered and bruised ensemble, a vivid reminder of our recent struggles. With the sun sinking lower, the city seemed to hold its breath. I watched as the Palatine Guard took their positions, their disciplined formation an imposing sight. The anticipation was palpable, a heavy collective anxiety in the air. Then, the emperor's carriage came into view, a luxury beacon amidst the old Rega city.

And - oddly enough, I could feel my heart pounding. I deduced that it was not from fear but from a burdensome sense of responsibility plaguing me already. I pushed it down as best as I could - but I knew well that the Kaiser being here personally was likely not good for the future of Lord-Commander Duclaire, who was recovering steadily.

Once I had pushed my thoughts away from myself - I gazed at the young Emperor Wolfgang stepping down from his carriage. He was just a youth - similar in age to me, yet already swathed in the heavy robes of state. His gaze swept over those gathered, his face an unreadable mask sculpted in the regal disdain and detached curiosity taught to him since birth. He was flanked by advisors whispering into his ear, their hands surreptitiously adjusting scrolls and documents as they walked. His presence brought a hush over the crowd, the kind that speaks of reverence and fear, a stillness that anticipates thunder.

As he approached, the crowd parted, a hushed silence falling. The murmurs ceased; even the clink of armor from the Palatine Guard seemed to quiet. All eyes were on him—on us.

"Soldiers!" His voice carried an accent that belonged clearly to the upper nobility, clear and commanding. "You have served the province of Ostland well in its hour of need." His eyes scanned our lines, perhaps looking for signs of dissent or fear. "And yet we find ourselves at a crossroads," he continued, "where leadership must be redefined and trust must be reestablished."

He paused for effect, allowing his words to saturate the twilight air. The silence lingered, oppressive and thick, before he resumed. "I have not come to chastise or to mourn the past but to secure our future. As such, changes will be implemented effective immediately."

The word 'changes' echoed ominously among the assembled soldiers and nobles. Murmurs began to rise, hushed but frantic, as everyone wondered what this youthful emperor had planned. His advisors appeared equally tense, their eyes flicking nervously about, gauging the crowd's reaction.

"Effective this sunset," Emperor Wolfgang declared, his voice rising over the whispers, "the command of the Eastern Garrison will be reassigned." A brief pause followed, in which you could almost hear hearts sinking. "Commander Duclaire is relieved of his duties due to health concerns."

A collective wave of disappointment swept through the ranks. Despite the rumors and my private discussions with Duclaire, the cold finality of hearing it proclaimed thus was a shock.

"To ensure a smooth transition and maintain the discipline and effectiveness of our forces here," continued Wolfgang, his gaze sweeping over us like a lighthouse beam in foggy darkness, "Duke Heinrich von Löwe will take temporary command."

I felt my breath hitch in my throat, and a murmur rippled through the assembled soldiers as they turned to each other in confusion. For me, I clenched my fist—hard.

However, before the whispers could swell into overt expressions of dissent, the young Emperor raised his hand, commanding silence with an authority that belied his tender years. "Duke Heinrich von Löwe has served with distinction in other provinces," he declared, his voice imbuing the unknown captain with an instant, if unverified, valor. "I trust he will bring fresh perspectives and rigorous discipline to our efforts here."

Stepping out - a figure stepped forward from the shadow of the emperor's entourage. Duke von Löwe was unmistakable even at a distance. His hair was white, and the black eyepatch. Hatred bored through me as he scanned over us like one might survey a chessboard.

A chilling silence fell over the crowd. Still reeling from the shock of their commander's dismissal, the soldiers could only stare at Duke von Löwe in disbelief. The tension was palpable, and amidst the murmurs, one question seemed to echo louder than all others.

What would become of our commander, Duclaire?

The silence that followed was filled with many unspoken questions and trepidations. I watched Duke von Löwe take a few determined steps toward the assembly, his gaze never wavering from the sea of faces before him.

"Attention!" the Duke's voice boomed across the square, echoing off the stone buildings that lined it. Instantly, the murmuring ceased, and every soldier gazed over at him.

"Slackers." He growled out, pointing a gauntleted fist. "It's because of you lot that Ostland is in such shambles. Weakness is a luxury we can no longer afford." His steel-grey eye swept across our ranks, each of us feeling the weight of his glare. "We will begin immediate retraining. I will not accept anything less than excellence from my command."

"Good, a right ol' bastard." Grumbled out a sergeant quietly. The thought simmered in the back of my mind as I stood, rigid in formation, watching Duke von Löwe pace before us, glaring at each of us.

"You will be tested," von Löwe continued, his voice relentless as the wind swept through the plaza. "You will be pushed beyond what you thought possible. And some of you will undoubtedly falter." His gaze lingered on a few of the younger soldiers, their faces drawn with apprehension - and then, he came up to me.

"Kaelitz." He growled quietly and turned to me, glaring at me. A second or two of silence followed - as I realized he was addressing me, and I stood upright, giving a salute.

"Sir!" I stated saber at the position, heart beating heavily under his scrutinizing gaze. I hesitated - not wishing to reveal my hatred of the man.

"You came recommended as an aide-of-staff." He inspected me. "Yet, I've never met an aide with such a sloppy stance." His eyes seemed to pierce through me, assessing every detail of my posture and appearance. "Straighten your back."

I adjusted my position - and then, a violent kick to my gut sent me right into the dirt, displacing the breath from my lungs in a single, excruciating whoosh. Dust swirled around me as I lay on the ground, stunned.

"Oi! Lay off him, you bloody bastard." Grunted out a sergeant - one of the men who served with me back in Northolt. Duke Heinrich von Löwe's head snapped toward the voice, his eyes narrowing into thin slits. "Who speaks?" he demanded, his voice low and dangerous.

The sergeant stepped forward, his chest puffed in defiance. "Sergeant Rottmann." he declared, standing firm despite the palpable tension that had suddenly choked the air. I recognized him - the voice, just barely - I had talked to him for a brief few words back after Castelon, after that dreadful affair.

Von Löwe took measured steps towards Rottmann, his boots thudding ominously against the cobblestones. The assembled soldiers tensed, their hands instinctively moving closer to their weapons, a mutiny seeming in sight - as even other members of the Palatine Guard seemingly were making ready for conflict, halberds at the ready.

"Sergeant," von Löwe growled out, standing toe to toe with Hawthorn. "I see the dreadful state of discipline in this army begins with its sergeants." He continued, his voice cold and hard as flint. "Insubordination will not be tolerated."

The sergeant crossed his arms, growling. "So be it," Rottmann retorted, his voice a daring challenge that resonated through the silent square. The tension coiled in the air like a primed spring awaiting release.

Before more words could escalate the confrontation, I scrambled to my feet, dust clinging to my uniform. "Lord Commander," I began, my voice raspy from the impact but firm in resolve, getting up. He's a bit traumatized from the affair. The slaughter, you see—was brutal, and it has weighed heavily on us all." I hoped my words would bridge the palpable rift and lend some understanding to our new commander's perception of us.

Von Löwe's eyes lingered on me, still piercing. He returned to Rottmann, who stood steadfast under the commander's scrutiny. After a tense moment that seemed to stretch endlessly, von Löwe's expression hardened again, yet he stepped back.

"Retraining will begin at dawn." He stated. "Anyone who is caught deserting is to be hung. No exceptions - not even for those of noble blood." He looked at me, square in the face.

"Dismissed!" von Löwe barked sharply, his command slicing through the tense silence like a saber. The assembled soldiers shuffled, a low murmur buzzing through ranks now fraught with wariness and barely suppressed anger. As they dispersed, it felt like we were crossing a far more dangerous border than the Danubitz river.

That evening, as the sun dipped below the horizon, painting the sky with streaks of blood-red and purple, the barracks were alive with whispered speculation and uncertainty. Rottmann approached me, his heavy steps echoing in the dimly lit hall.

"Kaelitz," he said, his voice rough like gravel. "You ever had someone tell you how stupid you are?" His question hung in the air, a half-hearted attempt at humor masking the deep-seated unease that had settled amongst us. I managed a tired smile, still feeling the ache in my gut from von Löwe's kick. "More times than I can count, Sergeant."

Rottmann grunted, nodding solemnly as he sat beside me on the wooden bench. "That was a bold move today—speaking to von Löwe after all that. Could've ended badly for you," he said, his voice low but not unkind.

I shrugged, my eyes tracing the wood grain beneath our fingers. "It could have," I admitted. "But it seemed worse to stay silent," I stated as I took a long breath.

"This retraining he's planning... it's going to break some of us, isn't it?"

"I suspect so," He replied softly. "And that bastard will claim he's making us stronger for it. Always how it seems to work out."

Then - the door creaked open. A gust of cold, night air swept in - and a courier walked in.

"Kaelitz von Ardent..?" The courier's voice trailed off as his eyes scanned the room, finally settling on me. He strode over, holding an envelope sealed with dark wax, impressed with the emblem of the High Command.

"Yes, that's me," I replied, standing to greet him. The room fell silent, all eyes now fixed on the mysterious delivery.

"This came for you, sir. Direct orders." He handed me the envelope with a stiff bow before turning and exiting as swiftly as he had entered.

I hesitated for a moment, my fingers tracing the seal. The weight of everyone's gaze felt heavy on my shoulders. With a deep breath, I broke the wax and unfolded the parchment.

The message was brief, but its content sent a cold shiver down my spine:

Kaelitz Ardent, report to my chambers at first light. You are to be appointed to the rank of Field Captain of the First Arkehovst Battalion.

- Lord Commander von Löwe.

Rottmann raised an eyebrow as he watched me absorb the words. "What's it say?"

I folded the letter, tucking it into my tunic. "It seems I'm not out of the fire yet, Sergeant," I murmured, my voice a mix of disbelief and resolve. "I'm to be appointed Field Captain of the First Arkehovst Battalion."

"Who in the bloody hell is the First Arkehovst battalion?" He grumbled out. "Not something I recognize." I sighed, running a hand through my hair. "Neither do I, Sergeant. Perhaps a restructuring..?"

Rottmann leaned back, his eyes narrowing thoughtfully. "Aye, likely. Probably took ten minutes to talk to Duclaire about the situation, and now he thinks he knows the whole problem." He snorted, shaking his head with disdain and reluctant admiration for von Löwe's decisiveness. "Either way, you're stepping into deeper waters, Kaelitz. Commanding a battalion is no light task. Especially one that doesn't exist." He smirked.

I couldn't help but laugh softly at his remark. "Most likely. I can only wonder what made him appoint me - I doubt it was Duclaire's recommendation alone." I stated aloud as Rottmann shrugged.

"You might be a young man, Kaelitz. A good decade or so younger than I - but you made it out of Castelon and out of the slaughterfield... With commendations and a decent track record." He stated. "Frankly, I don't think he has much of a choice. If he's smart - he likely knows that putting green officers in charge of a newly formed battalion could spell disaster. But someone like you? You've already been through hell, came back, and kept your head straight."

His words, though gruff, carried a weight of truth that settled in my chest. The room around us grew quieter as the soldiers, pretending not to eavesdrop, shifted their attention elsewhere, the initial curiosity fading into the background hum of pre-sleep rustlings and muttered conversations.

I nodded, acknowledging the compliment hidden within his blunt observation. "Thank you, Sergeant."

"Aye, Captain Kaelitz. Least I could do for you." Rottmann clapped a solid hand on my shoulder, his grip firm but reassuring. As he stood up, the wooden bench creaked under his weight, and he turned to walk - before he glanced back at me, sighing. He didn't say anything - as he walked away, and I respected that - after all, I was a bit overwhelmed.

The Way Things Are, and Were

At some point - you became used to being a soldier. The dreams. The fatigue. The constant need to remain vigilant. It wove into your being, as much a part of you as your blood and bone. That night - I had dreams of Alaric. The old village. My father - the old barony.

Dreams swirled in the murky depths of sleep, blurring the lines between past and present, reality and remnants of memories. Old Strossberg, with its cobblestone lanes drenched in the golden hues of sunset, came alive behind my closed eyelids. The gaze of my father - staring at me. Stern. Proud - but worried. That was the last thing I remember on his face - when I went to war. Would that stay with me?

"Kael, my boy." He whispered to me in those ethereal, dreamlike tones. "Don't repeat an old man's mistakes.: That whispered warning resonated through the layers of my slumber. Regret surged through me.

"I won't. I'll be back - sooner than you think." I said. The look on my father's face softened slightly, a ghostly smile flickering at the edges of his lips as if he understood the heavy burden on my shoulders. His voice faded like mist as dawn approached in the dream world, and I jolted awake to the sounds of a slam on the wooden door to the barracks.

"Wake up, you louts!" The voice barked through the still air, relentless and sharp. It was Sergeant Ullman, his face as stern as a judge's gavel in session. We knew better than to linger beneath the covers; those who did receive a harsher awakening by his boots or the icy splash of water - the sole exemptions were those of nobility.

Yet - the voice of Ullman was not what I feared. I jolted awake - strapping on my boots and rushing my way - I had to make it to the new Lord-Commander's office before the sun breached the horizon. The early morning air was crisp, filled with the scent of dew and the distant clatter of the morning guard's preparations. My footsteps echoed on the cobblestone as I hurried towards the towering structure that housed the Lord Commander's chambers, exhausted and out of breath as I finally entered the keep.

The stronghold was beginning to stir, the clatter of armor and murmur of voices slowly growing as dawn spread its pale light across the stone walls. I had skipped breakfast, so I rushed to the heavy oak door marked by the crest of the Lord-Commander, that of a lion's maw grasping a broken sword, and knocked.

"Enter," came the resounding, authoritative reply from within.

Pushing open the door, I entered a room that felt more like a war council chamber than a personal office. Maps littered the large central table, pinned down at corners with daggers, and weighed with stones. Von Löwe stood at the balcony, his back to me, hands clasped behind him as he gazed out over the training fields of Rega. Beside him - sitting in a chair with a cane, was the old commander, Duclaire, looking at me warmly.

"The young Kaelitz." Von Löwe said. "Just on time, as I expected." His voice was calm yet carried an undercurrent of something that could only be described as expectation mixed with a trace of urgency. I approached the table, my boots sounding against the stone floor, each step echoing in the high-vaulted room as I saluted.

"Sir," I began, nodding first to Von Löwe. "You summoned me?"

"Yes," Von Löwe turned from the balcony, his gaze piercing as it landed on me. His stern face softened slightly as we stared at each other. He stepped forward, his heavy boots thudding against the stone floor, until he stood directly before me.

"Kaelitz," he began. "I am aware of the history between our families, Kaelitz. It is a small world - an even smaller Empire." He said. A ghost of a smile touched the Duke's lips and was gone the next moment.

"Now, have you been briefed?"

"Not yet, sir."

Von Löwe nodded, understanding flickering across his features. "Very well. Arch-Duke, if you could?" He signaled to Duclaire, who rose from his seat with a slight effort, leaning heavily on his cane, as he smiled.

"Nobody has called me that in a long time, Von Löwe. You must have been sticking around the little Wolf too long." He grinned as Von Löwe growled.

"Your nephew spends more time in your old tales than studying in his tutorship," Von Löwe shot back, the corner of his mouth grimacing. I stood there - perhaps a bit shocked at the fact I had impressed the uncle of the Emperor, and Duclaire looked at me with a grin.

"Somebody never paid much attention to their tutorship either." He said, grinning. "I think this young man turned out rather fine himself without all that nonsense." Duclaire's words hung in the air, mingling with a warmth that momentarily lifted the steady weight of duty from my shoulders. His gaze shifted to the documents spread across the table, his expression turning severe once again as he beckoned me closer. "Come here, Captain Kaelitz. Look at this."

I approached, my boots clicking on the cold stone floor, and leaned over the map that dominated the table. It was a detailed depiction of our borders and beyond, marked with various symbols that denoted troop movements, strategic locations, and conflict areas. Duclaire's finger tapped a particularly dense cluster of marks near a narrow pass through the mountains—Feynrich's Pass, a critical point on the map and now, it seemed, in our upcoming strategy.

"The old Order of the Black Griffon once had a castle here, back when these lands were even more teeming with savages and pagans than they are today," Duclaire began his voice a mix of nostalgia and gravity. "It's now a derelict fortress, but its strategic position remains unmatched. Especially..."

He pointed eastward. The vast, gigantic Tzardom of Kholodia stretched across the map. Perhaps - even past it.

"Especially, should the worst happen, with the Kholodian Tzardom. They are volatile, dangerous neighbors."

Von Löwe took a step closer, his eyes narrowing as he followed Duclaire's gesture. "Indeed," he murmured, "if Kholodia decides to push westward, Feynrich's Pass will be the first line of defense. It could determine the fate of the entire eastern front in an invasion... Though frankly, with the great revolution in Eclaire, I feel we're better prepared than most think." He paused, allowing the weight of his words to sink in before continuing. "Captain Kaelitz, the council has decided you will lead the expedition to re-establish the garrison at Feynrich's Pass. Your mission is twofold: fortify the pass and scout for any Kholodian movements towards our borders."

"...Excuse me, revolution?" I stated that I was unaware of any such developments in the East. Von Löwe's eyes flickered with a hint of surprise, then frustration that I had not been informed earlier.

"Yes, a revolution," he confirmed with a heavy sigh. "Eclaire has finally reached its boiling point. Details are a bit..." He grimaced. "Thin. But - from my understanding, it's quite serious. Especially with the radicals from the Low Church..."

Duclaire coughed pointedly, drawing our attention back to him. His eyes shone defiantly as he spoke, his voice ringing with conviction. "The Low Church may be seen as radical by some such as you, Heinrich. But - I must remind you, the last thing we must do is split our forces in terms of denomination."

Von Löwe's jaw tightened, a flicker of irritation passing over his features. "Careful, Arch-Duke," he warned his tone low and measured.

Duclaire's warning hung in the air, a palpable tension diffusing between us. Lord Commander Von Löwe's eyes stayed locked on Duclaire for a moment longer than comfortable before turning back to the map, his finger tracing lines and symbols as though pondering his following words.

"Very well," he continued, redirecting the focus of our strategy meeting. "Back to Feynrich's Pass. We must secure it quickly. Not just due to its strategic importance, it may also serve as a valuable rallying point for those still loyal to our cause in the east." He paused, his gaze drifting toward a small insignia hidden among the myriad of troop placements—an insignia I recognized as that of the Order of the Black Griffon.

I followed his gaze to the symbol again, remembering tales my father told me about the ancient Order of the Black Griffon—a group shrouded in mystery and bound by complex oaths and allegiances. Traditionally, they had been warrior monks defending against ancient threats beyond our borders. Still, their presence had waned after many of their strongholds were lost or abandoned during the last Crusade - the last Crusade my grandfather fought in.

"The Order has a new Grandmaster," Von Löwe continued as if reading my mind. "A young and ambitious knight named Siegfried. A bit hot-headed - proclaiming he'll spear a new crusade to the heart of Moscova, but that's exactly what we need." He grinned. Duclaire glared.

"It's the last thing we need. The people of Baltiva are already largely good, god-fearing folk who listen to the Church. The last thing we need is those fanatics... Especially if they were to rile up fears about another Goetic incursion..."

I stared at the map, my mind churning with this influx of revelations. An uprising in Eclaire, the new Grandmaster of the Black Griffons eager for a crusade, the simmering tension between Von Lowe and Duclaire was almost overwhelming. But I needed to maintain focus. My duty was clear: secure Feynrich's Pass against any incursion from the east.

Then - I snapped back to the conversation.

"...Filthy, goetic heathens. Downright blasphemers, like the Arlenians and their *radicals*." Von Löwe's tone darkened with each word, his hands tightening into fists.

"That is, perhaps, the sole good thing the Order has done here - and the Baltzers, for that matter," Duclaire announced. "The old order of Goetics are long gone, for at least two generations. And as for the Arlenians and their *particular...* Blasphemous ways..."

"Von Löwe, with all respect, focus," Duclaire interjected sharply, his voice firm. "We're soldiers, far away from such things. The affairs of Arlenia are the affairs of Arlenia."

"Of course, Arch-Duke," he said, returning to me. "Captain Kaelitz... I would strongly recommend against sharing any news about the revolution.

Especially to the..." He glanced back to Duclaire, displeased. "Especially to the more free-minded sergeants."

"Understood, sir," I replied, nodding solemnly.

Von Löwe's demeanor shifted slightly as his gaze lingered on mine, probing.

"Captain Kaelitz," he began again, his voice dropping to a hint. "Before I dispatch you to Feynrich's Pass, there are matters that require deeper discussion that cannot be fully explored in this crowded room." He turned his steely gaze towards Duclaire, who was now absorbed in annotating another map segment with careful, precise strokes. "Arch-Duke, might I request a moment alone with Captain Kaelitz? There are specific instructions from the High Command which I need to convey privately."

Duclaire looked up, his piercing eyes flicking from Von Löwe to me and back before he sighed, holding the cane more tightly in his grip as he pushed himself up from the table. "Of course," he said with a nod, his tone carrying a hint of resignation mixed with curiosity. He moved away slowly, each step deliberate, leaving behind the faint echo of his cane tapping against the stone.

Von Löwe waited until Duclaire had left the room before he spoke. "Captain Kaelitz," he said - sitting at a desk near the corner of the large, dimly lit chamber. He motioned for me to sit across from him. As I obliged, the air seemed to thicken with an unspoken urgency.

"Captain," Von Löwe began, his voice low and steady. What I am about to discuss must not leave this room. But you are to stop associating with the Arch-Duke immediately."

His statement sent a chill down my spine, contrasting sharply with the musty warmth of the chamber. "I beg your pardon, sir?" I asked my voice barely a whisper, laden with disbelief.

Von Löwe leaned forward, his eyes boring into mine with an intensity that charged the air between us. "The Arch-Duke has been under surveillance for some time now," he revealed slowly, each word measured and heavy. There are suspicions regarding his ideals—not just to the crown but to the principles that hold our society together."

I sat frozen in place, trying to reconcile this stark proclamation with the man I had known and served with for half a year. The Arch-Duke, a traitor?

It was inconceivable. Yet here was Von Löwe, a man of impeccable reputation and loyalty to the crown, laying bare such damning suspicions.

"The evidence is not yet concrete," Von Löwe continued his voice almost a whisper now. "But we must act cautiously. Your assignment at Feynrich's Pass is critical, but your role in observing the Arch-Duke is more critical. We need to ascertain his true intentions. As you see - he has a layer of sympathy for the Eclaireans... The Low Church, in particular."

"I-I see. Isn't this an affair for the... Inquisition?" I stated, in a quiet breath.

Von Löwe's lips curled slightly with a smirk. "Indeed. You are quite right."

He leaned back, folding his hands in front of him on the desk. "Captain, Father Johann—whom I know you worked with briefly in Northolt —is not merely a simple town priest as most presume. He works closely with the Inquisition."

I felt a knot tighten in my stomach. Father Johann, a quiet and unassuming figure, always cloaked in his dark, flowing robes, had seemed to me nothing more than a man of faith. But Von Löwe's words painted a picture far more intricate and shadowed.

"As a man of noble blood - I'm sure you know what happens when the Inquisition starts prying into our affairs. Things get messy. Very messy. Especially if you've been working with the wrong people..." He said, his fingers tapping a slow, deliberate rhythm on the dark wood of the desk. "There is no room for error here, Captain—no room for divided loyalties. You will serve me. You will serve the Iron Church and our lord, God."

I felt the weight of his gaze, heavy and unyielding, pressing down upon me. "Yes, sir," I managed to say, my voice steadying despite the turmoil inside me.

"You are to report directly to me," Von Löwe continued, his tone brooking no argument. "Any communications with the Arch-Duke must cease immediately unless explicitly through channels I approve."

"Yes, sir," I said again as Von Löwe glared at me. A second of silence he followed as he gazed at me.

"I know what you're thinking. That I'm harsh, many more words would be well-suited for the gutter rather than a gentleman's conversation. But let me be clear, Captain. I would not appoint you to a position this important if I did not have a clue of respect."

"...Then why the threats?" I challenged back. "Were it not for Rottmann - you would have beat me bloody, I know it,"

Von Löwe's face hardened, the lines around his eyes growing more profound as he growled.

"You forget history, Captain." His voice was low, a controlled growl that seemed to vibrate the very air of the cramped chamber. "It is not love that governs men but consequences. You speak of brutality as if it were my pleasure. No, it is merely a tool."

He stood up and walked towards a large map that hung on one side of the room, its edges worn and colored as he gazed at it.

"Kaelitz. Some day - you'll understand. Surrounding us is a wall. Monsters. Heathens. Devil-worshippers." He turned back. "We are blessed. Truly - to live in God's chosen Empire. Anywhere else - and what would your life be?" He glanced back at me. "A life in Arlenia? Ruled by atheistic despots - to be denied salvation at gunpoint? To live in the old, decayed Arkenthian Empire as a slave? Or to be ruled over by the savage wolfmen as a serf?"

His words, though harsh, carried the weight of undeniable truths. I remained silent, digesting the gravity of Von Löwe's arguments and the broader implications of my mission.

"Yes, sir," I replied, finding my footing in this discourse. "I understand the stakes."

"Good." He nodded. "Now - get to it. I've wasted enough time on lecturing - you have your orders." He slid a letter towards me - a requisition order for men and supplies. "Take this to Major Brenner at the eastern garrison. He will provide you with what you need."

I took the letter, examined it, and felt the heavy seal. I couldn't help but notice the symbol of the Iron Church embossed upon it. What had I gotten into?

Assembling the formation of the First Arkehovst Battalion was much easier said than done. I found Major Brenner - a stout man with a bushy mustache, greeted me briskly as I approached.

"Here to get started?" He said, examining the letter. "Three hundred men, six horses - and two six-pound cannons... To be formed as a line infantry company, blah blah blah..." He stated, and then his eyes went wide.

"...And three hundred muskets. Muskets? The bloody hell are we going to get a hundred muskets on such short notice?" He shook his head with a blend of disbelief and irritation.

"Muskets?" I said, looking at the parchment again, my brow furrowing. "Is there an error, Major?"

Brenner shook his head, his mustache bobbing slightly. "No error on the paper, Captain. It's just... Ambitious." He stated. "The only muskets I know of come from Vien and perhaps a few of the Free Cities - and they're far from here, Captain." He sighed heavily, running a hand through his thinning hair. "I'll see what I can do. But I can hardly make any promises. Perhaps a month - or two, and we might get forty or so in."

I stared at him.

"Surely, at the very least, you can give us some arquebuses?" I asked.

Major Brenner nodded slowly, his expression turning contemplative. "Arquebuses, yes." He scribbled something briefly in his ledger, then looked up at me with a slight frown. "It won't be the firepower you expect with muskets, but it'll give your men something to hold. I'm surprised - frankly."

"Surprised?"

"Well - who the bloody hell ordered muskets?" He stated - before looking at the parchment. His eyes went wide - as he looked at the seal, he opened it more carefully.

"Oh, Savior..." He grumbled.

He stared at the seal with a new level of reverence, his gruff demeanor momentarily replaced by a cautious respect. He set the paper down carefully on his cluttered desk, then rubbed his eyes tiredly. "Captain, I'll do what I can. But tell the Church after this - I'm done." He picked the letter back up and waved it slightly. "This will stretch us thin—very thin."

I nodded, understanding his position but bound by my duties. "I appreciate your efforts, Major. I know it's not easy."

Brenner looked me straight in the eye, his gaze sharp yet not unkind. "No, it's not easy, Captain. But we do what we must, don't we?" He paused as if considering his following words carefully. "You're caught in a tough spot, young sir. I can't say I envy you very much, taking orders from the Inquisition."

I could only nod again, feeling the truth of his words like a weight upon my shoulders.

"Very well," he said briskly, breaking the brief spell of solemnity that had fallen between us. "I will send word to my contacts in Vien and the Free Cities immediately. We might not secure three hundred muskets, but I'll be damned if I don't get close."

I nodded gratefully, knowing that Major Brenner was going above and beyond to fulfill this challenging request. But as I stood there in his office, surrounded by the trappings of his position, a question gnawed at me.

"Major," I began, trying to phrase my query diplomatically, "forgive me if this seems impertinent, but I must ask - why are we not producing more of these muskets internally? Surely, we could outfit our troops more efficiently with the resources and craftsmen at our disposal?"

Brenner leaned back in his chair, a wry smile playing across his weathered features. "Ah, Captain Kaelitz, you've stumbled upon a contentious issue." He steepled his fingers, his eyes looking distant as he gathered his thoughts.

"You see," he continued, "the Handwerkskammer - the craftsman guilds... For generations, they have prided themselves on creating the finest goods in Aurisca. So - what do you think happens when they get a bulk order for muskets - something new, something exciting?"

I momentarily pondered Major Brenner's question, the implications slowly dawning on me. "I imagine the guilds would be resistant," I ventured. "New methods, new designs... It would disrupt their traditional way of doing things."

Brenner nodded, his smile turning rueful. "Precisely, Captain. The guilds feared that mass production of muskets would undermine their livelihood and way of life. They argue that it would flood the market with inferior goods and that somehow, the Imperial Army in all its brilliance will turn to Arlenia or Kholodia, or even Arkanthian for their muskets."

He sighed, leaning forward to rest his elbows on the desk. "And so, they lobby against it. They petition the nobles, the merchants, and anyone who will listen. So, no - we don't get to have rows upon rows of line infantry, like a real country, all because with the way things are now - they can sell an arquebus for a fortune because who the bloody hell still makes them?"

I absorbed Major Brenner's words, a deep frown etching my face. The political machinations at play, the entrenched interests resisting progress - it all seemed so frustratingly shortsighted in the face of our current predicament.

"So we are held hostage by the very craftsmen who should be supporting our cause," I said, unable to keep the bitterness from my voice. "While our enemies march ever closer, armed with the latest weapons, we are left to scrounge for outdated relics."

"Young Kaelitz - you haven't even seen the sheer price the Free Confederation charges for shipping goods and supplies here." He grinned.

I shook my head in disbelief, the weight of our predicament pressing heavily upon me. "So we're caught between the guilds' self-interest and the exorbitant prices of foreign trade," I said, my voice tinged with frustration. We face obstacles at every turn.

Major Brenner leaned back in his chair, his expression a mix of resignation and grim determination. "Welcome to the realities of war, Captain Kaelitz. It's not all glory and heroism - sometimes it's just a bloody mess of politics and economics."

He stood up, his chair creaking under the sudden movement. "But we'll make do, as we always have. I'll pull every string I can call in every favor owed to me. We'll get you those muskets, or at least as close as we can manage."

I stood as well, feeling a renewed sense of respect for the grizzled Major. "Thank you, sir. I know you're doing everything in your power to support us."

Brenner waved off my gratitude, his demeanor gruff but not unkind. "Just doing my job, Captain. Now, you'd best be on your way. I'm sure you have plenty of other matters to attend to."

I nodded, saluting crisply before turning to leave. Brenner's voice called out after me as I walked through the door.

"And Captain? Watch your back out there."

Two weeks later - we had assembled an actual, somewhat functional battalion armed with nearly as many muskets as we had hoped for. A few cannons to boot - and plenty of ammo. It seemed Brenner had pulled a miracle.

No pikemen. No halberdiers - only bayonets and muskets. It was progressing away from the old system of the Terijco - modernization. But, our first drills could have been more cohesive and well-practiced. Besides the actual firing mechanisms, Socket bayonets were the most impressive to witness. Not as cumbersome as one would think at first - and soon, our reloading drills began to pick up pace. After a few days, the men fumbled less with their cartridges, getting to the average expected of an arquebusier. And eventually - even the Lord Commander came to inspect.

"Not bad." He grunted. "Though, it pales to the Arlenians or the Streltsy in Kholodia."

"Thank you, sir," I said, saber at the ready, as he looked at me and grunted.

"It's a start." He said. "But - in their first real battle, they'll all die." He stated calmly. "The Kholodians, they fire three rounds a minute. I doubt you have to be educated to put the math together."

I stood straight, absorbing his harsh analysis. "We are training them harder, sir. We'll improve," I responded firmly, though inside, I felt the chasm of doubt that his words had carved.

The Lord-Commander paced slowly in front of the ranks, his eyes narrowing as he watched each soldier loading and firing. "You'd better," he muttered. "Because your whole command is riding on this. Get them up to... Four rounds a minute." He stated, as I blinked.

"Four..?"

"Four."

He then turned sharply on his heel and marched off, leaving a heavy silence in his wake. The men's faces, previously lit with the strain of effort and concentration, now mirrored my apprehension. We had only a week to refine our skills to meet an almost unattainable standard. As the Lord-Commander's figure disappeared into the distance, Sergeant Rottman walked past him, approaching our drilling grounds.

"Captain Kaelitz, sir." He saluted. "The old Lord-Commander requested me to serve with you." He handed me a sealed envelope. "And he wished you to have this." I took the envelope and looked at it.

The seal of the Lord-Commander, cracking it open, was written in High Valtorean, the court dialect.

Captain Kaelitz von Ardent,

In light of Von Löwe's appointment to the first Battalion, you are granted all the privileges befitting a *Feldhauptmann*. Immunity to prosecution, the right to requisition goods and services necessary for the war effort, and the right to conscript, alongside twelve acres of estate in Ostland, upon completing the campaign, bestowed to you from Archduke Frederich Duclaire.

With all due reverence - Archduke Frederich Duclaire.

I read the letter twice and blinked, glancing over at Rottmann.

"...Is Duclaire sticking around? I would have thought he would have headed back."

Sergeant Rottmann shifted uncomfortably, his eyes darting to the letter and then back to me. "He's staying, sir. Even after being stripped of command, he serves as an advisor to Von Löwe. In terms of... Regional matters. Not to mention - evidently, he's disliked at court."

"I see. Well - at least I'll have a familiar face here." I stated. "I've been running this battalion without a single sergeant." Rottmann nodded, his face settling into a grim line of understanding. "I'll do my best to serve you well, Captain. Just say the word, and I'll set to work."

"Thank you, Sergeant," I replied, feeling a slight ease at having an experienced non-commissioned officer by my side. There was much to do, and Rottmann's arrival could not have been more timely. With a week to increase our firing rate and a long campaign ahead, his experience would be invaluable.

"Fire!"

The command echoed across the drill field, sharp and imperative. The soldiers, now standing in rigid formation, executed the order with a swiftness that surprised even me. Muskets roared in unison, sending a cloud of smoke drifting across the cool morning air. The acrid smell of gunpowder stung my nostrils as I walked down the line, inspecting each man's handling and readiness.

Sergeant Rottmann stood beside me, his gaze equally critical. "Improving," he muttered under his breath, though his voice carried a trace of reluctant approval. "But not yet four rounds." I nodded, my mind racing through the possibilities. "We'll extend training hours," I decided aloud. "And break them into smaller squads for more focused drills."

Rottmann responded with a grunt.

"We're already up to nearly sixteen hours. Any more and you'll grind them into dust, si-"

"Make way!" Shouted from behind us and cut through our intense discussion, pulling our attention sharply towards the source. A courier mounted on a lathered chestnut mare galloped into the grounds, his uniform caked with the dust of hurried travel. The horse's sides heaved, and her nostrils flared red as she skidded to a halt before us.

The young and breathless courier hopped down from his saddle and extended a sealed envelope towards me. His eyes flickered with an urgency that tightened my chest in anticipation. "Captain Kaelitz Ardent?" he panted, confirming my identity before I nodded. Handing over the envelope, he added with rigid formality, "Orders from the Lord Commander."

I accepted the message, noting the seal – the symbol of the Lord-Commander, pressed deeply into dark wax. Breaking it open, I scanned the contents as Rottmann and a few nearby officers gathered closer.

"Sir?" Rottmann's voice was low, querying as always.

I gulped nervously.

You are to head out to Feyrnich's Pass immediately, at a double pace, alongside the 20th Saxonian Regiment led by Colonel Galland and the forces of the Black Band.

-Von Löwe

The handwriting was rushed; whatever situation awaited us there was escalating rapidly.

"Assemble the men," I commanded without hesitation, glancing back at Rottmann.

"Understood, Captain." Rottmann saluted sharply, then turned to relay the orders. Once filled with the repetitive sounds of training, the drill field quickly transformed into a hive of urgent activity. Men scrambled to gather their gear, their faces set in determined, anxious lines. Most of them were green - conscripts. It was hardly like the force that had set out here eight months ago - which was shocking in its way, to remember that I was now among the more senior officers.

As the urgency of the situation settled around me like the morning mist, I felt a weight pressing uncomfortably against my chest. Walking alongside Rottmann, who seemed ever stoic and unflustered by the sudden change, I couldn't help but allow my thoughts to drift into doubts and uncertainties about my capabilities.

"Rottmann," I began, my voice barely above a whisper as we moved towards the assembling troops, "I must confess something to you."

He glanced at me, his brows arching slightly in that characteristic manner which usually prefaced his patience for my occasional bouts of self-doubt. "Yes, Captain?"

"...Is it always like this?" My words trembled slightly, betraying the calm demeanor I strained to maintain.

"Ah. Feeling a bit inexperienced, eh?" He chuckled softly, the sound somehow reassuring amidst the clamor of preparation. "It's always a whirlwind, sir. War waits for no man, and neither do the orders that drive it. But you'll find your footing soon enough."

I nodded somberly, appreciating his confidence in me even as my stomach churned with nerves. "And if I stumble?" The question was out before I could hold it back.

Rottmann squared his shoulders, looking me directly in the eyes. "Then you get up and keep marching, sir. We all stumble. It's getting back up that counts. That's what makes a leader worthy of his title."

I sighed softly. "Thank you, sergeant," I said as he nodded, and we both looked out to the field, a blur of motion, as they made ready to march.

We set out on the eastern roads - little more than dirt tracks worn down by countless military boots. The rhythm of marching feet merged with the clinking of gear and the occasional cough or murmur from the ranks. The sky, a brooding canvas of gray, seemed to press down on us as if warning of the problematic march ahead.

Ahead of us - was the 20th Saxonian Regiment, recruited by Von Lowe himself. Quickly, it was a thousand men strong - and then, you had us in the middle. A battalion of musketeers assembled as the First Arkehovst Battalion - though none of us came from such a place. None of us could even name it on a map. We were a makeshift unit, composed of men from different regions of the Empire, each with their dialects and customs, yet thrust together.

It was uneasy. The brotherly bonds from a regiment such as the Saxonians - all brothers in blood, surpassed our own.

Behind us - was the Black Band. A five-hundred-strong mercenary force of locals. Their presence was a stark reminder of the desperation of our situation—hiring mercenaries was always a last resort in such campaigns - and they hardly looked like the type that became so famous in Casteloria and Valtorea. It's more like armed brigands than anything thoughtfully organized. They were locals - evidently 'sympathetic' to us.

Gradually, the landscape around us changed as we approached Feyrnich's Pass. The flat plains gave way to rolling hills and, soon, steep inclines that tested the stamina of every man. The once distant mountains now loomed large, their peaks shrouded in mist, casting long shadows over our path, and I saw a rider bearing down on us - a courier, from ahead.

"Sir - Colonel Galland from the 20th Saxonian Regiment," the courier panted as he reined in his horse lathered with sweat. "He sends urgent word."

I rode forward, feeling every eye upon me. "Report," I commanded, my voice steady despite the flutter of nerves within.

"The enemy has been sighted, Captain," the courier said, his face grave. "Three miles north of Feyrnich's Pass. Kholodians, sir. He wants your men in the front - to screen."

"Very well," I started, my response clipped and decisive, masking the burgeoning apprehension that gripped me. "Tell Colonel Galland we will move into position immediately."

As the courier wheeled his horse around and galloped off towards the Saxonian lines, I turned to address my battalion. The men looked back at me with anticipation and fear; their faces a stark canvas against the grim landscape. The first battle was always shaky when theories and drills hardened into harsh reality. I surveyed their ranks, catching snippets of muttered prayers and last-minute affirmations. To say their morale was low - was an understatement. Fear coursed through my own body looking at them - my confidence shaky.

"Listen up!" I called out, my voice cutting through the murmur of unease. The men straightened up, turning their attention towards me. The clinking of gear subsided as silence took hold, each man bracing for orders, leading them into the unknown embrace of war.

"We have been called to stand at the front," I stated. "The holy flag of the Empire stands behind us - and we will not dishonor it." I stirred. "Now - onward!"

With a persistent shout, the battalion rallied behind me. We shook off the stagnation of our march with renewed vigor, our pace quickening as we approached the mouth of Feyrnich's Pass, taking the lead ahead of the Saxonians, who looked at us with indifference as we passed them up.

Colonel Galland was a tall man - a few medals pinned to his greatcoat, and a few of Arlenian origin, as I rode up beside him. His eyes, sharp and calculating, surveyed the terrain with a practiced gaze that spoke of many battles waged and won. As we approached, he nodded curtly, his expression betraying no emotion. "Captain," he greeted me, his voice carrying the weight of authority and experience - a slight twang of a posh, Arlenian tone.

"Colonel," I stated. "I wasn't expecting an Arlenian to lead us," I said - more out of interest rather than chauvinism. He grinned at that, a sharp grin that lasted no more than a second.

"It's an interesting, worldly thing - politics," Galland replied, his tone tinged with ruefulness as his eyes drifted from the road ahead to meet mine. "Half a decade ago, I wouldn't have expected to be in Valtorea. But - things change, do they not?"

We fell into silence, the only sound being the rhythmic thudding of our horses' hooves against the hard-packed earth. Galland seemed lost in thought, his gaze distant. After a few moments, he broke the silence, his voice carrying a note of urgency that drew my attention back to him.

"The Kholodians are ahead - up there," he continued, pointing towards a series of rocky outcrops that jutted out like the jagged teeth of some great beast. "They have cannons, and their musketeers are well positioned. It will not be an easy assault, though we do outnumber them."

"...I see," I stated. "So - they're interdicting us from reaching the fortress?"

"Yes, precisely," Colonel Galland confirmed, his eyes narrowing as he assessed the situation further. "They aim to hold us here, bleed us before we make it there - at which point, we'll likely be running low on manpower... Making a quick assault impossible." He stated.

Both of us looked ahead, noticing two folks walking forward. Both of them - tall Vuks, standing tall and proud - the flag of parley out.

"At least, they seem gentlemen enough," Galland growled.

I nodded, adjusting the hilt of my sword, which hung uncomfortably against my side. We watched as the Vuks approached, their strides measured and purposeful. There was a brief silence as they drew closer, the tension between our forces palpable even in the still mountain air.

The Vuks—these tall wolfmen wearing courtly robes—seemed to rival the poshness of the nobles at court in our Empire. They walked over to us, giving a brief courtly bow—even though they were as tall as our horses. The lead Vuk spoke, his voice growly for his imposing size. "Valtoreans," he began, his common tongue laced with an accent of deep forests and ancient traditions. "I am Boyar Kievelov. You have heard of me, yes?"

I looked towards Galland - who's face seemed paled in comparison.

"Yes," Galland mumbled out. "I believe I have."

"Good," he continued, his broad shoulders shifting slightly as if to settle more comfortably into the gravity of our conversation. Then, you'll know very well that it is in better interests for you to head back." Boyar Kievelov's voice carried a note of finality, his eyes scanning our assembled faces with a discerning look. His gaze lingered on the imperial flag fluttering behind us as he smirked, a fanged smile that unnerved me.

"We cannot." I pressed. "Our orders are clear, sir."

Boyar Kievelov's fanged smile faded into a stern line, and he shifted his weight, somehow towering over us ominously. "Orders," he echoed disdainfully, his voice booming slightly in the cool air of the pass. "Orders that send young men to their deaths for a patch of dirt. Our empires have no reason to fight - and yet, we do so, for what?"

Perhaps sensing he had struck a cord - he looked at me.

"We believe in the same Savior, yes? Then - what reason do we have to fight each other? Has war not taken enough from you, young man?" He said, looking at me. "Your eye - those claw marks. You understand the cost of war." He states - before gazing over at Galland, unimpressed.

"And I am sure he does not." Colonel Galland's jaw clenched visibly, his eyes hardening as he faced Boyar Mikahelovich. "Boyar," he said, his tone cold and measured, "it is not for you to judge what I have or haven't endured. We stand here by orders of our Emperor to secure this pass and push forward. Higher powers dictate the politics of our nations than any of us on this field."

Boyar Kievelov gave a low chuckle, "True enough. Such is the fate of men like us. Bound by the whims of those above." His gaze glanced towards the horizon for a brief second - and then.

A gunshot rang out.

The boyar, who once stood before us, collapsed onto the snowy ground, his large frame creating a soft thud as it met the earth. Blood began to pool around him, a stark contrast to the pristine whiteness that engulfed us. The other Vuk - shocked, bared his fangs - rushed over, exchanging words with the fallen wolfman as I looked over.

Galland's pistol was out, smoking.

"Such - is the fate of monsters." He glared - before glancing at the Vuk - who looked at him with utter, intense hatred. The air, already thick with tension, now shimmered with the undeniable threat of violence.

"You have sealed the fate of many today." The wolfman stated, a hateful glare focused on Galland, who seemed indifferent.

"So I have. So I have." Galland said. The Vuk continued to glare - going to grab the body, but Galland interrupted.

"If you touch his body - I will not hesitate to have you killed."

The Vuk's eyes blazed with fury, yet there was a momentary pause, a calculation in the tension-laden silence. "And what then of your honor, Valtorean?" he spat bitterly. "You dishonor the dead with such threats. Is this the righteousness your Empire preaches?"

Galland's expression remained stone-like, unfazed by the accusation, his grip on the pistol unwavering. "Say whatever you'd please, monster. But do so in the company of your troops far from here. We claim this ground now, by blood and decree."

The Vuk's seething gaze held Galland's for a moment longer before he turned, leaving the body of the wolfman there - as I gazed over to Galland. I couldn't help but feel like the accomplice in a murder, foul and cruel.

"You may think me of being harsh - but these wolfmen are savages. You've seen them." He said. "You lost your eye to them - after all."

I nodded slowly, feeling a heavy churn in my stomach. My eye—a wound that never fully healed, a constant reminder of the brutal clash between our species. It was true; I had lost it to the Vuk during an earlier skirmish. Yet, staring down at the lifeless form of Boyar Kievelov, I couldn't suppress the surge of empathy. "Perhaps," I started, my voice barely above a whisper, "but he spoke of peace. Something we might someday strive for."

Colonel Galland turned his sharp gaze towards me, his eyes narrow slits of calculation. "Lieutenant, let not your heart be softened by the pleas of a monster." He said. "Once this is over - and we make out of here alive, I will tell you full well what that monster Kievelov is. A bullet between his eyes was a mercy."

"If you say so, sir."

The Battle of Feydrich Pass

At the time - perhaps I was shocked by such a display. But - Galland's murder had accomplished two things. Firstly - the commander of the Kholodian detachment was dead. Secondly - they could not simply sit there on the ridgeline for all matters of honor and not avenge their fallen leader. It was then inevitable that the roar of conflict would soon shatter the cold silence of the snow-covered pass.

My battalion - assembled at the front in a thin one-line row, bent down on their knees in a skirmishing formation, awaited the first move of the Kholodian army.

"They have a good two or, perhaps, three thousand men." Colonel Galland said - surveying with his spyglass. "Perhaps a hundred Streltsy." He said. I nodded, scanning the ridgeline nervously. Two or three thousand men was no small force, and their Vuk Streltsy were lethal - both from afar and close-up. We were severely outnumbered.

My eye throbbed, and I gripped my saber tightly and steadied my breath. This was it - the climax.

The Kholodian forces, like a steady wave, all at once, let out a fierce yell as they charged down the slope.

"By the Lord - what do they hope to accomplish by charging us?" Colonel Galland said - immediately looking around. He was wary, and so was I - undoubtedly, the death of the Boyar couldn't have led his army into such a foolish display.

The wave of charging Kholodian soldiers swept down the slope, their fierce cries and thundering footsteps stirring the frigid mountain air. I gripped my saber tighter, bracing myself for the brutal clash. From afar, I had a decent look at them, their ranks consisting entirely of muskets. Their cavalry, light hussars - pressed around the flanks, behind the men, waiting for a chance.

Yet as they neared, the horde suddenly split - half wheeling to the left, half to the right - and they stopped. Forming a wedge, as they stopped - and then started digging in.

They were a good four hundred meters away from us, well out of range of rifle fire. Cannon fire was a different story - yet we held off. They held enough of a slope that a round shot would have been a waste - after all, we were carrying light. We may have twenty cannonballs in each gun. Hardly enough to blast apart their lines.

I watched with unease as the Kholodian forces dug into the frozen earth, quickly establishing defensive positions along the ridge. Our cannons remained silent, conserving the limited ammunition we had brought on our trek through the mountains. The wintry wind whipped at our uniforms as we waited, huddled behind sparse cover on the open hillside - and their cavalry began maneuvering. The light hussars began to trot steadily around us, and Galland's face paled. He looked behind us - and looked forward. We were in an impasse - and I sensed danger. Incredible danger.

"Sir - what are your orders?"

Galland blinked.

"O-order the men to fall back at once. We cannot - and must not let their cavalry cut us off."

"But, sir..." I stated. "Our orders were clear," I started - looking ahead. Through the dim fog of the snowy pass - the old castle stood. I nodded slowly, though my heart was heavy. Our orders had been unambiguous - secure the ridge and the ancient fortress that stood upon it at any cost. Yet now, our position seemed hopeless.

Galland's face was pale but determined. "Damn the orders, lieutenant. We must choose life today if we are to fight again tomorrow."

I steeled myself, knowing he was right. Returning intact is better than throwing our lives away for pride. "Yes, sir," I replied. "I'll pass the order."

Quickly, I moved among our ragged lines, voices low but firm. "Fall back, lads. We're pulling out." Confusion flashed across some faces, but discipline held firm. Quietly, we withdrew, step by cautious step. The Kholodians held their positions, perhaps as surprised as we were at this sudden development—and they began to follow us at a quick pace...

We began falling back down the slope - a dangerous prospect, as the Kholodians seemed to delight in our organized retreat. The circling hussars went to the double-quick, hoping to flank around us - and then, there was a shout from the Kholodians.

Emboldened perhaps - by intimidating our force, they began to run forward now - and the hussars, the hussars charged in, hoping to shatter us completely. This - was, perhaps, the worst situation of warfare. An organized retreat could quickly turn into a rout - and one had to act hastily!

"First battalion! Square! Form a square!" I shouted - hoping off my horse. We must buy time for Galland's forces to regather themselves - otherwise, we would face destruction.

The men around me were confused at first—weren't we falling back, after all? These green-faced conscripts wished nothing more than to stay on the run with the safety of the bulk of the forces. But a chorus of shouts, ordering to form a square, echoed enough that some men hastily began to try and create it as the hussars bore down on us, wooden lances pointed towards us, hooves thundering on packed snow.

Around me - out of three hundred good men, I had perhaps a hundred or maybe two hundred, the rest either unaware - or fully content to leave us to our fate.

"Steady lads!" I shouted out over the chaos.

"Fire!"

A ripple of smoke and flame erupted - as lead and balls tore into men and mounts. Horses reared and screamed - riders tumbling lifelessly into the snow, as the hussars faltered - for a second, but a trumpet's blare announced their renewed charge.

"Reload!" I shouted again - My men scrambled to reload their muskets with shaking hands as the thunder of hooves grew louder. Louder - the earth-shaking. I almost broke my nerve until I heard a horn blast behind us.

Galland's forces were regrouping to join us. Heartened - my men let loose another volley just as the hussars smashed into our fragile little square. Men and beasts went down, but more came behind. It was hardly the charge of the famed Valtorean knights or the Eclairean cuirassers - but still, among us, lethal enough.

A hussar's lance caught me in the shoulder, knocking me to the ground and shattering against my breastplate - breaking my arm. I struggled to rise as a shadow fell over me - the Kholodian officer raised his saber for the killing blow. Then his face exploded in a shower of gore as Rottmann came over me.

"Sir! Sir!" He shouted - hefting me up. Around us - a melee was ensuing. A desperate one - as the bulk of the Kholodian force was perhaps a minute or two away.

The sounds of battle faded as I slipped in and out of consciousness. Rottmann had dragged me behind our ragged lines, propping me against an icy boulder. Through the screams and smoke, I saw our men again falling back as the main Kholodian force descended the ridge. We had bought some time, but at a significant cost. The snow around me was stained crimson, bodies and wrecked mounts strewn about. My shoulder throbbed where the lance had struck, and my arm hung limply at my side. Still, I knew I must rally what men remained.

"Sir - come on. We're getting the hell out of her-"

"No - no, we mustn't," I said, getting up. A handful of men rushing past me was perhaps a chance.

"To me!" I cried hoarsely. "Reform on me!"

A few men of our battalion turned, and a few others looked towards us and kept rushing downhill. But the fear of being a coward was enough to motivate a man, especially in front of an officer.

I steadied myself against the pain - raising my saber high.

"Volley fire into their flank - now!" I shouted. The Kholdian and Valtorean armies had clashed now - the Kholodians letting loose a volley of gunfire that tore apart our ranks as their hussars pulled away.

"Steady lads! One more volley!" I cried. My shoulder ached fiercely, but I pushed the pain aside.

The Kholodian's regimental banners were snapping in the icy wind - as they launched into their charge. They were a few seconds away from overwhelming the bulk of our forces entirely. A few bullets whizzed past - skirmishers who sought to pick us off, no doubt setting up for a retreat.

"Aim!" I shouted hoarsely. Muskets leveled at the oncoming tide of enemy soldiers, the mountains themselves shaking under this ferocious charge.

"Fire!"

A roar of smoke and thunder. Men fell on both sides. The Kholodian advance - numbering in the thousands, failed to be slowed, but - for a second, I saw their banner fall over—a small consolation.

"Kaelitz, damn it - it's lost. We need to go!" Rottman shouted. Our little force of a hundred men would do very little here - it was true.

I gritted my teeth as Rottmann tried to pull me away. The battle raged around us, but my eyes were fixed on the Valtorean banner. We still fought on - how could I abandon our forces?

"No. Not yet," I said firmly, wrenching my good arm from Rottmann's grip. I would not abandon my men. Not while I still drew breath. At this crescendo of battle - another volley would be too slow. There was - only one thing left to do.

I staggered forward, raising my sword high. "Bayonets!" My voice shouted out. These men - my men, were shaken already. Who was I - to call them into the fray, to send them to death? As if ignoring me - they continued to load their muskets. Even Rottmann blinked.

"Damn you - bayonets! Now! There's not a minute to lose!"

At my second command, the men slowly fixed bayonets with shaking hands. I could see the fear in their eyes but also their resolve. They knew what I asked of them and that many would not return from the charge. But it was our only chance—the only thing that could save us. The whizz of bullets flew past us, the men flinching and ducking down as they braced themselves.

It was time for audacity - for courage. I drew my saber, glancing back, waving it about as I grabbed a fallen Valtorean banner.

"Who will come with me?!" My voice, hoarse and strained from shouting, barely carried over the din of battle. Despite the pain that roared through my shoulder and arm, I lifted the banner higher, hoping it would ignite a spark of resilience among the tired and frightened soldiers.

A few men stepped forward, their bayonets fixed, eyes locked on me as if searching for my stance's last vestiges of courage. I didn't dare look back - to see how many were following - it was do or die.

Ignoring the searing pain in my shoulder, I broke into a run down the slope. The men followed, boots pounding the frozen earth as we built speed. The Kholodian ranks grew closer with each stride.

One hundred paces now, and the Kholodians had still not reacted to our desperate charge. Their focus remained on the main body of our army - as we plunged into the fray.

Bayonet charges were a shocking thing. Pike warfare was bad enough - but a brawl with a bayonet was primal and brutal. As we smashed into the Kholodian flank, I felt my men's bayonets thrust forward in desperate, violent jabs. The clash of steel on steel sang out over the roar of gunfire and the shouts of dying men. We were few, but our momentum, surprise, and desperation lent us a temporary advantage.

The snow beneath our feet turned to a horrible slush of mud and blood as we carved a path through the Kholodian line. My shoulder screamed with pain with each movement, threatening to buckle under the strain. My head was dizzy. Perhaps the Kholodians thought there were more of us in our charge than a beleaguered force numbering no more than forty men as they relented from pushing the Valtorean lines for just a second. Just enough to focus on us - those precious few.

It was a desperate melee. It lasted no more than, perhaps, a minute or two of a fool's glory before our defiant charge was cut short by the teeming number of Kholodians. We fought - we slashed, we stabbed. Yet - it was as if we were engulfed in the deluge of men. As I fought - a Kholodian infantryman smacked me with a stock, sending me into the snow - unconscious.

Coldness enveloped me, thoughts coursing through my head.

Was I dead? The first sensation was the icy embrace of the snow, cradling me as a mother would her child, yet somehow dispassionately indifferent. My senses were dulled, the din of battle now distant, almost like a dream. A numbness crept over me, not just of body but of spirit.

I lay there, the weight of my failure pressing down upon me like the heavy Valtorean banner that had spurred my foolhardy charge. Thoughts of my father surged through the fog in my mind. He had always stood firm in his beliefs, his honor untarnished despite the swirling court politics and war vortexes. What would he think now, knowing that his only son had seemingly squandered his life in a reckless gesture? The pain of disappointment seemed far more significant than any wound inflicted by enemy steel.

The air was filled with the iron tang of blood and the harsh scent of gunpowder; these scents mingled with the salt-heavy winds sweeping from Rega's coast, creating an intense reminder of where I lay dying—or so I thought. My heart ached more with sorrow than with the pain from my shoulder or the chill seeping into my bones. I had envisioned glory, perhaps some heroic end. Instead, here I was, seemingly on death's doorstep, cloaked not in victory but in defeat and disgrace.

My thoughts began to drift to darker places, and I wondered whether Alaric faced similar fears in his final moments at Castelon Fields. Did he, too, regret the path taken, lamenting what might have been if only different choices had been made? Was his spirit now wandering, restless, and tormented by the specter of unfinished deeds and unspoken words?

The realization of my isolation deepened, and a bitter sense of irony took hold as I thought of Von Löwe. My father's estate - those acres that I would never see again. His cold, calculated gaze - how could I lay here, dying?

No, I refused to accept this fate quietly. With great, tremendous will - I forced myself awake - to confront reality.

I didn't expect to wake up. No one does - in the aftermath of a battle.

I awoke with a start, my head throbbing. For a moment, I thought I was dead, but the stench of blood and smoke told me otherwise. I was lying in a pile of bodies, Valtorean and Kholodian alike. As I looked around, the battlefield was quiet. Not even for the cries of the wounded - it was deadly silent.

Had our charge failed? Was our brave last stand for nothing? I clutched my shoulder and sat up with much-pained effort. My uniform was caked in snow and gore - and only now did I feel how cold I was. My fingers were stiff - an early onset of frostbite. Rottman and the others were nowhere to be seen - had they fled? Or were they among the dead?

I staggered to my feet unsteadily. Looking around - were bodies. It felt as if another Castelon to me. I couldn't help but swallow and start moving forward down the slope towards hopefully friendly territory - however far that might be.

Cold - I shuddered, and I stumbled through the carnage, my limbs stiff from the cold and injuries. The snow fell steadily now, covering the gruesome scene in a serene white blanket. Ahead, I spotted a figure slumped against a tree - one of our men, though I could not tell who.

As I approached, the soldier raised his head. It was Rottmann, his uniform stained dark with blood. He clutched a ragged bandage to his side, face pale and eyes glassy with pain and blood loss. Yet he was alive.

"Captain," he rasped. "We held them off. The line held."

I knelt beside him, too exhausted to feel much relief. "The others?"

He shook his head. "It was a near thing. But we turned them, for a time. The Streltsy - they're on the prowl." He stated in a hushed tone.

"...The Vuk?"

"Aye. They're not taking prisoners." I nodded solemnly, peering through the snowfall toward the distant tree line. If the Vuk were here, the wounded Valtoreans remaining on the field lived on borrowed time. After the whole affair with Galland - I was sure they wouldn't give us any mercy.

Rottmann coughed a wet rasp that made my chest constrict in sympathy. The jagged wound in his side did not bode well. I tore a strip of cloth from my ragged uniform and helped brace the saturated bandage.

"You should go, sir. Rejoin the main force," Rottmann said. "You should know how these things go."

I didn't say a word - I picked him up with my one good arm.

"Let's just give it a damned shot."

He protested as we marched through the pass. Snow fell down around us, and a fog covered us as we moved. Both of us tried to help each other. His protests had faded to pained whimpers with each faltering step. I knew he wouldn't last much longer without care, but what choice did we have?

The icy wind cut through my blood-soaked uniform like daggers. My shoulder screamed in protest, threatening to give out completely. Still, I pushed on through sheer force of will, one agonizing step after another. Rottmann had fallen silent now, his head lolling against my good shoulder. I feared he had already slipped away when I felt the faint warmth of his breath against my neck.

"Stay with me, old friend," I muttered through chattering teeth. "Just a bit further."

The snow swirled thicker now, obscuring my view of the surrounding forest. We could be walking right into an ambush and not even know it. But what choice did we have? Stopping here meant freezing or bleeding to death. It was better to keep moving towards hope, however faint.

My legs buckled as I crested a slight rise, sending us both tumbling to the ground. Rottmann gave a faint groan as I struggled upright, squinting into the blizzard. I lay there for a second. Both of us lay there. - exhausted wrecks.

"...This... This isn't the worst place to die." Rottman said as I coughed. The wind howled around us as we lay in the snow, too spent to go on. My vision blurred, darkness creeping in at the edges. Perhaps it would be a relief to finally let go, to be free of pain and cold. I was tired of the struggle - tired of it all.

I felt my eyes close as the cold seeped into my bones. Perhaps this was it. Possibly, our story would end here, swallowed by the storm.

Some part of my mind turned to what they would say at home. My soul swooned slowly as I listened to it.

The howling wind carried faint shouts through the swirling snow. At first, I thought it a trick of my fading mind, but the calls grew louder, accompanied by the crunch of boots on snow. Glancing upward - I saw it. It would seem they weren't Valtoreans - Kholodians, and hussars at that. A glint was in their eyes - as they came up to me. The Kholodian hussars approached through the swirling snow, their sabers glinting menacingly. I struggled to rise, knowing there were no rescuers.

A voice sneered out - the lead hussar, prodding me with his boot. I cried out as he pressed against my mangled shoulder, pushing me against the snow. Alien murmurs - as the hussars discussed no doubt what to do with us - and I heard the draw of a blade rasping out of a sheath.

Then - a softer, quieter tread of footprints. A harsh, guttural grunt - and then, something hefted me out of the snow before I lost consciousness.

I awoke again - this time, somewhere warm. Wooden paneled walls surrounded me, and I lay on a rough cot piled high with furs. My shoulder had been tightly bandaged, the searing pain now just a dull ache.

I tried to sit up but found my arms and legs bound, alongside an unwelcome wave of dizziness washing over me. I was weak - so weak I could barely lift my head from the pillow. How long had I been unconscious?

A door opened, and an older man with a bushy gray beard entered carrying a tray of vials and towels. He was dressed in a simple tunic and a surgeon's apron tied around his waist - one of the healers in this place, wherever it was. He noticed I was awake - opening the door outward and barking something out in his language before approaching me.

"Ah, finally awake," he said in broken Valtorean. "We were starting to worry." I stared at the bearded man, confused. "Where am I?" I croaked, my throat dry.

He poured me a cup of water from a pitcher and helped me take a few sips. "You're in the demesne of Grand Prince Vladislav Michaelovich. Our men found you and your companion collapsed in the snow. It's a miracle you survived as long as you did."

I blinked, trying to clear the fog from my mind. Rottmann! Where was he?

As if reading my thoughts, the healer continued, "Your friend is here too. He lost a lot of blood, but we were able to stitch him up. He's resting in the next room... Though, he didn't recover exactly as well as you have."

"...I-I see."

Relief washed over me. Rottmann was alive. We had made it through the blizzard, somehow. But that raised another question...

"Why did the Grand Prince take us in?" I asked warily.

The healer smiled. "Nothing chivalrous, mind you." He said. "Effectively - you are hostages, far from home. I do not envy you - really, I don't." Despite the room's warmth, the healer's words sent a chill through me. Hostages - a fate I had desperately hoped to avoid. Though we had been saved from the storm, it seemed we were still prisoners of this endless war.

I tested the ropes binding my wrists. They held fast. Even if I could break free, I was in no condition to attempt escape or combat.

"What will happen to us?" I asked quietly.

"Who knows? Though - I reckon the Grand Prince will meet with you in a minute." The surgeon stated. "I'd get some rest if I was you. He's a very intense man since his father died."

I laid back, sighing. When would this cloud of fatigue end?

The door opened - perhaps a few hours later. A large wolfman entered the room, his sharp claws clicking against the wooden floorboards. I recognized him immediately as the companion of Boyar Kievolov, and he glared at me intensely.

"Mmh." He stated growly. His black fur ruffled as he glared at me - as if delighting in what torture he would inflict on me. He pulled out a seat - sitting down, staring at me. An uneasy silence followed as I stared back at the wolfman, trying not to show any fear. His eyes gleamed with a predatory light as he looked me over.

"So, you are awake," he growled. His voice was guttural, with that tell-tale Kholodian accent.

I said nothing, clenching my jaw and meeting his gaze steadily. After a moment, he barked out a harsh laugh.

"Brave, for a human. Or foolish." He leaned forward, lips curling back to reveal sharp, yellowed fangs. "We shall see which, soon enough. My name is Vladislav Michaelovich. Or, you can call me the Grand Prince - your grace... So on, and so forth." He paused, scratching his chin with a claw and a slight grin.

"...Ah. I see." I murmured out.

I nodded slowly, assessing my situation. Bound and at his mercy, I knew I must choose my following words carefully.

"I am Kaelitz von Ardent..." I said evenly. "Thank you for saving me from the storm... But - holding me as a hostage will prove fruitless."

"Fruitless?" The large wolfman's eyebrow raised.

"...I'm from junior nobility. A small village - any ransom you'd request, you'd likely find difficult to obtain."

The wolfman listened silently, his expression unreadable. For a long moment, he studied me, his dark eyes glinting in the firelight.

"You speak of mercy," he finally growled. "Yet your people show none when they kill our serfs and burn our fields. The suffering of this war is not equal."

He leaned forward, fangs bared. "But you are right about one thing. You are worth little to me as a hostage. Your life now depends on how useful you can make yourself here."

I tensed, unsure what he meant but knowing I had few options. I was at the mercy of this Kholodian lord and his men. And Rottmann - what had become of him?

"What would you have me do?" I asked quietly, steadying myself for the answer.

The wolfman sat up - grinning as if he delighted in my suffering.

"It's simple. Whatever knowledge you have - you will share."

"I know little of value," I said carefully. "I am but a junior officer."

The wolfman studied me, then barked a laugh. "Come now. You're the first officer I met leading a battalion of musketeers. The Valtoreans - as divided as they are, are starting to get wise to warfare."

I stared warily at the Grand Prince, unsure of how to respond. He was fitting that the Valtoreans had adapted our tactics in recent years to match the more advanced Kholodian forces. But I could hardly admit the full extent of our military knowledge without endangering my homeland.

The wolfman snorted, clearly unimpressed with my evasion. "Do not play me for a fool. You know more than you let on and will share it in time."

He stood, his clawed feet scraping against the floorboards. "I will give you a day to consider your position. Either you provide me with useful information about Valtorean plans and capabilities for their plans to re-organize their forces, or your fate will be...unpleasant."

With that vague but chilling threat, he turned and stalked from the room, the door slamming shut behind him.

I waited in that room - still bound to the bed, unable to move much except for the slight twitching of my fingers and the slow rise and fall of my chest. The room grew dark as the hours passed, and the demons of war haunted me - even in here, as I waited. It was true - I was a haunted man at this point. A year's worth of service had etched itself deeply into my soul - and left alone, the constant echo of cannon fire rang in my ears even during the silent nights, and the faces of fallen comrades visited me in sleepless fits. Perhaps - for a man like myself, the worst thing to do - was to give them nothing to do.

As night deepened, shadows danced across the wooden walls thrown by the flickering candlelight, mimicking the march of phantom soldiers. Some part of me - my immortal soul, recognized them as my own. I turned my thoughts towards them - how many of us had survived? Who was ultimately responsible for the fate of those men - was it I, rushed into duty, or was it the burden of men such as von Lowe? These questions weighed heavily on me, pressing down on me.

But then - the door creaked open once more - relief flooding me. This time - it was not the imposing figure of Grand Prince Vladislav but instead - a Vuk in gray fur who gazed into the room, wearing what seemed to be an expression of curiosity and caution. The Vuk's ears twitched as it walked softly into the room, its large, lupine eyes scanning the shadow-filled corners before settling on me. I saw it wore a pendant around its neck in the dim light, glimmering faintly with an ethereal blue light that seemed to pulse with life. On its back was a leather pouch bulging with unknown contents.

Her golden eyes glinted with a curious intelligence, and she moved silently, her paws making no sound upon the wooden floor.

"Good evening," she murmured, her Valtorean smooth and melodic, tinged with that guttural growl native to the Vuk. "I see my brother has left you in quite a dilemma."

I blinked - perhaps a bit shocked. I nodded.

"So - you know the man who killed our father then. Podpolko... I mean - Colonel Galland, yes?" She said.

"I-I do. I served with him - for a brief week's march." The wolflady's eyes narrowed slightly, and a ripple of tension passed through the air, palpable and sharp. "A week," she repeated softly, almost to herself. She approached closer, her movements deliberate, the pendant on her neck swinging gently with each step.

I struggled to maintain composure under her intense scrutiny. "Yes," I confirmed, my voice steady despite the tightness in my chest. "Colonel Galland was a man of... Considerable resolve."

She paused by the side of the bed, looking down at me with an unreadable expression. After hesitating, she sat down on a small wooden stool nearby, her tail gracefully curling around her feet.

"Yes. Judging from the way he killed my father - he very much was." She sneered before turning to me. "...Resolve. Foolish. Many words could be used. I'm not as fluent with high Valtorean as I once was." She sighed. "But I digress," she continued, changing the subject slightly - her eyes settling on me.

"Could I perhaps get a kholop to get you some porridge?" She stated. A hungry, long growl came from my gut as I nodded.

"Yes, please," I stated. "Could I perhaps - be let out of my bonds?"

She nodded. "Of course. So long as you swear not to try and do anything violent in my halls." She stated firmly. The thought hadn't crossed my mind - I hardly knew how far away from home I was, and besides, I was not in any condition to put up a fight.

Seeing my acquiescence, she reached towards the leather straps binding my wrists and deftly loosened them. The relief as blood began to flow more freely through my limbs was immense, though I kept my movements conservative, not wanting to alarm her or seem ungrateful for this small mercy.

With my hands-free, she stood and moved toward the door. "Stay here. I'll return shortly with your food," she said without looking back.

Left alone once again, I flexed my fingers to ease the stiffness - still sore. My shoulder, too - ached. I unwrapped the bandage - delicately - and noticed.

A significant, scarred mark and signs of infection - though abating. I allowed a deep breath to escape my lips, the sheer reality of my condition settling into the depths of my mind. I was fortunate to be alive, let alone with all my limbs.

As I rewrapped the bandage, my mind wandered to the Vuk woman. She seemed such a matter of fact - accepting almost of her father's death. These were a strange people.

The door creaked open again, snapping me out of my reverie. She returned, carrying a wooden bowl filled with steaming porridge and a water jug. Setting them down on a small table near the bed, she sighed and watched me with those intense golden eyes.

"None of the servants are up at this hour. So - you'll have to do some of my cooking." She said, looking over at me, grinning with all those sharp teeth. "Vuk stew. Very hearty." She said, passing a bowl of meat - a white gravy filled with sausage, ham, and meats - so rich that I had to stop myself. I was hardly used to this - more used to the gruel they served in our camp.

"Thank you," I managed, my voice hoarse from disuse. "For this...and for unbinding me... Why?"

She looked at me and blinked for a second before smiling.

"Because you remind me of my brother," she replied, her voice softening slightly as she settled back on the stool. "A warrior. Foolish - and scarred." She purred out, almost worried. "And young. Too young for such dark times."

Her warm demeanor momentarily belied the fierce warrior presence I had noticed when she first entered. She seemed lost in thought, her gaze drifting towards the flickering candle that cast eerie shadows along the walls. Then she turned towards me again, her eyes piercing through the dimness. I almost failed to notice the jewelry adorned by her - she was undoubtedly from the upper class. Arlenian robes - Eclairean jewelry. Some of the finest in the world.

"Not to mention - I enjoy guests." She states. "It's been far too long since our estate has had someone visit. Even if they're our junior." She stated, sighing.

"Oh," I said. "I... Well, I'll be honest. I don't know a hell of a lot about the Vuk. Or the..."

She glared at me, crossing her arms, irritated. Her eyes narrowed, the flicker of the candlelight reflecting a stormy gold. "Vuk," she repeated sharply, her voice carrying a weight that stilled the air between us. "That is not our name, not anymore." Her jaw clenched as she looked away, her expression cloaked in shadows.

"...Apologies," I said. "I didn't realize."

"You are fine. But us - as a people, are the Dvoryanstvo..." She said, stopping. "The manor-dwellers. The Dvoryans." She started listing them off - as I blinked. "The Vuk - the Vuko, that is a name associated with the pagans of Baltiva. We are not that. As much as the world likes to call us that." She stated.

"I'm not familiar with the history of your people," I admitted, the porridge momentarily forgotten. My curiosity peaked; the weight of my ignorance felt suddenly oppressive in the presence of her intense gaze.

She seemed to consider this, her expression softening. "Most aren't," she conceded. "It is simply the way things are - and most of the Dvoryanstvo wish to forget our people's past in favor of who we are now." She stated. "Which - sounds perhaps, terrible - but it is also good. The Kholodians - the people here are a backward sort. Were it not for us - they would still be tending to small villages." She stated matter-of-factly.

"The serfs," I stated. A basic familiarity of the Kholodians settled over me. "The Kholodian humans. Is it not slavery?"

She paused, glaring at me. Perhaps irritated - as she growled.

"...You can ask more offensive, stupid questions after you finish your soup." I stared down at the bowl, chastised, and started eating - as she began to answer.

"Here, it is...different. It is bound by ancient codes and traditions that intertwine our lives. The Kholodians are not slaves in the manner you imagine. They are tied to the land and the Dvoryanstvo through bonds of duty and protection." She stated. "I know the Valtoreans do things differently. With freemen, and... Politics." She said - an apparent distaste in her mouth. "Far too much politics."

"That much is true." I agreed. "It took nearly a year for me to wrap my head around our ducal's legal code. Let alone the Empire's legal code."

"My brother would say it's because you are a weak, corrupt people who profane the Lord." Her words stung, and I paused, spoon halfway to my mouth, and met her gaze squarely.

"A strong accusation from someone who spent their lives killing Valtoreans," I remarked, setting the spoon down with a clatter that seemed overly loud in the peaceful confines of the dim dining room. She leaned back, assessing me with a thoughtful tilt of her head. "Perhaps," she conceded after a moment. "But, I agree with him. Valtoreans are an ungodly people." Those words - I couldn't take them as anything but a challenge, as the change in atmosphere was palpable. I couldn't sit here. Her eyes widened - as she looked at me.

"You speak of my people as if already condemned! But - you savages, you kill us - you murder us - and enslave us, and invaded our lands on a whim..." I began as she hardened her face - and held back.

"It is too late for such arguing and vitriol." She states - before sighing. "But, I apologize. Things here in Kholodia are much simpler." She picked up the bowl and moved to pick up the empty jug,

"Yes - things are much simpler here." She said, closing her eyes. "I should retire." She says, "We'll talk more later. It was an..." She cocked her head. "Interesting conversation." She stated before retiring for the evening.

Left alone in the dimly lit dining room, my thoughts drifted unbidden to Strossberg and the life I had left behind. The grand ballrooms of the ducal palace were adorned with glittering chandeliers that cast a warm glow upon the smiling faces of the nobility. The fair ladies, resplendent in their flowing silk and lace gowns, their laughter like the tinkling of silver bells. I could almost smell the rose gardens' heady perfume and hear the orchestra's gentle strains as couples twirled and glided across the polished marble floor.

My heart ached with a deep longing for those carefree days, now lost to me forever—or perhaps to the moment. Regardless, sentimentality clouded my thoughts as I drifted to sleep.

Chains of the Tzardom

The next day, I was permitted to travel to the estate grounds with an armed guard. He was a burly man, wearing the buttoned-up white uniform of the Kholodian military - with a fur cape, a saber at his side, and a tall fox-fur hat. An elaborate mustache of the Eastern style added only to his swagger as I walked beside him in the crisp morning air; the estate revealed its grandeur with each step we took. The estate's main house was a staggering tower of dark stone and wood, surrounded by expansive gardens that seemed to fight against the cold with bursts of color from hardy winter blooms. Beyond the gardens were the fields of the serfs, stretching out for many miles. And beyond that - in the distance, seemed to be a city.

My guard, Mikhail, whose name I learned, spoke little but observed much. His eyes constantly roamed the perimeter, and his hand rested near his saber, always on alert. As we walked, the gravel crunched under our boots, breaking the morning silence with each step.

"Do you speak Valtorean?" I asked - after a few minutes of wandering the grounds. Mikhail glanced at me, his eyes narrowing slightly as if assessing my intent behind the question. "A little," he replied curtly, his voice tinged with a noticeable accent. "Enough to understand plotting or pleading." He said - a grin curling across his lips.

His response elicited a small chuckle from me despite the seriousness of his demeanor. "I suppose that's as much as you need," I acknowledged, watching a pair of crows take flight from the nearby trees, their caws echoing eerily across the fields. "Where are you from?"

"Zheltokholodia," Mikhail confirmed, his gaze following the birds momentarily before returning to scan the horizon. "The new, Eastern territories."

We continued our walk in silence for a few moments, the only sounds being our footsteps and the distant calls of working serfs in the fields. The stark contrast between the lush gardens of the estate and the more somber, utilitarian fields where the Kholodian serfs labored was striking, and then I turned back to him. As I studied Mikhail's features more closely, I noticed subtle details hinting at his true heritage. The slight curve of his nose, the shape of his eyes, and the way he carried himself with a proud, almost defiant bearing - these were all hallmarks of the southward cossack people, the fierce horsemen who had once roamed the steppes between Arkanthia - and Kholodia.

"You're not just from Zheltokholodia, are you?" I ventured, my curiosity piqued. "You have the look of a Cossack about you - and I'd wager, likely from one of the Hetmanates?"

Mikhail's steps faltered momentarily, and he turned to face me, his eyes widening in surprise. "You have a keen eye, Valtorean," he acknowledged, a hint of respect creeping into his voice. "Though, those days are long past. Now - we are all Kholods."

A silence settled over us as I gazed outward. I wondered how to respond - I did not wish to challenge his notion openly - and yet, I felt fascinated.

"It would be a shame to extinguish the flame of the East. The cossacks have always been something of a romantic tale back in Valtorea." I said.

Mikhail grunted, his expression clouding momentarily as if the weight of those memories pressed down upon him. "Romantic, perhaps, to those who haven't lived it," he said slowly, his eyes distant. "But there's little romance on the steppes, trapped between Empires, playing you for their Great Game."

We resumed our walk, the estate's vastness enveloping us in its quiet majesty.

"The Great Game," I said, sighing. The tremendous political project of our era was wrapped around Auroientalis.

"The all-mighty interplay of empires, each hungry for land and power, makes pawns of us all. Arkanthia, Kholodia, and Arlenian—mighty titans are encircling a board of infinite complexity." Mikhail spoke with bitterness. His words lingered in the frosty air, resonating with a truth I had often contemplated in quieter, more reflective moments. These thoughts led my gaze back to the horizon, where the gray outlines of distant mountains marked the borders of empires and the boundaries of man's ambition.

"I wonder," I began, pausing to choose my words carefully, "if there will ever come a day when men will tire of this game when the map's lines cease to dictate who must be enemy and who ally."

Mikhail looked at me, his expression softening slightly. "In a world driven by hunger — for power, land, resources — peace is but a fleeting dream. It is the nature of empires to expand; stagnation is decay."

His perspective was jaded, yet there was wisdom in his resignation. Walking alongside him, I felt the weight of centuries of conflict and strategy that defined our lands. Each step seemed to echo with the silent screams of those who had fallen victim to this never-ending struggle.

We approached a part of the garden where the path wound beside a frozen pond. The crispness of the air seemed to sharpen every detail around us — from the delicate frost on the shrubs to the stark nakedness of the trees.

"It seems a cruel fate," I remarked softly, "to be born into such a world."

Mikhail stopped and faced me again, his eyes intense. "Perhaps," he conceded. "But there is glory in it. There is glory in the challenge, in the rise and fall of nations, in the clashing of empires that sculpt the destiny of millions."

As he spoke, his demeanor changed. The usual hardness in his posture softened into something more contemplative and profound as if he were about to reveal a part of his rarely shared philosophy.

"Yes, the Tzars—they sought expansion, dominion over lands and peoples, a mere extension of power for power's sake - both of themselves and to protect Kholodia. But see," he gestured broadly with a sweep of his arm towards the horizon, where the land stretched out beneath the heavy sky, "Soon, that will all change. The Grand Prince will make sure of it."

Mikhail paused, letting the gravity of his statement settle between us before he continued. His voice grew soft, almost conspiratorial, as if the frost-laden branches might overhear and whisper secrets to the wind. "The Grand Prince, you see, has visions beyond conquests and crowns. He dreams of a Kholodia reborn—a realm where its people are liberated from the yoke of serfdom that has bound them for generations."

He began walking again, slowly, as his words painted a picture of a future unlike any told in the tales of old Tzars and their iron-fisted rule. "Imagine a Kholodia where each man's worth is determined not by the blood or soil of his birth but by his grit and mind. Where serfs are not chattel to be traded and toiled, but citizens with rights to hold and horizons to chase."

Arlenian Empire's shimmering ideals of liberal governance seemed to linger around us as Mikhail spoke, yet he quickly delineated his vision from theirs. "Do not mistake me—I speak not of adopting foreign decadences but forging our path. Away from the Western powers of Aurisca. A new covenant between Tzar and subjects where power is respected but checked by duty and the welfare of the common man, led by one - ruled by one."

The realization that such thoughts were brewing in the heart of Kholodia's prospective ruler struck me profoundly. It was an audacious hope that seemed almost too fragile for the harsh realities of our world—one so steeped in the blood-soaked soil of relentless ambition and age-old enmities.

Yet, despite the stirring portrayal of a future Mikhail envisioned, my thoughts kept returning to the palpable ideology that permeated the chilly air, an almost tangible essence that filled every corner of this expansive territory. Each person, from the humblest serf to the highest noble, seemed a staunch believer in some grand idea or another. It was as if ideology itself was the lifeblood of Kholodian society—a contrast stark against the practical and often cynically motivated politics of a Valtorean mind.

"Everyone seems the ideologue here in Kholodia," I remarked, the observation escaping my lips more pointedly than intended. The words hung between us, a subtle challenge to the noble aspirations Mikhail had just laid out.

Mikhail paused mid-step, his large wolfish form casting a long shadow on the frost-covered ground. A frown briefly crossed his features before he turned to face me with a sarcastic half-smile, an expression not entirely devoid of warmth. "Apologies, Captain," he said with a slight incline of his head. "It is true that we are perhaps overly passionate about our convictions here. It is both our strength and our ailment. We Kholodians will talk about change - and yet, nothing will change. Such is the way of things."

"It sounds awfully like Valtorea when put like that." I grinned. Mikhail smiled back slyly.

"Or perhaps, more like Arlenia."

"God damn you - don't mention them," I said - laughing. "Those bastards have more debates than decisions, and their parliament's a circus."

Mikhail chuckled, a deep rumbling sound emanating from the soil we stood upon. "I can agree with you on that."

We continued the stroll for a few more minutes, in silence - before my mind turned elsewhere - towards Rottmann.

"My companion. Rottman. Could I visit his chambers?" Mikhail paused, his expression unreadable momentarily, before giving a slight nod. "You can," he said gruffly, "but I will be with you. Of course."

I nodded in understanding, appreciating at least that small mercy. Following Mikhail, we veered off from the serene path through the gardens, taking a more secluded route to the servant quarters situated behind the main building.

The quarters were a stark contrast to the estate's opulent facade. The buildings here were built from more straightforward materials: wood mostly grayed with age and stone blocks that had seen better days. There was a sad pragmatism to their construction, reflecting perhaps the lives of those who resided within.

As we approached what I assumed was Rottman's chamber, Mikhail stopped and gestured toward a small, sturdy door. "Wait here," he instructed before stepping forward and knocking sharply twice.

A moment passed before the door creaked open, revealing Rottman lying in the bed. He looked somewhat surprised but quickly masked it with a formal nod. "Sir," he greeted Mikhail first and then turned towards me. I immediately noticed—his arm was gone. The old soldier had grown thinner, his face drawn tight with fatigue. "I wasn't expecting visitors," he said, his voice husky, probably from lack of use.

Mikhail stepped aside to let me in. The room was spartan, with minimal furniture and a small window that let in only a sliver of light. It brought out the lines of hardship etched deeply into Rottman's features.

"Sit," Rottman gestured to a wooden chair beside the bed. As I sat, he looked at me with an intensity that felt like he was assessing my soul. "You're the only other bloody Valtorean here. And one who's not a fluffball." He grinned. "I trust the wolves have been circling you - more than they have me." His laughter was dry, almost hollow. I nodded slowly.

"Yes, it feels that way," I admitted, trying to find comfort in the shared hardship, though his situation seemed far graver than mine. "Your arm..?" I asked cautiously, my eyes flicking to the bandaged stump where his left arm should have been.

Rottman's face stiffened momentarily, a shadow passing over his features. "Frostbite." He said grimly, the word weighed down with a gravity that filled the small room. "And then gangrene set in. They cut it off not two weeks past." His gaze drifted to the window, pinched with pain or perhaps memory. "At least it wasn't the leg. And - I've still got one good arm."

His frankness was unsettling yet oddly comforting; it was a truth laid bare, unembellished, and stark as the walls around us. "How are you managing?" I inquired, my voice low, respecting the gravity of his loss.

Rottman chuckled dryly, the sound rasping from his throat like gravel. "Like any soldier would. Hardly the end of the world - one arm," he replied, as he blinked and sighed...

"Did you grab breakfast for me, by any chance? I'm starved." His sudden shift from solemnity to mundane matters was jarring, yet it gave me a faint smile. "I didn't, I'm afraid," I confessed. "But I can certainly fetch something for you."

"Would you?" Rottman's eyes brightened slightly, a spark of life flickering within. "Just some bread and cheese will do. Oh, and if they have any of that stew that lady made last night..."

"Mmmh. So you had the pleasure to meet the lady as well, then?" I asked as he grinned.

"Aye. Y'know, for being a lad with one arm and halfway in the grave, she treats me decent enough. The Kholodians don't know what gems they have for women if they're all like her." Rottman continued, his tone lightening a touch with the mention of her. "Brings me my meals, and sometimes we share a word or two. Doesn't nag. Honest." He said, grinning. "Aye, now that - that's something worth keeping around. Hopefully, I don't recover too fast now." His eyes twinkled with a mischievous light that momentarily dispelled his condition's gloom.

I couldn't help but grin, a retort - as filthy as it was, settling in on my mind. "So what - are you some kind of wolf-fucker now?"

Rottman burst into laughter - unexpected, unprepared. His joy, so raw and hearty, filled the space between the cold stone walls, echoing off them as if to defy the somberness that had settled in our hearts. "Kaelitz," he gasped between fits of laughter, his remaining hand clutching his side as if to hold himself together. "You'd make a sailor blush with that tongue! Lord help us!" He said - making the sign of protection with his one good arm.

I leaned back against my chair, allowing a smug smile to curl at the edges of my mouth. "Well, when you're in the service of scoundrels, miscreants—and more..." I started, my voice dripping with mock solemnity. You learn a few things about colorful conversation."

His chuckle subsided into a series of chuckles, and he shook his head in disbelief. "Never thought I'd hear such crude jesting from you, Kaelitz."

His assertion sparked a playful glint in my eye. "Well, Rottman, war changes many things: our limbs, souls, and evidently, sense of humor."

He nodded sagely, then his gaze shifted slightly, softening as he looked past me towards the small window. There was a brief silence, a rare pause in the constant rhythm of jest and retort.

"It does at that," Rottman murmured, his voice barely above a whisper. "And it's taken more than it's given, I reckon." His eyes held a distant look that spoke of too many battles, too much lost. "But anyways - as I was saying... That last-"

"Lord forgive you," I sighed as he grinned at me. "I'll fetch your breakfast then; perhaps some fresh air might do you good later."

Rottman nodded appreciatively. "Maybe a little stroll would do these old bones some good. You're right." He leaned against his pillow, a contemplative look crossing his weathered face. "It's easy to forget there's a world outside these four walls when cooped up like this."

As I exited the door, Mikhail was waiting outside, leaning against the wall with his arms crossed. He followed me - as I went to the kitchens, his heavy boots thudding softly against the dirt path.

"Sweet Lord," Rottman grumbled in awe. "They have gravy." The old soldier let out a mumbled prayer of thanks - practically ravenously devouring the biscuit in one go as the two of us sat - practically devouring our meal. I couldn't lie - I hadn't eaten gravy or a real bite in nearly a year. Sausage and meat were mixed in - hearty and delicious. I couldn't help but thank God at least twice for it. Both of us ravenously ate up - strength returning.

After a few moments dedicated to devouring the meal, Rottman wiped his mouth with the back of his hand and looked up at me with renewed energy. "Tell me," he began, his tone shifting towards something more serious,

"...Did any of them tell you what has happened to our forces in Baltiva? Anything at all?" He said curiously.

I shook my head, swallowing the last bite of sausage before speaking. "No, I've heard nothing." My brow furrowed with concern.

"I'm sure we'll learn soon enough," Rottmann grumbled. "Hopefully, that bastard Von Lowe has his head on a pike." Rottman's expression turned dark, his single fist clenching visibly at the mention of Von Lowe. "That man has cost us much... Too much." His voice was a low growl, filled with a venom that surprised me, given his earlier levity. We fell into a momentary silence, but he sighed. Mikhail - the guard, coughed.

"To answer the question - nothing. It has been a stalemate." Mikhail's voice cut through the thick atmosphere, providing a sense of grim reality that neither of us wished to acknowledge. "Nobody wishes to push the other to an all-out war, " he continued solemnly.

"That's a relief," Rottmann grumbled. "At least they saw reason." He grumbled. "Nothing worse than dying for a shithole in nowhere, for someone who hates you. Those Baltzers - and Von Lowe, can suck on m-"

The door opened abruptly, and the tall, wolf lady entered - her eyes scanning the room with a stern efficiency that momentarily halted Rottman's tirade. Her presence filled the space, commanding and formidable, yet there was a gentleness in her gaze when it finally rested on Rottman. "Good morning," she said, her voice carrying a firm but soothing timbre. "I see our guests are in good spirits today."

Rottman's gruff exterior softened ever so slightly, a half-grin breaking through his usual scowl. "Thanks for your cooking, ma'am," he replied, gesturing towards the remnants of our hearty breakfast. She grinned - or smiled; honestly, I couldn't tell which, as she seemed to appreciate the compliment at most minor. "Well, I'm glad to hear it," she responded, her voice still carrying that sternness that seemed an inherent part of her yet mixed now with a touch of warmth.

"Now - you..." She said, looking at me. "Captain - my brother wishes to see you." She said, nodding towards the door. "He's in the council room waiting... And I'd wipe some of those crumbs off if I was you." She helpfully added, staring over at Rottman, who sighed.

"Go on then," Rottman urged, waving a dismissive hand as I hesitated. "Don't keep the man waiting."

Grand Prince Michaelovich awaited me in his study. Judging from it - he seemed to be a worldly man. An entire parchment of Aurisca hung on his wall like a tapestry, alongside maps of several disputed territories and drawings of various military fortifications. The room was dimly lit, the faint scent of incense mingling with the musty odor of old books and parchment. His desk was an organized chaos of scrolls and papers, over which leaned the Grand Prince himself, glaring at me.

"Captain," he greeted, his voice neither warm nor cold but commanding respect by its sheer firmness.

"Your lordship," I replied, bowing slightly.

"I trust the accommodations have been satisfactory?" he asked, gesturing for me to sit opposite him.

"Very much so, sir," I replied, settling into the chair. The air in the room felt heavy with anticipation of the conversation.

"I see. Have you decided about my offer?" He said - an eyebrow-raising. "I hope I will not have to rely upon more..." His claws gleamed sharply. "Persuasive measures," he concluded.

I shifted in my seat, acutely aware of the delicate situation I found myself in. "Sir," I began cautiously, "I don't believe I have much choice. My honor as a gentleman - and a nobleman... Or my life. I think you very well know which one I favor."

Grand Prince Michaelovich steepled his fingers, considering my words. "I understand your predicament, Captain. I would likely agree if I were in your place." He paused, his gaze piercing through the dim light as if he could unearth my deepest thoughts. "Yet," he continued, his voice a low rumble, "I hardly have the time - or the care, to play at games like this about honor and chivalry." He stated.

"I suppose you don't," I stated. "But - I have nothing to lose myself," I said, gazing at him. For a second, the wolfman concealed a grin. He leaned back in his chair, the leather creaking under his weight, and his eyes, sharp and discerning, continued to study me. "I see," he said finally, a tinge of respect coloring his tone. "I admire your honesty and your spirit, Captain. It reminds me of... old times. Times when such virtues were commonplace among men of action, such as ourselves." He paused, gazing towards the window where the early morning light began sifting through.

"From my understanding - you came from a rural village outside Strossburg." He stated that he was taking a document in hand. "Rural nobility. Little of note. Prior military service - minimal." He said before looking at me. "Usually - a man of your caliber would remain in your little demi-lancer corp or advance to a low-ranking officer rank. But, instead of that..." He said. "They put you in charge of a battalion and name you Captain. After only a year's worth of service."

He placed the document back on his desk, deliberately emphasizing his words' gravity. "This is highly unusual in Valtorea. I'm sure you're aware of that. Tell me, what about you warranted such a rapid promotion?"

I felt my throat tighten under his scrutinizing gaze, "I believe it was due to a demonstration of loyalty to the Empire at Castelon," I replied, my voice steady despite the undercurrent of anxiety. "It was a foolish thing. But romantic, I suppose."

"Romantical, indeed." Grand Prince Michaelovich nodded slowly, his eyes never leaving mine. "I've heard of young noblemen jumping to the front - getting themselves killed. But rarely have I heard them coming back alive. Let alone doing it again - and again." He said before adjusting the papers. "Not to mention - advancing in rank without bribes, without title... You know what that leads me to conclude?"

"...What?" I asked.

"Perhaps the fools in the Imperial Army are starting to learn something." He grinned. "Cultivating a new officer class - a remarkable thing. Yet - I cannot simply let that happen as a foe of Valtorea." Grand Prince Michaelovich's expression suddenly shifted, the grin fading into a more contemplative frown. "A weak Valtorea means a strong Kholodia," he continued thoughtfully, his fingers tapping on the polished surface of his desk. "You see, Captain, the existence of men like you complicates my plans. Men who rise through merit rather than money or birthright."

"A pity," I stated ironically. I held back a smirk - perhaps enjoying the compliments a bit.

Grand Prince Michaelovich let out a low, appreciative chuckle at my response. "Indeed, Captain. A pity for me but perhaps a stroke of fortune for your Empire." He leaned forward, his eyes narrowing slightly as if reassessing me through a new lens. "Tell me, what drives a man like you?"

It was a question I had often posed to myself during the lonely, cold nights at camp when my only company was the thoughts swirling in my mind. "Duty," I responded, my voice firm, reflecting the conviction that had anchored me throughout the trials of battle and beyond. "Duty to my comrades, my family, and the Empire."

The Grand Prince listened intently, sighed, and threw the document aside.

"Utter nonsense. You preach these romantical notions - but what have your eyes - or rather, eye, told you about how war is conducted now?" He waved his hand dismissively toward the maps and papers on his desk, each depicting various strategic points and battle lines. "Look at these, Captain. This is no longer the age of gallant knights riding into battle for honor and glory. It's an era of strategy, geopolitical maneuvering, and realism."

With my remaining eye, I followed his gaze, tracing the intricate lines and markers that defined territories and troop movements—a stark reminder of the cost of such 'romantic' notions. "War has indeed changed, Your Highness," I conceded, my voice tinged with a bitterness honed by experience. "Perhaps - I've questioned an order or two about Baltiva. But - regardless, we were sent there. It's of importance to the Empire..."

He laughed boisterously. The cynical wolfman slammed his fist on the table - practically crying.

"You poor, deluded fool. What purpose do those lands serve for your people?" He smirked.

"Perhaps none to you, sir," I replied, maintaining my composure despite the heat of his scorn. "But every inch of soil under Valtorea's flag is sacred to us. Every field and river we claim holds the blood and sweat of those who believe in what our Empire stands for."

His laughter subsided as he leaned back in his chair, the amusement fading from his expression to be replaced by a grudging acknowledgment. "And therein lies your strength—and your weakness, Captain. Your fervent loyalty blinds you to the larger picture." He tapped a clawed finger against the map. "These lands, as you call sacred, are merely pawns in a much larger game.

The Baltzers use the Empire and their vainglorious notions of conversion to keep in power." He stated. "I'm sure you're very aware of that."

"The Baltzers are of the same blood," I stated. "And does it matter who rules who?" I said, tightening in my chest. The wolfman grinned.

"Yes. It does. Your people claim monsters rule over the Kholodians like tyrants - I'm very aware of this. But - is it not true that the highest ranks of your nobility - are, indeed, old Valtorean blood from the first Empire? Nobles like you, tied to the land, hail from Volkia. Not from Valtorea."

The Grand Prince's words struck a chord, unsettling yet undeniable.

"True," I admitted reluctantly, shifting in my seat, uncomfortable under his probing gaze. "Many of the upper nobles hail from Valtorea, and few are Volkian by descent. But our allegiance..." My voice trailed off as I searched for conviction in my argument.

"Your allegiance?" The Grand Prince leaned forward; his interest piqued as if he sensed the wavering in my voice.

"Is to Valtorea, to the Empire we serve." I declared, reinforcing my loyalty with a sterner tone. "We may come from varied ancestries, but the banner we fight under unites us."

"My people rule over a vast Empire of at least eighty different cultures." He stated. "We know who we are and who our people are. Unlike with you humans - there's no way for the Dvoryanstvo to hide themselves." He stated proudly. "We hail from one blood - one people. We rule as one entity under a clear vision. And you, Captain, are caught in an Empire of divided ethnic loyalties and shadowed truths."

And yet, Grand Prince," I responded, my voice steady despite the turmoil he stirred within me, "Diversity within an empire can also be a source of strength. It brings different perspectives, different strengths."

"A foolish notion," he snickered with a dismissive wave of his hand, "What value does a woodsman have to say to a leader of man?" He stated. "Such notions are Eclairean in thought. Erudite, bold - and foolish, utterly, preached by men who believe a people don't have a shared interest."

I paused, considering his point but unwilling to concede entirely. "Yet, the very woodsman knows the forest's secrets, who can navigate its mysteries and utilize its resources." I leaned slightly forward, my eye fierce and unyielding. "Each person, regardless of their station or origin, holds knowledge that can benefit the whole. An Empire that listens only to the voices of its highest nobles risks overlooking the wisdom found in quieter corners."

Grand Prince Michaelovich smiled. "And that's exactly true with both Empires, right?" As he laid back, he paused, his smile lingering with an edge of irony. "A question to ponder. Autocracy - or democracy. The voice of one - or the voice of all." He said. "I'm sure the great philosophers of old would have much to debate. But here, in the stark reality of our world, we find ourselves at a crossroads of ideology."

He stood, pacing slowly around the room, his heavy steps resonant in the silence that followed. "You see, Captain, while you speak of duty and loyalty as if they are unshakeable pillars, I find them more fluid. They shift and adapt according to the needs and survival of the people - as a whole." He stopped by the window, gazing out at the bustling city below. "Perhaps it is time you consider that what binds an empire is not just loyalty to a flag or a piece of land, but loyalty to its people. The voice of the Dvoryanstvo speaks for all Kholodians - and thus, our great Tzardom will outlive yours."

I blinked.

"From what you would say - the state would hardly matter at all."

"Oh, but the state does matter—the people who rule the state. Us - the Dvoryanstvo, we rule with an iron fist - but we are fair. Just. Prone to romanticism, sure - but at least not subservient to mercantile powers or foreign influences that dilute the essence of governance," he continued, his tone now infused with pride.

I sighed wearily.

"Grand Prince - I find it hard to believe you brought me here to discuss the very notions of governance," I stated.

"You are right." He stated, hands clasping behind his back. "But - how could I resist? Rarely do I get to discuss my ideas. Autocracy. Orthodoxy. Nationalism," he enunciated each word distinctly as if tasting the flavor of his ideals. "National identity is not just something made up in a Perusian coffee house by radicals, Captain. They are the embodiment of what it means to be Kholodian. Or - what it will mean once I become Tzar. Once that happens - old Kholodia will finally become a nation-state. No longer bound by the whims of lesser nobility, of those who don't see the future."

He paused, letting the words hang in the air between us. Then, with a sudden shift in his demeanor, he approached me briskly, his eyes narrowed. "Such a notion in Valtorea would be impossible. Forty different nations, subjugated by the whims of an Emperor who must placate every dissenting voice to maintain a fragile peace," he continued, the fire of conviction burning in his gaze. "In Kholodia, there will be unity—absolute and unyielding under my rule. A counter-balance to the centuries of Valtorea's domination of the continent. A clash of our empires is inevitable."

I swallowed hard - feeling like I was trapped in the presence of a madman. Yet, there was a compelling truth to his words that gnawed at the edges of my loyalty. How many times had I complained about the Baltzers myself? Or a disaffectionate nobility - seemingly impartial to the struggles of their people? Though extreme, the Grand Prince's vision was rooted in a desire for profound unity and strength—an appeal that resonated with my deepest fears and aspirations.

"I can't say I agree," I stated. "But - I suppose you are right on some matters. Valtorea is..." I bit my tongue. "It is a good land. But - there are flaws. Like any other land."

The Grand Prince grinned - turning and looking at me. A fanged, predatory grin that sent a shiver down my spine. "Indeed, Captain," he murmured, his voice low and resonant as if he reveled in the admission of imperfection from an enemy. "I reasoned that the only reason your little Empire had stuck around for so long - was from the Iron Church's doctrines alone. Though, I suppose now I see a new reason." He stated before shrugging. That grin never left his face as we delved deeper into conversation.

Shadows danced across his study—the long shadows of evening. This meeting with the Grand Prince resembled more of a political debate than an interrogation of military maneuvers—or perhaps political maneuvering. I couldn't tell the difference—as we discussed and postured, my brain was exhausted.

"I tire of this." He stated - before ringing a bell. A kholop came forward. "...Wine?" He said, in the bit of Kholdish I knew. Of course, I nodded, feeling the weight of each word we exchanged still lingering between us. The wine would offer little respite from the intensity of the conversation, but it was a necessary pause—a momentary truce in a battle of ideals and convictions.

The kholop poured the crimson liquid into two glasses with a practiced hand, then quietly exited the room, leaving us again in our secluded arena. The Grand Prince handed me a glass; his movements were deliberate as if each motion was another move in a grander strategy.

The Grand Prince's demeanor softened as we sipped the rich, velvety wine. "You must understand, Captain, that all this talk of governance and philosophical ideals isn't merely academic for me. It is a career." He continued his voice now a blend of weariness and passion, "This is the fabric of our future—the narrative that will define the Kholodian Tzardom under my rule. The consolidation of power, the unification of our diverse regions into a single, indomitable force. It is to be my legacy." He said.

His eyes flickered with a hint of vulnerability as he stared into his wine glass, watching the light play in the deep red liquid. "It is an obsession. Something I can hardly escape from, myself." He wearily mumbled, drinking down his goblet in one fell swoop.

"Obsession is a dangerous bedfellow," I murmured, my gaze fixed on the swirling depths of my glass. The wine was excellent, and it was no doubt a product of the southern vineyards of Eclair.

The Grand Prince nodded slowly, acknowledging the truth in my words. "Indeed, it can consume a man whole if he is not careful. But what is a ruler if not one who dares to dream dangerously? To achieve greatness, one must dream. Dream relentlessly." He said. "I have no faith in the Eclaireans or the Arlenians. Their new little republic. It will not be a peasant who becomes elected or a common man who dreams of tilling his fields and waking the next morning to a full harvest. It will be nothing more than professional con artists and thieves." He paused, letting the disdain dripping from each word. "They play at democracy, an illusion to appease the masses, while they'll steal and plunder, and the people will long for an autocrat. A great man."

We sat silently for a moment, the only sound being the soft clink of our glasses as we set them down on the table.

"And you, Captain," he began anew, leaning forward slightly, his gaze piercing into mine, "Your empire, stuck in the middle of new ideas. Of autocracy and democracy." He said, smiling. *"Liberalism - and Reactionism."*

"Where do you see your allegiance?" He probed, the question hanging between us like a drawn sword. "With those who dream of democracies or with those who envision a consolidated power?"

"...Why would I care?" I stated. "It is not I who decides the fate of nations," I stated. "Though, for that matter, I wouldn't know who does, ultimately - beyond the will of God."

"A reactionary viewpoint - and true." He leaned back in his chair, the shadows from the flickering candles playing across his angular face. "God does will the fate of nations and empires. Though - we don't know his divine plan." He stated, sighing and stroking his lupine muzzle.

"But your voice does mean something, Captain. Every man's voice contributes to the chorus that builds or destroys empires," he said, his tone sharp yet inviting. "You wield influence, whether you accept it or not. The actions of a single soldier can turn the tide of battle; so too can the beliefs of a single officer sway the hearts of his men. And - I wish to see where my foe's hearts lie. That, to me, is the greatest thing to know. Whether you like it or not - you have conceded one thing to me this afternoon."

"And what's that?"

"Valtorea - will fall." The statement hung in the air, dark and potent as the wine we had just consumed. I felt a chill, not from the cool stone walls of the chamber but from the implications of his words. The Grand Prince looked at me, his eyes shining with triumph.

Weeks passed by. My containment in the estate - became more tolerable as my verbal jousting with the prince continued. He seemed to delight in having someone to spar with intellectually who could challenge his assertions and provide a different perspective. Clearly, he respected my mind, if not my allegiances, and this bizarre camaraderie we developed became an odd comfort in my isolation. I even had begun to pick up a hint of Kholodian from the books he had graciously allowed me access to - and Mikhail's limited tutelage. Occasionally, he would press on me with questions, perhaps testing himself against a Valtorean strategy game.

"Hypothetically - while Freydich's Pass is quite defensible - what about the Baltivan Sea?" He remarked - a claw pointing towards it. "Valtorea has never had a formidable navy."

"Neither has Kholdia." I countered, glancing at the map sprawled between us. "But the potential for naval power exists as much in your realm as in any coastal nation. It merely requires the will to harness it."

The Grand Prince stroked his muzzle, a gesture I had recognized as one signaling deep thought. "Indeed, Captain, indeed. Though - what about the Scandiarians?"

"And what about them?" I said. "They're irrelevant. They keep to themselves, away from continental matters."

"Perhaps." He stated. "But - say, the Svendish fleet took a side. Valtorea - or Kholodia, would be blockaded." Prince Michaelovich's fingers tapped a rhythmic beat on the hardwood table, his eyes narrowing slightly as he thought.

Then - the doors to the chamber opened. Holding a letter, a courier brought it over to the Prince, who blinked.

"Mmh." He stated, reading it, his eyes focusing on me, and he grinned.

"On behalf of the Lord-Commander... A generous ransom of 9,000 Castelorian gold denarios..."

The prince's smile widened as he folded the letter delicately, placing it on the table beside the map. "It appears your value is finally recognized, Captain. Not just by me, but also by your people." His tone was teasing as he grinned. "Some part of me wishes to contain you - I know you'll prove to be a threat." He stated. "But alas," he continued, his voice lowering into a contemplative murmur, "I do need the funds. The campaign has been taxing." He leaned back and surveyed me with a look that mingled admiration with a trace of regret. "I suppose this means our discussions will soon end, Captain. It is a pity; I have grown rather fond of our exchanges. And the break from the frontline."

Indeed, the notion of leaving this gilded cage stirred within me a mixture of relief and an unexpected pang of loss. It was comfortable. Unknowingly - I took a deep breath.

"I dare say I do not wish to return," I grumbled. "I know there's bound to be a disaster awaiting me back."

"You are quite right in that." He said, smiling. "All of my strategic goals - have been accomplished. Valtorea - for now, at least, will not be a threat."

"Mmh," I stated. "Another attempt to demoralize me?"

"You'll hardly need that. But - for now, at least, we are unlikely to be foes."

The Grand Prince stood up, his towering figure casting a long shadow across the chamber. "Come, Captain," he said with an uncharacteristic warmth in his voice. "I'll have the servants pack you and ready to go."

When Rottmann discovered we were to be freed - he was amid drink, lecherously in the soldier's barracks. He had picked up a rustic form of Kholodian, enjoying himself, telling stories to the younger soldiers here, and drinking heavily.

Upon hearing of our imminent release, Rottmann's expression transformed from jovial amusement to stark realization. He slammed his mug on the wooden table, ale splashing over the brim. "Freed, are we?" he barked, his tone laced with a bitter tinge of irony. "Back to the grinding wheels of war?!" He said, angered almost at the prospect, and his question hung in the air, unanswered, as the soldiers gathered around fell silent, the rowdy atmosphere dissipating like smoke. I touched his shoulder, feeling the tension knotted in his muscles.

"Yes, back to it," I replied solemnly. "It's our duty.

Rottmann looked up at me, his eyes bloodshot but sharp with a piercing clarity. "And what's that, Captain? What have we gained besides a delay in our inevitable end? I'll not go back." He defiantly.

"Rottmann," I began, my voice steady, "you know as well that abandonment of our post would mean more than just our lives at stake. It would betray everything we've fought for, every sacrifice made in the name of Valtorea."

He scoffed a hollow sound that echoed slightly in the now quiet barracks. "What of it? Our lives were chewed up and spit out for what? For honor? For duty?" Rottmann shook his head, his gaze turning toward the distant walls where twilight cast long shadows across the cold stone. "I spent too damned long on the front. Fifteen damned years." His voice trailed off into a weary grunt, and he turned away to pick up his mug again, taking a harsh swig of the remaining ale. The bitterness seemed to linger, not just on his tongue but in the very air between us.

I sighed and left - alone.

I continued down the Kholodian road the following day, a dirt road headed towards Baltiva. Mikhail rode beside me, escorting me to the border, which is a week's travel from here.

"Your friend did not come," Mikhail remarked, an undercurrent of curiosity weaving through his usual stoic demeanor. His eyes, constantly scanning the horizon for unseen threats, flicked momentarily towards me.

"No, he did not," I admitted quietly, my gaze fixed on the winding path that cut through the dense forest. "Though, I can't say I blame him any."

Mikhail nodded slowly, processing this information with a measure of respect. "It is a hard thing," he finally said, "To receive comfort - and then be told to march back into hell."

"Indeed," I responded. "I wonder what will become of him now."

"Likely mercenary work," Mikhail grunted. "Or the bottle." He paused, then added, "Perhaps both."

I nodded, understanding the truth in his words. The road ahead seemed to stretch endlessly, and I gazed back longingly at the estate. The sole friend I had found in this war - left behind.

We reached the border, at long last, under a sky heavy with the threat of rain. Mikhail reined in his horse, and I followed suit, staring at the river Benoltz that marked the end of his domain and the beginning of Valtorea.

"You've been a worthy adversary, Captain," Mikhail said, extending his hand towards me. I took his hand, the clasp of our gloves marking a formal farewell. "And you, sir," I replied. "May I see you again."

He nodded, a brief downturn of his lips betraying his skepticism. "One can hope," he murmured.

With a final nod, Mikhail turned his horse around and rode back toward his lands. I watched him disappear into the distance before urging my horse forward into the Baltiva. Lord only knew what awaited me—back home.

A Return in Ignominy

I rode along the old roads - quietly drawing a brown burlap cloak over myself. I had my saber returned to me, but I dared not get accosted alone out in the woods of Baltiva. I rode hard and fast for Rega - hoping that perhaps, some emissary of Valtorea would come, some patrol willing to guide me back to the safety of our fortified walls. The journey was arduous, fraught with uncertainty and the occasional bandit lurking in the dense thickets, eager to prey upon solitary travelers.

Despite the dangers, I pressed on, driven by a deep-seated sense of duty that would not allow me to rest until I once again stood on Valtorean soil. Each day presented its challenges: muddy paths that threatened to swallow my horse, sudden downpours that turned the world gray and indistinct, and nights so cold they seemed to leech the warmth from my bones.

On the fourth night, under a sliver of moon peeking through scudding clouds, I heard the distant clatter of hooves striking stone—a sound that tightened my grip on my saber's hilt. I slid from my horse, pressing against a large oak as shadows moved along the road.

Emerging from the darkness were two riders cloaked like myself. Their faces were obscured, and their postures were wary. One raised a hand, signaling a halt. My heart pounded in my chest as I waited for their approach.

An alien tongue yelled out - I recognized it quickly as being Lapsid.

One of them dismounted - axe drawn, and I lurched out, saber at the ready. The other one dismounted, too, quickly positioning himself with a crude, jagged blade that glinted under the intermittent moonlight. Their movements were practiced but raw, carrying the unmistakable mark of marauders used to confrontation and quick theft.

The first Lapsid, broad and menacing, charged without preamble. His axe swung in a wide arc aimed at my head. I ducked low, the edge of the blade whistling mere inches above my scalp, and retaliated with a swift thrust of my saber. The blade met chainmail but failed to penetrate deeply, only enraging him further. He grunted, swinging his axe back around in a low, sweeping attempt to catch me off-guard.

Meanwhile, the second marauder circled to my left, attempting to flank me. Anticipating his strategy, I swiftly pivoted my foot to kick up a cloud of dirt toward him, momentarily impairing his vision and disrupting his advance. This brief respite allowed me to focus back on the first attacker.

Our dance was deadly and precise; his axe strokes were powerful yet increasingly predictable. I dodged another vicious swing and countered with a piercing jab that finally found its mark beneath his arm. He staggered back with a curse, clutching his side.

At that moment, the second Lapsid recovered and lunged towards me, his blade aimed straight for my chest. I sidestepped, and his momentum carried him forward, exposing his back. With a rapid turn, I drove my saber into him, feeling the resistance as it punctured the leather jerkin he wore beneath his cloak. He cried out and fell to the ground, gasping as he clutched at the protruding blade, and I drew it back - and ducked at the last second as the other Lapsid hurled himself at me with a desperate, ragged shout. His axe came down hard, aiming for where my head had just been. I rolled away, my heart pounding, the ground brutal and unforgiving beneath me. As I approached my feet, I saw his figure looming over me again, the moonlight casting his shadow long and menacing across the leaf-strewn road.

Breathing heavily from exertion and pain, he raised his axe for another strike, but his movements were slower now, labored from the wound I had inflicted. Seeing my chance, I surged forward with all the speed and strength I could muster. My blade arced through the air with lethal precision, slicing through the gap in his armor and into his chest. With a choked grunt, he stumbled backward and collapsed onto the cold, hard road.

I stood over him, breathing heavily, watching as life ebbed from his body. The silence followed was piercing, only broken by the distant hoot of an owl and the rustling of leaves in the faint breeze. Resting my hands on my knees, I tried to steady my breathing and calm the adrenaline that still coursed through my veins. Both of the men were dying - and I had no cause to stay and help them after accosting me. A growl came from my belly - and I lurched over one of their bodies, scavenging...

Foodstuffs - a letter...

A letter - which I curiously opened, written in Kholodian.

"Kill the traveler on sight," it read, *"and then burn this message."*

From who it was - it was unmarked. The handwriting was unfamiliar to me - and I pocketed it. First and foremost - I had to reach Rega safely. With one last wary glance at the lifeless bodies sprawled on the road, I mounted my horse, urgency spurring me forward.

The remainder of the journey was tense and silent, save for the occasional distant howl of a wolf or the rustle of leaves above. My thoughts repeatedly drifted back to the letter - each scenario I conjured was more treacherous than the last. By dawn, when the first light filtered through the dense canopy, Rega's towering spires finally came into view, a sight that brought relief and a melancholy feeling over me.

I reported to the front gate. I had only realized - in the weeks I had been gone, I had not shaved, and my hair and goatee had grown thick, making me look instead Kholodian. The guards eyed me with suspicion as I approached, their hands resting on the hilts of their swords until a witness finally remembered me from the training drills I held months ago. However - instead of sending me to the Lord Commander - they bound me up in chains and escorted me to a dimly lit chamber deep within the fortress walls.

"Let go of me - damn you!" I struggled. The guards remained deaf to my protests, their grip ironclad as they shoved me into the chamber. The heavy door clanged shut behind me, echoing ominously through the cold air. A single torch flickered on the wall, casting long shadows that danced across the stone floor.

In front of me was von Löwe, standing with a look of irritation.

"...Ah. Kaelitz." He regarded me with a mixture of disdain and amusement as if my disheveled appearance was both tragic and pathetic in his eyes, and now I found myself shackled before him like a common criminal.

"Von Löwe," I replied, trying to maintain an even tone despite the rage burning within me. "What's the meaning of this?"

Von Löwe paced slowly in front of me, the faint light from the torch casting his shadow against the rough stone walls like a looming specter. He finally stopped and faced me squarely, his expression hardening.

"Conspiracy, Captain Kaelitz," Von Löwe began, his voice resonating with a cold authority that seemed to seep into the very stones of the chamber. "A most vile and treacherous plot, weaving its tendrils deep within the heart of our Empire."

My heart clenched at his words, though I kept my face impassive. "Explain yourself, Lord Commander," I demanded, though the shackles bit into my wrists, a reminder of my precarious position under his scrutiny.

He walked closer, his steps deliberate, the sound echoing off the walls. "It has come to my attention," he continued, each word dripping with venomous implication, "that you, Kaelitz, have been in clandestine correspondence with that treasonous Arch-Duke Duclaire. And not just him—but with agents from Kholodia. To think, a Captain in our glorious army conspiring with our enemies!"

The accusation was ludicrous yet delivered with such conviction that even I blinked for a moment. "You are mistaken," I replied firmly. "I serve the Holy Valtorean Empire with every breath in my body. I have no dealings with Duclaire or any Kholodian."

Von Löwe's laugh was a harsh sound that made the torchlight flicker more aggressively. "Oh, come now, Kaelitz. Do you take me for a fool? We've intercepted messages—coded letters that speak of meetings and promises of aid. They tell of a plot to restore your family's lost estates as a reward for your... 'services.' Services that would see me displaced—or worse."

He paused, allowing the weight of his words to settle like a cloak upon my shoulders. His gaze was piercing as he studied my reaction. I met his eyes squarely, refusing to let him see any trace of doubt or fear.

"What fabrications have you made in my absence?"

Von Löwe's eyes narrowed, his lips curling into a sneer. "Fabrications, Kaelitz? The truth needs no embellishment. Your guilt is as plain as the scars upon your face." He began to circle me slowly, like a wolf toying with wounded prey.

"The evidence is irrefutable. Signed documents, Kaelitz - in your hand! Detailing troop deployments, fortification plans, and supply routes. A treasure trove of intelligence, all promised to our foes." His voice rose, echoing off the dank walls. "And for what? The chance to reclaim your lost prestige? To get back at me?"

I shook my head, my mind reeling. This was insanity. "I have signed no such document!" I declared.

I strained against my shackles, the metal biting into my wrists as I leaned forward, my eyes blazing with fury. "This is your doing, Von Löwe! An elaborate scheme to disgrace me and my house, to rid yourself of a rival once and for all."

Von Löwe's lips curled into a cruel smile, his eyes glinting in the flickering torchlight. "You give yourself too much credit, Kaelitz. As if I would need to stoop to such theatrics to eliminate a one-eyed disgrace like you."

"Lies!" I spat, my voice ringing off the damp stone walls. "You've hated my family for years, coveted our lands and titles. And now, you saw your chance to strike. Forging documents, spinning tales, all to paint me as a traitor to the very Empire I've bled for!"

I could feel the rage coursing through my veins, hot and molten, fueling my words—Schemers and manipulators, weaving webs of deceit in the shadowed halls of power. You care nothing for honor, for loyalty. Only your ambition."

Von Löwe's face hardened, his jaw clenching. He stepped closer, his breath hot against my face. "You dare accuse me? Here, in the heart of my fortress? You forget yourself, Kael."

He stepped closer, his breath hot against my face. "I have tolerated your presence this long out of respect for your bloodline. But no more. The House of Kaelitz will be erased from history; its treachery cauterized from the Empire's flesh. I have written to the Emperor - informing him of the disgrace of your bloodline."

"Where's Duclaire?" I said. "He can clear this mess up."

Von Löwe's lips twisted into a sardonic smile that didn't reach the coldness of his eyes. "Duclaire? You truly are out of the loop. He's no longer among the ranks of the Empire, Kaelitz." He leaned closer, his voice dropping to a whisper with a chilling hint of threat. "Your patron is gone."

"Now," Von Löwe continued, straightening up and stepping back. "Tell me everything about your visit to Kholodia. Leave out no detail, no matter how trivial you think it might be. Your life quite literally depends on it."

I felt my blood turn to ice at Von Löwe's words, a cold dread seeping into my bones. Duclaire - gone? It couldn't be. He was my last hope, the only one who could vouch for my loyalty and integrity. Without him...

I swallowed hard, trying to maintain my composure even as the world seemed to tilt beneath my feet. "What do you mean, gone?" I asked, my voice sounding distant to my ears.

Von Löwe's smile widened, a predatory flash of teeth in the gloom. "Fled, Kaelitz. He vanished into the night like the coward he is when his betrayal came to light. Now he's with the Black Band... Outlaws, pillaging the countryside."

He began to pace again, his boots echoing on the stone. "But then, what else could one expect from a man like you? Dishonored, disgraced, clinging to the coattails of greater men in a desperate bid for relevance."

Each word was a dagger twisting in my gut. I wanted to deny it, to shout my innocence until my throat was raw. But what good would it do? With Duclaire gone and these damning accusations laid at my feet...

"So what now?" I asked, hating the way my voice wavered. "Am I to be executed as a traitor without even a chance to defend myself?"

Von Löwe paused, considering me with a cold, calculating grin that sent shivers down my spine. He savored the moment, letting the silence stretch until it was almost unbearable before finally speaking.

"Executed? No, Kaelitz. That would be too kind a fate for one such as you." His voice was smooth as silk but laced with venom. "I have a far more fitting punishment in mind."

He stepped closer, his eyes glinting with malicious glee in the flickering torchlight. "I have written to the Emperor, recommending that your noble title be stripped away. The House of von Ardent is forever stricken from the annals of the Empire's history."

My heart stopped, my blood turning to ice in my veins. Stripped of my title? It was a fate worse than death for a nobleman. Without my title, I would be nothing. A nameless, faceless outcast wandering the fringes of society. And my family's estate in Strossberg... Any chance of it being regained - would be lost.

"You can't," I whispered, my voice hoarse with desperation. "The estate... it's all I have left."

Von Löwe's laughter was cruel, echoing off the dank stone walls. "Oh, I can, Kaelitz. And I have. The Emperor trusts my judgment implicitly. He knows I only have the Empire's best interests at heart."

He leaned in close, his breath hot against my face. I could smell the wine on his breath and see the flecks of gold in his cold, merciless eyes. "I already owned your estate, of course. But - now it will finally be mine - after it's formally stripped from your family. A fitting summer retreat, don't you think?"

I strained against my shackles, wanting nothing more than to wrap my hands around his throat and squeeze the life from him. But it was futile. The chains held fast, biting into my wrists until I could feel the warm trickle of blood.

"You bastard," I snarled, my voice shaking with impotent rage. "You won't get away with this. The truth will come out. Duclaire will—"

"Duclaire will do nothing!" Von Löwe roared, his composure slipping for a moment. "He's a fugitive, a wanted man. His word means less than nothing now."

He took a deep breath, smoothing his features into a mask of icy control. "No, Kaelitz. You are alone in this. Utterly, completely alone."

I felt the weight of Von Löwe's words crashing down upon me, as heavy and oppressive as the dank air in this forsaken chamber. The flickering torchlight cast distorted shadows across his face, making his features appear even more twisted and sinister.

"Why?" I demanded, my voice raw with desperation and anger. "Why do you hate my family so much? What have the von Ardents done to earn such venom from you?"

Von Löwe regarded me silently for a long moment, his eyes glittering with a venom that seemed to have been nurtured over lifetimes. His voice was low and measured when he finally spoke, each word deliberately chosen.

"You truly are ignorant of your family's history, aren't you, Kaelitz?" He began to pace again, his footsteps echoing ominously in the confines of the chamber. "The bad blood between our houses stretches back generations, a festering wound that time has only deepened."

He paused, facing me squarely, his gaze boring into mine.

"Your great-grandfather, the esteemed Lord Reinhard von Ardent, was a man of insatiable ambition," Von Löwe continued, each word dripping with centuries-old bitterness. "He schemed and plotted, using every dirty trick in the book to expand his holdings and influence. And my family? We were just one of many obstacles in his path."

He stepped closer, the torchlight casting half his face in shadow, giving him a demonic appearance. "He fabricated evidence, bribed officials, even resorted to outright murder - all to strip my ancestors of their rightful lands and titles..." He stated. "Were it not for the intervention of the Crusades - no doubt, he would have succeeded in stripping away our last holdings. The duchy of Saxonia-Pomerdania."

I listened in stunned silence, my mind reeling. I had always been told that our family's wealth and status were the rewards of generations of loyal service to the Empire. But this...

"I... I had no idea," I stammered, hating how weak and uncertain I sounded. "But surely, the sins of the past..."

"The blood of the present pays for the sins of the past," Von Löwe snarled, his face twisting with rage. "Your family's treachery has gone unanswered for far too long, Kaelitz. But no more."

A sudden knock on the chamber door shattered the tension, echoing through the dank space like a thunderclap. Von Löwe's head snapped towards the sound, his eyes narrowing in irritation at the interruption.

"Enter," he barked, his voice laced with impatience.

The heavy wooden door creaked open, revealing a small group of figures silhouetted against the brighter light of the corridor beyond. As they stepped into the chamber, the flickering torchlight illuminated their features - the severe black robes and silver symbols of the Inquisition.

Leading the group was a tall, gaunt man with a hawkish nose and piercing grey eyes that seemed to cut right through me. His thin lips were set in a perpetual frown as if he had long forgotten how to smile.

"Lord Commander," he said, his voice a husky whisper that somehow filled the room. I am Father Martinez of the Holy Inquisition. We have come to... assist in the interrogation of the prisoner."

Von Löwe's jaw clenched, a muscle twitching in his cheek. It was clear he didn't appreciate the intrusion, but even he dared not challenge the authority of the Church.

"Of course, Father," he said, his tone neutral. "I was just beginning to...delve into the depths of Captain Kaelitz's treachery. But I welcome your expertise in such matters."

"Excellent." He said - Father Martinez turning to a compatriot - speaking in Castelorian before looking at Von Löwe.

"It is time you leave."

Von Löwe bristled at the dismissal, his eyes flashing with anger. But he knew he had no choice. The Inquisition's authority superseded even his own, and to defy them openly would be to court disaster.

"As you wish, Father," he said through gritted teeth, giving me one last nasty glare. "I trust you will be thorough in your interrogation. Captain Kaelitz's crimes against the Empire are many and grievous."

Father Martinez inclined his head slightly, conveying both acknowledgment and dismissal. "We are always thorough, Lord Commander. You may rest assured that the truth will be brought to light, no matter how deeply it may be buried."

With a curt nod, Von Löwe turned on his heel and stalked out of the chamber, his boots ringing on the stone floor. The heavy door slammed shut behind him with a resounding clang, leaving me alone with the Inquisitors.

Father Martinez turned to face me; his grey eyes bore into my soul. Despite the severity of his appearance, there was a hint of something else in his gaze - a glimmer of curiosity, perhaps even a touch of sympathy.

"Captain Kaelitz," he began, his raspy voice somehow softer, more measured than before. "I understand you find yourself in a most precarious position. The accusations leveled against you are grave indeed... I believe Heinrich had read them off to you."

He stepped closer, the faint scent of incense and parchment clinging to his robes. In the flickering torchlight, the silver symbol of the Inquisition gleamed on his chest, a stark reminder of the power and authority he wielded.

"But I am not here to condemn you," he continued, his words measured and deliberate. "My role is to seek the truth, no matter where it may lead. And I sense there is more to your story than meets the eye." He stated that he was taking a seat in a chair. Two other men stood beside him.

Father Martinez paused, folding his hands neatly atop the intricately carved table that separated us. The room, dimly lit and cloaked in shadow, seemed to close around us, the walls whispering secrets of their own. Dust motes danced lazily in the slivers of light, casting ghostly patterns across the stone floor.

"Now, Captain Kaelitz," he resumed his voice a low rumble that rumbled through the still air like distant thunder. "It has come to our attention that while you have been detained here in Kholodia, certain... developments have occurred back in the Empire that require our immediate concern."

He paused, surveying me closely to gauge my reaction before continuing. "Your patron, Duclaire—whom you've served loyally for the last year—has been found consorting with factions sympathetic to both the Eclairean revolution and members of the Low Church. This was not merely a matter of personal faith or political alignment; it was a deliberate act of subversion aimed at undermining the stability of our Holy Valtorean Empire."

The air seemed to thicken with each word he spoke, pressing down upon me with the weight of implications yet to be fully revealed.

"Given these circumstances," Father Martinez continued slowly, "We have begun our investigation. Already - a dozen officers have been burned at the stake for heresy." He turned to one of the inquisitorial attendants.

"List them off, if you would please."

The attendant, a stern-looking man with sharp features and cold eyes, unrolled a parchment and read the names in a monotone voice. Each name echoed around the stone walls, a grim litany of doom that sent a chill down my spine. I recognized some of them—men I had trained with, dined with, and fought alongside. The reality of their fiery fates struck me with horror and a gnawing sense of betrayal.

"Jürgen Halt," the attendant announced, his voice devoid of emotion. "Markus Freil, Tobias Rennert..."

Father Martinez watched me closely as he listed each name, observing every flicker of expression that crossed my scarred face. When the list was complete, he folded his hands again and focused on me.

"These were not mere soldiers, Captain Kaelitz," he said, his voice steady and implacable. "They were officers, conspiring against the Empire—and by extension, against the divine will of God. Their execution was not only just; it was necessary to preserve the sanctity and stability of our realm."

I swallowed hard, struggling to maintain my composure. The weight of my potential fate bore me like a physical burden.

"Your reaction is telling, Captain Kaelitz," Father Martinez observed quietly. "You are shocked—perhaps even appalled—by these actions. Good. It means you have not yet been numbed by the cruelties required to maintain order in the Empire."

"However," he continued, his voice lowering to a more intimate register, "it also places you in a precarious position. You were, after all, under the command of Duclaire. His actions indirectly cast suspicion on all those who served under him. This includes you, Captain Kaelitz. Your loyalty to the Empire is now in question."

I met his gaze squarely, feeling the sharp edge of accusation slicing through the dimly lit room. "My loyalty has never wavered," I replied firmly, my voice steady despite the tumult inside me. "I've served the Holy Valtorean Empire with honor and sacrificed much in its name. I knew nothing of Duclaire's treasonous activities."

Father Martinez frowned slowly as if weighing my words against some unseen scale. "Perhaps," he conceded. "Let us start at the beginning, then."

He leaned back in his chair, steepling his fingers as he regarded me with that unyielding gaze. He nodded to one of the attendants, who took out a parchment.

Father Martinez's eyes never left mine as the attendant unwound the new scroll, but it seemed he had forgotten the document for a moment. "Tell me, Captain Kaelitz," he began, his voice dropping to a whisper, barely filling the small, shadow-infested chamber. "Did Duclaire ever confide in you about the depths of his conspiracies? Was there ever a moment when he revealed any alliances that struck you as... Unconventional?"

I held his gaze, feeling the weight of each word like stones in my belly. "No, Father Martinez. Duclaire was always reserved about his plans. I knew him as a commander and sometimes as a confidant on matters of battle strategy and personnel, nothing more."

The old priest's eyes narrowed slightly, scrutinizing me further. "And what of connections to powers or beliefs outside our Holy Empire?"

"Father," I said slowly, each word careful and deliberate. "I witnessed no practice nor heard any endorsement of such darkness from Duclaire or anyone else under his command. Had I known, I would have reported it without hesitation."

Martinez nodded slowly, apparently satisfied with my response for the moment, yet the room seemed colder now, the shadows deeper. I felt the eyes of the other inquisitors upon me, their silent judgments mingling with the chill stone air.

"What will happen to me now?" I asked, my voice low.

"Torture." He stated mundanely. "We will see if you are speaking the truth. If you aren't, you'll be burned at the stake, like the rest." He stated.

Father Martinez paused as if sensing the weight of his words in the heavy air. The flickering candlelight cast shadows across his gaunt face, accentuating the stern lines that marked his years of service to the Inquisition.

"However," he added after a moment that stretched like an eternity, his voice softening slightly, "should your words prove truthful under scrutiny, I am prepared to advocate on your behalf. I know well the complexities and the corrosive nature of deceit within our ranks. It can trap even the most loyal of servants."

The room fell silent, save for the occasional pop and crack of the firewood burning in the hearth. I absorbed his words, each syllable laden with a blend of dread and hope.

"Should you stand resolute in your honesty and integrity, demonstrating without falter that you had no part in Duclaire's schemes," Father Martinez continued, leaning forward, his eyes piercing into mine, "then I shall personally recommend to the War Ministry that any punitive measures against you be reconsidered and, if justice permits, overturned entirely."

The possibility of redemption seemed almost too fragile to grasp, yet it was there—a thin thread amidst the looming darkness. "I understand, Father," I responded, my voice steady but my heart racing. "I am ready to face whatever trials are set before me. My conscience is clear."

Father Martinez gave a curt nod, a gesture that seemed to finalize our grim covenant. "Very well, Captain Kaelitz. We shall proceed at once."

I explained my story again and again, but the inquisitors seemed unimpressed. At every turn, they tried to point out the worst flaws.

"Did you not take the opportunity to escape at all?" The lead interrogator said. "What kind of soldier are you?"

I clenched my fists, feeling the cold metal of the shackles bite into my wrists. "How would I flee," I retorted, my voice tight with frustration. "In the heartland of Kholodia - in an alien country, with nothing to my name?"

"Suicide." He stated bluntly. Those words stung, echoing within the confines of the cold stone chamber. I felt a surge of anger boiling beneath my calm facade, but I knew better than to let it spill over. Instead, I drew a deep breath and stared at him, my eyes hard.

"I did what was necessary for survival." I countered, my voice firm yet controlled. "It almost sounds like you'd prefer me dead."

The corner of Inquisitor Martinez's mouth twitched slightly, betraying a flicker of irritation. His gaze intensified, the deep creases around his eyes growing more pronounced as he leaned closer. "Survival," he echoed, the word dripping with disdain as if it were unworthy of even being considered. "Survival without grace is but a hollow shell of existence. You were entrusted with the mantle of our Empire to uphold its values even unto death."

His words hung heavy in the air, like a guillotine poised to sever the last threads of any sympathy I might have hoped for from this tribunal. The cold, dampness of the room seemed to seep deeper into my bones, each word from Martinez a chilling reminder of the unforgiving nature of our creed.

"But let us consider that you did indeed prioritize survival," he continued his voice now a controlled, almost mesmerizing cadence. "Tell us then, how did your actions serve the greater good of the Holy Valtorean Empire?"

The question stung, more painful than any physical blow could have been. It challenged my decisions and my very identity as a soldier of the Empire. I searched for an answer to satisfy and justify my choices under such dire circumstances.

"I...I..." I stammered, grasping at the shards of my fractured dignity. "What else could I do?" The downright admission - it broke something in me. I struggled at the chains.

"That's enough. Take him to the torturer." Martinez sighed. "We'll reconvene in an hour."

The sting of the scourge lashed against my back, cutting through flesh and resolve with ruthless precision. Initially, anger surged within me towards the torturer. Yet, as the pain intensified, self-reproach crept in, filling me with a desire to vanish from existence. Muttering bitter words under my breath, I directed curses at the heavens, pleading for release, all while Inquisitor Martinez observed with detached indifference, his gaze frigid and calculating.

"That is sufficient for now," he declared as the restraints loosened their grip on me, sending me crashing onto the unforgiving cobblestones below. Paralyzed by agony and shame, I lay there motionless, tears mingling with the blood on my cheeks. Inquisitor Martinez advanced towards me, his footsteps echoing ominously in the chamber as he neared my crumpled form.

"I trust you, Kaelitz," he uttered.

Struggling to lift my head from the cold ground, I warily eyed Inquisitor Martinez's boot, still pinning down my foot. A glimmer of hope flickered within me at his unexpected declaration, though I dared not fully embrace it.

"You trust me?" I rasped incredulously. "Then why..."

Inquisitor Martinez silenced me abruptly with a voice as sharp as a blade of ice. "I believe that your actions did not purposefully betray our cause. However, whether intentional or not, they have cast suspicion upon you. And in these difficult times, suspicion alone can be damning."

As he raised his boot off my foot and excruciating sensation flooded back into it, I suppressed a pained gasp. With hands clasped behind his back, Inquisitor Martinez turned away.

"Nevertheless," he continued coolly. "I am not devoid of compassion. You will be allowed to vindicate yourself and demonstrate your allegiance."

Glancing back at me with eyes gleaming faintly in the dim light, I stared at Inquisitor Martinez through blurred vision filled with uncertainty about the fragment of hope stirring within me.

"An opportunity?" I croaked weakly. "What do you require of me?"

Turning fully now so that torchlight sculpted his features into stark shadows on his face, Inquisitor Martinez replied cryptically: "The moment will present itself in due course. For now... heal."

He gestured towards his attendants standing nearby. "Escort him to the healers."

Strong hands hoisted me up by my arms as fresh waves of agony rippled across my raw back like liquid fire, new rivulets of blood tracing down my skin.

"Consider this an act of leniency," remarked Inquisitor Martinez as they led me away forcibly. "Not everyone who enters these chambers emerges breathing."

I was half-dragged, half-carried through the winding corridors of the fortress, my feet stumbling and sliding on the slick stone. The rough hands of the attendants dug into my arms, their grip unrelenting even as I hissed in pain with each jarring step. The world swam in and out of focus, the flickering torches on the walls blurring into streaks of amber light that seared my vision.

At last, we reached a small, dimly lit chamber. The pungent scent of herbs and medicinal oils assaulted my nostrils, making my head spin. A robed figure emerged from the shadows - the healer, I presumed.

"Set him down there," the healer instructed, gesturing to a narrow cot in the corner. The attendants complied, dumping me unceremoniously onto the thin mattress. The rough fabric chafed against my ravaged back, eliciting a strangled groan from my throat.

The healer approached, his weathered face coming into focus as he leaned over me. His eyes, a pale, watery blue, held a mixture of pity and resignation - the look of a man who had seen too much suffering in his time.

"This will hurt," he warned, his voice rasping. "But it is necessary for the healing to begin."

I nodded weakly, bracing myself. The healer began to apply a salve to my wounds, and I grunted - passing out.

And there I was, trapped in the deep dungeons of a Baltivan castle.

Days turned into nights, and nights back into days within the stone walls where no sunlight dared touch. The physicians treated my wounds, applying salves and stitching flesh. Despite their cold efficiency, relief was slow to come. I learned to quiet the groans of pain as the healing began; every movement reminded me of the ordeal, threatening to tear open the fragility my body felt.

As misery ebbed marginally each day, replaced by growing desperation for clarity and purpose, I forced myself to focus on what lay ahead rather than what had transpired. The Empire had shaped me once as a soldier; now von Löwe sought to reshape me—into what, I was not sure.

One evening—or it might have been day hidden under night's cloak—the bolt of my cell door screeched open. A figure stepped inside, adorned in an imperial functionary's austere black and yellow garb.

His face was stern, yet a peculiar softness in his eyes seemed out of place in the harsh regimen of Baltivan castle.

"Kaelitz," he began, his voice resonant in the damp dungeon air. "My name is Gerhart. There's a bit to go over - before your release."

I stared up from the thin, straw-filled mattress, muscles tensing instinctively. Despite my weakened state, my survival instincts drilled into me as a soldier stirred within.

"Release?" I managed, my voice raspy from disuse.

Gerhart nodded, pulling a chair with a screech across the stone floor and sitting across from me. He placed a small, leather-bound book on his lap, fingers resting on the cover to emphasize its importance.

"Yes," he continued. "You are to be given an assignment—a mission that could not only redeem you in the eyes of the Empire but also prove crucial for our current endeavors. But first..."

Gerhart opened the leather-bound tome, the pages crackling with age as he thumbed through them. "The Inquisition has taken an interest in your case, Kaelitz. Father Martinez himself reviewed the charges levied against you by Lord Commander von Löwe. After much deliberation and prayer, he has found them...lacking in merit."

I sat up straighter, ignoring the twinge of pain that shot through my battered body. The Inquisition was not known for its leniency or mercy. If they had genuinely intervened on my behalf, it could only mean that there was something they wanted from me in return.

Gerhart must have sensed my skepticism, for he leaned forward, his voice low and urgent. "You must understand, Kaelitz, that this is no small matter. The Inquisition does not overturn the rulings of a Lord Commander lightly."

I remained silent, my mind racing with the implications of Gerhart's words. The Inquisition had the ear of the Emperor himself. If they believed in my innocence, or at least in my usefulness, then there was still a chance for me to regain my honor and standing within the Empire.

Gerhart closed the book with a soft thud, his eyes boring into mine. I remained silent and wary but intensely curious about what kind of mission would require a broken soldier like myself. Gerhart opened the leather-bound book, revealing pages filled with dense, meticulous script. He began to read aloud, his voice measured and clear in the oppressive silence of the cell.

"By decree of the Lord-Commander, Heinrich von Löwe, Captain Kaelitz von Ardent is now assigned to the Verlorener Haufen..." He began

- before coughing, noticing my eyebrow raise - the High Valtorean barely unfamiliar. "The Forlorn Hope."

He paused to gauge my reaction. I merely stared back, blinking, unresponsive.

Gerhart went on, his voice echoing off the dank stone walls. "You are to lead the assault on the traitorous Arch-Duke Duclaire, the leader of the Black Band, which has taken refuge in the Tartuvian marshes, and to execute them to the last man."

He closed the book with a soft thud. I sat up straighter despite the pain, my mind whirling. The Tartuvian marshes. A lonely, treacherous place rife with bogs that could swallow a man whole and strange creatures that lurked in the mists. And now I was to venture there, still bearing the marks of the inquisitor's cruel attention - and to put Duclaire to the sword.

The revelation hung heavy between us, Gerhart's words echoing in my mind. Duclaire, the man who had once been my mentor, my friend, had betrayed me, betrayed the Empire. And now I was being sent to hunt him down like a dog, to end his treachery once and for all.

I let out a slow breath, my ribs aching with the effort. "And if I refuse this...generous offer?"

Gerhart's expression hardened, his eyes glinting in the flickering torchlight. "Refusal is not an option, Kaelitz. The Inquisition has spoken. You will carry out this mission, or you will face the consequences of defying the will of the Empire."

I closed my eyes briefly, the weight of my fate pressing upon me like a physical burden. When I opened them again, Gerhart watched me intently, gauging my reaction.

"Very well," I said at last, my voice sounding hollow to my ears. "I will do as the Inquisition commands."

Gerhart nodded, a flicker of something like respect crossing his stern features. "As you say, Captain. The Empire expects great things."

"...I... When do we begin?" I asked, my voice steadier than I felt.

Gerhart's lips twitched into what might have been a smile. "At dawn, three days hence."

Morning passed. The food became remarkably better as I was left alone in the cell, the silence broken only by the distant water drip and the rasp of my breathing. The only interruption came one sudden morning when the heavy iron door finally creaked open, and a guard entered, holding a sealed letter. He tossed it at my feet with a sneer before turning on his heel and slamming the door shut behind him.

I picked up the letter with trembling fingers, breaking the familiar wax seal of my family's crest.

"My dear son Kaelitz," it began. "I write to you with a heavy heart and grave tidings. That vile snake Von Löwe has used your supposed dishonor as a pretext to confiscate our ancestral estate here in Vien - formally, in the court of the Reichskammergeicht. A few family friends have helped out - in legal funds, to contest such a manner. Though it matters little - the estate has already fallen into his hands.

But even then, my greater fear is for you, my brave boy, fighting in those godless eastern lands against the Kholodians and the barbarians. Pray tell - when will you return?

I sighed wearily, tossing the letter to the side as I slumped back against my prison cell's cold, unforgiving stone. The words of my father, while filled with concern and familial love, bore into me like an icy wind slicing through the tatters of my uniform. I knew not what was coming next, but the dread loomed large and ominous, like the storm clouds gathering over Rega's grey, forlorn skyline.

I could only hope - I was prepared.

In the days that followed, I was subjected to a grueling regimen of training and preparation. My body, weakened by confinement and deprivation, was honed anew through hours of punishing drills and sparring matches. Wearing imperial plate armor again on my flayed back made me feel as if I was a penitent flagellant; the pain was a constant companion, a searing reminder of my fall from grace as I practiced. A dozen or so men would accompany me - they were the scum of the lowest.

They were the dregs of the Empire - rapists, murderers, thieves. Men who had nothing to lose and everything to gain by taking on this suicidal task. But could such men truly be trusted? Would they fight with me or turn on me at the first opportunity? Perhaps - that was what Von Löwe also feared.

In the pre-dawn hours of the third day, we gathered in the fortress courtyard, our breath misting in the chill air. Von Löwe stood before us, his face an impassive mask. "You know your mission," he said, carrying across the assembled men. "Find the Black Band. Uncover their purpose. And bring me the head of the traitor Duclaire." I nodded grimly, my hand resting on the hilt of my saber - finally gifted back to me. The weight of the steel was a comforting presence, a reminder of the oaths I had sworn and the duty that now lay before me. Around me, the men shifted uneasily, their eyes darting between Von Löwe and the looming gates of the fortress.

"You may take your leave. You have a week to return. Should you not come back - you will be declared outlaws and hunted down." With those final, ominous words, Von Löwe turned and strode away, his dark form soon swallowed by the shadows of the keep. I stood there a moment longer, the weight of my task settling upon me like a shroud. Then, with a deep breath, I turned to face the men who would be my companions on this challenging journey.

They were a rough lot, their faces scarred and weathered, their eyes hard and jaded. Some bore the marks of the lash, others the crude tattoos of prison gangs. They were men who had known little but violence and brutality, and it showed in their feral, hunted gazes.

I, perhaps - feared them more than the hundred men in the Tartuvian swamps awaiting us.

The life I had seen when I first arrived here on a campaign now seemed like a distant memory, a fading dream swallowed by the harsh realities of war and betrayal. As we marched through the bleak, ravaged landscape, my task bore down upon me like a physical burden.

I glanced at the men around me, these hardened criminals and outcasts who were now my reluctant allies. They moved with a sullen, predatory grace, their eyes constantly scanning the horizon for any sign of threat. I knew they would fight fiercely if called upon, but I also sensed their resentment and barely-contained anger at being pressed into this service.

As the sun began to sink towards the horizon, painting the sky in lurid shades of orange and red, we came upon the ruins of a small village. The buildings were little more than blackened husks, their windows gaping like sightless eyes. In the center of the village square, a single gallows stood, its timbers weathered and gray.

I called a halt, and the men gratefully sank to the ground, resting their weary limbs. I knew we could not linger long, but even a brief respite was welcome after the long march. I watched as the men tended to their blistered feet and gulped water from their canteens, their faces etched with exhaustion and strain as I overlooked the ruined village we had stumbled into. It was one we had marched past - back when Lord Commander Duclaire led us. I presumed it was little more than wasteland, like most of Baltiva.

"Oi, sir?" A voice said - a careless tone, coming from a trooper - what passed for a sergeant

I turned to face the man who had spoken, a wiry, sinewy fellow with a badly pocked face and a crude tattoo of a hanging man on his neck. "What is it, Sergeant?" I asked, my voice carefully neutral.

The man hawked and spat, wiping his mouth with his hand. "Beggin' yer pardon, sir, but some of the lads were wonderin'... What's our stake in all this? I mean, we're riskin' our necks out here, goin' after these Black Band bastards. Seems only fair we get a cut o' the spoils out here 'know?"

I felt angry at the man's audacity but kept my expression impassive. "Your 'stake,' Sergeant, is your life. You're here because the alternative was the gallows or the chopping block. The only spoils you'll see are the rations in your pack and the air in your lungs. Understood?"

The sergeant's face twisted into a sullen scowl, but he nodded grudgingly. "Aye, sir. Understood." He slunk away, muttering under his breath.

As the sergeant retreated, I let out a slow breath, feeling the tension coiled within me like a serpent ready to strike. I knew I walked a razor's edge with these men and that any sign of weakness or uncertainty could prove fatal.

I cast my gaze once more over the ruined village, taking in the charred remnants of homes and shops, the scattered bones that gleamed white amidst the ashes. How many had died here, I wondered. How many innocent lives had been snuffed out in the name of this bloody, senseless war?

A sudden movement caught my eye, and I whirled around, my hand flying to the hilt of my sword. But it was only a skinny dog, picking its way through the rubble on stick-thin legs. It paused and looked at me for a long moment, its eyes hollow and haunted, before slinking into the shadows.

I felt a sudden, irrational anger at the sight of the pathetic creature. What right did it have to live when so many good men had perished? But then the anger faded, replaced by a profound sense of weariness and despair - and something foreboding.

Bones - in the snow. I moved over to one of the skeletons - and kicked it over.

The bones clattered across the frozen ground, scattering in a macabre display. I knelt, my eyes narrowing as I examined the remains more closely. These were no ordinary bones, picked clean by scavengers and the elements. No, these had been deliberately arranged, the skull and limbs positioned in a grotesque pattern.

A chill that had nothing to do with the bitter wind crept down my spine as I realized the implications. This was no mere abandoned village - it was a warning. A message left by someone. Perhaps the Black Band - but did they dabble with the macabre and the sinister?

I rose slowly to my feet, my hand clenched tight around the hilt of my saber. The men had gathered around, their faces pale and uneasy as they took in the gruesome scene.

"Mount up," I said, my voice harsh and commanding in the eerie stillness. "We ride hard, and we don't stop until we reach the edge of the swamps."

There was a moment of hesitation, a ripple of unease passing through the assembled men. Then, grudgingly, they began to move, gathering their gear and saddling their horses with grim efficiency as the sun started to set.

We set up camp on the edge of the swamp, a flickering fire casting eerie shadows across the faces of the men as they huddled close for warmth. The air was thick and heavy with the stench of decay, and strange, chittering sounds echoed from the darkness beyond the firelight.

I sat apart from the others, staring into the flames as my mind raced with dark thoughts. The warning left in the ruined village weighed heavily upon me, a warning of the horrors that surely awaited us in the depths of the swamp.

I glanced up as one of the men approached, a grizzled veteran with a face like weathered leather. He squatted down beside me, his eyes glinting in the firelight.

"Ye feel it too, don't ye, sir?" he said, his voice low and rough. "The evil that lurks in this place. It's like a living thing, watchin' us, waitin' to strike."

I nodded grimly, my hand tightening on the hilt of my sword. "Aye, I feel it. But we have no choice but to press on. Our duty lies ahead, no matter the cost."

"'Tis' a fool's errand." He stated, sitting down next to me. "Chasin' ghosts and shadows through this accursed swamp. Ye mark my words, sir - we'll not find anythin' but our deaths in there."

I turned to face him, my eyes hard and unyielding. "Then so be it."

The grizzled veteran shook his head, a bitter smile twisting his lips.

"Aye, the Inquisitors worked you over alright." He said, his teeth bared in a snarl. "They filled yer head with all that nonsense about duty and sacrifice. Bugger them, 'n bugger the bloody Empire. It's every man for 'himself out here."

I pushed the thought away, my jaw clenched tight. "Watch your tongue, soldier," I snapped, my eyes boring into his. "Or I'll cut it out myself. We serve the Empire and the Emperor's will. That's all that matters."

The veteran spat into the fire, the glob of phlegm hissing as it struck the flames. "Do we now?" He leaned in close, his breath rank with the stench of cheap tobacco. "I've been servin' the Empire longer than ye've been alive, boy. And I'll tell ye this - the Emperor only cares about himself. Him and his pretty little lords and ladies, sittin' safe behind their palace walls while the likes of us die in the muck."

I felt angry at his words, hot and bitter in my throat. But beneath it was a flicker of doubt, a nagging whisper that perhaps there was some truth to what he said. I pushed it down, fixing him with a cold, hard stare.

"I'll not hear such treasonous talk, Corporal. You swore an oath, the same as I did. An oath to serve, to obey. To die, if need be. If you can't honor that, then you're no better than the scum we hunt."

"Aye, sir." He said, a grin playing over his mouth. He looked at me - as if I was defenseless.

And then - I lunged out with my fist.

The man fell to the ground - unconscious. A few others rose to their feet in alarm, hands gripping weapons as they stared at me in shock and anger.

"Anyone else wish to question their oaths? To spit upon their sacred duty?" I snarled, wrenching back. Blood gleamed dark and wet upon my knuckles.

The men glanced at each other uneasily, a palpable tension crackling. For a long, tense moment, I thought they might turn on me, the veteran's treasonous words finding fertile ground in their weary, disillusioned minds.

But then, they lowered their eyes one by one, mumbling oaths of loyalty and obedience. I nodded grimly, wiping my hand clean on my armor.

"Get some rest," I ordered, my voice hard and cold. "We march at first light. And let this serve as a reminder to you all - the Emperor's will is absolute. Always."

As the men dispersed to their beds - I knew I would not sleep easy that night.

Shadows over Baltiva

As the first pale fingers of dawn crept over the horizon, we broke camp and began our march into the swamps. A thick, cloying mist hung low over the fetid water, swirling around the twisted roots and gnarled branches that jutted up from the murky depths. Strange, eerie calls echoed through the gloom, the cries of unseen creatures that lurked just beyond the edge of sight.

I led the way, my hand never straying far from the hilt of my sword as we picked our way along the narrow, winding path. The men followed close behind, their faces grim and set with determination. Despite their earlier unease, they were soldiers of the Empire, trained and disciplined, and they would not shrink from their duty.

We had not gone far when we saw the first signs of the horrors that awaited us. A body lay half-submerged in the salty water, bloated and pale in the wan light. Its face was a ruin, the flesh torn and ragged, as if savaged by some terrible beast. I motioned for the men to keep moving, my jaw clenched tight against the rising bile in my throat.

As we pressed deeper into the swamp, the sense of unease grew more pungent, a palpable dread that seemed to seep from the earth. The mist thickened, swirling around us in eerie tendrils that clung to our skin like clammy fingers. Strange shapes lurked at the edges of my vision, glimpsed from the corner of my eye, only to vanish when I turned to face them head-on.

Suddenly, a scream pierced the gloom, high and shrill with terror. I whirled around, my sword leaping from its scabbard, to see one of the men thrashing in the water, his face a mask of pure horror. Something held him, dragging him down into the murky depths with inhuman strength.

I lunged forward, hacking at the thing with desperate fury. Black ichor spurted from the wounds, sizzling where it struck my blade, but still, the creature would not release its grip. All around me, the men were fighting for their lives as more creatures burst from the water, their hideous forms all grasping claws and gnashing teeth.

I slashed and hacked with a berserker's rage, black blood spattering my armor as I carved through the foul beasts. But for every one I felled, two more seemed to rise in its place, an endless tide of horror surging from the fetid depths.

"Fall back!" I roared over the chaos of battle. "Defensive formation, now!"

The men obeyed with the desperate discipline of those who knew they fought for their souls. They formed a tight circle, shields locked and swords jutting out like the spines of some armored beast. I took my place at the fore, grimly determined to sell our lives as dearly as possible.

The creatures surged forward in a writhing mass of putrid flesh and snapping jaws. They threw themselves upon our armor, scrabbling and clawing with mindless ferocity. Men screamed as talons found gaps in armor, flesh parting in bloody furrows.

I lost myself in the madness of battle, hacking, and slashing until my arms burned with fatigue and my blade dripped black with ichor. Time lost all meaning, the world narrowing down to the next parry, the next desperate thrust. We were an island of steel adrift in a sea of nightmares.

Just as I felt my strength beginning to fail, a clarion call cut through the air, pure and bright with holy purpose. The creatures faltered, some shying back as if burned by the sound. I glanced over my shoulder to see a lone figure standing atop a rocky outcropping.

He was clad in shining armor of purest white, a long cloak billowing in the fetid breeze. In one hand, he held aloft a great golden icon blazing with searing light. The other gripped a long, keen-edged blade that seemed to shimmer with its inner fire.

"In the Savior's name!" His voice rang out, clear and commanding. "Back to the abyss, foul abominations!"

He leaped into the fray like an avenging angel, his sword flashing in glittering arcs. Where he struck, the creatures burst asunder in gouts of flame; their death screams shrill and piercing. The light of his icon seared through the mist, and where it touched the creatures, they crumbled to ash and were blown away.

Emboldened by his presence, we surged forward, hope kindling in our hearts like the first embers of a blaze. We drove the monsters back, their numbers thinning under our onslaught.

We rested on the bits of dryland. Out of our company of fifty - we had lost a good dozen men, and several more were wounded. The stranger who had saved us - was clad in the armor of the Order of the Black Griffon. A tall, imposing figure, he removed his helm to reveal a young face, saddled with the weight of grim experience yet still possessing a fierce vitality. His eyes were a piercing blue, seeming to hold within them the sorrows and triumphs of a hundred battles.

"Well met, brothers," he said, his voice a low rumble. "I am Siegfried of the Black Griffon. It seems we arrived just in time."

I stepped forward and clasped his arm in the warrior's grip. "Your arrival was most fortuitous, good sir. I am Captain Kaelitz, and these are my men. We owe you our lives."

He inclined his head in acknowledgment. "Think nothing of it." He stated, forming a grin. His grin held a hint of arrogance, making me wary despite his timely aid. My instincts, honed by years of battle, whispered caution even as I clasped his arm in gratitude.

"What brings a knight of the Black Griffon to this accursed place?" I asked, my tone carefully neutral.

His piercing blue eyes met mine, a flicker of something mysterious in their depths. "The same as you, I imagine. Duty. Honor. A sacred quest to purge the land of evil."

His voice was challenging as if daring me to question his motives. I let the moment, weighing my following words with care.

"What *are* you doing out here?" He asked. "I rarely see Imperial soldiers this deep inland. Save for marauders - and deserters."

I bristled at the implied accusation, my hand tightening on the hilt of my sword. "We are no deserters," I said, my voice low and fierce. "We march at the Lord-Commander's order to seek out and destroy the traitorous Black Band."

Siegfried raised an eyebrow, a hint of a smirk playing about his lips. "I see. I do believe I've heard of them." He said.

"Truly?"

Siegfried nodded slowly, his gaze distant as if lost in memory. "Aye, I've heard of this Black Band. A bunch of uppity Polovanian peasants who do not understand *who* their betters are." He grinned. "Not to mention - led by that traitor Duclaire. A shame to the Valtorean race." He said, looking at me - speaking as if he wasn't one of us.

"Ah. I didn't realize - you are a Baltzer."

"Correct." He said. I studied Siegfried carefully, noting the haughty cast of his noble Baltzer features, no different from the rugged Volkian faces of my men. We were of the same blood, yet these Baltzers persisted.

"The Black Band are more than mere peasants," He said with disdain. "They are a formidable foe. When Lord Commander Duclaire ordered Polvanians and Lithurians to be armed, I knew they would turn on us." He said. "It would seem - my Order was right."

I blinked. While - I had passed the Black Band on occasion, during our march to Freydrich Pass - I chalked them up to be little more than rabble and mercenaries. But - it was understandable why a Polvanian and a Lithurian would desert our cause. Were we not their subjugators?

I considered Siegfried's words carefully, a pensive frown creasing my brow. His casual disdain for the Polvanian and Lithurian people unsettled me, even as his accusation about the Black Band's strength gave me pause. Our mission had become far more difficult if they were as formidable as he claimed.

"You speak as if you know much of these rebels," I said, keeping my tone neutral. "Have you faced them in battle before?"

Siegfried's lips curved in a mirthless smile. "Indeed I have, Captain. The Black Griffons have clashed with Duclaire's little band on multiple occasions. They fight with the desperate ferocity of cornered rats, knowing they can expect no mercy from civilized men of the Empire..." He stated.

"Captain - we are gentlemen, are we not?" I stated. "Surely, that is a bit far."

Siegfried's eyes flashed with a zealous light. "It is the Savior's will that the Empire should rule over the lesser peoples. To rebel against that divine order is heresy of the highest sort."

"Regardless of their reasons," I said, steering the conversation to safer ground, "the Black Band must be dealt with. We cannot allow their rebellion to spread further."

Siegfried nodded, a grim smile playing about his lips. "On that, at least, we can agree. My Order has tasked me to hunt down these traitors and bring them to justice. Perhaps we might join forces in this endeavor?"

I glanced over at the ranks of my wounded men, their faces worn and weary. We had already lost too many on this accursed march. If the Black Band was truly as formidable as Siegfried claimed, joining forces with the Black Griffons might be our best hope of success - and survival.

And yet, something held me back—a nagging doubt, an instinctive wariness of this haughty Baltzer knight with his talk of divine right and lesser peoples. The Empire had subjugated the Polvanians and Lithurians for generations, grounding them under our boot heels. Was it any wonder that some would rise in rebellion?

I thought of the faces of the Polvanian peasants I had seen on our march, gaunt and hollow-eyed - well used to the turmoil and desperation Baltiva seemed to hold in endless amounts for them.

I turned back to Siegfried, weighing my words carefully. "I appreciate the offer, Sir Siegfried," I said at last, choosing my words carefully. Perhaps the two of us can work together—for a time."

Siegfried's smile widened a hint of triumph in his eyes. "Excellent. I believe our combined forces will make short work of these rebels." He clasped my arm, his grip firm. "Together, we shall bring the Savior's justice to these lands."

I returned his grip, meeting his gaze steadily even as a flicker of unease stirred in my gut. There was a zealous fervor in Siegfried's words, a certainty that bordered on fanaticism. I had seen such men before, knights who believed themselves the Savior's chosen instruments, anointed to purge the world of all they deemed unclean. They were dangerous allies, as likely to turn on their own as the enemy if they perceived any hint of wavering conviction.

"We march at dawn," I said, my tone brooking no argument. "I'll not risk my men's lives by blundering through these accursed woods in the dark."

Siegfried inclined his head, a faint smile playing about his lips. "As you wish, Captain. My men are not too far away - we shall make camp nearby. We can discuss our strategy further in the morning."

With that, he turned and strode away, his black cloak billowing behind him. I watched him go, a sense of foreboding settling like a leaden weight in my stomach. I had bought my men a brief respite, but - I feel as if at some grave cost.

The Order's troops were far worse than ours in every metric. Conscripted peasants - of distant Volkian heritage disdained the noble Baltzer knights leading them. Instead of breastplate - they had chainmail, almost archaic in these times. They resembled the men-at-arms of old from arming manuals. As the Order's troops filed through our encampment, their presence cast a pall over my men. The Baltzer knights themselves marched with a haughty bearing, their polished armor and fine cloaks a stark contrast to the mud-spattered uniforms of my soldiers. Yet, for all their finery, something was unsettling about these knights, a cold ruthlessness that seemed to emanate from them like a miasma.

I watched as Siegfried conferred with his lieutenants, their heads bent together in quiet conversation. Occasionally, one of them would cast a disdainful glance towards my men.

"So. We're working the Imperials." One of the knights spat out.

The knight's disdainful words were clear to my ears, and I felt a flare of anger rising in my chest. It was one thing for Siegfried to offer his aid, however condescendingly—it was quite another for his men to openly mock mine. I strode over to the group of knights, my hand resting casually on the hilt of my saber.

"Is there a problem, sir?" I asked, my voice deceptively mild.

The knight who had spoken turned to face me, a sneer twisting his patrician features. "No problem at all, Captain," he drawled. "We were simply marveling at the... The rustic charm of your encampment. Did you find those men in the wild, or were they brought here in a dung cart?"

I fixed the knight with a steely gaze, my voice low and dangerous. "These men have fought and bled for the Empire, sir. They have endured hardships that would break lesser soldiers. I'll not have them mocked by the likes of you."

The knight's eyes narrowed, his hand dropping to the hilt of his sword. For a moment, he might draw on me. But then Siegfried stepped between us, his voice cutting through the tension like a knife.

"Enough, Wolfram," he snapped. "We are all servants of the Savior here. We do not question the courage of our brothers-in-arms, no matter their origin."

The knight called Wolfram looked as if he might argue, but a sharp glance from Siegfried quelled any further protest. With a final sneer in my direction, he turned on his heel and stalked away, his hand still gripping his sword hilt.

Siegfried turned to me, his expression apologetic. "Forgive Wolfram's intemperance, Captain. He is young and headstrong but a true believer in our cause. He will learn respect in time."

"See that he does," I growled. "I'll not have my men insulted - even if they may be scum."

Siegfried inclined his head, his expression contrite. "You have my word, Captain. It will not happen again."

I gave him a curt nod, my jaw still clenched with anger. "See that it doesn't. We have enough enemies without fighting amongst ourselves."

As Siegfried moved off to confer with his men, I let out a slow breath, trying to quell the fury still simmering in my veins. The Baltzer knights might be skilled warriors, but their arrogance would be problematic. I could only hope that Siegfried could keep them in line.

We marched through the swamp in a long column, trying to maintain some semblance of order and discipline even as the sucking mud threatened to swallow us whole. The air was thick with the stench of decay, a miasma that seemed to seep into our very pores. My men slogged forward with grim determination, their faces set in hard lines beneath the rims of their helmets.

Beside me, Siegfried rode at the head of his column, his black destrier picking its way carefully through the mire. The Baltzer knights followed close behind, their armor gleaming dully in the diffuse light that filtered through the overhanging branches.

We had been marching for hours, yet the swamp seemed to stretch endlessly, an unending expanse of fetid water and twisted trees. The rebels were lurking in the shadows, waiting for the opportune moment to strike. I could feel their eyes upon us, a creeping sensation that made the hairs on the back of my neck stand on end - and finally, after half a day of walking - we found it.

A stone, ancient-looking fortress deep in the swamp. Its origins were a puzzle to me - it hardly seemed to be an Imperial castle built by the Order, and it was so deep in the swamp that I questioned its use.

There were no roads that led to this ancient fortress, and there were no signs of recent habitation or use. It seemed to have risen from the depths of the swamp, a relic of some long-forgotten age. As we drew closer, I could make out more details - the weathered stone walls were covered in a thick layer of moss and lichen, and the narrow windows were little more than dark slits in the masonry. A sense of unease crept over me as I gazed upon the forbidding structure.

"What is this place?" I muttered, more to myself than to anyone else.

Siegfried reined in his horse beside me, his gaze fixed on the ancient fortress. "I know not its name or history," he said, his voice low and thoughtful. "But there is an old legend among my people of a cursed castle deep in the swamps, built by a mad tribe in the days before the Savior's grace saved us all. They say it was a place of great evil, where unspeakable rites were performed in the name of dark gods of these lands."

I shuddered at his words, feeling a chill that had nothing to do with the damp air. "You think this could be the place from your legend?"

Siegfried shrugged. "Who can say? The swamps hold many secrets, Captain. But if the rebels have taken refuge here, we must root them out, whatever the cost."

I nodded grimly, knowing he was right. We had come too far to turn back now. "Then let us proceed with caution," I said. "If evil exists here, we must be prepared to face it."

We formed into a tight column, with my men taking the lead and the Baltzer knights bringing up the rear. As we approached the crumbling gatehouse, I could feel a sense of dread settling over me like a shroud. The very stones seemed to exude an aura of malice, as if the fortress was aware of our presence and resented our intrusion.

The portcullis was raised, its rusted teeth like fangs in the gloom. Nothing seemed to greet us - as we watched, and an eerie silence enveloped us.

"Oh lord - ain't that something." One of the men mumbled. "They're just waiting for us; they' are."

I nodded grimly at the soldier's words. The ominous silence and the dark aperture of the gatehouse yawned before us like the maw of some slumbering beast. Every instinct screamed at me to turn back, to flee this accursed place and never look back. But I knew we had no choice. Our duty compelled us ever onward into the very heart of darkness.

"Steady, men," I called, surprised at the calm in my voice. "Remember your training. Keep your wits about you and watch each other's backs. The Savior is with us, even in this forsaken place."

I saw some men touch their crudely carved wooden Savior symbols hanging from their necks, muttering quick prayers. Siegfried and his knights likewise made the sign of the Savior's Flame across their breastplates. The holy gestures brought a small measure of comfort, but the oppressive dread still hung over us like a burial shroud.

With a deep breath, I drew my sword and stepped forward into the shadows of the gatehouse. My boots squelched in the damp moss and decaying matter underfoot. The men filed in behind me, their weapons ready, eyes wide and scanning the darkness.

The tunnel through the gatehouse was low and narrow, forcing us to proceed with a single file. The slimy stone walls pressed in on either side as if the fortress sought to swallow us whole. In the courtyard - was a scene unlike any other.

It was akin to an abattoir - the oppressive stench of death hit all at once as I saw rows of decimated men laying upon the grass.

The stench of death and decay hit us like a physical blow as we emerged into the courtyard. The scene before us was one of unimaginable carnage. Dozens of bodies lay strewn across the overgrown grass, their limbs twisted at unnatural angles, their lifeless eyes staring sightlessly up at the gray sky. Many bore blackened veins, while their mouths were filled with a bloody froth crusted around their lips.

I heard retching sounds behind me as some of the men lost the contents of their stomachs. Even Siegfried looked pale beneath his dark beard, his knuckles white on the hilt of his sword.

"Mother of mercy," he breathed.

"What?" I asked - looking over at him. He seemed alert - but he said nothing, staring at me. I have never seen a man so fearful that he trembled.

"Look at what... Look." He said. I gazed - and noticed the positioning of the way all these men were assembled

As I stared closer at the horrific scene, a chilling realization crept over me. The bodies were not strewn about haphazardly as I had first thought. No, there was a disturbing purposefulness to their arrangement, a sickening symmetry that spoke of a twisted intelligence behind this carnage.

The corpses were laid out in a precise grid, their splayed arms almost touching, forming a macabre lattice across the weed-choked courtyard. And at the center of this grisly tableau, a raised dais of crumbling stone bore a massive blazing brazier.

The flames danced and writhed, casting eerie shadows across the scene of butchery. A noxious black smoke poured from the brazier, carrying a stomach-churning stench that made my gorge rise.

"This is no rebel hideout," I managed through clenched teeth, fighting back my nausea. "This is something far worse."

Siegfried nodded grimly, his eyes never leaving the dais and its hellish brazier. "An altar," he spat. "To what dark god, I dare not guess."

"Captain!" One of my men called out, his voice quivering with barely restrained terror. "Over here!"

I turned to see the soldier pointing toward one of the crumbling walls with a trembling hand. There, daubed in what looked like dried blood, was a strange symbol - a jagged sigil that made me sign the Holy Flame.

It was the Sign of the Unholy, the mark of the Dark One - unmistakable. A shudder ran through me at the sight of that foul sigil, and I felt the icy touch of fear upon my soul as Siegfried approached me.

"We must burn them. These bodies - they carry the Plague." I felt my blood run cold at Siegfried's words. The Plague - a scourge so vile, so utterly horrific, that even the bravest of men quailed at its mention. It was a disease born of dark sorcery, a contagion that twisted flesh and corrupted the very souls of its victims before granting them an agonizing death.

"Are you certain?" I asked, my voice sounding hollow in my ears.

Siegfried nodded grimly. "I've seen it before - only once, and that was enough. The blackened veins, the bloody froth...there can be no mistaking it. We must burn the bodies before the contagion spreads." He stated.

I swallowed hard, my mind reeling at the implications. If the rebels had unleashed the Plague here, we were not safe. The disease could already be spreading, carrying on this accursed place's fetid air. We had to act quickly.

"We cannot tarry then," I said, surprised once more at the steadiness of my voice. "Gather the bodies. Build the pyres. We will send these poor souls to the cleansing flame and pray it is enough to halt the spread of this unholy pestilence."

The men leaped to the grim task with an alacrity born of fear. They hauled the twisted corpses onto heaps of broken furniture, and rotting timbers scavenged from the ruined keep. All the while, I kept a wary eye on the hellish brazier, its flames crackling and popping as if in gleeful anticipation of what was to come.

As the pyres were lit and the first wisps of greasy smoke began to curl upward, I turned to Siegfried. The knight's face was drawn and haggard, his eyes haunted.

"Now - what awaits us in there, I wonder?" He stated, looking into the castle proper - looming at us.

I could only fear what lay inside.

The Infernal Foe

The main hall was a vast, echoing space, its vaulted ceiling lost in shadows. Tattered banners hung limply from the walls, their colors faded and devices obscured by decades of dust and neglect. At the far end of the hall, a massive staircase led into darkness, its once-grand balustrade now crumbling and thick with cobwebs.

Our footsteps seemed unnaturally loud as we advanced cautiously into the hall, reverberating off the ancient stones. I could feel the weight of centuries pressing upon us, a palpable sense of age and decay that seeped from every crack and crevice.

"Stay alert," I whispered to my men, my voice sounding thin and strained in the oppressive silence. "There's no telling what horrors may lurk in this accursed place."

We spread out as we moved deeper into the hall, swords and halberds at the ready, eyes straining to penetrate the gloom. The air was thick and musty, laden with the scent of mold and something else, something far more foul - a sweet, cloying odor that clung to the back of the throat and made the stomach churn.

Suddenly, a sound shattered the sepulchral silence - a low, rasping moan that seemed to come from everywhere and nowhere. I spun around, my heart pounding, searching for the source of the unearthly noise.

The moan became louder this time, a wretched sound of unfathomable agony and despair. My men drew closer together instinctively, their faces pale beneath the flickering torchlight.

"There," Siegfried hissed, pointing toward a shadowed alcove with his sword. "Movement."

I peered into the darkness, my breath caught in my throat. At first, I saw nothing, but then a shape detached itself from the deeper shadows - a shambling, lurching figure that moved with a jerky, unnatural gait.

I recoiled in horror as it stepped into the wan pool of light cast by our torches. The creature had once been a man, but now it was a twisted mockery of humanity. Its flesh was blackened and necrotic, sloughing off in rancid sheets. Weeping sores covered its body, oozing a foul ichor that sizzled and smoked where it dripped onto the flagstones. But worst of all was its eyes - milky white orbs that burned with an unholy hunger as they fixed upon us.

"By the Holy Flame," one of my men whimpered, his sword trembling. "What is that thing?"

"Plague-spawn," Siegfried whispered, his voice tight with disgust and dread. "A victim of the pestilence, twisted into an abomination by the dark sorcery that animates their rotting flesh."

The creature let out another moan, a sound of such utter torment that it sent shudders down my spine. It began to lurch towards us, its movements growing more frantic with each shambling step.

"Stand firm!" I commanded though I could hear the tremor in my voice. "Skewer the fiend before it can get close!"

My men leveled their halberds, bracing for the creature's approach. But even as they did so, more shapes began to detach themselves from the shadows - a dozen, a score, a whole host of plague-ridden monstrosities shuffling forward with single-minded purpose.

"There are too many!" one of the soldiers cried out, his face ashen with terror. We'll be overwhelmed!"

The tips of our halberds pierced decaying flesh as the first wave of abominations reached us, foul black ichor spraying from their wounds. But for every one we struck down, two more surged forward to take its place, a relentless tide of pestilent horror.

"Fall back!" I shouted, desperation tinging my voice as I thrust my blade through the eye socket of a gore-encrusted skull. "Back to the entrance! We must not let them surround us!"

We gave ground, slashing and stabbing, a frantic melee in the flickering torchlight. The air was thick with the reek of decay, the wet squelch and crack of steel sundering rotten meat. A flailing, pus-covered arm caught Siegfried across the face, and he reeled back, spitting blood and broken teeth.

"The doors!" he cried, pointing with his gore-slicked sword. "We must bar the doors!"

I glanced over my shoulder and felt relief at the sight of the heavy oak doors still standing open on their rusted hinges. If we could reach them, we put a solid barrier between ourselves and the insatiable hosts.

We fell back towards the doors, our desperate retreat becoming a mad scramble as the dead pressed forward, their numbers seeming to multiply with every passing second. The cloying stench of rot and decay suffocated, the sickening squelch and crunch of our halberds hewing through putrid flesh and brittle bone echoing in the confined space.

At last, we reached the threshold and staggered through. Siegfried and I heaved our weight against the great doors, muscles straining as we struggled to force the warped wood closed against the relentless pressure of the horde.

"The bar!" I gasped. "Get the damned bar!"

Two soldiers heaved the heavy length of oak into place just as the first fists began to hammer against the other side, the wood shuddering under the impacts. For a breathless moment, I feared it would not hold - that it would splinter and burst, unleashing the nightmarish deluge upon us. But the ancient timbers held firm and the thud of rotting meat against wood receded to a dull pounding.

I slumped against the wall, my saber falling from my nerveless fingers to clang against the flagstones. The men collapsed around me, chests heaving, breastplates dark with blood and ichor. In the guttering torchlight, I saw Siegfried clutching his wounded face, blood seeping between his fingers.

"We cannot go back that way," he said thickly, his voice muffled behind his hand. "Those creatures - no halberd or blade can slay them. Surely - the Black Band are dead." He stated - looking up at the castle. I looked at him from the ground.

"How can we be sure? While - there are a few bodies... It's hardly been a company of five hundred." I stated. "Where's the rest of them?"

Siegfried looked at me grimly, his hand still pressed to his wounded cheek. "If they live, they are trapped in there with those... Abominations. And how can we enter without condemning ourselves to the same wretched fate."

I wanted to argue. My mission, sure enough, was to slay - or capture them, but now - what were we to do? The words died in my throat. The memory of those shambling horrors was still too raw, too visceral. The unholy hunger in their milky eyes, the clinging reek of decay that contaminated the air...

"What evil is this?" I whispered hoarsely, struggling to comprehend what we had seen. "What manner of devilry could twist the dead into such blasphemous mockeries of life?"

"The pestilence," Siegfried spat, his voice thick with disgust and dread. "Brought of devilry and diabolism. I'd wager the Black Band are in the presence of a Goetian - of considerable power."

"A Goetian - this far out?" I stated. The words tasted like ashes in my mouth. "I thought their kind was exterminated."

Siegfried shook his head grimly. "Not exterminated. Driven into the shadows, perhaps, their numbers thinned. But never wholly destroyed." He pulled his hand away from his face, revealing an ugly gash that wept crimson rivulets down his jaw. "And now it seems one has found a new lair to work their black arts. Far from the center of the Empire."

I felt a chill settle in my bones at the implications. A Goetian sorcerer, here, on the edges of the Empire. And in league with the Black Band, no less. It was a prospect to make the blood run cold.

I pushed myself to my feet, wincing as my battered muscles protested. "We must send word to the Lord Commander," I said. "Call for reinforcements, for inquisitors. We are ill-equipped to face such a foe alone."

"It is too late now. These minions - even an apprentice Goetic can see through their eyes. It's likely - he's scrying on us as we speak." He stated. Fear coursed through the knight's words as I glanced to our right - metal boots stomping on dead grass.

Brother Konrad approached, his weathered face grim beneath his battered helm. "What evil have you encountered within?" He glanced towards the barred doors, his hand tightening on the haft of his poleaxe.

I met his gaze, seeing my horror mirrored in his eyes. "The dead walk," I said softly, each word leaden on my tongue. "Animated by some unholy power, they assailed us within. We were fortunate to escape with our lives."

Konrad blanched, his grizzled features slackening in shock. "Necromancy? Here?" He made a sign of warding, his fingers sketching the Holy Sigil in the air.

"There is more," Siegfried added grimly. "We suspect the presence of a Goetian sorcerer. One in league with the Black Band we were sent to destroy."

A palpable ripple of unease passed through the assembled knights, a susurrus of muttered oaths and prayers. All knew the vile reputation of the Goetian warlocks—their pacts with the Dark One, their blasphemous rites, and their unspeakable cruelties.

"If this is true, we are sorely outmatched," Konrad said heavily. "Our forces are too few to challenge a Goetian and their minions directly, let alone whoever is in league with them..." He stated. Then - Konrad's face turned white.

"This whole yard - it explains everything. This is a ritual site - for blood magic." He stated. "...But - it doesn't make sense. They use the blood of virgins, typically, not of common folk - I haven't seen a site like this for a very, very long time..."

I followed Konrad's gaze, a cold dread seeping into my veins as I entered the scene with new eyes. The dead grass, the unnatural stillness, the faint metallic tang that hung in the air...

"Virgin blood..." I whispered, bile rising in my throat at the thought. "Truly, these are cursed lands."

Siegfried's face was ashen beneath the blood and grime. "The Goetian's power waxes with the spilling of innocent blood. And what purer source than the untouched maidens of the outlying villages?" His voice shook with barely suppressed rage. "Raising the dead here - I hardly doubt it was the extent of the ritual."

"What other foul purpose could such a ritual serve?" I asked, dreading the answer even as the question left my lips.

Konrad's weathered face was etched with grim lines as he replied. "Blood magic of this scale, fueled by the life essence of the pure and innocent... It could grant the sorcerer immense power. Power to twist the very fabric of reality, to call forth nightmares from the abyss."

A heavy silence fell over our battered group as we contemplated the enormity of the threat we faced. A Goetian warlock, bolstered by the darkest forbidden arts, perhaps allied with the savage might of the Black Band.

"We must burn this place - and flee at once." Brother Wolfram stated.

We worked double time, piling kindling against the oak doors. Men chopped down trees at the edge of the swamp - as a dark, fetid fog rolled in,

The fog crept in from the swamp, tendrils of sickly grey mist that writhed and coiled like living things. It swallowed the trees, the tumbled stones of the yard, and even the muted sounds of our frantic labor. In moments, the world had shrunk to a few paces in every direction, and the rest lost to a clammy, clinging blankness.

I shivered, and not just from the sudden chill. There was something unnatural about this fog, something that set my teeth on edge and made the hairs on my nape prickle. It felt tainted, malevolent, as if some vile presence lurked within, watching us with cruel, unseen eyes.

"Hurry," Konrad urged, his voice muffled and eerie in the deadening murk. "We must put the torch to this accursed place before..."

He trailed off, leaving the ill thought unspoken before the Goetian could mount a counter-attack. Before the walking dead could shamble forth once more. Before something even worse emerged from the unhallowed depths of the swamp.

We redoubled our efforts, piling the last of the wood against the barred doors. The damp and cloying fog clung to us as we worked. It seeped into our clothes and skin until we were shivering and miserable. But still, we did not slack.

Finally, with sweat and grime coating our brows, the last kindling was heaped against the cursed doors. Brother Siegfried approached with a lit torch, its flickering light a feeble thing in the gloom. With a muttered prayer, he thrust it into the pile.

For an agonizing moment, nothing happened. I held my breath, fearing some eldritch power would snuff out the flame. But then - a wisp of smoke. A crackle. The dry wood caught, and hungry flames began to lick at the ancient timbers.

"Back!" Konrad commanded, his voice cracking like a whip. "Put distance between us and this unholy place!"

We needed no further urging. As one, we turned and began a stumbling retreat, desperate to escape the festering blight we had uncovered. But the fog pressed in like a living thing, clinging and cloying, muffling our steps and clouding our vision.

Each breath was a struggle, the air thick and foul in my lungs. Tendrils of mist curled around my limbs like fingers, tugging at my feet as if dragging me down into some lightless abyss. Nameless dread clutched at my heart, a certainty of doom that went beyond mere fear.

Behind us, the fire was an angry red glow in the murk, painting writhing shadows on the fog. I glanced over my shoulder - the old, venerable castle beginning to catch ablaze.

As the flames consumed the ancient wood, a terrible wail arose within the castle walls. It was a sound no human throat could make, a keening cry of rage and anguish that seemed to pierce the soul. The earth trembled beneath our feet, and the fog convulsed as if in pain.

"Faster!" Siegfried shouted, his voice raw with urgency. "The sorcerer knows their work is undone!"

We ran, crashing through the underbrush, heedless of the grasping branches that tore at our clothes and skin. The wailing grew louder, joined now by a cacophony of shrieks and howls that chilled the blood. The unholy denizens of this place were roused to fury by the destruction of their sanctum.

Shapes moved in the fog, darting shadows that were there and gone in the blink of an eye. Glowing eyes peered from the gloom, evil and hungry. Fear spurred us on and lent speed to our weary limbs. To falter now was to die—or suffer a fate far worse.

The ground grew soft beneath our pounding feet, the soil turning foul-smelling mud. The swamp was reclaiming its own, eager to swallow us whole. Each step was a struggle, the mire clutching at our boots, threatening to drag us down into its bottomless depths as we sped through it.

The sun was sinking below the horizon, painting the sky in lurid shades of crimson and orange, by the time we finally allowed ourselves to collapse, exhausted and shaken, on a stretch of relatively dry ground. The fog had thinned as we put distance between ourselves and the cursed castle, but still it clung to us in wispy tendrils, as if reluctant to relinquish its hold.

I gulped air into my burning lungs, my heart pounding a furious tattoo against my ribs. Every muscle ached, pushed far beyond the limits of endurance. But it was not just physical exertion that left me trembling. The horrors we had witnessed, the malevolent power we had felt, weighed heavy on my soul.

I looked to my companions, seeing my own haunted expression mirrored in their faces. Brother Konrad, usually so stoic and unshakable, was ashen beneath his beard, his eyes shadowed. Siegfried had sunk to his knees, his head bowed.

The rest of the men - those who remained of the Forlorn Hope, and the Order's own stalwart brothers - were in little better state. They sprawled or sat in poses of utter exhaustion, gulping water from skins and tending to the scratches and bruises earned in our desperate flight. In their eyes I saw the same shadow that haunted my own thoughts - the knowledge that we had brushed against something profane and unholy, a darkness that would forever mark our souls.

In the distance, the castle was a pillar of greasy smoke and angry flame, spitting sparks into the darkening sky like the fires of hell itself. Even from this remove, I fancied I could feel the heat of it on my face, could hear the crack and roar as ancient timbers succumbed to the blaze. The wailing had ceased, but an oppressive silence lay heavy on the land, as if even the natural creatures sensed the evil we had unleashed and fled.

"What manner of devil's work was that?" One of the Forlorn Hope, a grizzled man-at-arms, broke the silence. His voice was hoarse, either from exertion or fear. "Sorcery and walking corpses...I've never seen the like."

"Pray you never do again," Konrad said grimly. He had produced a roll of parchment and a stick of charcoal from some hidden pocket, and now he sketched rapidly, his hand flying over the paper.

"We have struck a blow against the Goetian this day," Brother Siegfried said, his voice low but fervent. "But I fear our work is far from done. That foulness, that corruption...it spreads deeper than we know."

I nodded, my throat tight. The horrors of the swamp, the abominations we had put to the sword and the flame, were seared into my mind's eye. They would haunt my dreams for years to come, I had no doubt.

"What is our course now?" I asked, dreading the answer even as the question left my lips. "Do we press on, seek out the source of this evil?"

Konrad looked up from his parchment, his eyes hard as flint in the fading light. "We must. But first, we send word to the Grandmaster. He must know what we have found here, the threat that festers in this godsforsaken place."

He rolled up the parchment, his mouth a grim line. "We must make haste back - to civilized lands."

As we trudged through the mire, each step a struggling effort, my mind raced with the implications of what we had seen. The Goetics, that ancient and foul order, had always been spoken of in hushed whispers, their name a curse. To see their handiwork firsthand, to witness the depths of their depravity... It shook me to my core.

Brother Konrad, ever the scholar, muttered to himself as he walked, his brow furrowed in thought. "The sigils, the incantations...I've seen their like before, in the forbidden tomes. But to think they would dare unleash such abominations..."

His hand never straying far from his sword hilt, Siegfried nodded grimly. "Aye, it is a black day when such filth walks the earth unchallenged. We must root it out, burn it like the cancer it is."

The men of the Forlorn Hope, for all their base nature, shared our revulsions. They huddled close as we walked, casting wary glances at the lengthening shadows. Even the most hardened among them had been shaken by what they had seen.

And then - we saw a dozen shadowy silhouettes in front of us.

As we drew closer, the shadowy figures resolved into the unmistakable forms of men - ragged, filthy, but men nonetheless. A ghost from our past stood at their head, a specter that sent a chill down my spine. It was Duclaire himself, alive and whole. How - I did not know. I was hardly informed about his death - and now, perhaps, a sick churning began in my gut.

Beside Duclaire stood the men—who seemed to be cutthroats and brigands, their eyes glinting in the fading light. They had made camp here in the swamp, just ahead of us.

The two groups stared at each other across the misty expanse for a moment, hands twitching towards sword hilts. The air crackled with tension, a bowstring drawn taut.

It was I who broke the silence, my voice ringing out with a mix of shock and anger. "Lord Duclaire! They say you are dead, back at Rega!" I said, standing in front of everyone. Now, you take the company of traitors?"

Duclaire's eyes narrowed as he regarded me, his face a mysterious mask. "Kaelitz. You might have been mixed up in this sorry business." As I remembered, his voice was low and gravelly, but there was an edge to it now, a bitterness that had not been there before.

He stepped forward, his hand resting on the hilt of his sword. "As for my supposed demise - you may thank your new Lord-Commander for his treason. And these men are no traitors. They are loyal soldiers, true to the cause."

"The cause?" I spat, my hand tightening on my weapon. "What cause could justify consorting with the Goetia, with unleashing such abominations?"

Duclaire looked at me - a sour look on his face. A look of betrayal.

"You accuse me of consorting with the diabolists? Have you gone mad?" He said. "They are Löwe's pets." He spat out. "Not mine."

Duclaire's words hit me like a physical blow. Löwe, the Lord-Commander, in league with the Goetics? It was unthinkable. Impossible - even. Despite my hatred of the man - it seems far-fetched. It seemed far more likely that this was an elaborate ruse - have us storm that fortress, be slaughtered by the abominations within, and then outflanked by the Black Band.

"You lie," I said. "The Empire would never tolerate such deviancy."

Duclaire laughed, a harsh, humorless sound. "Do I? Think, Kaelitz." He took another step forward, his eyes blazing with a fervor I had never seen before. "I was so naive. So foolish..." Duclaire's face twisted with anguish as he spoke, his words tumbling in a bitter rush. "I was blind, Kaelitz. Blind to the truth that was staring me in the face all along. The Empire, even this blasted Order... All of it is rotten to the core. All of it."

I shook my head, refusing to believe what I was hearing. "No - no. You've gone mad." I stated.

Brother Konrad spoke up then, his voice trembling with barely suppressed rage. "You speak of betrayal, yet here you stand with brigands and cutthroats. How are we to believe a word you say?"

Duclaire's gaze shifted to the knight, and for a moment, I thought I might strike him down on the spot. But he merely smiled a cold, predatory thing.

"I would hardly think a fanatic belonging to the Order would listen to me - listen to the truths of the Low Church."

I felt a chill run through me at Duclaire's words: the Low Church - that heretical sect. To hear him openly declare allegiance to them was shocking. Blasphemous, even.

"The Low Church deals in lies and sedition," Brother Konrad said coldly. "You damn yourself with every word."

Duclaire merely shrugged. "I have seen the truth that the High Church tried to bury. The Goetics are not some rogue element - they act with the blessing of the Church and the Inquisition itself."

I stood there stunned, trying to process Duclaire's shocking revelations. My mind reeled at the implications - that the rot of corruption and heresy reached the highest echelons of the Empire. It was almost too much to fathom.

Siegfried stepped forward, his hand gripping the hilt of his sword and his jaw clenching in anger. "Enough of this prattle. I care not for your tales of conspiracy and betrayal. All I see before me is a traitor and a heretic in league with the vilest scum imaginable. In the name of the Lord, I condemn you to death."

Duclaire's men tensed at this, hands flying to weapons, but he held up a hand to stay them. His eyes never left Siegfried as he spoke, his voice low and dangerous.

"You are a fool, Siegfried—a blind, ignorant fool, like all the rest. You cling to your precious Order, your diabolical religion, even as it crumbles around you. But I have seen the truth. I know what is coming. When the Goetics ascend, and the Empire is drowned in blood, I will pick up the pieces. To forge a new order from the ashes of the old."

I shook my head in disbelief and disgust. "I will not hear these treasonous words. You dishonor yourself, Duclaire. You dishonor the Empire - and your dynasty."

At the mention of his son, Duclaire's face contorted in a mask of grief and rage. "My dynasty - no longer!" Duclaire's voice trembled with barely suppressed emotion as he spoke of his son. "They are lost to me, Kaelitz. Lost to their ambition's machinations, they turned against the Lord's truth."

His gaze hardened then, a steely resolve settling over his features. "But I will save the Emperor. I will save all of us from the rot that eats away at the heart of the Empire. Even if it means tearing it all down and starting anew." He said - staring at me. He took a shuddering breath, visibly trying to compose himself. "I had hoped you might see reason, Kaelitz, that you might join our cause. But I see now that the Church's poison runs too deep in you."

His hand dropped to his sword, and the men behind him tensed, ready to spring into action. Siegfried and the others likewise readied their weapons.

"So be it then. If you do not join us, you will die with the rest of the Empire's lapdogs."

With a roar, Duclaire's men surged forward, a tide of bared steel and passionate fury. I leaped into the fray with my saber flashing in the murky light as I slashed and jabbed forward - gunshots and yelling echoing through the night.

Duclaire himself drew his blade and lunged at me, his eyes blazing with hatred and the conviction of his twisted cause. Our swords clashed in a shower of sparks as we traded blow after furious blow. Around us, the chamber erupted into a chaotic melee of clashing steel, flashing pistols, and the screams of the dying.

I parried Duclaire's savage attacks, my blade a blur of shining metal. His swordsmanship was superb, honed by years of battle, but I matched him stroke for stroke, calling upon all my training and skill. We danced a deadly waltz amidst the swirling violence, oblivious to all else.

Duclaire's face was painted with rage as he pressed his assault. "You cannot stop what is coming, Kaelitz!" he snarled over the din of battle. "The Empire is rotten to the core, and I will see it burned to ashes before I let it fester any longer!"

I gritted my teeth and redoubled my efforts, my blade slicing the air in a dazzling pattern of cuts and thrusts. "You're insane, Duclaire!" I shouted back.

I deflected a vicious slash and riposted, my saber scoring a thin line across Duclaire's cheek. He snarled in pain and redoubled his assault, his blade a whirlwind of steel.

"You blind, ignorant fool!" Duclaire raved, spittle flying from his lips. "You're too indoctrinated to see the truth, even when it's right before you!"

We circled each other amidst the melee, blades flashing in the guttering torchlight. Duclaire's face was a mask of manic zeal, his eyes wide and fevered - and then, I heard something come from behind me.

A man of the Forlorn Hope - jabbed a dagger right into my shoulder, and I collapsed. Pain exploded through my shoulder as the dagger sank deep. I staggered, my saber falling from suddenly nerveless fingers. Duclaire saw his opening and lunged forward, murder in his eyes.

But even as I fell, I lashed out with a booted foot, catching Duclaire in the knee. He stumbled, his strike going wide, and I used the momentary respite to rip the dagger free with a spray of blood. The man behind me - seemed shocked, backing up, as I viciously lunged forward like a man possessed against the traitor. Caught off guard, he barely managed to elude my savage attack, his blade deflecting off my dagger, until I caught him in the neck.

He struggled - gasping as the knife plunged.

The knife plunged deep into the man's neck, blood gushing out as he gurgled and choked. His eyes widened in shock and pain before the light faded from them, and he crumpled to the ground.

I whirled, ignoring the searing agony in my shoulder, to face Duclaire once more. He had regained his footing, fury, and madness blazing in his eyes as he raised his sword. He was upon me in an instant - his sword arcing down...

I threw myself aside at the last moment, the blade cleaving the air where I'd been a heartbeat before. I hit the ground hard, pain lancing through my wounded shoulder, but I pushed it aside and rolled to my feet, snatching up a fallen pistol as I did - and it roared, the sound deafening. Duclaire staggered back, a red stain blossoming on his chest. He looked down at the wound in shocked disbelief, then back up at me.

"Y-you... You fool." Duclaire swayed on his feet, his sword slipping from his grasp to clatter. He pressed a hand to the wound in his chest, his fingers coming away slick with crimson. He sank to his knees, a trickle of blood running from the corner of his mouth. Around us, the battle still raged, but I scarcely noticed. My entire focus was on the broken man before me, my former mentor, now revealed as a traitor and a madman.

Slowly, I got up, grabbed my saber, and walked over to him.

"You... It ends here." I stated, my breath ragged with exhaustion and grief. "Your treacherous ways - your little band... It is over. I should have seen this coming - traitor." I spat out.

Duclaire looked up at me, his face ashen, eyes glassy with impending death yet still alight with feverish conviction. "No... you're wrong, Kaelitz," he rasped, each word a struggle. "This is only the beginning. The truth... cannot be stopped. Even if I fall... others will rise to finish what I started."

A coughing fit wracked his frame, and specks of blood flecked his lips. I gazed down at him, my heart heavy.

Duclaire fixed me with one last piercing stare, a ghost of his old intensity. "You'll see, Kaelitz... in time, you'll understand..." With those final words, Duclaire slumped forward and was still, his lifeblood pooling beneath him on the dirt.

I stood over his body, numb with exhaustion and the weight of all that had transpired. Around me, the sounds of battle were fading as the last of the Black Band fell to my men's blades and bullets. In the distance, I could hear Siegfried barking orders, securing the perimeter.

But I scarcely registered any of it. My gaze remained fixed on Duclaire's corpse, my mind reeling. This man had been my mentor. He had taught me so much and shaped me into the soldier and officer I was today. And now... now he lay dead at my feet, cut down by my hand, revealed as a madman and a traitor to the Empire he had once sworn to serve.

Had it all been a lie? A facade to mask his true intentions, his descent into treachery and madness? I couldn't reconcile the man I had known, the man I had admired and respected, with the twisted fanatic bleeding out at my feet.

Questions swirled in my head, taunting me with their elusiveness. What had driven Duclaire to such extremes? What was this "truth" he spoke of with his dying breaths? Had I been blind to the signs, too naively trusting to see the darkness festering in his heart?

I had no answers, only a yawning void of uncertainty and betrayal. It threatened to swallow me whole, to drag me down into the same abyss that had claimed my former mentor. I pushed it aside and continued jumping into the last flickering moments of the battle.

A Lonely Testament

The battlefield lay strewn with the bodies of the fallen, a grim testament to the day's struggle. I surveyed the carnage with a heavy heart, knowing each lost life was a devastating blow to our already diminished forces. Siegfried approached, his wizened face etched with concern.

"Kaelitz," he said gravely, placing a weathered hand on my shoulder. "It was hard work you did."

I nodded solemnly, unable to tear my gaze from the lifeless form of Duclaire littering the blood-soaked earth. "It was not enough," I replied, my voice hoarse from shouting commands over the clamor of battle.

Siegfried squeezed my shoulder, a gesture of solidarity amidst the desolation. "You fought with courage and honor, as befits a captain of the Holy Valtorean Empire. The men who di-"

"I'm not worried about the men." I said. I gazed into the distance, gripping my saber, glancing back at Siegfried.

"The politics - that's what I'm worried about."

I turned to face Siegfried fully; my brow furrowed with the weight of my concerns. "It's clear to me now. Since the beginning - I have been nothing but a pawn." I stated. "What is going on here - at the heart of the matter? Duclaire - and Von Löwe at each other's throat - the accusations of heresy and treason..."

Siegfried's weathered visage grew somber, his eyes darkening with unspoken knowledge. "What are you implying?" He stated.

I clenched my jaw, a simmering anger rising within me. "Duclaire was my mentor, Siegfried. A man of honor - when I knew him." I shook my head, unable to finish the thought. "Now - dark sorcerors, rebels - what else lies at the heart of Baltiva? What else do I not know?"

Siegfried's weathered face grew stern, his eyes flashing with warning and resolve. He grasped my shoulders firmly, his voice low and urgent.

"Kaelitz, you must stop this line of questioning at once," he said, his tone brooking no argument. "The Empire is facing grave threats from all sides, and we cannot afford to sow seeds of doubt among our ranks."

I opened my mouth to protest, but Siegfried cut me off with a sharp gesture. "Listen to me carefully, young Kaelitz. Von Löwe is a loyal servant of the Empire who has dedicated his life to protecting our people from the dark forces that threaten to engulf us. To suggest that he is in league with the Goetics is absurd and treasonous."

I felt a flicker of uncertainty, my resolve wavering under Siegfried's words. Could I have been mistaken? Was my grief over Duclaire's betrayal clouding my judgment?

Siegfried must have sensed my hesitation, for his grip on my shoulders tightened. "You are a man of the Valtorean Empire, Kaelitz."

As Siegfried spoke, I noticed something peculiar on his arm - a jagged symbol peeking beneath his torn sleeve. It was the same symbol I had seen etched into the stone walls of the castle we had burned down mere days ago. Seeing it sent a chill down my spine, and I felt a sudden, inexplicable sense of unease.

I narrowed my eye, studying the symbol more closely. The harsh, angular lines seemed to pulse with malevolent energy as if imbued with some dark power. As a soldier of the Empire, I had seen many strange and unsettling things, but this symbol was unlike anything I had encountered before.

"Siegfried," I said slowly, my voice low and cautious. "What is that mark on your arm?"

The knight's eyes widened, and he quickly pulled his sleeve to cover the symbol. "It's nothing," he said gruffly, avoiding my gaze. "Just an old battle scar."

But I knew he was lying. The way he had reacted, the flicker of fear in his eyes - it was clear that the symbol held some deeper meaning, some secret he was desperate to keep hidden. His hand went to his blade.

In a flash, I drew my sword, the rasp of steel against the scabbard ringing out in the tense silence. Siegfried's eyes narrowed, his weathered face twisting into a scowl.

"Stand down, Kaelitz," he growled. "You don't know what you're doing."

"I know enough," I retorted, my voice cold as the winter wind. "That mark on your arm - I've seen it before. In a den of sorcery and darkness, where the very air reeked of evil."

Siegfried let out a harsh bark of laughter, a sound devoid of joy. "You think you've stumbled upon some grand conspiracy? You know nothing of the true nature of this war."

I tightened my grip on my saber, the weight of it steadying my resolve. "Then enlighten me, Siegfried. What is the true nature of this war? What secrets have been kept from me?"

Siegfried's eyes glinted with a dangerous light, his hand tightening on the hilt of his blade. "The secrets I keep are not mine to share, Kaelitz. They are the Empire's secrets and are kept for good reason."

I shook my head, unwilling to back down. "The Empire's secrets? Or the secrets of those using dark sorcery to further their ends? I have seen too much, Siegfried. The Goetics, the rebels - they are all connected somehow. And now, that mark on your arm..."

Siegfried's face hardened, his jaw clenching with barely contained fury. "You dare to question my loyalty? After all, I have done and sacrificed for the Empire?"

"I question everything now," I replied, my voice heavy with the weight of my suspicions. "Duclaire's betrayal has shown me that nothing is as it seems. Not even those I once trusted with my life."

We stood locked in a tense standoff for a long moment, our blades poised to strike. The men of the Forlorn Hope stood by, and the knights of the Order stood ready.

How could I even take on several Order knights - presumably alone? My mind raced, searching for a way out of this impossible situation. I could not hope to defeat them all in open combat. But - I didn't need to. I had to outlast.

I stood my ground, refusing to be cowed. "Then tell me, Siegfried. What is this game? Who are the players?"

Siegfried laughed, a harsh, grating sound. "You think I would reveal such things to you? A mere captain, a loyal dog of the Empire? No, Kaelitz. You are not worthy of such knowledge."

He lunged forward, his blade flashing towards my throat. But I was ready. I parried the blow, the steel clash ringing across the battlefield. Another knight stepped forward - swinging at me with a greatsword sparkling with magic. I leaped back, narrowly avoiding the magically-charged blade as it cleaved the air inches from my face. The heat from the enchantments seared my skin. I swiftly countered with a thrust of my saber, aiming for a gap in the knight's armor, but he deflected it with unnatural speed.

Then Siegfried was on me again, his blade a blur of steel as he rained down a flurry of blows. I parried frantically, my arms aching with the effort of turning aside his relentless assault.

"You - kill them all!" Shouted Siegfried to the rest of the knights. "Don't let a single one of them get away."

I heard the shouts of alarm and clashing steel erupt behind me as the knights of the Order fell upon my men. But I couldn't spare a glance, locked in a desperate duel with Siegfried. His eyes blazed with fanatical fervor as he pressed his attack, driving me back with the sheer ferocity of his bladework.

"You cannot win, Kaelitz!" he snarled, punctuating each word with a crushing blow. "The Empire will prevail, and all who stand against it will be destroyed! Once - and for all!"

I gritted my teeth, parrying madly as I sought an opening. Siegfried was a master swordsman; his technique was flawless, and his strength was unrelenting. But I had not survived countless battles by yielding to despair.

With a burst of desperate energy, I slipped inside his guard, my saber flashing up to score a line of crimson across his sword arm. Siegfried stumbled back with a hiss of pain, his sleeve darkening with blood.

I pressed my momentary advantage, raining down blows upon Siegfried's defenses. But even wounded, his skill was formidable. He dodged my strikes with uncanny precision, his blade always there to intercept mine at the last instant.

Behind me, I could hear the desperate clash of steel and the cries of the dying as my men fought for their lives against the deadly knights of the Order. I knew I had to end this quickly, or all would be lost.

"Why, Siegfried?" I demanded, my voice ragged with exertion as our blades locked together. "Why betray everything the Order stood for? What could be worth such treachery?"

To my surprise, Siegfried laughed - a cold, mirthless sound. "You understand nothing, Kaelitz. The only way this Empire survives - is through us."

I summoned my remaining strength and shoved Siegfried back, disengaging our blades. We circled each other warily, our ragged breathing mingling with the clash of steel and cries of pain that surrounded us.

"Through the Order?" I demanded. "Through sorcery and dark magic? Is that truly what you believe?"

"Believe?" Siegfried spat. "I know it, Kaelitz. I have seen what will come and what will occur in the Empire if we do not act. The Order is the only hope. Do you truly believe the men of the Empire can stand against Eclairea - against Arlenia, against Kholodia?" He spat out. "That castle was proof. Proof of what we can do."

"Summoning demons - summoning the undead?" I stated. "No wonder you knew so much about the monsters within. They were of your Order's doing, weren't they?" I stated.

A look of dark satisfaction twisted Siegfried's features. "You begin to see, Kaelitz. The power we wield. The depths to which we will go to preserve the Empire. There is nothing we will not do, no forbidden art we will not employ, to ensure the Empire's survival."

I shook my head in disgust, revulsion rising like bile in my throat. "You're mad, Siegfried. You and the rest of the Order. This isn't preservation; it's a perversion. An abomination against all that is holy and just."

"Spare me your sanctimony," he sneered. "I have seen the face of the divine, Kaelitz, and it cares nothing for your prattling. There is only power and those strong enough to seize it."

He lunged at me again, his blade humming with unholy energy. I parried desperately, the force of the blow sending shockwaves up my arm. We traded blows back and forth across the blood-soaked ground, the bodies of the fallen lying strewn about our feet. I could feel my strength flagging, each parry and riposte draining me further. Siegfried seemed indefatigable, buoyed by the unnatural power suffusing his blade and armor. The battle raged around us, the remaining Forlorn Hope fighting grimly against the implacable knights.

Then - Siegfried's blade slipped past my guard, the tip nearly severing my hand straight through my metal gauntlet - and I stumbled back, biting back a scream as searing pain lanced through my hand. My saber to the ground, clattering to the ground. Siegfried loomed over me, his eyes alight with unholy glee, his blade poised for the killing blow.

This was it then. After all the battles, all the years of struggle and sacrifice, to meet my end here, at the hands of a traitor and heretic. A bitter laugh bubbled up in my throat.

Siegfried's blade descended, the wicked edge gleaming in the firelight. Time seemed to slow to a crawl. A strange calm descended over me in that crystallized moment, suspended between heartbeats. I thought of the brave men I had led, those who had followed me into the mouth of hell without hesitation. I thought of my home - of my family. I could not - would not - let it end this way. Not while a single breath remained in my body

I threw myself to the side at the last second, Siegfried's blade cleaving the air where my neck had been an instant before. I hit the ground hard, rolling desperately to avoid his follow-up strike. My severed hand screamed with pain, but I pushed it down, forcing myself to focus through the red haze of agony.

Siegfried advanced on me, his eyes alight with murderous intent. "It's over, Kaelitz," he boasted. "You have nothing left. Yield and I will grant you a swift death."

I barked a laugh, tasting blood in my mouth. "You never did know me very well, Siegfried."

With my last ounce of strength, I lunged for my fallen saber. My fingers closed around the hilt, and I brought it up just in time to deflect Siegfried's descending blade. The impact sent a fresh wave of agony searing through my mangled wrist, but I gritted my teeth and surged to my feet, adrenaline and desperation lending me strength.

"Die - damn you!" I shouted - lunging forward with a burst of desperate strength, I drove my saber forward, the point seeking Siegfried's throat. He tried to twist aside, but then - he noticed it. In my other, nearly severed hand was a small dagger. I saw recognition flare in his eyes as the blade flashed toward his exposed neck.

Time seemed to fracture into a series of disjointed images: the widening of Siegfried's eyes as he realized his peril; the dagger, its polished blade reflecting the chaotic flames around us, plunging into the gap between gorget and helm; the spray of arterial blood, shockingly bright against Siegfried's pale skin.

Siegfried staggered back, his hands scrabbling at his throat in a vain attempt to stem the crimson tide. His sword slipped from nerveless fingers as a wordless gurgle escaped his lips. I watched, numb, as he sank to his knees, a look of shocked disbelief etched upon his face.

"Kaelitz..." he choked out, blood bubbling from his lips... "I'll... Kill you... You worthless..." He said - before collapsing.

I stumbled away from Siegfried's fallen form, my vision blurring at the edges as the adrenaline that had sustained me began to ebb. The pain from my mangled hand threatened to drag me down into unconsciousness, but I fought against it, knowing that to succumb now would mean certain death.

Around me, the battle still raged, the Forlorn Hope locked in a desperate struggle against the remaining knights of the Order. The air was thick with the coppery scent of blood and the acrid tang of smoke, the screams of the wounded and dying mingling with the clash of steel.

I staggered forward, my feet dragging through the churned mud and gore. I had no destination in mind, only the primal urge to put as much distance between myself and this place of carnage as possible. So - I fled. I fled deeper into the swamps, as deep as I could go.

I ran for what must have been a day before I collapsed against one of the ancient pine trees of the swamp. I slumped against the gnarled trunk, my breath coming in ragged gasps, my wounded hand cradled against my chest. The pain had faded to a dull, persistent throb, but I knew that without proper treatment, I risked losing the hand entirely if blood loss or shock didn't claim me first.

Through the haze of exhaustion and agony, I tried to get my bearings. The swamp stretched out in every direction, an endless morass of brackish water and twisted trees. There were no landmarks, no signs of civilization. I was well and truly lost, and the day's light was fading fast.

A bitter laugh escaped my cracked lips. So this was to be my ignominious end. Not in glorious battle against the enemies of the Empire, but alone and bleeding in this godforsaken swamp. A fitting fate, perhaps, for a fool who had trusted such men.

As night fell, I huddled against the base of the tree, shivering as fever and blood loss took their toll. Twisted shadows danced at the edges of my vision, and eerie calls echoed through the swamp. I clutched my saber with my good hand - and a visitor approached.

"Stuck out here alone, Kaelitz?" He said. It was Alaric.

"...Alaric." I choked a laugh. "I thought... I thought you were dead. You *are* dead." I said. "I left you at Castelon." Alaric stepped closer, his figure resolving from the shadows. His face was pale and gaunt, his eyes sunken and rimmed with dark circles. He looked like a walking corpse. And yet, he stood before me, as natural as the tree I leaned against.

"Dead?" He chuckled, a dry, rasping sound. "No, not quite. Though not for lack of trying on your part, eh Kaelitz?"

I shook my head, trying to clear the cobwebs from my mind. This couldn't be real. Alaric was dead; I had seen him fall with my own eyes. This must be some fevered hallucination, a trick of my exhausted mind.

"You're not real," I muttered. "Just a figment of my imagination. A ghost comes to haunt me."

Alaric squatted down beside me, his face inches from mine. I could feel his breath, cold and clammy, against my skin. "Oh, I'm real enough, old friend. As real as that wound in your hand. You left me there, Kaelitz. I was there - shivering. They thought I was dead."

I recoiled from Alaric's proximity, my back pressing against the tree's rough bark. His words stung with the bitter truth. I had left him at Castelon, abandoned him to an uncertain fate. I had thought him lost in the chaos of the battle and the desperate flight that followed. Yet here he was, returned like a ghost to torment me.

"I...I thought you were dead," I repeated lamely, my voice hoarse. "In the confusion, the retreat...there was no time... You told me to take the banner... For the Empire..."

Alaric's laugh was sharp and mirthless. "The Empire?" He stated. "When has it ever cared about men like you and me? Look where it brought you, Kaelitz. You fought in this shithole for two years. Lost your eye - and now, your hand."

I stared at Alaric in confusion and growing unease. Though spoken with his voice, his words seemed alien, laced with a bitterness and cynicism that I had never known him to possess.

"What happened to you, Alaric?" I asked, my voice barely above a whisper. "What changed you so?"

Alaric's eyes seemed to bore into me, twin points of smoldering resentment amidst the pallor of his face. "What happened to me?" he spat. "I'll tell you what happened, Kaelitz. It was all worthless. All of it."

Alaric settled down next to me, his back against the ancient pine. For a long moment, he was silent, his gaze distant, as if seeing something far beyond the shadowed confines of the swamp. When at last he spoke, his voice was low and laden with a weary bitterness.

"You know - you'll never go home. They don't let men go back anymore." He stated. "It's for life now, this life. The army." He said.

"I know," I said remorsefully. "I-I know, damn you. It wasn't my choice. You..."

"It wasn't your choice?" He smiled. - and it was a twisted, bitter thing. "No, it wasn't your choice, was it? Just like it wasn't mine. We're just pawns,

Kaelitz. Pieces to be moved about the board at the whims of our betters. Until we're spent."

I shook my head, trying to summon some argument, some defense of the choices that had led me here. But the words wouldn't come. Because deep down, I knew he was right.

"What would you have me do, Alaric?" I asked, my voice heavy with exhaustion and defeat. "Desert? Flee like a coward? I took an oath..."

"An oath," Alaric scoffed. "An oath to what? To whom? The Emperor? The Empire? What have they ever done for us except send us to die in places like this?"

He gestured expansively at the swamp around us, his hand sweeping through the fetid air. "This is our reward, Kaelitz. This is the glory we were promised. A lonely death, far from home."

The fever was taking hold now, my thoughts growing muddled and disjointed.

"I want to go home." My bitter words hung between us, heavy with the weight of hard truths. I could feel the last vestiges of my strength ebbing, my vision blurring at the edges as the fever tightened its grip.

"Home," I murmured, the word tasting strange on my tongue. It seemed like a distant dream, a half-remembered memory from another life. "Do you remember, Alaric? The golden fields of Strossen in the summer? The way the light glinted off the spires of the Cathedral?"

A wistful expression flitted across Alaric's gaunt face, a fleeting echo of the man I once knew. "I remember," he said softly. "But that was a long time ago, Kaelitz. In another life." The fever's grip tightened, the world spinning around me. Alaric's face swam in and out of focus, his words echoing as if from a great distance. Golden fields and cathedral spires danced in my mind's eye, visions of a home I feared I would never see again.

Then - another visitor appeared, edging closer. Sergeant Rottmann. He glanced at me - a look of displeasure, annoyance.

"You bastard," I stated, glaring up at him. "You left me to die out here."

Rottmann looked down at me dispassionately, his face etched with the lines of hard years and more complex decisions. "I did what I had to do, Kaelitz," he said, his voice gruff but not unkind. "I knew what would happen. I had a chance to leave it. All of it behind."

I let out a bitter laugh, the sound scraping my throat raw. "You left us," I spat. "What about loyalty? What about the men who bled and died for us?"

Rottmann squatted down, bringing his weathered face level with mine. I saw a flicker of something in his eyes - regret, perhaps, or understanding. "Loyalty is a luxury, Kaelitz. Out here, it's survival. Each man for himself. You should know that better than anyone."

I shook my head, anger and fever making my thoughts churn. "No. That's not how it's supposed to be. We're brothers-in-arms. We look out for each other."

"Brothers?" Rottmann scoffed. "There are no brothers out here. Just ghosts and the damned."

He stood then, his form blotting out the meager light filtering through the canopy. "You're on your own now, Kaelitz. Best make your peace with that."

With that, he turned and melted into the shadows, leaving me again with Alaric's specter and the bitter tang of betrayal on my tongue.

I slumped back against the tree, my strength spent. Hatred and fever are burning in my one good eye.

"Is mankind so irredeemable - so demented?" I murmured, my voice a hoarse rasp. "Are we all damned, scrabbling for survival in this godforsaken place?"

"No." A familiar voice cut through the swirling fog of my fevered mind - a calm anchor amidst the storm of bitterness and betrayal. I glanced over—another visitor.

"Not all of mankind, Kaelitz," she said softly, crouching beside me. Her keen eyes - looking into mine. It was familiar - it was the lady. The lady whose name I never got was back in Kholodia. The Vuk - the wolf...

"There is still goodness in this world, though it may be harder to find in times such as these without the Savior so present," she said softly. I blinked, trying to focus on the woman's face through the fever haze. Her presence was unexpected, a glimmer of light in the darkness that had engulfed me.

"You..." I rasped, my parched lips struggling to form the words. "I remember you. From Kholodia. The wolf-woman. The Grand Prince's sister..."

She smiled then, a gentle curve of her lips that held a world of understanding. "Yes, Kaelitz." She said. "You don't have to remember my name if it's too hard for you."

"You were beautiful." I stammered out awkwardly, tears starting to form. "I wish I stayed. I wish that miserable bastard Rottmann forced me to stay there." The Vuk woman's smile softened, her eyes filled with a gentle compassion that cut through the haze of my fevered despair. She reached out, her cool hand resting on my burning forehead.

I leaned into her touch, the simple comfort easing the ache in my soul. "I'm so tired," I confessed, my voice cracking. I'm tired of fighting, losing, and watching good men die for a cause I no longer understand."

She nodded, her gaze distant, as if seeing through me the tangled web of my life. "It is a heavy burden, the one you carry. The weight of duty, of loyalty, of honor." She stated. "But - it is a worthwhile one."

"Is it?" I asked bitterly, my voice hoarse with exhaustion and despair. "What has honor brought me but pain and loss? What good is a duty to a world that has forgotten the face of its Savior? I've lost everyone. There's nothing left - nowhere to go."

The Vuk woman's eyes sharpened, her gaze piercing through the veil of my anguish. "Honor is not about reward, Kaelitz. It is about doing what is right, even when the world tells you otherwise."

She shifted, her hand moving from my brow to rest over my heart. "You have a good soul, Kaelitz. One that has been battered and bruised, yes, but never broken. Much like Kholodia, or of Valtorea."

Her words stirred something within me, a faint ember of the faith and conviction I had once held so dear. I closed my eyes, focusing on the steady beat of my heart beneath her palm, as I sighed, relief filling me.

"...Will I ever see you again?" I said with longing. The Vuk woman's smile turned wistful, her eyes shimmering with an emotion I couldn't quite place. "Perhaps, Kaelitz. If the Savior wills it."

She withdrew her hand, drifting down to it - and a pain filled me. I grunted my teeth - and then, as I glanced down at my mangled hand, I saw the Vuk woman's delicate claws hover over the twisted, mutilated flesh. A soft glow emanated from her palm, bathing my ruined skin in a warm, golden light. I watched in awe as the light seemed to seep into my very bones, knitting together the shattered remnants of my hand.

The pain that had been my companion began to ebb, replaced by a soothing warmth that spread up my arm and into my chest. I flexed my fingers tentatively, marveling at the newfound strength and agility - the feeling of being whole again.

But even as I reveled in the relief, I noticed the healing was incomplete. A brutal scar remained, stark against my pale skin - a jagged reminder of the price I had paid. I tried to twist it - to feel it. But I could feel nothing through it - it was like a brick attached to my hand. I looked up at the Vuk woman, questions brimming in my eyes. She met my gaze steadily, a knowing look on her face.

"Why?" I asked, my voice a hoarse whisper. "Why would you heal me - how?"

Her smile was enigmatic, her eyes holding secrets I could only guess. "Perhaps - if you survive this swamp. I will tell you." She said sweetly. "I would recommend making haste - before the Order finds you."

I blinked, my mind reeling from the Vuk woman's words. The Order. They were coming for me. I had to move and find a way out of this accursed swamp before they could catch me.

With a grunt of effort, I pushed myself to my feet, swaying slightly as a wave of dizziness washed over me. The Vuk woman reached out to steady me, her touch a cool balm against my fevered skin.

"Easy, Kaelitz," she murmured. "You're still weak. The healing I gave you will help, but it will take time for your body to recover fully."

I nodded, gritting my teeth as I forced my battered body into motion. Each step was agony, the dull throb of my wounds a constant companion as I pushed myself forward through the murky water and tangled vegetation.

"Where will you go?" the Vuk woman asked, her voice drifting to me through the mist.

"...To Rega," I stated. "I have to figure out the truth. Once and for all. But, I do have one question for you."

"What?" She asked, curious, as I sighed.

"I never got your name."

She grinned - and for a second, I saw an ambitious, calculating cunning in there.

"Catherine."

To Kill a Traitor

As I stumbled forward out of the dank, fetid swamp, I felt the fever that had been wracking my body for days finally begin to recede. The cool night air was a balm on my flushed skin as I emerged from the marsh's humidity.

My hand throbbed with a dull ache. I glanced down at it in the moonlight, flexing my fingers experimentally. Though the strange healing I'd been given had stopped the deadly infection from spreading further, the damage to the nerves was permanent. My once steady sword hand trembled slightly, the fingers curling into a claw. I knew instinctively that I would never wield a saber with skill again.

Despair threatened to overwhelm me at the thought. What good was a one-eyed, crippled soldier to the Holy Valtorean Empire?

I shook my head, pushing those dark thoughts aside. I was alive. Permanently maimed, yes, but I still drew breath. And more importantly - I had grievances to avenge.

I pressed onward, gritting my teeth against the throbbing ache in my hand and the residual weakness from the fever. The solid ground felt strange under my feet after slogging through sucking mud for so long. Crickets and night birds called from the underbrush, the ordinary sounds, as I walked onto one of Baltiva's many dirt roads, sighing in relief as I stumbled forward.

My mind whirled with thoughts as I trudged along the dark, empty road. Heavy with the scents of loam and wildflowers, the night breeze cooled the sweat on my brow. High above, the stars glittered coldly in the moonless sky, ancient and unchanging. How small and insignificant I felt beneath that vast, infinite expanse. My eyes - drifted down to my hand yet again.

Though I had rendered my sword hand a clumsy shadow of its former self, I was astounded that I still had a hand. Was this the divine intervention of the Savior Himself? Had He laid a healing touch upon me, sparing me from certain death so I may continue serving the Holy cause? It seemed almost too wondrous to believe. The priests always spoke of the Savior's grace and benevolence, but I had never witnessed such direct intercession in all my years.

And yet, a small, doubtful voice in the back of my mind whispered of another possibility. Of diabolism - of witchcraft. I pushed it aside - I didn't dare think about it. Instead - my thoughts turned towards other damnable things.

Namely, what would await me back in Rega? Did they whisper my name among the dead and defeated - Sir Ardent Kaelitz, the promising young captain, cut down alongside his men in that cursed marsh? What slander would there be - against my name once I arrived?

The thought made my stomach clench painfully. Honor was the pillar of a Valtorean gentleman - and the treacherous Von Löwe, that cruel, Machiavellian schemer - he had set me up to fail from the beginning. Sending my company into that godforsaken swamp on a fool's errand, all so he could undermine me, get rid of me - assuming I was a loyalist to Duclaire. I could picture his scarred, sneering face as he penned the damning reports that would destroy my career - my commission, gone in tatters.

I clenched my fist, ignoring the throb of pain from my injured hand. No, I would not let that conniving snake Von Löwe destroy my honor and reputation so quickly. I was a Kaelitz from a proud lineage that had served the Empire for generations. My father had not raised a coward or a failure.

Gritting my teeth, I struggled to my feet, swaying unsteadily for a moment before finding my balance. My armor felt like a leaden weight, my muscles screaming in protest, but I forced myself to stand tall. I would march back to Rega, injury be damned, and demand an audience with the Emperor himself if I had to. I gazed heavenward afterward, gritting my teeth.

I could almost hear Alaric's voice, that roguish grin on his bloody lips: "Come now, Kaelitz. Don't let a few scratches stop you - the Empire still needs men like us."

Perhaps it still does.

The cold city of Rega sat on the shoreline of Baltiva like a blister as I approached, slinking along.

The weathered gray walls of Rega loomed before me, and ancient stone fortifications built by Valtorean engineers in ages past were now manned by the mongrel Baltzers who styled themselves as the city's rulers. I could see their banners snapping in the chill sea breeze atop the battlements of one of the castles - a black griffin rampant on a field of crimson. The same symbol flew by that young Sir Siegfried and the delusional Order knights.

As I limped closer, I finally saw the prized banners of the Valtorean Empire. Some small comfort washed over me as I stumbled down the road - disturbingly, the only refugee.

Two guards in salt-stained chainmail eyed me warily as I approached the main gate, their halberds held at the ready. "Halt! Declare yourself," one barked in crude Valtorean, his accent thick with Baltivan consonants.

I drew myself up to my full height, ignoring the scream of abused muscles. "I am Captain Ardent Kaelitz. I have returned."

The guards exchanged a skeptical glance before the speaker nodded gruffly. "Wait here," he grunted, turning to confer with his companion in what I understood to be Lapsidian. After a moment, the second guard hurried off into the city while the first returned his suspicious gaze to me.

I stood my ground, refusing to show weakness despite my battered state. The wait seemed interminable as I listened to the distant cries of gulls and the lapping of waves against the seawall until, finally, the guard returned with a severe-looking officer in tow.

The man was clad in the uniform of an Imperial major, though his breastplate bore the scars of hard use. He looked me up and down, taking in my blood-crusted armor and haggard face. "Captain Kaelitz. We had thought you lost with the Forlorn."

"I yet live, sir, and I bring urgent news. I must speak to the Lord Commander." I said - my hand perhaps, tensing up and grabbing at my empty holster.

The major's eyes narrowed. "The Lord-Commander is indisposed at present. But I will hear your report, Captain." He motioned for me to follow him through the gate.

I limped after him into the castle courtyard, trying to ignore the stares and hushed whispers of the soldiers and servants we passed. The lieutenant led me to a small side chamber and shut the door behind us.

"Now then, Captain Kaelitz. What news from the Forlorn?" He folded his arms, fixing me with an intent stare.

I took a deep breath, wincing as my cracked ribs protested. "The Forlorn has fallen, sir. Betrayed."

The lieutenant frowned. "That is grave news indeed. But - the mission..."

"It's complete," I said, growling. "The Black Band, and Duclaire. They're dead." I said - spitting out to the ground.

The major's eyes widened in surprise at my words. "All of them?"

I nodded grimly. "Aye, though it cost us dearly. I'm the only one left of the Forlorn. At least, I assume so."

The major was silent for a long moment, absorbing the news. Finally, he spoke. "You've done the Empire a great service, Captain Kaelitz. The traitorous Duclaire - brought to justice, alongside his heretics..."

The major's voice trailed off as he noticed the dark look that had come over my face at the mention of Duclaire. My fists clenched and unclenched spasmodically as a tide of bitter memories washed over me - memories of blood and betrayal.

"Justice?" I spat, my voice low and dangerous. "Is that what you call it? Sending us to slaughter Duclaire and his followers like dogs without even telling us why? Without telling me? I hardly knew the man betrayed us - yet, to my surprise..."

The major took an involuntary step back at the venom in my tone. "Captain Kaelitz, I understand your distress, but surely you know it was necessary-"

"Necessary for WHAT?" I roared, all pretense of respect forgotten. "You send me to kill a man - a great, honorable man - and for what? On whose orders?" I advanced on the major, my eyes blazing with barely controlled fury. "I demand to see the Lord-Commander. NOW."

The major paled and reached for his sword, but the door burst open just then. The Lord-Commander himself strode in, his regal bearing at odds with the concerned expression on his face.

"That's enough, Captain Kaelitz," he said sternly. "Stand down."

I rounded on him, my voice shaking with rage and anguish. "Why? Why did you send us to kill Duclaire? He was a good man once - now, spouting off about treason - and I believe him!" I declared - and then, in a daring instant of boldness fueled by my rage, I lunged at the major, catching him off guard. My fist connected with his jaw in a sickening crunch. He crumpled to the ground, out cold.

In one fluid motion, I drew the pistol from the unconscious major's holster and leveled it at the Lord-Commander. The weapon felt heavy and cold in my hand as I thumbed back the hammer with a menacing click.

"Enough lies," I snarled through gritted teeth, the scar tissue on my face pulling taut. "I want the truth, Von Löwe. No more secrets, no more betrayal. Why did you order me to kill Duclaire?"

The Lord-Commander regarded me with an inscrutable expression, seemingly unfazed by the gun pointed at his heart, as he took a seat. Von Löwe looked at me, steadfast in the face of the pistol pointed at his chest. He leaned back in his chair, steepling his fingers. "Why don't you have a seat, Captain Kaelitz," he said calmly, gesturing to the chair across from him. "Let's talk about this like civilized men."

I kept the gun trained on him, my arm unwavering despite the exhaustion seeping into my bones. "I'll stand, thanks," I growled. "Just give me one good reason why I shouldn't pull this trigger and rid the Empire of your treachery right now."

Von Löwe raised an eyebrow. "Treachery? Come now, Captain. Everything I've done has been for the good of Valtore. Duclaire and his ilk were cancer, eating away at the very foundations of our great nation. They had to be excised, no matter the cost."

"You bloody bastard," I said, my finger tightening on the trigger. "They were our men. Our men! You wanted us dead - us, all of us." My voice cracked on the last bit, raw grief welling up to mingle with the rage.

"Sacrifices must be made for the greater good," Von Löwe said, his tone maddeningly reasonable. "The cancer Duclaire was spreading - had to be excised." He sighed, looking at me with weariness. "But - now I see."

Von Löwe's eyes seemed to soften slightly as he gazed at me, a flicker of something akin to respect passing over his hardened features. "I must admit, Captain Kaelitz, I underestimated you. When I first heard the whispers of sedition among the ranks, I suspected you might be involved. A junior nobleman, scarred and maimed, mentored by the old Lord-Commander himself. Uppity for his position - and bold... From a little-known family."

He leaned forward, his voice low and intense. "But I see now that I was wrong. You are a true son of Valtore, Kaelitz. Your devotion to the Empire is unwavering, even amid unimaginable adversity and betrayal."

I kept the gun steady, but I could feel a tremor beginning to build in my arm as I glared at him.

"And what about the Order? I killed that heretical bastard, Siegfried. Gutted him. I could swear Duclaire said you were in league with them."

Von Löwe's expression changed, a flicker of surprise passing over his stern features before he quickly regained his composure. He chuckled, a deep rumbling sound emanating from his barrel chest. "The Black Order? Really, Kaelitz. I thought you were smarter than that."

He stood slowly, ignoring the gun still pointed at his heart as he walked over to the grand fireplace that dominated one wall of the side chamber. Ornate carvings of dragons and knights danced in the flickering light cast by the flames. Von Löwe rested a hand on the mantle, his back to me.

"Do you know the history of this building, Captain? It dates back over four centuries, to the early days of the Empire." His voice took on a storyteller's cadence as he continued. "Legends say that the first Grandmaster of the Order built this castle - the first Valtorean castle in Baltiva."

Von Löwe turned back to face me, the firelight casting harsh shadows across his scarred visage. "The Order and the Empire have always been intertwined, Captain Kaelitz. Two sides of the same coin. Both working tirelessly to maintain order and suppress the enemies of Valtor - within Baltiva."

He took a step towards me, seemingly unconcerned by the pistol I still had aimed at his chest. "Siegfried was a useful tool, but he allowed his ambition to outgrow his loyalty. He thought of using the forbidden arts of Goetia to challenge the rightful rule of the Emperor. To try and reform the Empire into his vision - one that I - and the rest of my colleagues, do not share." He grinned.

"Colleagues?" I said.

Von Löwe nodded slowly, his eyes never leaving mine. "Oh yes, Captain Kaelitz. Did you think I was acting alone in all of this? Many within the highest echelons of the Empire share my vision. A vision of a Valtore restored to its former glory, purged of the weak and the disloyal."

He took another step closer until the barrel of my pistol pressed against his broad chest. I could feel the heat radiating off him and smell the smoke and steel that seemed to cling to him like a second skin.

"The Order has lost its way, corrupted by the heresies it once sought to destroy. But there are those of us who remember the old ways. The true path." Von Löwe's voice dropped to a whisper. "Join us, Kaelitz. Take your rightful place among the sons of Valtore. Together, we can burn away the rot that eats at the heart of the Empire and usher in a new age of strength and purity."

I stared at Von Löwe, my mind reeling from his words. The zeal in his tone and the way he spoke of "burning away the rot" and "ushering in a new age" was all too familiar. I had heard similar sentiments before from the lips of fanatics and madmen.

"You sound just like him," I said slowly, my gaze never wavering from Von Löwe's scarred face. "Like Siegfried when he tried to convince me to join his twisted cause. The same righteous fervor and talk of 'restoring glory' and 'purging the weak.' He thought he was doing Valtor's work too."

Von Löwe's eyes narrowed, but I pressed on before he could interject. "And not just Siegfried. Your words echo those of another man I once knew - Grand Prince Michaelovich. His dream - of an autocratic, unified Kholodia."

I kept my gun trained on Von Löwe's chest as I spoke, my voice steady despite the turmoil roiling inside me. "Michaelovich dreamed of a 'great' Kholodia ruled with an iron fist, where dissent was crushed mercilessly. He saw himself as a visionary, a savior of his people." I let out a harsh laugh. "He sounds more noble than a man such as you."

Von Löwe's face darkened, his eyes glinting dangerously in the firelight. "You dare compare me to that Kholodian dog? I am nothing like him, Kaelitz. I serve the Empire, not my selfish ambitions."

"Do you?" I challenged, taking a step forward, the pistol never wavering. "Because from where I stand, you're willing to sacrifice anything and anyone for your so-called 'vision.' The men under your command, the very people you swore to protect, are just pawns to you, aren't they? Disposable pieces in your grand game of Imperial restoration. And - that's not to mention that this is *personal.*"

Von Löwe's jaw clenched, a vein throbbing in his temple. "You understand nothing, Kaelitz. The sacrifices I make, the hard choices - they are all necessary for the greater good of Valtore. A soldier like you should understand that better than anyone... You dishonor Valtorea, even bringing up your *personal* dispute with me."

I shook my head slowly, a grim smile tugging at the corner of my mouth. "You're right, von Löwe. I am a soldier. I've made hard choices and sacrificed more than you can imagine for the Empire. But I know a traitor - that much is clear when I see it."

Von Löwe's eyes blazed with fury. "You naive fool," he spat. "The Empire needs men like me, willing to do what must be done! Have you been to the court at Vien? Do you know - what lies back at home for men like us? Whelps like you - you think you know it all, the day you march to war, the moment you see your comrades die..."

Von Löwe's face twisted into a sneer as he stared me down, his voice dripping with scorn. "You think you understand sacrifice, Kaelitz? You know nothing of what I've endured for the Empire. Nothing!"

He took a step towards me, seemingly uncaring of the pistol aimed at his heart. "Now, let me enlighten you about the difference between us. You were born into nobility, a silver spoon in your mouth, even if it was just a minor noble spoon. Your family's estate, name, small comforts—you had them handed to you. And now? Now, you swaddle yourself in this cloak of martyrdom as if it comforts you from the cold truth."

His voice dropped to a soft, menacing cadence. "Your family's lands, seized by me after the sheer staggering debt—orchestrated by whom? Himself. Your disgrace was not just a product of war but of politics. Tell me,

Kaelitz," he paused, his lips curling into a grimace of disdain, "how does it feel to fight not only for an empire that cares nothing for you but also stand before the man responsible for your disinheritance?"

I lowered my pistol slightly, struck not by fear but by the piercing accuracy of his words. The fires of anger and betrayal flickered in my heart alongside the haunting memories of my father's crestfallen face when we were turned out of our home. My world had crumbled that day—brick by brick.

Yet, I steadied my voice; my aim unwavering again as I met Von Löwe's icy gaze. "You mistake understanding for acceptance," I retorted sharply. "Yes, you stripped me of everything. My home, my rights, nearly my honor. But unlike you, Lord Commander, I am not here clawing back for power."

Von Löwe's eyes glared into me before he barked a harsh laugh. "Enough of this, Kaelitz." He stated. "You wanted your answers. Now - you have it. Don't you dare play the martyr here?" Von Löwe's eyes bored into me with unsettling intensity.

"Here is how this is going to play out, Kaelitz. You have two choices before you now. Two paths. On the first, you pull that trigger and strike me down where I stand. Maybe you even get away with it; slip out of the city before they catch you. But how far do you think you'll get? How long until they hunt you down like a dog, brand you a deserter and a traitor? They'll hang you from the gallows and leave your body for the crows."

He took a step closer, seemingly uncaring of the flintlock pistol aimed at his heart. "Or, you lower that gun and get back to service. Maybe scrap enough gold together after all this - and you might be able to afford a title of nobility." He smirked.

My mind raced as I stared down the barrel of my pistol at Von Löwe, his ultimatum hanging between us. The moment's weight pressed down on me, the gravity of the choice before me almost suffocating.

And so - I tightened the finger around my pistol.

The flintlock cracked like thunder in the enclosed chamber. Von Löwe's eyes widened in shock as the lead ball tore through his chest, a crimson blossom rapidly spreading across the front of his tunic. He stumbled back, one hand clutching at the wound as his legs gave out beneath him.

I stood frozen, pistol still raised, a thin wisp of smoke curling from the barrel. At that moment, the world seemed to hold its breath. Then, with a final rasping gurgle, Von Löwe collapsed to the stone floor and lay still, glassy eyes staring sightlessly at the vaulted ceiling above.

The reality of what I had just done crashed over me like a frigid wave, as he was now lying in a slowly spreading pool of his blood at my feet. My pistol slipped from numb fingers and clattered to the floor.

Suddenly, the heavy oak door burst open with a splintering crash. Imperial guards poured into the room, blades leveled and faces grim beneath their steel helmets. At their head strode a captain, his weathered face set in a scowl.

The Imperial Captain's steely gaze swept over the scene before him - Von Löwe's still body, the expanding crimson stain on the stone floor, and me standing over him, the dropped pistol at my feet all but proclaiming my guilt.

"Arrest this man," the Captain barked, his voice cracking like a whip in the shocked silence. Two guards surged forward, roughly seizing my arms and wrenching them behind my back. I offered no resistance, my mind still reeling, barely comprehending.

As they hauled me towards the door, the Captain stepped into my path, his grizzled face inches from mine. "You've just made the biggest mistake of your life, soldier," he growled. "Murdering a superior officer? You'll hang for this."

Despite the circumstances, I met his glare blankly, a curious sense of calm settling over me. "He was a traitor," I heard myself say, my voice sounding distant to my ears. "He would have destroyed the Empire for his ambitions."

The Captain's eyes narrowed. "That's not for you to decide." He turned to the guards. "Get him out of here. Let him rot in the cells until the magistrate arrives to pass judgment."

As they dragged me from the chamber, my boots leaving smeared trails in Von Löwe's blood, a grim sort of resignation settled in my gut. I had made my choice, for better or worse. Now, all that remained was to face the consequences.

Slowly, I was getting used to a prisoner's cell. It seemed like a companion almost as I rested my scarred, bare back against the wall. The cold, damp stone of the cell wall seeped into my bones as I sat in the darkness, the only light a thin sliver seeping under the heavy oak door. The shackles around my wrists and ankles chafed with every slight movement, the metal long since warmed to my skin.

Time seemed to lose all meaning in this place. Had it been hours since they'd thrown me in here? Days? With no windows to mark the passage of the sun and no sounds beyond the occasional scurrying of rats in the corners, I could only measure time by the slow, steady drip of water somewhere in the blackness. I wondered if they were readying the executioner's rope for me - could I blame them?

Suddenly, the scrape of a key in the lock jolted me from my grim musings. I squinted against the sudden flare of torchlight as the cell door swung open with a groan of rusted hinges. A figure stepped inside - one that seemed all too familiar. Gerhart.

"Captain Kaelitz." He stated. "We ought to stop meeting like this." The functionary stated, sitting on a stool.

My eyes narrowed as I regarded Gerhart in the flickering torchlight. His tone was light, almost conversational, but I wasn't fooled.

"What do you want, Gerhart?" I asked, my voice rough from disuse. "Come to gloat before they string me up?"

Gerhart tutted, shaking his head. "So pessimistic, Captain. I'm here to offer you a deal."

I barked a harsh laugh, the sound grating in my ears. "A deal? Like the same deal that had me march nearly to my death? Forgive me if I'm not leaping at the chance."

Gerhart leaned forward, his elbows on his knees, hands clasped. The torchlight cast deep shadows across his angular features.

"Hear me out, Kaelitz. Yes, you killed a superior officer. Yes, that would normally earn you a short drop and a sudden stop. But these are not normal times." His eyes glittered in the semi-darkness. "The Emperor asked about you - after all. It's not very often men like you come to his attention."

I eyed Gerhart warily, not trusting the calculating glint in his eye. "The Emperor asked about me. Why?"

Gerhart leaned back, steepling his fingers. "You see, Captain, your actions, while... unorthodox... It has solved a few issues." He paused, letting his words hang in the dank air of the cell. "You did the Empire a service, even if your methods were... questionable. Dishonorable - and ungentlemanly. The

Inquisition seems to be in your favor as well. Likely - that's what stayed the Emperor's hand."

"So, Von Lowe was a traitor after all?"

"Not an obvious one, at least. But - hardly a friend of the Inquisition..." A grim smile tugged at the corner of Gerhart's mouth. "Von Löwe was a complicated man. Loyal to the Empire, in his way, but his methods were becoming increasingly... Troublesome. It was likely a matter of time."

I shifted against the cold stone wall, the shackles clanking with the movement. "So what, I did you all a favor by putting a bullet in him?"

"In a manner of speaking." Gerhart leaned back, crossing his arms. "Your actions, while reckless and insubordinate, have potentially saved the Empire from great turmoil. Von Löwe's death, while unfortunate, has eliminated a growing threat... Not to mention the death of Lord-Commander Duclaire."

I digested this information, furrowing my brow. "And what does this mean for me? Am I to be rewarded for my 'service' with a quick execution instead of a slow one?"

Gerhart chuckled, the sound devoid of humor. "Perhaps. The Emperor is not at all pleased over Duclaire's death. After all, they were relatives."

"I see. Such are things in the Empire." I said, grinning. "What happens now if the Emperor decides to spare me?"

Gerhart studied me, his expression unreadable in the dim light. "Well, Captain, the fact remains that you killed two high-ranking officers of the Empire. That's not something that can be easily swept under the rug. Your commission, at the very least, is gone. Your noble title - while that was under review pending the courts..."

I let out a bitter laugh. "My commission - my title. As if that matters now, sitting here in chains." I rattled the shackles for emphasis. "So what's the alternative? A life sentence in these charming accommodations?" I gestured sarcastically around the dank cell.

Gerhart leaned forward, his eyes glinting in the torchlight. "Not quite, Captain. In his infinite wisdom, the Emperor has decided to offer you a choice."

I couldn't help but scoff. "A choice? How generous of him. And what might these choices be?"

Gerhart ticked them off on his fingers. "Option one: you face a noble's tribunal for your crimes. With the evidence and witnesses against you, alongside Von Lowe's connections in court, a guilty verdict and execution is all but guaranteed."

I grimaced. It's not an appealing prospect. "And option two?"

A slow smile spread across Gerhart's face. "Option two: You take a commission in the Emperor's army - not the Imperial Army since that would be untenable at best, at the moment."

I stared at Gerhart, trying to process his words. The Emperor's army? It was an offer I hadn't expected, especially given my current circumstances.

"The Emperor's army?" I repeated slowly. "You mean the Palatine Guard?"

Gerhart shook his head. "Not quite. Technically - as a retainer. Some discussions are being had - about appointing you to a battalion of irregulars along the border with Arkanthia..." He stated. "But, I recommended you for another post."

"And that would be?"

He smiled.

"Well, there's a small battalion of riflemen—a good eighty or so men - Arlenian rifles, expensive stuff. The best foresters the Empire could gather together were from all the provinces. That includes Hortharia, Celija..." He said. "From the troublesome military frontier provinces."

I leaned back against the cold stone wall, considering Gerhart's words. The Emperor's army - it was a chance at redemption, a way out of this dank cell and the looming specter of the noose. But I knew it would come with a price.

"And what would be expected of me, in this... Battalion of riflemen?" I asked cautiously. "I assume the Emperor isn't offering me this out of the goodness of his heart."

"He is not. And frankly - you have a rather dour history with your commissions." He stated. "The Forlorn Hope - despite being scum, are presumed to be dead. The first Arkhovost Battalion shattered... A few dead superior officers..." He said, grinning.

I met Gerhart's grin with a scowl of my own. "My 'dour history,' as you put it, is a direct result of the incompetence and betrayal of those superior officers. The Forlorn Hope, the Arkhovost Battalion - their blood is on the hands of men like Von Löwe and Duclaire, not mine."

Gerhart held up his hands in a placating gesture. "I'm not here to debate the past, Captain. The Emperor is offering you a future, albeit a dangerous one. This battalion - they're good damned men, but they're scum, disorderly - and undisciplined."

I nodded slowly, the appeal of the challenge growing stronger with each passing moment. "And what of the men themselves? What kind of scum are we talking about here?"

Gerhart chuckled darkly. "Thieves, brawlers, poachers - men who have spent more time on the wrong side of the law than the right. But they're tough, Kaelitz, and they know how to fight."

"You could say that about most of the Imperial Army's troops," I stated. "I keep seeing younger and younger lads - and more and more scum."

Gerhart sighed and nodded solemnly. "You're right about that, Captain. But I'm afraid the situation is even more dire than you realize. The Emperor has just enacted a state of conscription across the empire. Men between 17 and 25 are being called up to serve. The training camps are already overflowing with raw recruits, most of whom have never held a rifle in their lives."

I felt a chill run down my spine at Gerhart's words. "Conscription? But why now? What's happened?"

Gerhart leaned forward, his voice low and urgent. "The revolution, in Eclair. I'm sure you've heard of it. They *executed* the king just a month ago - and now, worst of all, the *Radicalists* took over. As we speak - the clergy of the Church are being persecuted, and the faithful perish under the hands of these revolutionaries."

"And the Emperor fears the revolution will spread to Valtore," I said grimly, piecing it together. "He's building up his armies, preparing for war."

Gerhart nodded. "Precisely. The Emperor believes the only way to protect the empire from the radical contagion is to put it down in its cradle."

"And so - what about the Baltivan campaign?" I stated. "Surely, we will not just give up our position here. Not after so many men have been lost."

Gerhart's expression darkened. "The Baltivan campaign will have to be either forfeit - or succeed. These - will be its final days before its conclusion.

The Emperor's top priority is securing our borders and stamping any hint of revolutionary sentiment within the empire. That means recalling troops from the frontlines and redeploying them to key strategic locations."

I shook my head in disbelief. "So all the blood spilled, all the sacrifices made - it was all for nothing?"

"Not for nothing, Captain," Gerhart replied firmly. "We've made significant gains in Baltiva, and now - it's time to push our luck and go all in. Regardless of our failure here, the Emperor must focus on the greater threat now. If the revolution spreads to Valtore, it could mean the end of the empire as we know it."

I sighed heavily, the weight of the situation settling on my shoulders like a lead cloak. "So be it. When do I leave?"

"This afternoon - after the paperwork for your release is secured." He said. "I recommend never to mention the Von Lowe situation again."

"Of course - and I don't plan to," I stated before stopping.

"And what about my father? Does he... Does he know yet?"

Gerhart's eyes shifted uncomfortably, a pained expression briefly crossing his weathered face before he mastered himself again. His following words fell heavily, like stones, into the still waters of my soul. "Captain Kaelitz, I also regret that I bear ill tidings on that front. Your father...he passed away a week ago, not long after receiving word.."

The room seemed to tilt, the edges blurring as though I were viewing the world through a fogged glass. "Passed away?" My voice sounded detached, foreign to my ears.

"Yes, from grief," Gerhart continued softly. "After the Emperor stripped him of his nobility due to the alleged misconduct tied to your family's name — a decision spurred by Lord Commander Von Löwe's accusations — your father could not bear the dishonor. It...it broke him, Kaelitz."

Dishonor. A cold fire kindled in my chest, spreading its icy tendrils through my veins. My father had been a stalwart man, stern but fair, and his life was a testament to service and loyalty to the Empire. That he should leave this world, not with the glorious dignity he deserved but shadowed by disgrace, was a cruelty beyond reckoning.

"I...I see." I said. A silence fell between us - heavy and thick.

Gerhart cleared his throat, adjusting his collar uncomfortably. "I must leave now, Captain. Your release should be processed by the end of the day. Prepare yourself for the journey ahead."

He stood, his chair scraping softly against the stone floor. As he moved towards the door, he paused and returned to me before deciding to say nothing.

I remained seated, staring at the vacant spot where Gerhart had been just moments ago. The cell's oppressive silence enveloped me again, broken only by the distant echoes of marching feet and clanging armor from outside the corridor.

The world felt hollow, dim - and cruel as if the very essence of life had been sucked from its marrow.

The Grenziers

I arrived at the military encampment on the outskirts of Rega later that afternoon, my meager belongings slung over my shoulder in a weathered pack. The camp was a sprawling maze of tents and makeshift structures, bustling with activity as soldiers hurried to and fro.

I went to the command tent at the center of the encampment, where I was to report for duty. As I approached, I caught sight of a tall, stout man with a thick beard and a fierce scowl etched onto his face, organizing out commands amongst junior officers—no doubt - a colonel of some kind and fresh-faced to boot.

"You there!" the man barked as I drew near. "State your business."

I drew myself up to my full height and met his gaze steadily. "Captain Ardent Kaelitz, reporting for duty with the battalion of riflemen."

The man's eyes narrowed as he looked me over, taking in my scarred face and missing eye. "Ah, the infamous... Major Kaelitz, I believe is what it is now." he sneered. "I've heard of you. They say you're a troublemaker, a rabble-rouser who can't follow orders. And so, they promoted you to Major. How excellent."

The man stepped closer, his face mere inches from mine. "Let me make one thing clear, *Major*," he said, his voice dripping with disdain. "I am Colonel von Olenstross and run a tight ship here. I won't tolerate any insubordination or disrespect from the likes of you."

I stood my ground, refusing to be intimidated by the colonel's bluster. I looked Colonel von Olenstross up and down, taking in his crisp, freshly pressed uniform with nary a wrinkle or smudge of dirt. His boots gleamed with a mirror-like shine, clearly having never seen a day of hard marching or trudging through muddy battlefields. The man's hands were soft and uncalloused, his skin pale and unblemished - a far cry from a seasoned military commander's weathered, battle-hardened hands.

I couldn't help but smirk as I addressed the Colonel, my voice dripping with sarcasm. "Forgive me, sir," I said through gritted teeth, barely containing my anger. "But it seems your commission hasn't even had time to dry before you started issuing orders." My tone was laced with disdain.

Colonel Olenstross's face turned an alarming shade of purple, and he jabbed a finger into my chest. "You listen here, Kaelitz," he snarled. "You're nothing but an insult to nobility. I ought to have you flogged - or worse." He grinned.

I met Colonel von Olenstross's fiery gaze with an icy glare of my own. Slowly and deliberately, I raised my scarred hand, the twisted flesh.

"So let me make one thing clear," I continued, my words dripping with contempt. "I don't give a damn about your threats or your posturing. I've fought and bled for this army and continue to do so - with or without your approval. Now, tell me where my damned regiment is."

Colonel von Olenstross's face twisted into a sneer of pure loathing. His eyes glinted with malice as he jabbed a finger towards the far side of the encampment. "Your rabble is camped over there, Kaelitz. Try not to get them all killed with your reckless insubordination."

I gave a mocking salute. "I'll do my best, sir. Wouldn't want to sully your spotless record now, would we?" Without waiting for a response, I turned on my heel and strode off in the direction the colonel had indicated.

As I made my way through the maze of tents, I could feel the eyes of the soldiers on me. Some regarded me with awe or respect, having heard tales of my exploits on the battlefield. Others looked at me with suspicion or outright hostility. I paid them no mind - as I finally reached the cluster of tents.

My boots sank into the soft mud as I approached the ragged assembly of tents that housed the 22nd Horthian Grenziers. The scene before me was one of utter chaos—men milled about aimlessly, their uniforms in varying states of disarray. Some lounged by cookfires, lazily stirring pots of what passed for stew, while others engaged in smoking pipes and lying about.

I scanned the disorderly camp, my eyes searching for any semblance of authority amidst the sea of unwashed bodies and slovenly attire. Finally, my gaze settled upon a figure who seemed to be barking orders in a guttural tongue I recognized as Horthian. I strode purposefully towards the man, my bearing radiating the confidence and command befitting my rank.

As I drew closer, I could make out more details of the Horthian captain. He was a stout, barrel-chested man with a thick beard completely against regulations that obscured most of his weathered face. Small and piercing eyes darted about as he shouted at the men, his words punctuated by wild gesticulations of his meaty hands.

I cleared my throat, drawing the captain's attention. He whirled to face me, his expression a mixture of annoyance as he took in my rank insignia.

"Captain Márton, I presume?" I asked in Valtorean.

The Horthian captain squinted at me suspiciously, his eyes lingering on my scars and eyepatch. "Aye, that's me," he grunted in heavily accented Valtorean. "And who might you be..?"

"Kaelitz," I supplied, extending my hand in greeting. "Major Ardent Kaelitz, your new commanding officer."

Captain Márton's bushy eyebrows shot up in surprise. He ignored my proffered hand, crossing his arms over his broad chest. "Is that so? I wasn't informed of any change in command."

I met his challenging gaze unflinchingly. "I assure you, Captain, the orders come directly from the Emperor. I've been assigned to whip this sorry excuse for a regiment into shape."

Márton's eyes narrowed. "The 22nd Grenziers are some of the finest soldiers in the Empire," he growled. "We don't need some prissy Valtorean nobleman telling us how to fight."

I took a step closer, my voice low and dangerous. "Prissy?" I hissed. "Do these scars look stuffy to you, Major? I've spilled more blood for the Empire than you've had hot meals. And as for being a nobleman..." I glanced around at the squalid camp with disdain. "It seems nobility is in short supply here."

Márton let out a harsh bark of laughter, his eyes glinting with a newfound respect. "You've got guts, Kaelitz, I'll give you that," he said, his voice gruff but not entirely unkind. "Maybe you're not just another pompous ass after all."

I allowed myself a small, wry smile. "Glad to exceed your expectations, Captain. Let's see about getting this regiment into fighting shape, shall we?"

Márton nodded, then turned to bellow at the lounging soldiers in Horthian. The men scrambled to their feet, hastily straightening their uniforms and falling into haphazard ranks. I surveyed the motley assortment of soldiers, my critical eye taking in their shabby appearance and lack of discipline.

"Any of these lads speak Valtorean?"

"A few, sir," Márton said. "But they're the worst lot. Learned to kill prissy Valtorean nobles. Like yerself?" He said, grinning.

I fixed Márton with a steely glare, my voice low and dangerous. "Is that so, Captain? Let's hope their skills at killing Valtorean nobles extend to killing Eclaireans." I said before smirking.

Márton's grin continued. "Aye, sir. I'll make sure they understand that."

"Now, you lot - listen up."

I turned to face the assembled soldiers; my posture was straight and commanding. In a clear, authoritative voice, I addressed them in Valtorean:

"Men of the 22nd Grenziers, I am Major Ardent Kaelitz, your new commanding officer. I have been sent here by direct order of the Emperor to instill discipline, hone your skills, and forge you into an elite fighting force that will strike fear into the hearts of our Eclairean foes. If you have any questions - I recommend asking them now."

As I concluded my speech, I was met with confused and somewhat skeptical faces. The men glanced at one another, murmuring in Horthian as they tried to make sense of my words. Captain Márton, standing off to the side, stifled a chuckle.

"I was expecting something longer, Major." He mumbled, still grinning.

With that, I strode into the ranks of disheveled soldiers, my boots crunching on the frosty ground. I stopped before a particularly scruffy-looking private, his uniform more patches than fabric, a sneer plastered on his unshaven face.

"You there," I barked. "What's your name, soldier?"

"Székely." He grumbled. "Sir."

I slowly surveyed the ragtag group of soldiers again, taking in every tattered sleeve, every scuffed boot, and every missing button. The uniforms were a patchwork of faded colors and fraying edges, barely held together by a few stubborn threads. It was as if these men had been dragged through the mud and left to dry in the sun. Székely's uniform, like many others, hung off his frame in tatters, the sleeves threadbare and the hem ragged.

I turned to face Captain Márton, my eyes narrowed and my voice low. "Captain, what in the Savior's name is the meaning of this? These uniforms are a disgrace to the regiment and to the Empire itself. I demand an explanation for why your men are parading around in such a sorry state."

Márton shifted uncomfortably, avoiding my gaze. "We're light infantry, sir." He stated. "But the rifles are clean."

I fixed Captain Márton with a piercing stare. "Light infantry or not, there's no excuse for this level of slovenliness," I said, my voice sharp with disapproval. "Clean rifles are all good, but discipline starts with attention to detail."

I turned back to Private Székely, who stood rigidly at attention, his eyes fixed straight ahead. I circled him slowly, taking in every frayed edge and missing button of his uniform.

"Private Székely," I said, my tone deceptively calm. "Do you take pride in serving in the Emperor's army?"

Székely swallowed hard, glancing around at his fellows. A chuckle went through the regiment.

Székely's eyes darted nervously as he struggled to find the right words. "Of course, sir," he mumbled, barely audible. "It's an honor to serve."

I stepped back, surveying the ranks of disheveled men once more. Their uniforms may have been tattered, but I could see the glimmer of potential in their eyes. These were soldiers of the Empire, and by Valtorean steel, I would make them look and act the part.

"Listen well, all of you," I said, my voice carrying across the frosty parade ground. "I care little for the mud and dirt on your uniforms. We are light infantry, and a little grime comes with the territory. But there is no excuse for poor personal hygiene and unkempt appearances."

I paced along the front rank, meeting each man's gaze. "From this day forward, every soldier will be clean-shaven before morning muster. Hair will be kept short and tidy. I expect half-decency in your grooming and bearing. Is that clear?"

A ragged chorus of "Yes sir!" rang out.

I nodded, satisfied for the moment. "Good. Captain Márton, see to it that each man has a razor and soap later this afternoon."

Márton saluted crisply. "Yes, Major Kaelitz. It will be done."

I clasped my hands behind my back, ignoring the dull ache from my maimed fingers. "Now - to the heart of it. Let's see how well these boys can shoot."

I led the regiment to the shooting range on the outskirts of Rega. The weather was overcast and dreary, and a drizzle dampened our greatcoats as we marched. Mud squelched under our boots.

When we arrived, I had the men form up in a long firing line facing the distant targets - simple wooden cutouts of men at one hundred and fifty paces. I walked behind them, studying each soldier as they loaded their rifles and took aim.

To my surprise, their movements were smooth and practiced, not the clumsy fumbling I'd expect from such a ragged-looking regiment. There was no wasted motion as they bit open paper cartridges, poured the powder, rammed the ball, and primed the pan.

"Ready!" I called out. The men in front of me brought their rifles to their shoulders in unison. Again, their form looked excellent.

"Aim!" Sixty rifle barrels leveled at the targets, unwavering.

"Fire!"

The volley crashed out, a rippling blast of smoke and flame. I peered downrange through my spyglass, studying the targets.

To my amazement, at least fifty of the sixty targets were hit, many with multiple holes punched clean through the center of mass. It was uncannily accurate shooting for a single volley at this range, better than I'd seen from my first commission with the 1st Arkhevost Battalion.

As the smoke cleared, I watched the men hurriedly reload their rifles for another volley. The process was laborious and time-consuming compared to the smoothbore muskets I was accustomed to. Each soldier had to carefully pour the powder, ram the ball, and prime the pan individually. Even with their practiced efficiency, it took well over a minute before they were ready again.

At that time, I contemplated the benefits and drawbacks of these rifles. Their accuracy was astounding, no doubt. But the slow loading time could be a liability in the heat of battle when every second counted. A well-drilled infantry with muskets could likely get off three or even four volleys in the time it took for a single rifle volley.

As if reading my thoughts, Sergeant Kósa, a grizzled veteran with a scar running down his weathered cheek, spoke up. "Begging your pardon, Major Kaelitz, sir."

I turned to face Sergeant Kósa. "Yes, Sergeant? Speak your mind."

The old sergeant scratched his stubbled chin thoughtfully. "If I may ask, sir - what manner of soldiering did you do before this posting?"

I smiled wryly. The question was forward but not disrespectful. Kósa was a sharp man, trying to take my measure as a commander.

"I began my service as a demi-lancer. Dangerous work, that."

Kósa nodded, a glint of respect in his eye. "Aye, sir. Demi-lancers, they're a breed apart. Riding hell-for-leather into the thick of it, drawing fire so the heavy horse can smash the line. It's an honorable trade, of sorts."

"Just so," I agreed. "After that, I held a commission leading the first Arkhevost battalion, though that hardly lasted more than a month - and I trust you're familiar with the recent deployment of the Forlorn?"

"Aye, that I am." Kósa nodded. "We were second on that list to be sent to that damned marsh."

I nodded grimly at Kósa's words. "Then you understand well the kind of butchery you avoided."

Kósa spat on the muddy ground. "Aye. Probably hacked to pieces in the swamps before they could get off a shot."

"Either by beast or man, as it would seem," I stated. "I hope we're sent westward rather than pursuing this Kholodian campaign."

Kósa nodded.

"This campaign will be over either once Valtor is dead - or when Kholodia is dead."

"On that cheerful note," I said wryly, "let's see another volley, men. Reload!"

I pondered the sergeant's words as the soldiers hurried to reload their rifles. Perhaps he was right.

Regardless, my mind drifted back to the days I spent with Grand Prince Michaelovich in Kholodia and all those campaigns on his maps. I missed the soaring onion domes plated in gold leaf, the palatial halls adorned with vibrant frescoes depicting Kholod's mythic history, and the exotic smells of incense and perfume.

The long hours away from the front - instead, poured into a private study, debating strategies and alliances. The fate of both our nations hung in the balance. It took me back.

"Valtorea seeks to expand its borders, to consume its neighbors like a ravenous beast," Michaelovich growled, his long claws tapping the map. "Naturally - I must stop their advance here, at the Lyvov River, past Freydrich's Pass and the mountains. If they cross it, all of Kholodia will be vulnerable."

As I studied the map, a plan began to form in my mind. I traced my finger along the winding path of the Lyvov River, flanked on both sides by steep, forested ridges. The terrain was treacherous, but therein lay an opportunity.

"Why not bypass it entirely - and head southward, through the Zaroska Gorge?"

Michaelovich leaned forward, his amber eyes flashing with interest.

"Ah. But - that would open up the entire Valtorean army to an encirclement. Cut off from supplies - and too far to defend Baltiva proper."

"Precisely," I said, tapping the narrow defile of the Zaroska Gorge on the map. "A small force could move through - and strike deep inside Kholodia without much resistance. I doubt the garrison troops are splendid - garrison troops rarely are."

Michaelovich rumbled deep in his chest, a contemplative sound. "And from there, they could push forward and cut off the Kholodian army. Catch them between the Valtorean center - over the river and skirmishers in the rear." He stated. "It would be audacious - daring. I doubt very many would be capable of such an act." I leaned back in my chair, a slight smile playing across my lips. "Audacious, yes. But that is precisely why it could work. You would never expect such a bold move."

Michaelovich regarded me thoughtfully, his massive paw-like hands steepled before him—a glimmer of respect in his eyes.

And then a sudden realization struck me like a bolt of lightning. The pieces began to fall into place in my mind, forming a picture I had not seen before.

"Perhaps - we'll be in Kholodia before we know it."

As the men finished reloading their rifles and stood at the ready once more, I was jolted out of my reverie by the sound of hoofbeats rapidly approaching. I saw a courier galloping towards us, his horse lathered with sweat. He reined in sharply and dismounted, snapping a hasty salute.

"Urgent dispatch for Major Kaelitz, sir!" the courier said breathlessly, holding out a sealed envelope.

I took the dispatch with a nod of thanks, breaking the seal and scanning the contents. As I read, I sighed. An audience - with his Imperial Highness."

"Ready the troops, Sergeant," I said to him. "I believe we'll be marching out soon enough."

Passing through the old castle gates, I dismounted my steed and handed the reins to a waiting stablehand. The courtyard was abuzz with activity - nobles in resplendent finery, guards in polished armor, and servants hurrying to and fro. I couldn't help but feel out of place in my battle-worn uniform, still stained with the dust and blood of recent skirmishes.

A pair of guards escorted me through the castle's grand halls, their footsteps echoing off the marble floors and vaulted ceilings. Tapestries depicting historic battles and the likenesses of past emperors adorned the walls, their colors muted by time but no less striking. I couldn't help but find this such a charming display by the Baltzers - like they were feigning friendship at long last.

Finally, we arrived at the throne room. The massive oak doors swung open, revealing a hollow chamber bathed in the soft glow of countless candles. A handful of figures were gathered - and I recognized him, the Emperor.

We both met eyes. He was still a young man - I had only seen him perhaps a year ago, and I had become something much more than a youth.

His pale blond hair was neatly coiffed, and his blue eyes were sharp and calculating.

"Major Kaelitz," the Emperor said, his voice ringing in the hushed chamber. "I have heard much about your exploits. Both the good - and the bad." He stated. "The rest of you - leave us."

I bowed deeply as the others filed out of the throne room, leaving me alone with Emperor Wolfgang. The silence stretched between us for a long moment before he spoke again.

"Walk with me, Major," he said, descending from the dais and gesturing for me to follow. We exited the throne room through a side door, emerging into an overgrown garden courtyard.

As we strolled along the winding paths, the Emperor clasped his hands behind his back and glanced at me sidelong. "I have heard the official reports of what transpired with Lord Duclaire. But I would hear the truth from you directly."

I hesitated, choosing my words carefully. "It was a difficult situation, Your Highness. Lord Duclaire had been compromised, working against the interests of the Empire. In the end, he left me no choice."

The Emperor nodded slowly. "And his final moments? How did he meet his end?"

I swallowed hard; the memory was still vivid and painful. "He was defiant to the last. Even as I ran him through with my sword, he spat curses at me and the Empire. But in his eyes...I saw a flicker of something else. Regret, perhaps. Or acceptance of his fate."

We stopped beside a burbling fountain, the Emperor gazing into the clear waters as if searching for answers in their depths. "My uncle, the Arch-Duke, was always headstrong and ambitious," Emperor Wolfgang said, his voice tinged with a hint of sadness. I fear his desires outgrew his loyalty to the Empire. It's a pity it had to end this way."

He turned to face me fully, his blue eyes boring into mine. "And - for Von Löwe - that was quite regrettable. He was a good man at heart - but I suppose that's what defines man in the Savior's eyes." He sighed.

"I'm still shocked I wasn't executed, to be frank," I said. The Emperor grinned.

"I'm shocked that the gentry didn't call for your head. Truly, we live in enlightened times."

The Emperor's words hung between us, a mix of irony and genuine surprise. I couldn't help but let out a short, humorless laugh.

"Enlightened times indeed, Your Highness," I said, shaking my head.

Emperor Wolfgang raised an eyebrow, a hint of a smile playing at the corners of his mouth. "And - I trust you met my peer. Grand-Prince Michaelovich." He stated. "A different side of the coin - like a Von Löwe for the Kholodians."

I nodded, recalling my encounter with the Grand Prince. "Yes, Your Highness. He is an impressive man—sharp and strategic. We had many discussions about military tactics."

The Emperor's smile widened slightly. "Ah, so you glimpsed the keen mind behind that exterior. Michaelovich is a formidable ally - and a terrible enemy." He stated.

We resumed our stroll through the gardens, the gravel path crunching beneath our boots. The Emperor seemed to be carefully weighing his next words.

"What do you think about the Kholodians, Major?"

I considered the Emperor's question for a moment, mulling. "What I think - is that there's a load of shite told about them, and they're not going to be easy to kill."

The Emperor stopped - almost breaking down in laughter, as he smiled.

"Precisely - precisely! That is what I keep telling the Reichskammergeicht, but they're steadfast on this brutal campaign. Undoubtedly, it's because of the Black Order and the secret societies providing a hefty contribution to their treasuries."

"You have a refreshingly frank perspective, Major Kaelitz. It's a rare quality in the circles of nobility and power." He paused, seeming to choose his following words carefully. "I fear that many in the Empire are blinded by greed and old hatreds when it comes to the Kholodians. They think of them of the savage tribes that existed there - perhaps, two hundred, maybe three hundred years ago." He sighed.

"But, the situation has changed, as I trust you've inferred. The Eclairean Revolution - ah, excuse me. They're calling it the 'Grand' Revolution." He smirked. "Now - of course, any monarch worth his salt would know republicanism is a disease to be stamped out - but, Michaelovich, just over the border... He's a bastard, a right bastard." He grinned.

"Mh?" I said.

"He knows very well - that he can outwait us. There's no heart in this war - there hasn't been for some time now. Indeed, Michaelovich is a patient man. He knows that time is on his side." Wolfgang gazed over the immaculately manicured gardens, the vibrant blooms swaying gently in the breeze.

"The situation in Eclairea grows more dire by the day. The revolutionaries gain ground, their fervor spreading like wildfire among the populace. It is only a matter of time before we must divert significant forces to quell the uprising."

He turned to me, his eyes sharp and calculating. "And therein lies the crux of Michaelovich's strategy. As we exhaust ourselves stamping out the flames of rebellion in Eclairea, the Kholodians will seize the opportunity to strike. They will pour over our borders, annexing the frontier territories while our armies are occupied elsewhere."

Wolfgang's hand clenched into a fist at his side. "Baltiva, Horthia, Polvania- all of our hard-won gains in the East will be lost. This Holy Empire would likely never recover. There CANNOT be a Holy Empire, with the existence of a Greater Kholodia - of a Greater Eclaria, a greater Arkanthia, or even of a Greater Arlenia."

The Emperor's words hung heavy in the air, the gravity of the situation settling upon me like a leaden weight. I could see the lines of worry etched into his face, the burden of an empire teetering on the brink of collapse resting squarely on his shoulders.

"And yet - we cannot slay our foes. No one - lest we upset the Great Game." He sighed. "Statecraft is treasonous business. It's being punished for the father's sins - if we had left the Polvanian-Lithurian Commonwealth intact, we could have avoided this whole debacle."

He sighed and looked at me. "I'm sure you're aware of Zaroska Gorge - and I'm sure Michaelovich is aware of it."

The Emperor's mention of Zaroska Gorge sent a chill down my spine. I knew the place all too well - a narrow, treacherous pass through the jagged mountains that separated Kholodia from the frontier. It was the only other viable route for a large army to cross the border, and whoever controlled the gorge held the key to the entire region.

"Yes, Your Highness," I replied, my voice grim. "Zaroska Gorge is a strategic chokepoint... Straight into the heartland of Kholodia, if I'm not wrong."

"You aren't. Freydrich Pass is no longer viable - we've lost too many men, and the pass is simply unassailable without greater commitment from the Empire." He said. "Perhaps - the most we can do- send a skirmishing force through it - harass and threaten their supply lines... However, the problem lies in that such a unit would be prone to destruction if it got bogged down."

I nodded solemnly. The Empire was stretched thin, fighting on multiple fronts while our enemies waited, ready to strike at our most vulnerable moment.

"Your Highness," I said, my voice steady despite the turmoil within, "I presume you mean to send me - and the 22nd Horthian Grenziers into the pass?"

The Emperor regarded me with a piercing gaze as if measuring the depth of my resolve. After a long moment, he spoke. "Absolutely." He stated. "We must make it untenable for them to stay where they are - although, you'll likely run into one of their skirmishing forces. The Kholodians are also probing - hoping to find a knock-out blow, but the hard fact is that our supplies come from the sea - not from overland." The Emperor's lips curled into a knowing smile.

"I understand, Your Highness," I said, respectfully inclining. "I'll get them into shape. Get'em ready."

The Emperor nodded a flicker of approval in his eyes. "I trust you will. So far - your commanders have written nothing but good remarks - despite the fact you've killed both of them." He grinned.

A wry smile tugged at my lips despite the gravity of the situation. "Well, Your Highness, all I can say is I'll try not to make a habit of it."

The Emperor chuckled a rare moment of levity amidst the heavy concerns weighing upon us both. "See that you don't, Major Kaelitz. The Empire needs men like you - loyal, capable, and unafraid to jump into the muck."

I felt a swell of pride at his words, tempered by the knowledge of the immense responsibility ahead. "I won't let you down, Your Highness. The

22nd Horthian Grenziers will go through the Zaroska Gorge, come what may."

"I do not doubt that," the Emperor replied, his gaze drifting back to the gardens below. "Perhaps - we can bring this war to an end, once and for all. Though - who knows what the future will hold for us."

The Emperor turned to face me fully, his eyes alight with a fierce intensity. "Now - get going."

I bowed deeply, the weight of his words settling into my very bones. "By your command, Your Highness."

As I strode from the imperial presence, my mind raced with plans and strategies. I could not fail again - not with the Emperor's attention firm on my shoulders.

A Confrontation at Valka

The drills intensified as they marched on, the sun beating relentlessly on the 22nd Grenzers. I watched them march past their peers, the crisp cadence of their boots on the hard-packed earth filling the air. To their side, I noticed the other regiments were also training hard, but something about their formations and armaments caught my eye. It was different—far different than what I was used to.

"Lieutenant Márton," I called out, gesturing for him to join me. He trotted over, a questioning look on his weathered face.

"What is it, Major Kaelitz?" he asked in his thick Horathian accent.

I nodded towards the other units. "I wasn't aware we were redrilling the whole army. No more tercios. They're all in line formation now. No more halberds - no more pikes. No more of those blasted, old arquebuses." I stated.

Márton nodded. "Aye. The whole army is to be redrilled. The Emperor's orders, straight from his mouth." Márton replied, casting an appraising eye over the precise lines and gleaming bayonets of the infantry regiments drilling nearby.

I frowned thoughtfully. "I wonder where they found the gold to re-equip so extensively. Let alone the muskets - only a few months ago, it was a royal pain in the arse to get a hundred - let alone a few thousand."

The lieutenant snorted derisively. "Where else? The damned merchants of the League and Free Cities. Loans. They're all too happy to outfit our forces, knowing we'll be spending Valtorean blood to expand their trade routes and fill their counting houses once it's all over."

I sighed heavily, knowing he was right. The merchant princes that ruled the Free Cities only ever acted in their self-interest. Even as nominal vassals of the Emperor, their loyalty was paramount to their ambitions and greed.

"Well, at least it means the army will be better equipped to face our foes," I said grimly. "Though I suspect those fat burghers will expect to be well-compensated in plundered gold and new markets for their 'generous' support."

"Aye, there's always a price to be paid," Márton grumbled, spitting in the dust. "I suppose the Emperor is going all in. They outfitted us with rifles only a year ago - but that was a specialized case." He grinned. "The only rifles made in Aurisca are from Arlenia. It's a shame no one's bothered to make them domestically."

"Too true," I stated before sighing. The workshops on the homefront were likely overflowing with pressed men and hasty orders to churn out the new arms, I thought to myself.

"Those gunsmiths are likely working overtime to fulfill the Emperor's orders for the army's new muskets. " Márton said. "They're saying this will be the biggest campaign in the East since the first Crusade here, over two hundred years ago."

I nodded solemnly, the weight of Márton's words hanging between us. The first Crusade into Baltiva was a pivotal moment in Valtorian history, a grand campaign that solidified the Empire's hold on these lands and opened up vital trade routes. But it had come at a steep cost in blood."

"Two hundred years..." I mused, my gaze drifting over the drilling soldiers. "And yet, it feels like little has changed in some ways. The weapons may be different, the tactics evolved, but the heart remains the same - men marching off to fight and die in foreign lands for the glory of the Empire and the profit of the merchant princes."

Márton grunted in agreement. "The more things change, the more they stay the same, as they say. But this time, Major, I fear the scale of it will be unlike anything we've seen before. The Emperor is staking everything on this campaign - wrapping up the Eastern Front and then pivoting westward."

"How are the men holding up?" I said.

"They're not eager. The Vuk have the advantage in the woods. Our boys might be foresters and poachers, but they'll get ripped apart there. And - if we can't use the woods, what good is a bunch of light infantry and skirmishers?" Márton sighed. I let out a heavy sigh, Márton's words weighing on my mind. The Vuk were renowned for their fierce forest fighting skills. Even with rifles and drilling, engaging them in the thick woods of Baltiva would be a death sentence for many of my men.

"Those damned wolfmen will tear us apart." I sighed. "Halberds and pikes would give us a fighting chance - at least, we'd have some reach on them..." I said before sighing. "We'll have to figure it out."

As we watched the men drilling with their new weapons, a courier galloped up on a lathered horse. Dismounting hurriedly, he saluted. "Urgent dispatch for Major Kaelitz, sir!"

I took the sealed missive, noting the Imperial seal. Breaking the wax, I scanned the contents, my brow furrowing. Márton looked at me expectantly.

"Orders, sir?"

"As always." I sighed grimly. "The Kholodians are striking first, it would seem - and we're to skirmish them at Valka."

I strode into Colonel von Olenstross's command tent, the canvas flaps whipping behind me in the chill breeze. Lantern light flickered over the large tactical map across the campaign table, casting dancing shadows. Von Olenstross stood hunched over it alongside a dozen other regimental officers.

Colonel von Olenstross stood at the head of the table, his hawklike features shadowed. "Gentlemen, the time has come. The Kholodian Army is on the march, aiming to cross into our territory near the border town of Valka. His Imperial Majesty commanded that we prevent and drive them back."

He paused, steely eyes sweeping the assembled officers. "Our scouts report their strength at approximately 25,000 men in seventeen battalions, with 170 cannons. We field around 16,000 in twelve battalions, with 122 cannons. The odds are not in our favor, but we can choose our ground to make a stand."

Mutters circulated the tent at the prospect of facing a significantly larger foe. Major Sternberg, commander of the 3rd Battalion, spoke up in his booming voice. "If I may, Colonel - we should immediately dispatch the cavalry and light infantry to harass their advance. Slow them down, force them to deploy early, and sap their energy and will to fight. By the time they reach Valka, they'll be exhausted and ripe for a counterattack."

Colonel von Olenstross nodded approvingly. "Of course - of course. The 22nd Grenzers will act alongside the 8th Saxonian Dragoons and the 12th Kroate Hussars. From what I understand, the land around Valka is open - though, there is some forest."

I stepped forward, the lantern light flickering across my face. "Colonel, with all due respect, I must express my reservations about this plan. While I understand the strategic necessity of slowing the Kholodian advance, sending my men - light infantry - against their main force in open terrain is tantamount to suicide..."

The Colonel fixed me with a steely gaze. "Major Kaelitz, your concerns are noted. But - we must buy time for the main army to arrive and fortify Valka."

"And what of the Vuk, sir?" I pressed on. "They can outrun us - and they have rifles of their own. The Kholodians have a significant skirmishing capability we're dismissing - and if they were to bypass us and skirmish the army..."

A heavy silence hung in the air. Major Sternberg cleared his throat. "The Major raises a valid point, Colonel. Perhaps we should reconsider-"

But Colonel von Olenstross cut him off with a sharp gesture. "Major Kaelitz - the orders stand," Colonel von Olenstross said firmly, his gaze unwavering. "We cannot allow the Kholodians to advance unchecked. Your Grenzers will skirmish them and slow their march, buying precious time for our main force to dig in at Valka. That is your duty, sir."

Von Olenstross turned back to the map. "The 22nd Grenzers will advance and engage the enemy vanguard. Delay them as long as possible. The cavalry will support you." He looked up, his gaze sweeping the gathered officers. "We'll fortify here, here, and here," he pointed at several critical positions around Valka. "And pray that reinforcements arrive in time. Another batch of 30,000 men will be arriving from Varsaw and Lithuria within about six days, should conditions hold..."

Eventually, the meeting concluded. It would seem this was the first act of a full-fledged war: About 100,000 Empire men against an estimated force of 170,000 Kholodians marched to seize the Frontier.

As I exited the command tent, the weight of the impending battle settled heavily on my shoulders. The cold wind nipped at my face as I returned to where my men were encamped, mulling over the Colonel's orders.

Márton fell into step beside me, his expression grim. "What's the word, Major?"

"We're to advance and engage their vanguard," I said, my jaw tight. "Skirmish and delay them as long as possible so that the main force can fortify Valka."

Márton let out a low whistle. "That's a day's march at a light infantryman's pace. We'll get ready right away."

My mind raced as we walked, the enormity of the task ahead sinking in. Skirmishing against the Kholodian vanguard with their Vuk shock troops... It was a daunting prospect. But orders were orders, and I had a duty to fulfill, no matter the cost.

"Lieutenant Márton, have the men strike camp and prepare to march within the hour," I said, my voice steady despite the unease churning in my gut. "We'll need to move quickly to reach the enemy in time."

Márton nodded, his weathered face set in determination. "Aye, Major. The lads will be ready."

He hurried off to relay the orders, barking commands in his thick Horathian accent. I watched him go, grateful for his steadfast loyalty and competence.

I made my way to my tent, ducking inside to gather my gear and donning my battle harness, my mind still churning with the weight of the task ahead. As I reached for my saber, a sharp twinge shot through my maimed hand, the scarred flesh protesting as I tried to grip the hilt. I grimaced, flexing my fingers slowly, feeling the pull of the damaged nerves and tendons. The injury, a parting gift from Siegfried, left my swordsmanship a shadow of what it once was.

With a heavy sigh, I slid the saber into its sheath.

The 22nd Grenziers, all four hundred of them, marched with a sense of urgency through the rolling countryside of Lapsia toward the town of Valkia. The late afternoon sun hung low in the western sky, casting long shadows across the patchwork of golden wheat fields and emerald pastures that stretched out before us. A warm breeze rustled the tall grass, carrying with it the earthy scent of soil, adding to the anticipation of the impending encounter with the Kholodian forces.

In the distance, a handful of imposing hills rose from the plains like ancient sentinels, their slopes draped in a thick cloak of dark, brooding forest. Shafts of amber light pierced the dense canopy, dappling the forest floor in a mesmerizing play of light and shadow. The air grew cooler as we drew closer to the woods, a welcome respite from the heat of our march.

As the day wore on, the men, their faces glistening with sweat and streaked with dust kicked up by hundreds of marching boots, grew increasingly weary. But they pushed onward with grim determination, their exhaustion a testament to their unwavering commitment to the mission, and the knowledge that every step brought us closer to our objective - and the waiting Kholodian forces.

The sun was dipping below the horizon as we crested a final rise and caught sight of Valkia in the failing light. The small town huddled in the shelter of one of the more prominent hills, a cluster of sturdy stone buildings and thatch-roofed houses surrounded by a stout defensive wall. But even from a distance, I could see the banners of Kholodia fluttering - the garrison had already surrendered to the Kholodians.

"Orders, sir?" Márton asked. Nightfall was descending - and being out in the open was hardly ideal.

"We'll set up on the top of the hills."

I surveyed the hills overlooking Valkia; their slopes shrouded in lengthening shadows as dusk settled over the land. The dense forest would provide ample cover for my men to hunker down for the night, shielding us from prying Kholodian eyes - and hopefully, with a suitable picket around us, we should have enough warning against the Vuk.

"We'll make camp in the woods," I said, gesturing toward the dark tree line. "Have the men disperse and set up a perimeter. No fires, cold rations only. I want us hidden and ready to move at first light."

Márton nodded, already moving to relay the orders. "Aye, Major. We'll make sure the Kholodians never know we're here."

I watched as my men fanned out into the forest, their ragged, gray uniforms blending into the shadowy undergrowth as they moved to establish our perimeter. Despite the fatigue etched on their faces, they moved with the practiced efficiency of seasoned soldiers, setting up camp with minimal noise and fuss.

I went into the woods, picking a spot beneath a towering oak to lay my bedroll. As I settled down, my back leaning against the rough bark, I couldn't help but feel a pang of unease. The Kholodians were formidable foes, their Vuk shock troops renowned for their ferocity and skill in battle. And here we were, a mere four hundred men, tasked with delaying their advance.

It was a daunting prospect. But I had faith in my men, in their courage and determination.

As the last vestiges of daylight faded, the forest came alive with the sounds of the night: the hooting of an owl, the chirping of crickets, and the rustling of unseen creatures in the underbrush. I let the familiar noises wash over me, trying to calm my racing thoughts.

Sleep, when it finally came, was fitful and plagued by dreams. I saw the faces of the men I had lost, the friends I had buried. Alaric, his lifeless eyes staring up at me from the blood-soaked fields of Castelon. Would this be another Castleon? I wondered about that as I slept.

I woke with a start, my heart pounding, my maimed hand throbbing with phantom pain. The first pale light of dawn filtered through the trees, casting the forest in a ghostly half-light.

It was time to move.

I rose, shaking off the lingering tendrils of sleep, and roused my men. We had a long day ahead of us, and every moment counted.

As the camp stirred to life, I caught sight of Márton, his face grim as he approached.

"Major," he said, his voice low. "Sentries just reported in - the Imperial Army is a mile behind us - and the Kholodian host is moving into position."

We broke camp swiftly, our movements as silent as the forest around us. Márton led the way, his eyes scanning the path ahead while I brought up the rear, ensuring no man was left behind. The journey was arduous, the terrain treacherous, but we pressed on, driven by a grim determination. As we neared the crest of a hill, I signaled for my men to halt. Ahead lay our destination - and our destiny.

From the top of the hill, the view stretched out before us, a panorama of war and devastation. The fields below were churned and muddy, scarred by the passage of thousands of boots and hooves. In the distance, the town of Valkia huddled behind its walls, a fragile island in a sea of violence.

And arrayed before those walls, dug in like ticks behind a formidable line of breastworks, was the Kholodian army. Even from this distance, I could see the exhaustion in their postures, the way they sagged against their muskets. They had been digging all night, preparing for our arrival.

I allowed myself a grim smile. "Colonel von Olenstross will be in for a surprise," I remarked to Márton. "He was expecting to arrive first and fortify the town himself."

Márton grunted. "Aye. Your orders?"

I surveyed the enemy lines, my mind racing. The Kholodians had the advantage of position and fortification. But they were tired, and we had the element of surprise. If we struck hard and fast...

"How far out would you say we are from the edge of the Kholodian lines, Márton?"

"A good five-hundred paces or so, sir."

I considered for a moment, my eye narrowing as I studied the Kholodian lines. Five hundred paces - at the edge of our rifles' effective range. But these were no ordinary marksmen under my command. They were the 22nd Horthian Grenziers and the finest shots in the Empire. If any men could make those shots count, it was them.

"Márton, have the men drop prone along the crest of the hill," I ordered, my voice low and intense. "Instruct them to take careful aim at the flanks of the Kholodian line. Pick off their officers if they can."

Márton nodded grimly, then paused. "And our ammunition, sir? If this turns into a prolonged engagement..."

"Then we make every shot count," I said firmly. "These may be the most important volleys we ever fire. The fate of the Empire could hinge on what we do here in these next few moments."

As Márton moved to relay my orders, I gazed around - the morning mist swirled around us, wreathing the forest in a ghostly shroud. In the distance, I could hear the low rumble of the Imperial artillery, the prelude to the coming storm. A low, quiet cheer went through the ranks of prone riflemen.

"Steady, boys," I murmured, my voice barely audible over the pounding of my own heart. "Wait for my command."

The seconds stretched out, each one an eternity. I could hear the rasp of my breath and the creak of leather as my men shifted slightly, adjusting their aim.

The morning calm was shattered by the thunderous roar of Imperial howitzers and smoothbore cannons, their muzzle flashes lighting up the misty dawn like flickers of summer lightning. Moments later, fountains of dirt, splintered wood, and mangled bodies erupted along the Kholodian lines as the shells found their marks.

The Kholodian response was swift and furious. Their guns roared to life, sending a hail of iron and lead back toward the Imperial batteries. The ground shook with the concussive impacts, and the air was filled with the acrid scent of gunpowder and the screams of the wounded.

I watched in grim fascination as the two armies traded blows, each seeking to overwhelm the other with sheer firepower. The Kholodian earthworks began to crumble under the relentless Imperial bombardment, but their gun crews worked with desperate speed, keeping up a punishing rate of fire.

"Their artillerymen are no slouches," Márton observed, his voice tight with tension. "Think they know they have us outgunned?"

I nodded, my jaw clenched. "They'll figure it out soon enough," I grunted. "Wait longer - we'll engage once the infantry moves up.

As the minutes ticked by, the artillery duel intensified. It was a bloody scene—the breastworks the Kholodians dug did little against explosive shots and cannonballs. The quality of our Imperial artillery was indeed higher despite being outgunned, and it began to win the artillery duel as the morning wore on. The Kholodian guns fell silent one by one, smashed into ruin by the relentless bombardment. Plumes of smoke and dust rose from their shattered emplacements, obscuring the carnage.

As the last Kholodian battery was silenced, a cheer rose from the Imperial lines. The men knew that the tide was turning in their favor. The way was clear for the infantry to advance and finish the job.

I watched as the first regiment of Imperial infantry began to move forward, their black uniforms and gleaming bayonets striking contrast to the drab earth tones of the battlefield. At their head rode Major Lazarević, his saber raised high. The regimental banner fluttered proudly in the breeze, the golden double-headed eagle of the Empire resplendent upon a field of rich purple—the banner of Kroate.

The Kholodians saw them coming and scrambled to form a defensive line. Their officers shouted hoarse commands to instill some sense of order amidst the chaos. Men rushed to take up positions along the remnants of their earthworks - the few working cannons they had were loading canister as fast as they could.

"Now!" I shouted. "Open fire!"

As one, my men squeezed their triggers. The crack of the rifles shattered the morning stillness, a rolling volley that echoed off the hills. Through the drifting smoke, I saw Kholodian soldiers tumbling, their bodies jerking and twitching as our bullets found their marks.

For a moment, the enemy line wavered. I could see the confusion and panic as they realized they were under attack from an unexpected quarter.

Officers shouted orders, trying to rally their men, but the continuing volley from my Grenziers drowned out their voices.

"Reload!" I shouted, "Let's keep the pressure on, boys!"

We fired again and again, our rifles spitting lead and smoke. Each volley struck the Kholodian flanks like a hammer blow, sowing chaos and destruction. I saw gaps opening in their lines, men falling, and others turning to run. The first layer of breastworks was largely devastated.

The enfilading fire from my Grenziers was devastating, ripping significant bloody gaps in the Kholodian line. Men screamed and fell in droves, cut down like wheat before the scythe.

And then - the first Kroate Regiment charged in with a mighty roar, their uniforms flashing amidst the smoke and chaos. They surge over the breastworks like a tidal wave, bayonets gleaming as they crash into the faltering Kholodian line.

A fierce melee erupts - men grappling and stabbing in desperate hand-to-hand combat. The clash of steel, the cries of the wounded and dying, and the sharp cracks of pistol shots all blend into a hellish cacophony that assaults the senses.

The Kroatians fight savagely, hacking and slashing, driving the Kholodians back. The enemy's right flank crumbles under the onslaught, dissolving into a rout as men throw down their weapons and flee for their lives - a cheer erupting from among us.

But then - to our left, the wooded hills erupt with gunfire and war cries as Vuk skirmishers materialize from the shadows. Large shapes dart from tree to tree - bullets whizzing past us. A few unfortunate Grenziers crouched - rather than prone, fall, twitching as I glance over.

I dropped to the ground, pressing myself flat against the earth as bullets whizzed overhead. Around me, my Grenziers did the same, taking cover wherever they could find it. I cursed under my breath - we had been so focused on supporting the Kroatian charge that we had neglected to watch our flank.

"Return fire!" I shouted, my voice hoarse from the smoke. "Pick your targets, boys!"

My men needed no further encouragement. They rolled onto their bellies, rifles at the ready, and began to fire back at the Vuk skirmishers. The crack of our rifles was almost lost amidst the din of battle, but I saw several of the enemy fall, tumbling from their perches in the trees.

But the Vuks were canny fighters, well-versed in the art of ambush and skirmish. They used the terrain to their advantage, darting from cover to cover, never presenting an easy target. And they quickly adapted, shifting their fire to concentrate on my exposed position.

I felt a hot, searing pain in my left shoulder as a bullet glanced past me. I grunted, gritting my teeth against the sudden agony. But there was no time to dwell on the wound - not with the battle still raging around us.

"Márton!" I called out, spotting my second-in-command a few yards away. "Take a good third - move around the side and flank these bastards!"

Márton nodded, his face grim beneath the soot and grime of battle. He barked orders, directing the men to shift their fire and keep the Vuks pinned down.

I forced myself to my feet, ignoring the searing pain in my shoulder. I realized the Kroatian charge was faltering - they had driven deep into the Kholodian lines, but now they were bogged down, the momentum of their attack blunted by the sheer weight of numbers.

They needed support - and fast. I looked around, assessing the situation with a commander's eye. The Kholodian left flank was still holding, pouring a withering fire into the Kroatian ranks. If we could shift our fire, take some of the pressure off...

"Boys!" I shouted. "Shift fire left! Target those Kholodian bastards pouring it into the Kroatians!"

The Grenziers - most of them not speaking Valtorean, hesitated at my shouted command. They glanced uncertainly at each other, gripping their rifles with white-knuckled hands. But Márton was there, bless him, barking the order again in their native Horthian, his voice cracking like a whip. They reluctantly began to comply, shifting their fire to the left.

The effect was noticeable almost immediately. The punishing barrage the Kholodians had laid into the Kroatian flanks slackened as the Grenziers' fire found its mark. Men fell, screaming and writhing, as the bullets punched through the fur of officers and the flesh and bone of their enlisted men. The Kroatian line surged forward again, a defiant roar rising from their ranks as they pressed their advantage.

But the Kholodians were far from beaten. Even as their left flank crumbled beneath the Grenziers' onslaught, their right flank suddenly erupted with a thunderous barrage - slamming into our position.

I threw myself to the ground as the Kholodian artillery opened up, the ground shaking beneath me from the impact of the shells. Dirt and debris rained down, and I could hear the screams of wounded men amidst the chaos.

"Rifled cannons," I breathed. It was the only explanation for that kind of accuracy. The Kholodians must have somehow gotten their hands on the latest Arlenian artillery designs. This changed everything.

I racked my brain furiously—what were those cannons supposed to be doing anyway? Common sense would dictate battery fire. But they were well-concealed, dug in on the reverse slope of a hill, virtually immune to our small arms. And we had no artillery of our own in this position to counter-battery them—and now, they were firing shots at skirmishers.

I peered over the hill's edge to get a better look at the enemy's position. The smoke from the cannons obscured much of the hill, but I could make out the glint of metal in the sun - the barrels of the rifled cannons pointing directly at us.

Something didn't add up. Why would the Kholodians waste their precious ammunition on a small force of skirmishers like us? We posed no real threat to their position. The placement of those cannons was almost as if they were expecting a much larger force to attack from this direction.

A sudden thought struck me, and a chill ran down my spine. What if this was all a trap? What if the Kholodians had deliberately left their flank exposed, luring us in with the promise of an easy victory, only to unleash hell upon us with their concealed artillery?

I turned to my second-in-command, Lieutenant Janus, who crouched beside me in the trench. "Something's not right here," I said, my voice low and urgent. "Those cannons - they're not firing like they should be. It's almost as if they're waiting for something."

Janus frowned, his brow furrowed in thought. "You think it's a trap, sir?"

"I don't know," I admitted. "But we can't afford to take any chances. Send word back to the main force - tell them to hold their position and wait for further orders. And have the men spread out and take cover. If the Kholodians are planning something, we must be ready."

Janus nodded and scrambled off to relay my orders. I turned my attention back to the enemy position, my mind racing with possibilities. If this was a trap, what was their endgame? Were they trying to lure us into a false sense of security, only to launch a devastating counterattack? Or was something else at play here, something we had yet to see?

The cannons continued to thunder, their shells exploding around us with loud booms. But now, each shot only served to deepen my unease. Something was coming - I could feel it in my bones. And whatever it was, I knew that we had to be ready for it.

For now, all we could do was wait and watch - and pray that my suspicions were unfounded. But deep down, I knew that this was only the beginning - and that the actual test of our mettle was yet to come as the battle reached its crescendo.

The Kholodian cannons continued their relentless barrage, each thundering shot shaking the earth beneath our feet. Plumes of dirt and shattered rock erupted around us as the shells found their mark, showering us with debris. I could hear the screams of wounded men amidst the chaos as we lay down behind the hill. It had been fifteen minutes of being surrounded - under an artillery barrage.

I gritted my teeth, trying to block out the cries of pain and focus on the task at hand. We couldn't afford to lose our nerve now, not with so much at stake. Janus returned, his face grim as he crouched down beside me.

"The men are in position, sir," he reported, his voice strained. "But they're getting restless. This waiting, it's wearing on them."

I nodded, understanding all too well the toll that this kind of uncertainty could take on even the most seasoned soldier. "Steady them as best you can," I said. "Soon enough, this will be over with!"

Janus gave a tight nod and moved off to rally the men. I turned my gaze back to the Kholodian position, my mind whirling with possibilities. What were they waiting for? Why hadn't they pressed their advantage yet?

And then, as if in answer to my unspoken question, I saw it - a flicker of movement on the far side of the hill, barely visible through the haze of smoke and dust. At first, I thought it might be a trick of the light, a phantom conjured by my overactive imagination. But as I watched, the flicker resolved into a solid shape, then another, and another.

My blood ran cold as I realized what I was seeing. Troops—Kholodian troops, hundreds of them, marching in perfect formation up towards the hill—a detachment sent to root us out. Smoke from cannon fire and musket volleys had obscured the rest of the field. Did the Kholodians finally have a free hand to do away with us?

"Grenziers! Grenziers - to me!" I shouted - standing up over the crest, pointing downwards. A cannonball screeched by my head, the shockwave nearly knocking me off my feet. Around me, the Grenziers were scrambling into position, their faces etched with fear and determination.

"Steady, boys!" I shouted over the din of battle. "Pick your targets carefully. Make every shot count!"

The Kholodian infantry was closing fast, their bayonets glinting in the sunlight as they charged up the hill. I could see the whites of their eyes - the steady drumbeat.

"Fire!" I roared, raising my smoothbore pistol towards the oncoming horde, firing.

A thunderous volley erupted from the Grenziers' line, a sheet of flame and lead that tore into the Kholodian ranks. Men screamed and fell, their bodies tumbling and cartwheeling down the slope. But still, they came on, heedless of their losses, driven onward by their Vuk officers.

"Reload!" I shouted, saber raised. "Second rank, fire!"

Another volley, another wave of death and destruction. The air was thick with smoke and the coppery scent of blood. We fired repeatedly, each volley tearing bloody gaps in the Kholodian ranks. But it wasn't enough. For every man that fell, two more seemed to take his place, surging forward with grim determination.

I felt a surge of despair as I realized the hopelessness of our situation. We were hopelessly outnumbered, outgunned, and outflanked. It was only a matter of time before we were overrun.

But even as the realization of our dire straits sank in, I felt a sudden surge of defiance rise within me. We might be doomed, but by the gods, we would make the Kholodians pay dearly for every inch of ground they took.

"Grenzers!" I bellowed, my voice rising above the din of battle. "Ready yourselves!"

There was a rasp of steel as my men obeyed, locking their long, wicked-looking blades onto the ends of their rifles. They knew as well as I did that it would soon come to hand-to-hand fighting. The Kholodians were almost upon us, a sea of snarling faces and gleaming steel only a few paces below.

I raised my saber, preparing to give the counter-charge order to meet our fate head-on. But the ground beneath our feet began to tremble before I could speak. At first, I thought it was the impact of the artillery, but then I realized it was something else entirely.

Hoofbeats. The thunder of hooves, hundreds of them, grew louder by the second. And then, cresting the hill behind us, I saw them - a sight that made my heart leap with a sudden, wild hope.

Cavalry. Imperial cavalry, a whole brigade of them, their pennants snapping in the wind as they counter-encircled the Vuk behind us. I recognized them as two battalions - the 8th Saxonian Dragoons and the 12th Kroate Hussars. Their arrival could not have been more timely. With a thunderous roar, they rushed into position - stopping, leveling their carbines - and letting loose.

The Vuk Streltsy skirmishers, caught entirely by surprise, faltered and whirled to face this new threat. Lieutenant Márton's picket detachment was finally relieved - just as the climatic showdown between us and the column of Kholodian line infantry ahead of us was on the verge of cresting over. The whole valley seemed to resound with the clash of steel on steel, the screams of men, and the ceaseless roar of gunfire.

As the dragoons and hussars swept down upon the Kholodian flank, I glimpsed a momentary disarray among their ranks as they scrambled to reorganize against this unexpected assault. It was our chance, our only chance.

"Charge!" I cried out, thrusting my saber forward and signaling the Grenziers. "For the Empire! Charge!"

With a defiant yell that echoed off the hillsides, my men surged forward - bayonets fixed, faces set with a fierce resolve - a desperate charge over that left no time for the Kholodians to let off a shot.

The impact was devastating. Bodies collided with a sickening crunch of bone and metal. Men grunted and screamed as they pushed and shoved, stabbed and slashed in a fierce melee, as bayonets rang out - and just as quickly as we had surged forward, the Kholodian line began to crumble under the combined weight of our ferocity and the blistering cavalry onslaught. Already muddy from an earlier downpour, the ground became slick with blood and trampled debris. Boots slipped, and men fell, rushing away and downhill - the once imposing formation of hundreds of men now scattering like leaves in the wind. The Kholodian officers tried vainly to rally their men; their voices were drowned out by the clamor of battle and the panicked cries of the routed infantry.

I pressed forward with savage determination - we had them on the ropes. Our dragoons and hussars were harassing them - the sudden charge. The Kholodians would likely - at the base of the hill and forest below us, form a square to deter a cavalry charge - and keep cohesion. The perfect target for harassment - at last, our battalion of rifles was having an impact!

"Detach bayonets! Prepare to open fire!" I commanded, my voice hoarse from the strain of battle. The Grenziers responded efficiently, unlocking their bayonets and readying their rifles. Below us, the remnants of the Kholodian column were retreating towards the tree line, their formation dissolving into a disorganized mass as they sought shelter from our cavalry's withering fire in what *appeared* to be a disorderly square.

"Level!"

The Grenzers obeyed, their weapons trained on the milling Kholodians below. We had the advantage of the high ground and the element of surprise. We might turn this rout into a full-fledged victory if we could break their command structure and sow further chaos in their ranks.

"Fire!" I roared; the hillside erupted with a cacophony of gunfire as the Grenziers unleashed a blistering volley into the enemy's midst. Dozens fell - and they realized quickly that they were going to suffer horrific losses from the enfilade fire from both us and the dragoons. The Kholodians, realizing their dire situation, began to scatter in all directions, forming into a panicked mob - a few others throwing their arms down - surrendering wildly.

"Cease fire!" I called out, not wanting to waste ammunition on a broken foe. The Grenzers obeyed, lowering their smoking rifles as they watched the Kholodians' disorderly retreat.

I turned to survey the battlefield, taking in the scope of victory on our flank. The hillside was littered with the bodies of the fallen, Kholodian and Valtorean alike. But we had held our ground and, with the timely arrival of our cavalry, had turned the tide of battle.

As I watched, the dragoons and hussars began to round up the surrendering Kholodians, herding them into makeshift prisoner groups - ushering them away as I looked out over my men, battered and bloodied but unbowed. They had fought with the courage and tenacity that exemplified the finest traditions of a Horthian battalion. Against all odds, we had prevailed.

But even as I savored this hard-won triumph, I knew we could not rest here. Just then - the Kroatish major rode up to me, his steed's hooves churning the blood-soaked mud. He was a striking figure, tall and broad-shouldered, with a sweeping, fierce mustache and a hawkish gaze.

His skin was olive-toned, smooth, and sun-kissed, reminiscent of the seafaring people of southern Aurisca. Yet his jaw was hard, and his brow had a bold set that spoke of resolve forged in the crucible of countless battles against the Kholodian menace.

"Major Miroslavios, 12th Kroate Hussars," he declared, his voice rich and resonant, tinged with the melodic cadence of the south. "My compliments, Major. Your Grenziers fought with exceptional bravery today."

I nodded my thanks, too spent for a more elaborate reply. Horvat's gaze swept over the battlefield, taking in the scale of the carnage. His eyes, a striking blend of blue, narrowed as he appraised the situation.

"This is but a respite, Captain," I said gravely. "The Kholodians are far from beaten. Even now, their main force is pressing hard against our center. The rest of your brothers are down there - somewhere in that damnable smoke."

I followed Horvat's gaze, my heart sinking as I saw the thick plumes of smoke rising from the valley below. The distant thunder of artillery and the rattle of musketry told a grim tale of the desperate struggle unfolding there - the back and forth of charges - something of a standstill had been reached.

Our lines couldn't push past the first layer of breastworks, and now - it was up to the flank to make a decisive move.

"Then, it is up to us," I said, my voice hoarse with exhaustion and emotion. "The Grenziers are ready, Major Miroslavios. Give the word, and we'll march."

He nodded, his expression grim, wheeling his horse around. "I'll order the Saxonian dragoons to dismount and join you as you seize the second layer and the town itself - and my hussars will wheel around, bypass the bulk of their army - and cut off reinforcements." He said. The hussar's grin was tell-tale - a seasoned look, a golden tooth grinning.

"Or perhaps - get the first shot at plundering," I said.

Miroslavios let out a hearty laugh, his eyes twinkling with mischief. "Ah, Kaelitz, you know us hussars too well! But fear not, we'll save some spoils for your brave Grenziers."

I couldn't help but grin in return, even as the weight of the task ahead settled upon my shoulders. We still had a long, hard fight ahead of us, but with the hussars and dragoons at our side, I felt renewed confidence.

"Very well, Major," I said, straightening my shoulders. "Let us waste no more time. The sooner we strike, the sooner we can end this bloody affair."

Miroslavios nodded, his expression turning serious once more. "Agreed. I'll rally my men and brief the Saxonians. We'll be ready to move out within a few minutes.

With that, he spurred his horse and galloped off, his saber flashing in the sunlight as he rode to gather his troops. I turned back to my men, seeing the mix of exhaustion and determination in their eyes. They had already been through hell today, but I knew they would not falter now, not with so much riding on our actions.

"Grenziers!" I called out, my voice ringing with authority. "Reform the line! Check your ammunition and ready yourselves - we'll be the first bastards down there, mark my words!"

A ragged cheer rose from the Grenziers as they hastened to obey, their weariness forgotten in the face of this new challenge. I watched with pride as they fell into formation, their movements crisp and precise despite the toll of the day's fighting. As I surveyed my Grenziers, I felt pride rising within me. They were a ragtag bunch, to be sure - their uniforms were tattered and stained, their faces grimy with dirt and blood. Many of them sported bandages hastily wrapped around wounds.

But beneath the grime and the weariness, I saw something else—a fierce, unyielding spirit that refused to be broken—that unique, southern Auriscan spirit that seemed undaunted—always.

I had only been their commander for a short time, thrust into the role by the twists of fate and the fortunes, but already, I was proud.

In moments, the dragoons rode up alongside us, their mounts snorting and stamping eagerly. Major Miroslavios was at their head, his face set with grim determination.

"Ready, Kaelitz?" he called out, his voice carrying over the din of preparations.

I nodded, drawing my saber and raising it high. "Ready, Major! Grenzers, forward march!"

A Descent into Darkness

With a resounding roar, the Grenzers and Saxonian dragoons surged forward, a tide of determined men rushing down the hillside towards the chaos below. The ground shook beneath the infantry's thundering, pounding boots, a drumbeat of impending doom for the beleaguered Kholodians.

As we charged, the scene unfolded like a hellish tapestry woven from smoke, fire, and blood. The valley was shrouded in a thick haze, the acrid stench of gunpowder and burnt flesh assaulting our nostrils. Cannon fire echoed in a relentless symphony, each boom followed by the whistle of iron round shot and the eruption of earth and bodies where they struck. Explosions echoed from in front of us and behind us as howitzer rounds whistled overhead, sending shrapnel shredding through flesh and bone as they burst amidst the closely-packed ranks. The screams of wounded and injured men pierced the air, a haunting chorus mingling with the combatants' defiant battle cries.

Through gaps in the billowing smoke ahead of us, I caught glimpses of the desperate struggle raging across the field. Valtorean and Kholodian soldiers clashed in brutal hand-to-hand combat, bayonets flashing and sabers gleaming amidst the press of bodies. The ground was littered with the detritus of war - broken muskets, shattered wheels, and the twisted remains of men and horses—the two fluttering banners - the Valtorean War Eagle, clashing violently against the Kholodian red-and-white wolf banner.

But our focus was on the Kholodian left flank, where their breastworks stood as a formidable barrier against our advance. The earthen fortifications bristled with the barrels of muskets and the glint of sharpened stakes, and we closed the distance; the Kholodians unleashed a blistering volley, a hail of lead tearing through our ranks. Men stumbled and fell, some pitching forward to be trampled beneath the feet of their comrades, others clutching at grievous wounds as they crumpled to the blood-soaked earth.

Beside me, one of my lieutenants, Janus, let out a sharp cry as a musket ball found its mark right in his head - sending brain matter and bone splattering to anyone behind us. I gritted my teeth and pressed on, not daring to look back, knowing that to stop now would invite death.

We Grenzers followed close behind, our bayonets fixed and our faces set with grim determination. We slammed into the Kholodians like a human battering ram, jumping over the breastworks - the exhausted defenders were the same foes we had routed moments ago, having barely gotten a break, as the fighting quickly became brutal and intimate, a whirlwind of stabbing bayonets, slashing sabers, and the crunch of bone beneath rifle butts.

The melee within the breastworks was a maelstrom of savagery and desperation. Kholodian and Valtorean soldiers grappled and slashed at each other with bayonets and sabers; their faces contorted in snarls of rage and pain. The close confines of the fortifications turned the battle into a claustrophobic nightmare, where every step was treacherous and every moment brought the risk of a deadly blow.

I found myself at the heart of this brutal clash, my saber flashing as I parried and thrust, seeking to hold the line alongside my men. The old wound in my arm throbbed with each jarring impact, and my damaged eye made it difficult to track the swirling chaos of the fight. But I refused to yield, drawing upon every ounce of skill and determination I possessed to keep at the front.

A burly Kholodian soldier loomed before me, his bayonet lunging for my throat. I twisted aside at the last moment, feeling the cold kiss of steel grazing my neck as I brought my saber around in a vicious backhand slash. The blade bit deep into the man's shoulder, eliciting a howl before another Grenzier stabbed him - one I recognized as Székely.

These poor souls - left with no option, began to break and rout - towards the last bastion of Kholodian resistance—the city of Valkia.

As the Kholodian left flank crumbled under the relentless onslaught of the Grenzers and Saxonian dragoons, the situation across the rest of the frontline remained dire. The open ground surrounding the city of Valkia had become a killing field, where Valtorean battalions struggled to advance in the face of withering fire from the Kholodian defenses.

The 3rd Stadtenmark Infantry Battalion in the center found themselves pinned down in a shallow depression, their ranks decimated by the incessant barrage of artillery and musket fire. The regimental colors, tattered and stained with the blood of fallen comrades, fluttered defiantly amidst the carnage. Colonel Radzimir - who I could see from here, had his face streaked with grime and sweat, bellowing out orders to his men as they lay prone - providing dismal fire against the defiant Kholodian center.

To their right, the 7th Cavalry Regiment attempted a daring charge across the open field, their hooves thundering against the earth as they surged forward. The Kholodian gunners adjusted their aim, and a hail of canister shots tore through the advancing horsemen. Horses screamed in agony as they were struck, their riders tumbling from the saddle to be trampled beneath the hooves of their comrades. The charge faltered, the surviving cavalrymen wheeling away in disarray, leaving behind a trail of broken bodies and dying steeds - a pointless assault.

The Valtorean artillery, positioned on a low rise to the rear, labored to support the beleaguered infantry. Gunners swabbed the barrels of their cannons, sweat pouring down their faces as they rammed home fresh rounds. The ground shuddered with each successive volley, the acrid smoke from the guns mingling with the thick haze that blanketed the battlefield. Despite their best efforts, the Valtorean guns struggled to silence the Kholodian rifled cannons, which were cunningly positioned and well-protected in the hills surrounding Valkia.

Sweat beaded down - as I considered our options, surveying the chaos unfolding across the battlefield; a grim realization settled upon me. The Valtorean center was on the verge of collapse, and if we did not act swiftly, the hard-fought gains on the flank would be for naught. The decision weighed heavily upon my shoulders, but there was no time for hesitation. With a rallying cry, I gathered the remnants of the Grenzers and Saxonian dragoons; our ranks thinned, but our spirits were unbroken.

"Forward, men! To the center!" I bellowed, my voice straining to be heard above the din of battle. "We must support our brothers-in-arms!"

A ragged cheer rose from the men as they formed behind me, their bayonets gleaming in the smoky light. We set off at a brisk pace, picking our way through the corpse-strewn field, our boots squelching in the mud and blood. The sounds of battle grew louder as we approached the beleaguered 3rd Stadtenmark Infantry on their left, flanking the dug-in Kholodians, the crack of muskets, and the boom of cannons filling the air.

As we drew near, I could see the desperation etched upon the faces of the infantrymen, their uniforms torn and stained, their eyes haunted by the horrors they had witnessed. Colonel Radzimir caught sight of our approach, his expression a mix of relief and grim determination.

With a quick series of hand signals, I deployed the Grenzers and dragoons, sending them forward in a skirmish line. We advanced cautiously, using the uneven terrain and shattered remnants of wagons and carts for cover. The Kholodian defenders, focusing on the Stadtenmark Infantry, needed to react faster to our sudden flank appearance.

The crack of our rifles joined the din of battle as we opened fire, the Grenzer marksmen picking off Kholodian officers and gunners with deadly precision. The dragoons, their carbines at the ready, provided steady, if inaccurate, fire - at least, perhaps giving the Kholodians a pause.

The sudden onslaught from our flanking maneuver caught the Kholodians off guard, momentarily faltering their defenses. Colonel Radzimir seized the opportunity, his voice ringing across the battlefield. "Forward, men of the 3rd! For Valtorea and glory!"

With a roar of determination, the Stadtenmark Infantry surged to their feet, their bayonets fixed as they charged toward the Kholodian lines. The enemy soldiers, still reeling from our attack on their flank, struggled to reorient their defenses. The clash of steel against steel rang out as the two forces collided, the Valtoreans driven forward by a desperate fury born of near-defeat.

I led the Grenzers and dragoons in a relentless advance, our rifles and carbines spitting fire as we closed in on the Kholodian positions. The air was thick with smoke and the cries of the wounded, the ground beneath our feet slick with blood and viscera. Yet we pressed on, determined to break the stalemate as we rushed in.

The Kholodian defenses began to crumble under the relentless pressure of our assault. The Stadtenmark Infantry, their spirits rekindled by our timely arrival, fought with a ferocity that bordered on madness. Bayonets flashed in the smoky haze, the clashing of steel against steel punctuated by the cries of the wounded and the dying. The Kholodian soldiers, their faces etched with grim determination, fought back with equal ferocity, unwilling to yield even an inch of ground.

But the tide had turned, and the weight of our combined forces proved too much for the beleaguered defenders. Slowly, inevitably, we pushed them back, our advance marked by the growing piles of fallen bodies and the churned, blood-soaked earth beneath our feet. The Kholodian officers' voices, hoarse from shouting commands, struggled to maintain order amidst the chaos, but it was a losing battle.

As the Kholodian center began to waver, the impact of our success rippled across the battlefield. The Valtorean artillery, their spirits buoyed by the sight of our advance, redoubled their efforts. The ground shook with the thunder of their guns, the heavy round shots smashing into the Kholodian positions with devastating effect. Chunks of earth and shattered bodies flew through the air, adding to the hellish tableau of war.

The Kholodian rifled cannons, once the bane of the Valtorean advance, fell silent one by one as hussars overran their positions. Gunners lay dead beside their shattered pieces, their blood mingling with the spilled gunpowder and smoke. The Valtorean flag, its colors tattered but still proud, fluttered in the breeze atop the captured emplacements, symboling our hard-fought victory.

With a final, desperate push, the Stadtenmark Infantry broke through the last line of Kholodian resistance. The enemy soldiers, their will to fight, shattered, turned, and fled, casting aside their weapons and gear in their haste to escape the relentless Valtorean advance. The sound of their retreating footsteps mingled with the cheers of triumph from us.

As the smoke began to clear, the full extent of our victory became apparent. The once-formidable Kholodian defenses lay in ruins, their breastworks shattered, and their trenches choked with the bodies of the fallen. The fields before Valkia, once a verdant green, were now a muddy wasteland, the earth rent and torn by the passage of thousands of boots and hooves.

In the distance, the city of Valkia loomed, its walls and towers still intact, but its aura of invincibility shattered. The Kholodian flag, still fluttering, as I sighed - the gates closed.

This battle - was still far from over.

We reconvened in a command tent just a short distance from the frontline.

I stood before a makeshift table in the command tent, a map of Valkia and its surrounding environment spread out before me. The canvas walls did little to muffle the sounds of the army camp outside—the clatter of equipment, the neighing of horses, and the low murmur of conversation among the men. The air was thick with the mingled scents of smoke, sweat, and the coppery tang of blood that clung to us all.

Colonel von Olenstross, Major Radzimir, and Major Miroslavios were gathered around the table, their faces illuminated by the flickering light of the lanterns. Von Olenstross traced his finger along the map; his brow furrowed in concentration.

"Gentlemen," he began, his voice grave, "we have won a great victory today, but the task before us remains formidable. The city of Valkia is a fortress, its walls high and its defenders determined. To take it by storm would be a costly endeavor, one that our army, weakened as it is by the day's fighting, can ill afford."

Major Radzimir, his uniform still stained with the blood and grime of battle, leaned forward, his eyes alight with a fierce determination. "With all due respect, Colonel, we cannot afford to delay. The Kholodians are reeling from our assault, their morale shattered. If we give them time to regroup and reinforce the city, our task will become more difficult."

Von Olenstross shook his head, his expression somber. "You underestimate the strength of Valkia's defenses, Major. The city is built upon a hill, its walls studded with towers and bristling with cannons. The gates are reinforced with iron - and out of the 16,000 men we had, we now number perhaps 7,000. And that is only a rough guess."

Major Miroslavios spoke up, his voice calm and measured. "Then let us not assault it head-on, Colonel. Bypass it entirely - let them starve out while we plunder the lands behind them..."

I listened to the debate, my thoughts racing as I studied the map. The city of Valkia was indeed a formidable obstacle, its defenses honed over centuries of warfare. The walls were thick and high, constructed of sturdy stone and reinforced with earthen embankments.

As the debate continued, I felt a wave of exhaustion wash over me. The day's battle had taken its toll physically and mentally, and the thought of engaging in a prolonged siege or bypassing the city altogether filled me with a deep sense of weariness. The old wound in my arm throbbed painfully, a reminder of the sacrifices I had already made in this bloody war.

With a heavy sigh, I stepped back from the table, drawing the attention of the other officers. "Gentlemen," I said, tired but firm, "let us retire for the night. We have all fought bravely today, and our men deserve a chance to rest and tend to their wounds. The question of how to proceed with Valkia can wait until tomorrow when we have clearer heads and a better understanding of our situation."

Colonel von Olenstross nodded, glaring at me before relenting. "I suppose you might be right, Kaelitz," He grunted. "We'll have a rest - and reconvene at first light."

Before taking my leave, we saluted the colonel and stepped out into the cool night air. The camp was a hive of activity, with soldiers huddled around campfires, tending to their wounds and equipment. The scent of roasting meat mingled with the acrid tang of smoke, and the low murmur of conversation filled the air as Major Miroslavios and Radzimir walked with me.

"Well, Kaelitz. I suppose that was a good first showing." Radzimir chuckled. As we walked through the camp, Radzimir's expression turned somber. "But for all our valor today, I fear it may have been for naught. Von Olenstross's tactics have been questionable at best, and now we find ourselves mired before the walls of Valkia with no clear path to victory."

Miroslavios nodded, his brow furrowed with concern. "You speak the truth, my friend. The Colonel's insistence on arriving here *first* was dangerous. We've lost too many good men already, and for what? To be stuck here, our forces depleted, while the Kholodians move throughout the rest of the theater? While - tactically, it was a victory, the Kholodians still have a massive strategical advantage..."

I listened to their complaints, my doubts weighing heavily on my mind. Our victory today had been hard-fought, but it felt hollow in the face of the challenges ahead. I gazed over to the city of Valka—Kholodian flags still fluttered defiantly in the moonlight. It stood, unbowed and unbroken, a silent testament to the long night awaited us.

"What exactly *is* the point of taking Valka? It's a needless assault." Miroslavios grumbled. "And Savior, help us if that fool thinks we can settle in for a siege. Kholodian light cavalry within a week will overrun our supply lines, and we'll be starving instead of them."

"I fear you may be right," I said, my voice low and tired. "Von Olenstross has been too reckless, too eager for glory at the expense of sound strategy. And now we find ourselves in a precarious position, our supply lines stretched thin and our men exhausted from the day's fighting."

Radzimir kicked at a clod of dirt, his frustration evident. "The idea of 'containing' the Kholodians at Freydrich's Pass failed once - and the idea we can stop them here is absurd. Massive losses which we can't replenish - and likely, another frontal charge." He grunted. The infantry major shook his head. "As much as I enjoy seizing enemy colors, this is a Valtorean war - and the men know it."

I sighed, feeling the weight of my heritage heavier upon his shoulders with each word Radzimir spoke. "You're not wrong, comrades. But remember, we are all Valtoreans," I said, lifting my chin slightly, the last glint of the sun catching the proud yet tired lines on my face. "I would remind you - not to place your sympathies with regionalistic endeavors.

Radzimir and Miroslavios exchanged glances, their expressions hardening a bit, before Miroslavios cleared his throat, "Of course, Major. None of us mean to dismiss the importance of this battle to you or your people. But, as Kroatish subjects - we think differently. We think about the liberation of our homeland from the Arkanthians - not about petty disputes in Baltiva."

Ah - so that was their angle. At last - I glared at them, anger coursing through my veins. "Petty disputes? Is that what you call the fight? The Kholodians would see the Holy Empire dissolved - and then, who would be left to care for your precious Kroatia?"

Radzimir's face reddened, and his anger was evident. "And here, I thought perhaps, we had a comrade. I should have known better."

I opened my mouth to retort, but Miroslavios stepped between us, his hands raised placatingly. "Enough, both of you. This bickering solves nothing. We are all here, fighting a common enemy. Let us focus on that."

I took a deep breath, forcing down my anger, before I nodded curtly, my jaw clenched tight as I struggled to rein in my emotions. "You're right, Miroslavios. Forgive me, Radzimir. The day's events have taken their toll on us all."

Radzimir grunted in acknowledgment, his anger still simmering beneath the surface. "Let us hope tomorrow brings clearer heads and a better path forward."

With that, we parted ways, each seeking the comfort of our tents and the brief respite that sleep might bring. But as I lay upon my cot, my mind refused to quiet, the events of the day and the words of my comrades playing repeatedly in my thoughts.

I thought back to the lands of Strossberg, to the Reichskammergericht, where the nobles and diplomats of the Empire gathered to debate and scheme. I had always believed in the idea of the Empire, in its unity and strength. But now, faced with the harsh realities of war and the disparate desires of its many subjects, I saw it clearly.

The Kroatish, the Saxonians, and the Horathians had their agendas, their dreams of autonomy or dominance, all festering under the guise of unity.

The Imperial courts buzzed with languages as diverse as the landscapes from which its people hailed—forests, mountains, rivers, and urban sprawls—all held together by the fragile threads of tradition and the iron will of the Empire's bureaucracy. Yet those threads were unraveling, worn thin by internal strife and external pressures.

Images danced before my eyes as I lay there - of what must be in Vien. Those fools, clad in gold and shadows, where aristocrats draped in silks, whispered conspiracies over goblets of wine. These were men and women divided by wealth and bloodlines who viewed their territories not as part of a collective whole but as chess pieces in a never-ending game of power. Their loyalties to the Empire were conditional, pledged only so long as it served their interests.

And was it not for those unseen actors, those unaccountable schemes and plots - I couldn't help but wonder if I would still be a free man. I had killed Duclaire and Von Lowe, and they had deserved it, those traitors with their silver tongues and duplicitous hearts.

But was my survival simply due to luck? Or was there a deeper, more sinister purpose for which the Emperor had spared me? As the moon climbed higher into the night sky, a chilling realization dawned on me. The Emperor might have reserved me for later use in his grand design. It was not mercy that stayed his hand but calculation.

The thought gnawed at me, unsettling the foundations of my faith in the Empire. Had my life been nothing more than a pawn's existence, maneuvered by those in power for unknown reasons? My loyalty had been unyielding, my sacrifices immense. Yet here I was, lying in a humble tent, no longer possessing noble title, honor - or much of anything.

The fragrances of the earth around me, mixed with the distant smell of campfires and horse leather, seemed to mock my spiraling thoughts. Every sound of the night whispered betrayal: the rustling leaves spoke of secrets kept just out of reach; the distant hoot of an owl echoed like laughter at my expense.

I woke up in the morning—my sleep had been terrible. The cold light of dawn did nothing to ease my discomfort or quiet the turmoil that had claimed my heart through the night. I rose from my cot with a stiffness that spoke more of emotional weight than physical exertion. The camp was already bustling with activity: men preparing for the day's maneuvers, the clatter of pots, and muted conversations about the upcoming strategies.

I walked towards the morning gathering, where officers and men alike shared in the sparse breakfast being distributed. The smell of brewing coffee wafted through the air, mingling with the scent of fresh mud and sweat—an odd comfort in these trying times.

As I approached, I noticed Miroslavios engaged in a heated conversation with a young lieutenant, possibly about the day's plans. Radzimir was not far off, staring into his cup as if it contained answers to the deep questions that last evening had unearthed.

Joining them without a word, I received a nod from Miroslavios and an unreadable glance from Radzimir. The tension was palpable, but so was our need for unity against adversaries beyond our campgrounds.

"We're expecting reinforcements by midday," Miroslavios finally said, breaking the silence between us. "Olenstross hasn't decided what we're to do with Valka."

"And what of the Kholodians?" I asked, "Have there been any movements on their part?"

Radzimir looked up from his contemplation. "Scouts report minor skirmishes along the forestline. A few skirmishers - likely a few routing forces who regrouped, trying to assist the trapped army in Valka," He sighed heavily, setting his cup down with a decisive thud. "It's clear they're not giving up. Not yet."

I nodded, absorbing the weight of the information. The Kholodians were tenacious, known for their guerrilla tactics and unwillingness to surrender. Even with their main force trapped, they could still cause significant harm if underestimated.

"Well, let's get to that damned meeting already." I picked up my cup, the warmth barely seeping into my cold fingers, and followed Miroslavios and Radzimir to the large tent that served as our makeshift command center.

The canvas flapped in the brisk morning wind, a constant reminder of the impermanence of our encampment.

Inside, maps were strewn across a long wooden table, weighted down by stones at each corner. Officers from various regiments clustered around, their voices a low murmur as they discussed strategy. The atmosphere was thick with tobacco smoke and the underlying scent of tension. Von Olenstross didn't look like he had slept at all.

His reddened and sharp eyes darted across the room as he absorbed every detail of the accompanying discussions. Olenstross straightened as we entered, clearing his throat with a raspy grunt that commanded attention.

"Gentlemen," Olenstross began, his voice booming across the tent, "the situation in Valka is precarious. We stand on a knife's edge between victory and a disastrous defeat."

He moved to the map, his fingers tracing the lines marking our position and that of the Kholodians. With a pointed finger, he stabbed at the town of Valka, encircled in red. "Here! This is where we must strike. They are weakened and disorganized by our previous assaults. One solid push could tip the scales in our favor."

The Kroatish commanders exchanged uneasy glances before Radizimir stepped forward. His face was lined with the scars of many battles, his eyes weary yet resolute. "Colonel Olenstross," he said cautiously, "we risk much with an aggressive push. Our men are tired; our resources are stretched thin. Perhaps it is wiser to withdraw now, regroup, and re-strategize for a more favorable engagement."

Murmurs of agreement fluttered through some sections of the tent while others whispered dissent. The debate grew heated as tactics and strategies were argued back and forth like merchants haggling in a market square.

I was torn, listening to each argument with a growing dread. Both options bore significant risks—assault could lead to massive casualties if it failed; withdrawal might give the Kholodians time to regroup and strengthen their positions, possibly prolonging the war and costing more lives in the long run. Every decision seemed to balance on a razor's edge, and every outcome was soaked in blood.

Von Olenstross raised his hands, demanding silence. The clamor gradually died down until only the sound of the wind against the canvas walls remained. He looked around, sighing.

"We do not have the luxury of time," Olenstross said firmly. "Every moment we delay, the Kholodians fortify Valka further. Our spies confirm they're weak now; this might be our only chance to break them before they receive reinforcements."

A heavy silence settled over the tent. Each man seemed to wrestle with his thoughts, weighing lives against strategic gains. It was a grim calculus—the kind that haunts soldiers long after the war is done.

Finally, I spoke up, my voice rough from disuse that morning. "Perhaps - we ought to go around. Bypass them - and strike into the heart of their land. Stop reinforcements from flooding through." The suggestion hung in the air, unexpected yet bold. For a moment, all eyes turned towards me, assessing the viability of such a maneuver.

Von Olenstross paused, his expression unreadable. Then, slowly, he began to nod, the gears visibly turning in his head as he considered the implications. "A flanking operation," he murmured, almost to himself. "Through where? The Freydrich Pass is guarded - and I would wager it would take a week at least to go through..."

"Then, we head southward through the Zaroska Gorge."

The room paused. It was audacious - it was bold. The mere mention of the Zaroska Gorge drew a sharp intake of breath from those gathered. Known among the soldiers for its treacherous paths and the legends that haunted its rocky cliffs, the gorge was a narrow funnel into a sprawling, mist-shrouded marshland, hemmed in by towering mountains whose peaks seemed to scrape the very heavens. This was no ordinary route; it was a gambit of desperation and daring in equal measure.

"The Zaroska Gorge?" Radizimir repeated, skepticism etching his voice. "It's a death trap. The marshes at its end are riddled with sinkholes, and the cliffs are prone to landslides..."

Von Olenstross's eyes narrowed slightly, his gaze intense as he addressed the concerns. "Yes, it is dangerous," he conceded, his voice steady and confident despite the underlying risks. "But it also means the Kholodians will not expect us there. It is lightly defended, if at all. They, too, fear the gorge's wrath and its treacherous terrain."

An uneasy silence fell upon the room as commanders considered this unexpected proposal. The path through Zaroska Gorge was fraught with natural dangers that could decimate their forces before they met the enemy. However, it also offered a direct route into the heart of Kholodia, bypassing heavily fortified positions along traditional routes.

"We can send scouts ahead," suggested one of the younger officers, breaking the tense quiet. "They can find us a safe passage through. Such as the Grenziers..."

Von Olenstross nodded slightly, processing the contribution. "The Grenziers are the only light infantry we have... Prepare a detachment immediately," he ordered, his voice unwavering, cutting through any remaining hesitations like a sword through silk.

A murmur of assent rippled through the tent as officers began to mobilize, dispatching orders and rallying their troops with newfound purpose. Despite the risks, there was a palpable surge of energy—a mixture of fear and excitement—that charged the air.

I watched plans crystallize, feeling the weight of our decision. We were committing to a dangerous gamble, but it might just allow us to outmaneuver the Kholodians in a way they least expected.

"And what about you sir?" I asked, von Olenstross sighing.

"I will have to explain myself to the Emperor and likely hold off high command..." he began. The sweat on his face, though, told something different: cowardice.

But I didn't confront him - oh no. Let him run back to Rega's safety - it just meant one less rival in my way.

Total War

The southward march to the Zaroska Gorge was grueling, fraught with natural perils, and the constant threat of Kholodian ambush. The landscape seemed to conspire against us, the terrain growing increasingly hostile with each passing mile. The once-fertile fields and gently rolling hills gave way to barren, rocky outcroppings, where twisted, stunted trees clung tenaciously to the thin soil. The sun beat down mercilessly from a cloudless sky, its relentless heat

sapping the strength of men and beasts alike.

Dust billowed in choking clouds from beneath the feet of the marching soldiers, coating their uniforms in a fine layer of grime and turning their faces into masks of exhaustion. The clatter of equipment and the creak of leather mingled with the labored breathing of the men as they struggled beneath the weight of their packs and weapons. Horses, their coats streaked with sweat, strained to pull the heavy artillery pieces over the uneven ground, their hooves slipping on the loose shale.

The Grenzier pickets, ranging ahead of the central column, brought back discouraging reports. The way ahead was a treacherous maze of narrow defiles and steep, crumbling slopes, where a single misstep could send a man tumbling to his death. The few streams they encountered were little more than trickles, their waters brackish and unpalatable. Game was scarce, and the foraging parties returned empty-handed, their faces gaunt with hunger.

As the army wound deeper into the foothills, the air grew thick with a sense of foreboding. The towering peaks of the mountains loomed ever closer, their jagged silhouettes knife-edged. In the distance, the entrance to the Zaroska Gorge was a gaping maw, its shadowed depths seeming to swallow the light. The men muttered uneasily among themselves, speaking of the dark legends that clung to this place—tales of ancient battles, of vengeful spirits, and of malevolent creatures that stalked the unwary.

I rode at the head of the column, my mount's hooves kicking up puffs of dust as we picked our way along the narrow track. Beside me, Radzimir and Miroslavios were grim-faced, their eyes constantly scanning the surrounding hills for any sign of danger. We had left a token force to maintain the siege of Valkia, but most of our strength was committed to this desperate gamble, and we all knew the stakes.

The landscape became even more ominous as we drew closer to the gorge. The hills pressed close on either side, their slopes strewn with jagged boulders and scree. Stunted, twisted pines clung to the rockfaces, their branches gnarled and reaching like skeletal fingers. The air was still and stifling, heavy with the scent of dust and decay, and the silence was oppressive, broken only by the muffled clop of hooves and the occasional clatter of loose stones tumbling down the hillsides. As we reached the mouth of the gorge, an icy wind whistled through the narrow defile, carrying with it a chill that seemed to seep into our very bones. The towering cliffs rose on either side like the walls of a tomb, their strata twisted and buckled by ancient cataclysms. Overhead, the sky was a narrow ribbon of blue, barely visible between the encroaching stone walls.

I signaled a halt, and the column ground to a stop, the men sagging wearily against their packs. Scouts were sent to probe the gorge's depths, and the shadows soon swallowed their lithe forms. As we waited for their return, an eerie stillness settled over the assembled host, broken only by the uneasy stamping of hooves and the low murmur of nervous conversation.

Minutes stretched into hours as the sun climbed higher in the sky, its heat beating mercilessly upon the exposed rock. Sweat trickled down my back beneath my uniform, and my mouth was dry and gritty with dust. At last, the scouts returned, their faces grim and their eyes haunted.

"The way ahead is clear," reported the lead scout, a grizzled veteran named Haufler. "But there are signs of recent Kholodian activity. Campfire ashes, hoof prints, and discarded supplies. They may be lying in wait further ahead."

I glanced at Radzimir and Miroslavios, seeing my concerns mirrored in their eyes. If the Kholodians knew our presence, our gambit was in jeopardy. But we had come too far to turn back now.

"We press on," I said, my voice sounding hollow in the oppressive stillness. "But be on your guard. The enemy may be closer than we think."

With a nod, Haufler melted back into the shadows, and the column began to move once more, winding its way deeper into the gorge. The walls pressed ever closer, the path narrowing until it was little more than a rocky ledge, with a sheer drop on one side plunging into darkness. The air grew colder as we penetrated deeper, and a clammy mist began to rise from the depths, swirling around our feet and obscuring the way ahead.

Suddenly, a shout rang out from the column's rear, followed by the sharp crack of musket fire. Cries of alarm and pain echoed off the gorge's walls as the Kholodians sprang their ambush, hidden marksmen pouring a deadly hail of lead into our ranks from the heights above.

"Defensive positions!" I roared, spurring my horse forward. "Return fire!"

Chaos erupted as the Kholodian ambush tore into our ranks. Men screamed and fell, blood splattering the rocky ground as the crack of musket fire echoed off the narrow walls. Horses reared and plunged in panic, their hooves lashing out and adding to the confusion. The acrid stench of gunpowder mingled with the coppery tang of blood, and the gorge was filled with a swirling haze of smoke and mist.

I leaped from my saddle, hitting the ground in a crouch as a musket ball whined past my ear. Around me, the men were scrambling for cover, diving behind boulders and pressing themselves against the cliff faces as they frantically sought to return fire. The Kholodian marksmen were well-concealed, their positions hidden among the jagged rocks and twisted pines that clung to the heights above.

"Radzimir, Miroslavios!" I shouted over the din of battle. "Take your men and scale those cliffs! We must dislodge the enemy before they pick us apart!"

The two officers nodded grimly, already rallying their troops. Radzimir led a contingent of infantry up a narrow, winding path, their lithe forms darting from cover to cover as they climbed. Miroslavios and his Kroatish hussars, bogged down in the swamp, resorted to using carbines to support the infantry as they pushed forward.

I turned my attention to the rest of the column, ordering the men to form a defensive perimeter. The artillery crews wheeled their guns into position, the heavy barrels swiveling to face the heights. With a roar, the six-pounder cannons opened fire, sending explosive shells arcing up to burst among the Kholodian positions, showering the hillsides with deadly fragments.

The battle raged on, the narrow confines of the gorge turning it into a brutal, close-quarters affair. The Kholodians fought with a savage determination, clinging to their positions even as the Grenziers and Valtorean infantry closed in. The crack of muskets and the clash of steel echoed off the walls, mingling with the cries of the wounded and dying. It sounded as if we were surrounded on all sides - but in truth, it was an ambush formed together in an L-shape. Morale was declining - men weren't moving - the tell-tale signs of confusion and disorder.

So, I rushed forward, finding myself in the thick of the fighting as I rallied confused and disoriented men, my saber flashing above. The wound in my arm throbbed, but I pushed the pain aside, focusing on the desperate struggle at hand.

Slowly, inch by bloody inch, we began to turn the tide. The artillery fire and the relentless pressure of Radzimir and Miroslavios's troops took their toll, and the Kholodian fire began to slacken. The enemy marksmen fell back, yielding the heights as they sought to escape the vengeful bayonets of the Stadtenmark infantry, who surged forward, bayonets gleaming as they drove the enemy before them. The narrow gorge ran red with blood, the bodies of the fallen carpeting the stony ground.

I pressed forward with the main body of our troops, the men's spirits buoyed by the sight of the Kholodians in retreat. The artillery continued its relentless barrage, explosive shells bursting among the fleeing enemy, sowing further chaos and destruction. The air was thick with smoke and the stench of death, but we pushed on, determined to break through the ambush and secure the passage. But - with the conditions of the swamp, no cavalry could manage to chase them down - it was enough, though, I reckoned - they were likely to outright dissolve in cohesion and flee all the way back to Moskova.

I surveyed the aftermath of the battle, taking grim stock of our losses. Too many good men had fallen, their lives spent to purchase this bloody victory. But we had prevailed, and the way ahead now lay open.

Radzimir and Miroslavios rejoined me, their uniforms stained with sweat and gore. Radzimir's face was etched with a fierce, almost feral satisfaction, while Miroslavios looked haggard, the toll of the fighting weighing heavily upon him. Together, we set about tending to the wounded and gathering our dead for proper burial.

As the column reformed and prepared to march on, I couldn't shake the feeling that this was only the beginning. The Zaroska Gorge had tested us, extracting a heavy price in blood, but I knew that more significant trials lay ahead. The Kholodians would not relinquish their lands easily, and every mile we advanced would be bitterly contested.

With a heavy heart, I mounted my horse and signaled the advance. The men fell in behind me, their faces grim and determined. We had passed through the crucible of the gorge, but the actual test of our resolve was yet to come. As we marched deeper into Kholodian territory, I could only pray that our gambit would prove successful and that our sacrifices would not be in vain.

The sun beat mercilessly as we emerged from the gorge, the rocky defile giving way to a desolate, wind-scoured plain. In the distance, a line of jagged peaks marched across the horizon, their snowcapped summits glinting beneath the harsh light. Somewhere beyond those mountains lay our objective, the heart of Kholodia itself.

As we crossed the barren expanse, I couldn't shake the foreboding that gripped me. The Zaroska Gorge had been surpassed, and now we were deep in enemy lands.

With the Zaroska Gorge behind us, we pushed deeper into the Kholodian heartland, a vast expanse of rolling hills, dense forests, and scattered villages that had thus far been untouched by the ravages of war. The land was rich and fertile, a patchwork of golden wheat fields and lush pastures where herds of cattle and sheep grazed contentedly. The air was sweet with the scent of ripening crops and the hum of insects, a stark contrast to the acrid stench of smoke and blood that had haunted the gorge.

As we marched, I couldn't help but marvel at the beauty of the countryside, even as I steeled myself for the grim task ahead. We had not come as liberators or saviors but as a scourge, a vengeful tide sweeping across the land and leaving only ash and ruin in its wake. It was a bitter necessity, a cruel calculus of war that demanded we strike at the very heart of the enemy's power to bleed them dry and shatter their will to resist.

Our first target was a small town nestled in the foothills of the mountains. It was a bustling hub of trade and commerce that served as a vital link in the Kholodian supply chain. The town was ringed by sturdy timber and stone walls, with watchtowers standing sentinel at regular intervals. The alarm was raised as we approached, and the gates were swiftly barred against us.

I signaled for the Grenziers to deploy, and they fanned out in a wide arc, their forms melting into the surrounding woods. Radzimir and his infantry formed up in a tight column behind me, their bayonets fixed and their faces grim with determination. Miroslavios and his cavalry took up position on the flanks, ready to sweep in and cut off any attempt at escape.

With a nod to the artillery crews, the bombardment began. The heavy guns roared to life, their shells arcing over the walls to burst among the buildings with devastating effect. Flames leaped skyward as thatched roofs ignited, and the air was rent by the screams of the wounded and dying. The defenders returned fire from the walls, their muskets cracking and spurting flame, but the Grenzier sharpshooters picked them off with ruthless efficiency.

As the barrage continued, I led the infantry forward in a tight wedge, our boots pounding against the packed earth. The gates shuddered and splintered under the relentless pounding of the guns, and with a final, tortured groan, they burst inward. We surged through the breach, bayonets leveled, and the desperate hand-to-hand fighting began.

The town's streets were a maze of narrow alleys and winding lanes, where every window and doorway concealed a potential threat. The Kholodian defenders fought with savage determination, contesting every inch of ground with blade and bullet. Civilians sheltered in their homes as we quickly seized the small, largely undefended town - the sole defenders being a tiny garrison of national militia.

With the Kholodian defenders dispatched and the town firmly under our control, I halted the fighting. The men were exhausted, their uniforms stained with sweat and blood, but their eyes showed a fierce light of triumph. We had struck our first blow against the enemy, and the taste of victory was sweet upon our tongues, as brief as the battle had been.

As the soldiers set about securing the perimeter and tending to the wounded, I summoned Radzimir and Miroslavios to the town square, a broad, cobblestone expanse ringed by elegant buildings of whitewashed stone and timber. The burghers' homes and shops, with their gabled roofs and ornate facades, spoke of the prosperity and plenty that had reigned, as we discussed what to do with the Kholodian border town.

Miroslavios was the first to speak, his voice thick with a grim enthusiasm. "We should make an example of this place," he growled, his eyes alight with a feral intensity. "Burn it to the ground and put the civilians to the sword. Let the Kholodians see the price of defiance."

I felt a chill run down my spine at his words, a cold knot of revulsion twisting in my gut. I had seen too much of the savage cruelty of war, the wanton destruction, and the needless slaughter of the innocent. No matter the provocation, I would not be a party to such barbarism.

Radzimir, ever the pragmatist, interjected. "The town is a valuable prize," he pointed out, his voice calm and measured. "It is a nexus of trade and commerce, with storehouses full of grain and other supplies. We should seize what we can to provision our forces and deny the enemy its use."

I considered their words, weighing the competing demands of necessity and conscience. The town was a rich prize, its wealth and resources a tempting target. But to simply loot and pillage, to leave the civilians to the tender mercies of the soldiers, was a step too far.

"We will take what we need," I declared, my voice ringing across the square. "Food, supplies, and anything of military value. But the civilians are to be left untouched. They are not our enemy, and we will not stoop to the level of common brigands. Anyone who decides to start plundering - will be court-martialed and shot."

The storehouses were emptied of grain and provisions, and the livestock was herded away to feed our hungry troops. Skilled craftsmen were conscripted to repair our equipment and fashion new supplies. But true to my word, the civilians were mainly left unmolested, watched over by a contingent of stern-faced officers to ensure discipline was maintained.

Miroslavios grumbled at this, his eyes still alight with that unsettling look of his, but he deferred to my command. Radzimir merely nodded, his pragmatic nature satisfied by our secured resources.

As night fell, I retired to the mayor's residence, its opulent furnishings and well-stocked larder a welcome respite from the hardships of the march. But sleep eluded me even as I sank into the plush embrace of the feather bed. My mind raced with the implications of our victory and the challenges that yet lay ahead.

We had struck a blow against the Kholodians, but it was a mere pinprick compared to the full might of their armies. They would rally swiftly, marshaling their forces to drive us back and reclaim what we had taken. Our only hope was to press the advantage, strike hard and fast before they could regain their balance, to go deeper—to twist the knife deeper.

But as I lay there in the darkness, staring up at the ornate plasterwork of the ceiling, a deeper unease gnawed at me. The thrill of battle, the rush of victory, was a heady thing, but it could not entirely mask the bitter aftertaste of what we were doing. And we, the soldiers on the front lines, were but pawns in their game, our lives and honor sacrificed on the altar of their ambition.

Sleep finally claimed me in the early morning hours, but it was a fitful, troubled slumber haunted by visions of blood and fire. And when dawn broke, casting its pale light over the occupied town, I rose with a heavy heart, steeling myself for the trials to come.

We set out at first light, leaving nothing to hold the town and guard our rear. The men were in high spirits, buoyed by our victory and the prospect of further glory. They marched with a spring in their step, their voices raised in bawdy songs and boisterous laughter.

But as we pressed deeper into Kholodian territory, the mood shifted. The land grew wilder and more rugged, the villages fewer and farther between. The lush farmlands gave way to dense forests and craggy hills, where the only signs of habitation were the occasional charcoal burner's hut or lonely woodsman's cottage.

As we marched deeper into the Kholodian heartland, an eerie sense of familiarity began to creep over me. The dense forests, with their towering pines and carpets of needle-strewn loam, the craggy hills that rose abruptly from the earth, their slopes clad in scrubby brush and jagged outcroppings of weathered stone - it all stirred a deep unease within me, a nagging sense of déjà vu that I couldn't quite place.

The realization struck me like a thunderbolt when we crested a particularly steep rise, the land falling away before us in a sweeping vista of mist-shrouded valleys and distant, snow-capped peaks. I had been here months ago when the fortunes of war had seen me a captive in Kholodian hands, and I was released.

I felt a shudder run through me, a cold sweat beading on my brow despite the chill of the mountain air. Beside me, Radzimir cast a questioning glance, noting my sudden pallor. "Something wrong, Major?" he asked, his voice low and concerned.

I shook my head, not trusting myself to speak. The memories were too raw, too close to the surface. I spurred my horse forward, eager to put some distance between myself and the ghosts of my past.

As we descended into the valley, the signs of the Kholodian industry became more apparent. Tucked away in the folds of the hills were sprawling granaries and storehouses, their weathered timber walls bulging with the bounty of the harvest. Plumes of smoke rose from charcoal kilns and smelting furnaces, the air thick with the acrid stench of burning pine and molten metal.

I knew all too well the importance of these installations. They were the beating heart of the Kholodian war machine, supplying the food and materials that kept their armies in the field. And they were ripe for the taking, vulnerable and exposed.

With a calculating, smug smile, I turned to Radzimir and Miroslavios. "Deploy the skirmishers," I ordered, my voice hard and cold. "Burn the granaries, the storehouses, anything that might aid the enemy. Leave nothing standing."

They nodded, their faces alight with fierce anticipation. The men were unleashed like hounds on the scent, fanning through the valley with torches and tinder. Soon, the valley was ablaze, the granaries and storehouses engulfed in roaring flames that painted the sky a lurid orange. Thick black smoke billowed upwards, carrying the acrid stench of burning grain and timber. The men moved methodically through the conflagration, their faces lit by the hellish glow, as they ensured the destruction was complete.

I watched it all unfold with grim satisfaction, the cold knot in my gut easing somewhat as I witnessed the fruits of our grim labor. This was the ugly reality of war, stripped of all its glory and romance - a brutal calculus of deprivation and attrition, of bleeding the enemy dry by any means necessary.

But even as I savored this fleeting moment of triumph, I couldn't shake the unease that had gripped me since we entered this all too familiar valley. The ghosts of my past seemed to lurk in every shadow, their spectral fingers clutching at my mind, and their whispers echoed in the crackle and roar of the flames. I felt wrong for all of this - but it had to be done. At least, we were not monsters like the Arkinthians, who enslaved women and children, or butchered them outright.

As the last of the storehouses collapsed into smoldering ruin, I gave the order to move out. We had tarried here too long already, and the Kholodians would not be slow to respond to this provocation. We needed to press on, to strike deeper into their territory before they could muster their forces and bring their full might to bear against us.

We marched through the night, the glow of the burning valley fading behind us as we wound our way deeper into the mountains. The men were subdued by the adrenaline of the raid, giving way to a bone-deep weariness. They trudged along in sullen silence; their faces smudged with soot and their uniforms reeking of smoke.

Two weeks had passed since we set out from the smoldering ruins of that first Kholodian valley, and in that time, we had carved a swath of destruction through the heart of the enemy's territory. The land lay ravaged in our wake, a blighted wasteland of charred fields shattered villages, and broken bodies. We moved like a scythe through the ripening wheat, leaving only stubble and ashes behind us.

Each day brought new targets for our relentless advance. We struck at supply depots and armories, burning them to the ground and seizing their stores for our use. We sabotaged bridges, severing the arteries that fed the Kholodian war machine. We ambushed enemy patrols and raiding parties, leaving their shattered remnants to the crows and the wolves. Crowds of refugees headed for safety - towards Moskova.

A few odd serfs had even joined up with us in rebellion. But, just as often as they would join - we would fight vengeful militiamen who wanted us to be driven out.

But for all our successes, for all the damage we inflicted, I couldn't shake the feeling that we were merely flailing in the dark, lashing out blindly at an unseen foe. We had no way of knowing the true impact of our actions, no means of gauging how deeply we had wounded the Kholodian beast. The front lines were distant, a world away from our guerrilla campaign in the hinterlands, and the news that trickled back to us was sporadic and unreliable.

Still, we pressed on, driven by a grim determination to see our task through to the bitter end. The men were exhausted, their uniforms tattered and their faces gaunt from the ceaseless marching and fighting, but they never wavered in their resolve. They were veterans now, tempered by the crucible of war, and they would follow me into the very jaws of hell if I asked it of them.

Radzimir and Miroslavios were my constant companions, having become somewhat subjugated - they were eager to get home, to make a name for themselves - and were more than happy to let me pursue glory. These style of lieutenants in this campaign of fire and blood were invaluable. Miroslavios's hussars ranged ahead of the main force, scouting out targets and gathering intelligence, while Radzimir's infantry formed the backbone of our striking power, their bayonets, and bullets reaping a grim harvest wherever we went.

Yet even as we moved from triumph to triumph, I couldn't shake the sense of unease that had haunted me since that first fateful valley. The specter of my past loomed ever larger in my mind, a dark shadow that threatened to engulf me at any moment. I found myself staring at shadows, my hand flying to my saber at the slightest sound, my nerves stretched to the breaking point by the constant strain of the campaign.

It all came to a head one evening as we made camp in a sheltered glen, the men huddled around their meager fires as they tended to their wounds and cleaned their weapons. I sat apart from the others, staring into the dancing flames as I tried to still the tumult in my mind.

Miroslavios approached me, his face etched with concern as he settled himself on the log beside me. He offered me a tin cup of steaming coffee, the rich aroma mingling with the woodsmoke and the sharp tang of pine. I accepted it gratefully, wrapping my hands around its warmth as I took a long, slow sip.

"You've been quiet lately, Major," Miroslavios said, his voice low and gentle. "More so than usual. Is everything alright?"

I hesitated, weighing my words carefully. Miroslavios was a good man, a loyal friend, and a skilled officer, but there were some burdens that could not be shared, some wounds that ran too deep for mere words to heal.

"Just tired," I said at last, my voice sounding hollow even to my own ears. "It's been a long campaign, and there's still so much to do."

Miroslavios nodded, his eyes searching my face for the truth behind the lie. "We're all tired, Major. But there's something more troubling you; I can see it in your eyes."

I sighed, my shoulders slumping as the weight of it all seemed to press down upon me. "I know, Miroslavios. And I'm grateful for that, truly. But some ghosts are meant to be faced alone."

He was silent for a long moment, the crackling of the fire the only sound in the stillness of the glen. When he spoke again, his voice was heavy with understanding. "You aren't meant for this type of warfare." He said.

I sat in silence for a long moment, Miroslavios's words hanging heavy in the air between us. He was right, of course. This campaign of terror and destruction, this guerrilla warfare in the enemy's hinterlands - it was not what I had trained for, not what I had envisioned when I first took up the sword in service to Valtorea.

My thoughts drifted back to those early days when the war had seemed a noble and glorious endeavor. I had marched off to battle with a spring in my step and a song in my heart, filled with dreams of valor and victory. But the reality had been far different - a nightmare of blood and mud, of screaming horses and shattered bodies. And now, here I was, leading a band of raiders deep in Kholodian territory, burning and pillaging like a common brigand.

"You're right," I said at last, my voice heavy with resignation. "I'm a soldier, not a butcher. But what choice do we have? The Kholodians must be stopped by any means necessary."

Miroslavios nodded, his face etched with a grim understanding. "I know, Major. But at what cost? To them and to ourselves? When this war is over, when the killing is done - will we even recognize the men we've become?"

I had no answer for that. The weight of it all seemed to press down upon me, a leaden mantle of guilt and doubt. I thought of the villages we had burned, the lives we had shattered in our relentless advance. I thought of the hatred and fear I had seen in the eyes of the Kholodian peasants, the way they had cowered before us as we rode through their shattered homes.

Was this indeed the price of victory? To become the very thing we sought to destroy, to sacrifice our own humanity on the altar of necessity? I didn't know anymore. All I knew was that we had to press on to see this bitter task through to the end.

I drained the last of my coffee and rose to my feet, my joints aching from the long days in the saddle. "Get some rest, Miroslavios," I said, clapping him on the shoulder. "We have a long march ahead of us tomorrow."

He nodded, his eyes still shadowed with concern as he watched me go. I made my way through the camp; the men huddled around their fires, their faces gaunt and haunted in the flickering light. They looked to me for guidance, for strength, but I had none to give them. I was as lost as they were, adrift in a sea of blood and doubt.

I retired to my tent, the canvas walls flapping in the chill night breeze. I lay on my cot, staring up at the shadows dancing on the ceiling, my mind awhirl with dark thoughts. Sleep eluded me, as it so often did these days, and I found myself reaching for the battered flask I kept tucked next to me.

I could only hope it would end soon.

The Final Battle

The sun hung low on the horizon, casting long shadows across the cold landscape as I emerged from my tent, the weight of the campaign heavy on my shoulders. The men were gathered around the campfires, their faces drawn and haggard, the toll of the long weeks of raiding and plundering etched in every line and furrow.

I made my way through the camp, the murmur of low conversation and the clink of tin cups against stones echoing in the still evening air. The scent of woodsmoke and roasting meat mingled with the ever-present tang of sweat and horse, a pungent reminder of the hard miles we had traveled and the battles we had fought.

As I approached the central fire, where Radzimir and Miroslavios huddled in close conversation, a sense of unease prickled at the back of my neck. The men were restless, their eyes darting and their hands never far from their weapons. The easy camaraderie that had marked the early days of the campaign was gone, replaced by a sullen, brooding tension that set my teeth on edge.

Radzimir looked up as I drew near, his face grim in the flickering firelight. "Major," he said, his voice low and urgent. "We have a problem."

I felt a cold knot of dread settle in the pit of my stomach. "What is it?" I asked, dreading the answer even as I spoke the words.

Miroslavios cleared his throat, his eyes flicking nervously to the gathered men. "The scouts have returned from their reconnaissance. The Kholodians have mustered a response. An army of 14,000 men, well-equipped and heavily armed, is marching to intercept us. They'll be upon us within a day, two at most. Well before we make it to pressure Moskova."

I closed my eyes, the weight of the news settling over me like a leaden shroud. 14,000 men. It was a force that dwarfed our own, a vast host of fresh troops and seasoned veterans against our ragged band of raiders and guerrillas. The odds were stacked heavily against us, and every man in the camp knew it.

I looked out over the sea of faces, the men who had followed me through hell and back, who had trusted me to lead them to victory. They were gaunt and hollow-eyed, their uniforms tattered and their spirits worn thin by the long weeks of constant fighting.

I made my way to the center of the camp, where Radzimir and Miroslavios were already gathered around a makeshift map table. They looked up as I approached, their expressions somber.

"They're less than a day's march away," Radzimir said without preamble, his finger tracing a line across the map. "If we break camp now and push hard, we might be able to slip past them and reach Moskova before they can cut us off."

I studied the map, my brow furrowed in thought. Moskova, the Kholodian capital, lay just ten miles to the north, tantalizingly close after weeks of hard marching and bitter fighting. Its capture would be a devastating blow to the enemy, a dagger thrust into the very heart of their power.

But as I looked out over the camp, at the ragged, exhausted men who had followed me so far and so faithfully, I knew that it was not to be. They were at the end of their endurance, worn down by the ceaseless grind of the campaign, and now, flush with the spoils of their plundering, they had lost the will to fight.

I could see it in their eyes as they gathered around, a sullen, mutinous glint that spoke of a deep desire to be done with this war, to return to their homes and families with the riches they had seized. They had tasted the fruits of victory, but the bitter reality of the coming battle was a cup they would not drink from.

"We can't fight them," I said at last, my voice heavy with resignation. "The men won't stand. They're too tired, too demoralized. If we try to force them to face the Kholodians now, they'll break and run at the first sign of trouble."

Radzimir's face darkened with anger, his hand clenching into a fist on the map table. "So we're just going to turn tail and run? After all we've done, all we've accomplished? Moskova is right there, within our grasp!"

Miroslavios laid a calming hand on his shoulder, his eyes meeting mine with a look of grim understanding. "The Major is right," he said softly. "We've pushed them as far as they'll go. We'll lose them entirely if we ask any more of them now."

I nodded, my heart heavy with the weight of the decision. "We'll head west," I said, tracing a new line on the map. "Back towards our own lines - and cut off supplies as we make our escape."

I surveyed the camp with a heavy heart, the weight of the decision settling over me like a shroud. The men were gathered around in small groups, their faces etched with a mixture of exhaustion, fear, and a simmering resentment. They had followed me this far, through the long weeks of raiding and plundering, but now, with the specter of a vastly superior Kholodian force bearing down upon us, their resolve had faltered.

I could not blame them. They were soldiers, not martyrs, and they had already given more than any commander could rightfully ask. To force them to stand and fight now, against such overwhelming odds, would be to condemn them to a slaughter.

Radzimir paced back and forth, his face twisted with frustration and anger. "We can't just abandon the campaign!" he growled, his hand clenching and unclenching on the hilt of his saber. "We've come too far, struck too deep into their heartland to turn back now."

Miroslavios shook his head, his expression somber. "We've done all we can, my friend," he said softly. "To press on now would be folly. The men are at their breaking point, and to ask any more of them would be to invite disaster."

Radzimir looked as though he might argue further, but a sharp glance from Miroslavios silenced him. He nodded curtly, his jaw clenched tight with barely suppressed rage.

I turned to face the men, my voice ringing out across the camp. "Strike the tents and saddle the horses," I commanded, my tone brooking no argument. "We ride west, towards home and safety."

A ragged cheer went up from the men, a spark of their old fire rekindled by my words. They set to work with a will, tearing down the tents and packing their gear with a speed born of desperation.

As the camp dissolved into a hive of activity, I turned back to Radzimir and Miroslavios. "I want the swiftest riders out front," I said, my mind racing as I planned our withdrawal. "They'll range ahead, scouting our path - and hopefully finding us enough food to make it back."

When we set out, the sun had barely crested the horizon, and the camp was little more than a scattering of cold ashes behind us. The men rode in grim silence, their faces set and their eyes scanning the surrounding hills for any sign of pursuit. We had left a bitter trail of destruction in our wake, and we knew the Kholodians would not be far behind, hungry for vengeance.

I rode at the head of the column, Radzimir and Miroslavios flanking me on either side. Our swiftest horsemen ranged out ahead, scouting the path and watching for any sign of ambush or encirclement. The rest of the men followed close behind, a ragged serpent of horse and steel winding its way through the rugged terrain.

The first day passed without incident, the only sound the creak of leather and the muffled thud of hooves against the hard-packed earth. We pushed the horses hard, stopping only briefly to rest and water them before pressing on again. Every man knew the stakes - if the Kholodians caught us in the open, weighed down with our plunder and exhausted from weeks of hard campaigning, it would be a slaughter.

As dusk fell, we made a hasty camp in a sheltered hollow, the men huddling close around meager fires as they tended to their mounts and wolfed down a few mouthfuls of cold rations. I sat apart from the others, staring into the dancing flames as I struggled to come to terms with the bitter reality of our retreat.

Radzimir approached, his face lined with fatigue and frustration. He squatted down beside me, his voice low and urgent. "We should have made a stand," he growled, his eyes flashing in the firelight. "Turned and fought, instead of running like whipped dogs."

I shook my head, my own exhaustion and doubt writ plain on my face. "You saw the men," I said softly. "They're at the end of their tether. To ask them to face the Kholodians now would be to ask them to die for nothing."

Radzimir looked as though he might argue further, but Miroslavios's arrival forestalled him. The Kroatish officer's face was grim as he settled himself beside us, his voice pitched low to avoid being overheard.

"The scouts have returned," he murmured, his eyes darting to the surrounding darkness. "The Kholodians are closing fast. They'll be on us by midday tomorrow, unless we can find some way to slow them down."

I nodded, my mind racing as I considered our options. We were deep in enemy territory, with no easy path to safety. If the Kholodians caught us in the open, it would be a short, brutal fight.

"We'll need to buy time," I said at last, my voice heavy with resignation. "Send out a rearguard to hold them off, while the rest of the column presses on. It's our only chance."

Radzimir and Miroslavios exchanged a grim look, the weight of my words hanging heavy between us. We all knew what I was asking - for a handful of brave men to sacrifice themselves, to buy the rest of us a chance at escape with their lives.

"I'll lead the rearguard," Radzimir said, his voice steady despite the magnitude of what he was proposing. "My infantry are slowing down the rest of the army anyways. We'll make the Kholodians pay in blood for every step."

I clasped his shoulder, my throat tight with emotion. "You're a good man, Radzimir."

He nodded curtly, his jaw set with grim determination as he rose to his feet. "Just see the rest of the lads to safety, Major. That's all the thanks I need."

I watched him go, his form soon swallowed up by the gathering darkness as he went to muster his men. Beside me, Miroslavios let out a heavy sigh, his face etched with sorrow and resignation.

"He's a brave one, that Radzimir," he murmured, shaking his head slowly. "But I fear this is a sacrifice from which there can be no return."

I said nothing, my own heart heavy with the knowledge of what I had just asked of my comrade. But there was no time for regrets, no room for second-guessing. We had to press on, to use the precious time Radzimir and his men would buy us.

As dawn broke, we struck camp and mounted up once more, the column moving out in grim silence. Behind us, in the distant hills, we could hear the crack of musket fire and the distant roar of battle as Radzimir and his men made their stand.

We rode hard through the morning, pushing the horses to the limits of their endurance. The sounds of pursuit faded behind us, lost in the rugged folds of the terrain, as we made our way urgently for the Zaroska Gorge again. My heart was heavy with the weight of leaving them behind, but I had no choice. The survival of the rest of the column depended on us pressing forward, on reaching the safety of the Zaroska Gorge before the Kholodians could catch us.

Miroslavios rode beside me, his face grim and his eyes haunted. I knew he felt the loss of Radzimir as keenly as I did. The three of us had been through so much together, had faced death and worse in the name of Valtorea. To leave one of our own to die went against every instinct, every fiber of our being.

But this was war, and war demanded sacrifices. Radzimir understood that better than anyone. He had volunteered to lead the rearguard, to give his life so that the rest of us might live. It was a debt I could never repay, a burden I would carry with me for the rest of my days.

We rode in grim silence, the only sound the pounding of hooves and the ragged breathing of exhausted men and horses. The terrain grew more rugged as we neared the gorge, the hills rising steep and jagged on either side. The path narrowed, hemmed in by towering cliffs that cast deep shadows across the rocky ground.

I felt a prickle of unease between my shoulder blades, a sense of foreboding that I couldn't quite shake. The Zaroska Gorge had been treacherous enough on our outward journey, when we'd had the element of surprise on our side. Now, with the Kholodians hot on our heels and our men demoralized and exhausted, it felt like a trap waiting to be sprung.

As if in answer to my dark thoughts, a shout rang out from the head of the column. I spurred my horse forward, Miroslavios close behind, as we raced to see what new threat had emerged.

We crested a rise and pulled up short, our hearts sinking at the sight that greeted us. The entrance to the gorge was blocked by a hastily-erected barricade, a wall of felled trees and boulders that bristled with Kholodian pikes and muskets. Behind the barricade, the cliffs rose in a series of steep terraces, each one lined with more enemy soldiers, their weapons trained on the approaching Valtorean column.

It was a masterful ambush, perfectly positioned to cut off our escape. The Kholodians must have guessed our route and sent a force ahead to lie in wait. Now they had us trapped, caught between the hammer of their pursuing army and the anvil of the gorge's defenses.

For a moment, I simply stared in numb horror, my mind reeling as I tried to come to grips with the magnitude of our plight. The Kholodians had outmaneuvered us completely, using their knowledge of the terrain and their superior numbers to deadly effect. We were trapped, caught between the jaws of a vice that threatened to crush us utterly.

Around me, the men were coming to the same grim realization. I could see it in their faces, in the way their shoulders slumped and their eyes dulled with despair. They had followed me this far, had trusted in my leadership to see them through. Now, I had led them straight into a nightmare from which there seemed no escape.

Miroslavios reined in beside me, his face ashen. "God help us," he whispered, his eyes fixed on the bristling barricade ahead. "We're done for."

I wanted to argue, to rally the men for one last desperate charge. But the words died in my throat as I surveyed the situation with a commander's eye. The Kholodians had chosen their ground well. The barricade was positioned at the narrowest point of the gorge, where the cliffs pressed close on either side. Any attempt to storm it would be suicide, a brutal slog through a hail of lead and steel that would cut us to pieces long before we reached the enemy lines.

And even if by some miracle we managed to break through, there was no guarantee of escape. The Kholodians had the high ground, with more men positioned on the terraces above. They could rain down fire on us from every angle, turning the gorge into a killing ground from which there would be no retreat.

For a long moment, I simply sat there, paralyzed by the enormity of our predicament. The weight of command had never felt so heavy, the lives of my men resting squarely on my shoulders. I had to find a way out, had to salvage something from this disastrous campaign. But what could I do, against such odds?

As if in answer to my desperate thoughts, a figure emerged from behind the Kholodian barricade. A tall, wolfman - wearing that noble, haughty uniform so familiar to me. I felt a shock of recognition run through me. It was Grand Prince Michaelovich.

He strutted in a short distance from our lines, his bearing regal and his expression inscrutable. For a long moment, he simply stood, surveying the ragged Valtorean column with an unreadable gaze. Then, slowly, he raised a hand in a gesture of parley.

I exchanged a glance with Miroslavios, my heart pounding in my chest. This was unexpected - as I waved him over, as I spurred my horse forward, Miroslavios following close behind as we approached the Grand Prince. As we drew near, I could see the lines of weariness etched on Michaelovich's face, the toll of the long campaign evident in the shadows beneath his eyes. But there was a warmth in his expression as he inclined his head in greeting, a flicker of something like respect in his gaze.

"Major Kaelitz," he said, his voice carrying across the short distance between us. "It seems fate has brought us together once more."

I reined in my mount, my own expression guarded as I studied the Kholodian nobleman. "Your Highness," I replied, my tone carefully neutral. "I must confess, I had not expected to find you here."

Michaelovich's smile was wry, tinged with a hint of irony. "Nor I, Major. When last we met, it was under rather different circumstances."

I felt a flush of shame at the memory of my captivity, of the long days spent in the prince's company as I recovered from my wounds. Michaelovich had been a gracious host, treating me with a respect that had left me deeply unsettled. It was hard to reconcile the man I had come to know with the enemy commander who now stood before me.

"Much has changed since then," I said, my voice rough with emotion. "For both of us."

Michaelovich nodded, his eyes shadowed. "Indeed it has, Major. The fortunes of war are ever-shifting, and it seems they have brought us to this pass."

He gestured to the barricade behind him, to the grim-faced Kholodian soldiers who watched our exchange with wary eyes. "I have no wish to see more bloodshed this day, Major. You and your men have fought bravely, but surely you must see that there is no path to victory here."

I felt a surge of anger at his words, my hand tightening on the reins. "We will not surrender, Your Highness. We will fight to the last man, if need be."

Michaelovich sighed, his expression pained. "I do not doubt your courage, Major. But consider the cost. Your men are exhausted, your supplies dwindling. And my father, the Tsar, rides hard behind you with an army that far surpasses your own."

I felt a chill run through me at the mention of the Tsar. I had heard tales of the man, of his ruthlessness and his implacable hatred for all things Valtorean. To fall into his hands would be a fate worse than death.

Michaelovich must have seen the flicker of fear in my eyes, for his expression softened. "I offer you a choice, Major. Surrender to me now, and I will see that you and your men are treated with honor. You have my word as a prince of Kholodia."

I stared at Michaelovich, my mind racing as I weighed his offer. The prospect of surrender galled me, every instinct rebelling against the thought of laying down our arms. We had come so far, had fought so hard to strike a blow against the Kholodians. To give up now felt like a betrayal of all we had sacrificed.

And yet, as I looked back at my men, at the exhaustion and despair etched on their faces, I knew that Michaelovich was right. We were at the end of our endurance, trapped and outnumbered with no hope of victory. To fight on would be to condemn them to a futile death, to spend their lives for nothing more than my own stubborn pride.

Slowly, feeling the weight of every eye upon me, I dismounted and walked forward to stand before Michaelovich. Up close, I could see the weariness in his face, the toll of the long campaign evident in the lines around his eyes. But there was no triumph in his expression, no gloating satisfaction at having cornered his foe.

Instead, there was a solemn gravity, a quiet respect for the gravity of the moment. He understood the magnitude of what he was asking, the shame and the anguish of the choice he had forced upon me.

But - my own familiarity with the Prince, gave me an idea. Bold. Audacious.

I met Michaelovich's gaze, my mind racing as a desperate, audacious plan took shape. Licking my dry lips, I leaned in close, my voice low and urgent. "Your Highness," I murmured, "I have a proposal that may yet salvage something from this disaster. A way to end this campaign without further bloodshed, and to secure a lasting peace between our nations."

Michaelovich's eyes narrowed, his expression guarded. "Speak plainly, Major. What is it you suggest?"

I glanced around, ensuring no one else was in earshot. "A mock battle," I whispered, my heart pounding. "We will stage a fight, a grand spectacle to satisfy honor on both sides. My men will make a show of resistance, then surrender at a prearranged signal. Your forces will be seen as victorious, their honor satisfied."

The prince frowned, his brow furrowed. "To what end, Major? Why should I agree to such a deception?"

I leaned in closer still, my voice barely audible over the pounding of my own heart. "Because during the chaos of the staged battle, my men will find the Tsar. And will assassinate him, leaving the throne to you."

Michaelovich recoiled as if struck, his eyes widening in shock. For a long moment he simply stared at me, his expression unreadable. Then, slowly, a glimmer of understanding dawned in his eyes, a flicker of cautious intrigue.

"You play a dangerous game, Major," he murmured, his gaze searching mine. "The risks are immense, for both of us. If we are discovered..."

"The risks are worth it," I insisted, my voice low and fervent. "Both of us gain something from this."

Michaelovich was silent for a long moment, his expression torn. I could see the wheels turning behind his eyes, the ruthless calculus of statecraft warring with his own sense of honor and duty. At last, he let out a slow breath, his shoulders sagging almost imperceptibly.

"If Catherine heard about this - she would kill me." he said softly. "But - you may have a point." Michaelovich looked around furtively, then gestured for me to follow him a short distance away from prying eyes and ears. When he spoke again, his voice was hushed, laden with a mix of weariness and grim resolve.

"You have placed me in a difficult position, Major Kaelitz. What you propose is nothing short of treason, a betrayal of my own father and sovereign." He sighed heavily, his gaze distant as if seeing something far beyond the confines of the gorge. "And yet, I cannot deny the truth of your words. This war has been a disaster for Kholodia, a slow bleeding of our strength and resources that threatens to undo all that we have built. Already, the Arkanthians are posturing to intervene, alongside the Arlenians."

He turned to face me, his expression haggard. "Your campaign has been a thorn in our side, a constant drain on our forces as we sought to hunt you down. The Tsar grows increasingly erratic, his decisions guided more by paranoia and pride than sound strategy. He sees enemies in every shadow, traitors in every council chamber. Even I, his own son, am not immune to his suspicions."

Michaelovich began to pace, his hands clasped tightly behind his back. "The war goes poorly on all fronts. In the west, the Valtoreans have pushed us back, reclaiming territory that we had thought securely under our control. The Tsar's insistence on focusing our efforts on your capture has left our flanks exposed, vulnerable to counterattack. Our supply lines are stretched thin, our men exhausted and demoralized."

He paused, his gaze meeting mine with a piercing intensity. "And now, with your forces trapped here, it seems the Tsar's obsession has finally borne fruit. He rides hard to meet us, determined to crush you personally and parade your broken army before the gates of Moskova as a trophy of his triumph."

The prince's lip curled in a bitter smile. "He does not realize that it is his own neck he places upon the block. The nobles grow restless, weary of this endless conflict and the toll it takes upon their lands and people. There are whispers of discontent in the capital, murmurings that perhaps it is time for a change of leadership."

Michaelovich stepped closer, his voice dropping to a whisper. "And that is why your proposal intrigues me, Major. If the Tsar were to fall here, in the midst of battle, slain by Valtorean blades... it would be seen as a tragedy, yes, but also an opportunity. A chance for new leadership, for a fresh start and an end to this ruinous war."

He held up a hand, forestalling my response. "But the risks are immense, as you say. If we are discovered, if any hint of this plot reaches the wrong ears... It will mean both our heads upon the block."

"Doubtless, my head is already bound for the block." I stated. "And so is Kholodia - if what you say is true."

"It is."

Michaelovich straightened, his voice firming with resolve. "Very well, Major Kaelitz. I accept your audacious proposal. We shall stage this mock battle and use the chaos to eliminate the Tsar. But we must plan this carefully. There can be no margin for error."

I nodded grimly. "Agreed, Your Highness. We will need to select a small group of my most trusted men to carry out the deed. The rest will engage your forces in a convincing show of defiance before surrendering at the signal."

The prince's eyes narrowed thoughtfully. "I will instruct my officers to focus their efforts on the flanks, leaving the center more lightly guarded. That should provide your marksmen the opening they need to reach the Tsar's position."

We spent the next several minutes in hushed discussion, ironing out the details of our desperate ploy. It was a precarious balancing act, choreographing a battle realistic enough to fool any onlookers while still ensuring the key players were positioned to strike at the critical moment.

At last, Michaelovich stepped back, his expression set. "It is decided then. We will commence the attack at dawn. May God have mercy on us all if we fail."

I bowed my head in acknowledgment, feeling the weight of destiny settling upon my shoulders. "Indeed, Your Highness. The fate of nations hinges upon the outcome of this gambit."

We parted ways, each of us returning to our respective camps to make our final preparations. As I rejoined my men, I caught Miroslavios's questioning gaze, seeing the unspoken concern in his eyes.

I shook my head minutely, unable to risk explaining the full scope of the plot aloud. Instead, I gathered my most trusted officers close, speaking to them in hushed tones as I outlined their roles in the coming battle.

To Miroslavios, I entrusted the vital task of leading the feigned assault on the Kholodian center, drawing their attention and leaving an opening for the assassins to exploit. He accepted the assignment with a solemn nod, comprehension dawning in his eyes as he grasped the true nature of our plan.

As the first light of dawn began to paint the eastern sky, I took my position at the head of the Valtorean lines. My heart pounded in my chest, adrenaline surging through my veins as I surveyed the arrayed Kholodian forces before us.

Men would doubtlessly die today - a mock battle had to have casualties, and the common rank and file were unaware of the intricate nature of it.

The first rays of dawn crept over the jagged peaks, casting a pale, ethereal light across the mist-shrouded gorge. The air was still and heavy with anticipation, the only sound the soft jingle of harness and the muffled crunch of boots on gravel as the men moved into position.

I sat astride my horse at the head of the Valtorean lines, my gaze fixed on the Kholodian barricades ahead. Beside me, Miroslavios was a statue of grim determination, his hand resting on the hilt of his saber. The men were arrayed behind us in ragged ranks, their faces drawn with exhaustion but their eyes alight with a desperate, feverish energy.

Across the gorge, I could see Michaelovich marshaling his own forces, the ordered ranks of Kholodian infantry and cavalry gleaming in the early light. There was a palpable tension in the air, a coiled anticipation as both sides prepared to unleash the fury of feigned battle.

I closed my eyes for a moment, my lips moving in a silent prayer. So much depended on the outcome of the next few minutes. The fate of nations, the lives of thousands, all balanced on the razor's edge of our desperate gambit. If we succeeded, it could mean an end to this ruinous war, a chance for a lasting peace between our peoples. But if we failed...

I pushed the thought aside, my jaw tightening with resolve. Failure was not an option. We would see this through, no matter the cost.

At a shouted command from Michaelovich, the Kholodian lines began to advance, their movements precise and disciplined. I raised my saber high, the steel flashing in the pale light as I called out to my own men. "For Valtorea! For the Emperor!"

A ragged cheer went up from the Valtorean ranks as they surged forward, Miroslavios leading the charge toward the Kholodian center. The crash of steel and the crack of muskets split the morning air as the two forces collided, men crying out in real and feigned agony as they fell.

I led my handpicked group of assassins in a wide arc, skirting the main melee and angling for the Kholodian rear where the Tsar's standard could be seen fluttering above a knot of richly-attired officers. My heart pounded in my ears, every fiber of my being focused on the moment at hand.

As we neared the Tsar's position, a line of elite Kholodian guardsmen moved to block our path, their eyes hard and their blades bared. I felt a thrill of fear, wondering if Michaelovich had betrayed us, if this was all some elaborate trap. But then the guardsmen parted, making a show of resistance but allowing us through to the Tsar himself, just as Michaelovich promised. The Tsar sat astride a magnificent black charger, his bearing regal and his expression one of haughty disdain as he surveyed the swirling melee before him. He was surrounded by a knot of advisors and generals, their faces taut with a mix of fear and anticipation as they watched the battle unfold.

I spurred my horse forward, my hand tightening on the reins as I closed the distance to the Tsar. Around me, my handpicked marksmen fanned out, their rifles at the ready as they prepared to strike.

As our small band of assassins broke through the Kholodian lines, the din of battle seemed to fade into the background, replaced by the pounding of my own heart in my ears. The Tsar's entourage was just ahead, a knot of richly-attired figures clustered around the imposing form of the monarch himself.

The Tsar himself was an imposing figure, tall and broad-shouldered, black fur wearing a a resplendent uniform of white and gold, his chest adorned with a dazzling array of medals and decorations that sparkled in the sun. Atop his head rested a fur-trimmed hat, a golden double eagle perched proudly on its front.

As we drew closer, I could see the Tsar's face more clearly. His features were stern and regal, with high, sharp cheekbones and piercing blue eyes that seemed to bore right through me. His expression was one of haughty disdain as he surveyed the churning melee before him, as if the desperate struggle was little more than a mildly diverting spectacle for his amusement.

Around the Tsar, his entourage was a glittering throng of advisors, generals, and courtiers of the Vuk'ish race. They were clad in a rainbow of rich fabrics - silks, velvets, and furs in every hue imaginable. Gold and silver thread glinted on their uniforms, and precious gems sparkled on their fingers and at their throats. They formed a protective cordon around their sovereign, their eyes watchful and their hands never far from the jeweled hilts of their swords and daggers.

I glanced to either side, catching the eyes of my chosen marksmen. They were hard, grizzled veterans all, hand-picked for their skill and their unwavering loyalty. Their faces were grim and set, their jaws clenched tight with determination. They knew the stakes, knew that the fate of nations rested on the next few moments as they lined up a shot, the world held its breath, the very air seeming to vibrate with tension.

The crack of the rifles split the air like a thunderclap, a volley of shots ringing out in perfect unison. The Tsar jerked in his saddle, a look of shocked surprise flashing across his aristocratic features. A bloom of crimson blossomed on his chest, spreading rapidly across the white fabric of his uniform.

For a heartbeat, the world seemed frozen, the Tsar swaying slightly as if in a gentle breeze. Then, slowly, ponderously, he toppled to the ground crumpling to the ground in a tangle of limbs and billowing cloak.

Pandemonium erupted around us. The Tsar's entourage surged forward with shouts of alarm and anguish, fumbling for their weapons, unsure whether to attack or defend. The Kholodian lines wavered, dumbfounded by the sudden fall of their sovereign.

Seizing the moment of confusion, I spurred my horse forward, my marksmen close on my heels. We thundered through the disarrayed

Kholodian lines, taking advantage of the chaos to make good our escape. Behind us, I heard Miroslavios bellowing orders, rallying our main force into a fighting withdrawal now that our true purpose was accomplished.

As we galloped clear of the melee, I risked a glance over my shoulder. The Kholodian forces were in disarray, milling about in confusion, leaderless and stunned by the assassins' lethal handiwork. In their midst, I could see the still, sprawled form of the Tsar, a spreading pool of crimson staining the ground beneath his body.

A fierce, exultant joy surged through my veins, mingled with an overwhelming sense of relief. Against all odds, our desperate gambit had succeeded. The Tsar was dead, struck down by Valtorean bullets in the midst of battle. The course of the war, of history itself, had been irrevocably altered.

As we raced to rejoin the main body of our forces, my thoughts whirled with the implications of what we had done. Michaelovich would now ascend the throne, his path to power cleared by our actions. He had sworn to end the war, to forge a lasting peace between our nations - but only time would tell if he would keep his word. For now - the only avenue for us was to escape, and to perhaps surrender, should the opportunity present itself.

The Valtorean army rode hard through the narrow defile of the Zaroska Gorge, a battered serpent of exhausted men and lathered horses winding its way through the twisting rocky passage. Behind us, the towering cliffs seemed to press in from either side, their jagged heights lost in wreaths of swirling mist. The only sounds were the clatter of hooves on stone, the jingle of harness, and the labored breathing of the straining beasts.

I rode at the head of the column, my eyes fixed grimly ahead as I scanned the path for any sign of pursuit. The success of our desperate gambit had bought us a reprieve, but I knew it would be a temporary one at best. Once the Kholodians recovered from the shock of the Tsar's assassination, they would be after us with a vengeance.

Beside me, Miroslavios's face was drawn and haggard, the toll of the last weeks etched deep in the lines around his eyes. His once-immaculate uniform was stained and tattered, the gold braid tarnished and the fabric rent by sword cuts and musket balls. But his eyes still burned with the same fierce determination that had sustained us through the long campaign.

As we left the confines of the gorge and emerged onto the windswept expanse of the Valtorean plains, the true extent of our losses became grimly apparent. Where once we had been a proud army of thousands, now barely a thousand ragged survivors remained. The rest lay scattered across the length and breadth of Kholodia, their bones moldering in unmarked graves or picked clean by the carrion birds.

Those who remained were a sorry sight indeed. Men slumped wearily in their saddles, their faces gaunt and their eyes hollow with exhaustion. Horses stumbled on, their heads hanging low, the whites of their eyes showing as they were pushed beyond the limits of their endurance. The wounded rode or were carried by their comrades, their injuries bound up with dirty rags and their faces grey with pain and blood loss.

But even in our battered state, a fierce pride burned in every heart. We had done the impossible, had struck a blow against the Kholodian war machine that would be felt for generations to come. The Tsar was dead, and with him the driving force behind the invasion of our homeland. There would be a reckoning, we knew, a price to pay for our audacity. But for now, in this moment, we had achieved a victory beyond our wildest imaginings.

As the miles fell away beneath our horses' hooves, a strange thing happened. The expected pursuit never materialized. The horizon behind us remained empty, devoid of the dust clouds that would herald the approach of Kholodian cavalry. It was as if the enemy had simply lost our scent, had given up the chase before it had even begun.

A wild, desperate hope began to kindle in my breast. Could it be that Michaelovich had kept his word? That he had called off the pursuit, content to let us limp back to Valtorean lines unmolested? It seemed too much to hope for, a mercy unlooked for from an enemy who had every reason to want us dead.

And yet, as the hours turned into days and still no Kholodian forces appeared on our tail, that fragile hope began to blossom into something more substantial. Miroslavios rode up alongside me, his brow furrowed in puzzlement.

"I don't understand it," he muttered, his gaze flicking back over his shoulder for the hundredth time. "By all rights, they should be harrying us every step of the way. We assassinated their Tsar, for God's sake. Why let us go?"

I shook my head slowly, hardly daring to give voice to the thoughts that churned in my mind. "Michaelovich," I said softly. "It has to be. He's letting us escape."

Miroslavios shot me a sharp look, his eyes widening in surprise. "What do you mean? What did you and the prince discuss before the battle?"

I hesitated, weighing my words carefully. I had kept the full extent of my bargain with Michaelovich a secret, knowing the risk it posed if the wrong ears heard of it. But Miroslavios deserved to know - he was one of the few men I knew I could count on absolutely. If anyone deserved the truth, it was him.

"We made a deal," I said at last, my voice low and intense. "Michaelovich agreed to let us go, to give us safe passage back to Valtorean territory. In exchange..." I trailed off, the enormity of what I had done still scarcely believable, even to myself.

"In exchange for what?" Miroslavios prompted, his voice edged with a sudden wariness.

I met his gaze squarely, my jaw set. "In exchange for arranging the Tsar's death. Michaelovich wanted his father out of the way, wanted a clear path to the throne. He knew we had the capability to make it happen, right there on the battlefield. So we struck a bargain."

Miroslavios recoiled as if struck, his face draining of color. For a long moment he simply stared at me, his expression a mask of shock and disbelief. Then, slowly, a look of understanding dawned in his eyes, tinged with a reluctant admiration.

"My God, Kaelitz," he breathed. "You magnificent bastard. You played both sides and came out on top. I don't know whether to congratulate you or call you a dirty, rotten bastard."

A wry smile tugged at the corner of my mouth. "Let's wait until we make it back to Rega. We need a drink. Hopefully - Von Olstenstross didn't take all the credit."

Miroslavios chuckled darkly. "Oh, I have no doubt the good Colonel is already regaling the Emperor with tales of how he planned the whole damned thing. But the men know the truth. They know who led them through the fire and the blood, who brought them out the other side against all odds."

I grimaced, the thought of Von Olstenstross's self-aggrandizement leaving a sour taste in my mouth. The man was a glory hound of the worst sort, always ready to claim credit for the deeds of others. But Miroslavios was right - in the end, it was the respect of the men that mattered most. They would remember who had stood with them in their darkest hour.

As we rode on, the cold, rolling grasslands of the Baltiva opened up before us, the distant spires of Rega shimmering on the horizon like a mirage. The sight of the capital filled me with a profound sense of relief and homecoming, even as a new kind of dread began to gnaw at my gut.

What awaited us?

A Long-Awaited Peace

As the battered remnants of the Valtorean army approached the towering walls of Rega, a sense of trepidation and exhaustion hung heavy in the air. The men were bone-weary, their uniforms stained with the grime of the long march and the blood of fallen comrades. Horses plodded forward with heaving flanks and foam-flecked muzzles, their riders swaying in the saddles with the last vestiges of their strength.

Yet beneath the fatigue, a current of excitement thrummed through the ranks. They had achieved the impossible, had struck a blow against the Kholodian juggernaut that would echo through the ages. The assassination of the Tsar himself, carried out under the very noses of his elite guards, was a feat that would be celebrated in song and story for generations to come.

As the column wound its way through the outer districts of the city, the streets began to fill with cheering crowds. Word of their exploits had spread like wildfire, and the citizens of Rega turned out en masse to welcome their returning heroes. Flowers rained down from balconies, and children darted out to press sweets and small tokens into the hands of the grinning soldiers.

I rode at the head of the procession, Miroslavios at my side, our battle-stained uniforms a stark contrast to the bright finery of the city folk. The weight of command sat heavy on my shoulders, even as a fierce pride burned in my breast. These were my men, the ones who had followed me into the jaws of hell and back again. Their loyalty, their sacrifice, was a bond forged in blood and fire.

As we approached the towering gates of the castle, the crowds grew thicker, the cheers louder. The Imperial Palatine Guard, resplendent in their polished armor and crimson cloaks, snapped to attention as we passed, their eyes wide with awe and respect.

We dismounted in the great courtyard, stable hands rushing forward to take the reins of our exhausted mounts. Servants in livery bowed and scraped, ushering us towards the grand entrance with murmured words of welcome and congratulation.

As we strode into the vaulted halls of the old familiar castle that served as the headquarters for Valtorean high command, our footsteps echoed off the stone floors and ornate tapestries fluttered gently in the breeze from the high, arched windows. The air was filled with the scent of beeswax candles and the faint, lingering aroma of incense from the Imperial chapel.

Miroslavios and I made our way through the labyrinthine corridors, past saluting guards and bowing courtiers, towards the great double doors of the Emperor's audience chamber. My heart pounded in my chest as we approached, the magnitude of the moment hitting me like a thunderbolt. We were about to stand before Emperor Wolfgang himself, to report on a campaign that had achieved the unthinkable.

The doors swung open with a groan of heavy oak and iron hinges, revealing the opulent splendor of the audience chamber beyond. The vaulted ceiling soared overhead, supported by massive columns of veined marble. The walls were hung with rich tapestries depicting the great victories and heroes of Valtorean history, the colors still vivid despite the passage of centuries.

At the far end of the chamber, atop a raised dais, sat the Emperor himself. Wolfgang was an imposing figure, tall and broad-shouldered, with a neatly trimmed goatee. He wore robes of deepest purple, trimmed with ermine and hung with glittering chains of office. A heavy golden crown rested upon his brow, the light of the chandeliers glinting off the precious stones set into its surface.

As we approached the throne, I could feel the eyes of the assembled court upon us. Generals and admirals, resplendent in their dress uniforms, stood stiffly at attention, their faces a mix of curiosity, envy, and barely concealed annoyance. They were men who had spent their lives in service to the Empire, who had fought and bled on a hundred battlefields, and yet it was we, the ragged survivors of a desperate gambit, who were being hailed as heroes.

We reached the foot of the dais and sank to one knee, bowing our heads in obeisance. For a long moment, there was silence, broken only by the soft rustling of silken robes and the occasional cough or shuffle of feet.

Then, Emperor Wolfgang spoke, his voice rich and resonant, filling the chamber effortlessly. "Rise, Major Kaelitz, Major Miroslavios. You have done well, and brought great honor to yourselves and to the Empire."

We rose to our feet, meeting the Emperor's gaze with a mix of pride and humility. Up close, Wolfgang's features were lined with the cares of state, but his eyes were keen and piercing, missing nothing.

"Your Majesty," I began, my voice sounding thin and reedy to my own ears, as I awaited his response.

Emperor Wolfgang leaned forward on his throne, his eyes glinting with a mix of amusement and admiration as he appraised us. A faint smile played about his lips, softening the regal lines of his face.

"Major Kaelitz," he said, his voice warm and resonant. "Your exploits have reached our ears, even here in the heart of the Empire. The audacious counter-invasion, the daring scorched earth campaign - and the death of Tzar Nichovich I... It is a feat that will be remembered for generations to come."

A murmur rippled through the assembled courtiers, a mixture of awe and disbelief. I could feel the weight of their gazes upon me, some admiring, others envious or openly hostile. But I kept my eyes fixed on the Emperor, my spine straight and my chin held high.

"It was a desperate gambit, Your Majesty," I said, my voice steady despite the pounding of my heart. "One born of necessity, in the face of overwhelming odds. But it succeeded beyond our wildest dreams. The Kholodian invasion has been thrown into disarray, their leadership decapitated in a single stroke."

Wolfgang nodded slowly, his expression thoughtful. "Indeed. And in the wake of this great victory, a most unexpected development has occurred." He paused, letting the anticipation build before continuing. "Grand Prince Michaelovich, now Tsar Michaelovich I, has reached out to us through diplomatic channels. He wishes to open peace talks, to bring an end to this long and bloody conflict. To draw up permanent lines, separating the territories."

The chamber erupted into a cacophony of gasps and exclamations, nobles and generals alike gaping in shock at this stunning revelation. I myself felt a surge of disbelief and wild, desperate hope. Peace. After so many years of war, of sacrifice and suffering, could it truly be within reach?

The Emperor raised a hand, and the tumult gradually subsided. "It seems your actions have had consequences far beyond the battlefield, Major Kaelitz. In striking down the old Tsar, you have paved the way for a new era of peace and cooperation between our nations."

He rose to his feet, his robes rustling softly as he descended the steps of the dais. The court held its collective breath as he approached me, his eyes boring into mine with an intensity that made me want to look away. But I held his gaze, my heart hammering in my chest.

"For your service to the Empire, for the bravery and cunning you have displayed in the face of our enemies, I hereby restore to you the noble title of your forefathers," Wolfgang declared, his voice ringing out through the chamber. "Rise, Lord Kaelitz von Ardent, hero of the Valtorean Empire!"

A stunned silence greeted his words, followed by a rising tide of murmurs and whispers. I could feel the eyes of the court upon me, some filled with admiration, others with barely concealed rage. I knelt before the Emperor, my head bowed, scarcely able to believe what I had just heard. Lord Kaelitz von Ardent. The name echoed in my mind, a title I had never thought to hold again. My family's noble status had been stripped away months ago, lost in the mists of time and the vicissitudes of politics. To have it restored now, in front of the assembled might of the Valtorean court, was an honor beyond my wildest imaginings.

As I rose to my feet, Emperor Wolfgang laid a hand on my shoulder, his grip firm and reassuring. "But that is not all," he said, his voice ringing with a new note of solemnity. "For a deed such as yours, a simple restoration of rank is hardly sufficient recompense."

He turned to one of his attendants, who approached bearing a small, ornate casket of polished ebony and gold. With reverent hands, the Emperor opened the box, revealing what lay within. There, nestled on a bed of rich purple velvet, was a glittering starburst of gold and diamonds, a medal of such exquisite craftsmanship that it seemed to capture and reflect the very light of the chandeliers above.

"The Order of the Holy Eagle," Wolfgang intoned, lifting the medal from its resting place. "The highest honor that the Valtorean Empire can bestow upon one of its own. Only a handful have ever been awarded in all the long centuries of our history."

He turned back to me, his eyes shining with a fierce pride. "But you, Lord Kaelitz, have earned this distinction a hundredfold. You have shown valor beyond measure, have sacrificed all in the service of your Emperor and your homeland. You have brought low the mightiest of our foes and turned the tide of this war with a single, devastating stroke."

The medal glittered in his hands as he raised it high, the gold seeming to blaze with an inner fire. The diamonds caught the light and scattered it in a dazzling array, each facet a tiny, perfect star. The craftsmanship was exquisite, the details so fine and intricate that they seemed almost alive. The eagle at the center of the starburst was rendered in stunning detail, its wings spread wide and its beak open in a silent cry of triumph.

"Kneel," the Emperor commanded, his voice resonant with the weight of ancient tradition.

I sank to one knee, my heart pounding in my chest as Wolfgang lowered the medal over my head. The ribbon settled around my neck, the weight of the gold and jewels resting comfortably against my chest. It felt like a tangible manifestation of the honor and glory that had been bestowed upon me, a physical reminder of all that I had achieved and all that I had sacrificed.

"The Order of the Holy Eagle," Wolfgang intoned, his voice resonant with the weight of tradition. "The highest honor that can be bestowed upon a soldier of the Empire. It is given only to those who have displayed the utmost valor, the most selfless devotion to duty."

As I rose to my feet, the medal of the Order of the Holy Eagle glittering proudly upon my chest, I felt a swell of emotions too profound for words. Pride, certainly, in what I and my men had accomplished against all odds. Relief, that our desperate gambit had not only succeeded, but paved the way for a potential end to this long and terrible war. Gratitude, to the Emperor for recognizing our sacrifices and bestowing such high honors. But there was sorrow too, a deep and aching grief for all those we had lost along the way, for the friends and comrades who would never return home to share in this triumph.

I glanced to my side, to where Miroslavios stood tall and proud. He met my gaze, and in that moment, an understanding passed between us, a shared acknowledgment of all we had endured together, and all that was still to come.

Emperor Wolfgang's voice drew me back to the present, his tone warm with affection and respect. "Rise, Lord Marshal of the Eastern Forces, Kaelitz," he said, the new rank rolling off his tongue with an air of finality. "For that is what you are now, by my decree, in these pacified lands."

I bowed my head, scarcely able to believe what I was hearing. Lord Marshal of the Eastern Valtorean Armies. It was a position of immense responsibility, of trust and authority second only to the Emperor himself. To be granted such a role, after all that had happened, was a testament to the faith that Wolfgang placed in me, and the magnitude of what we had achieved.

As I straightened, my eyes roamed over the assembled court, taking in the sea of faces. Most wore expressions of shock, others of envy or calculation. I knew that not all would be pleased by my sudden elevation, that there would be those who sought to undermine or challenge my authority.

But I felt satisfied, grateful. Many emotions ran through me as I smiled for what felt like the first time in months.

The hot water enveloped me like a comforting embrace, the scent of lavender and rosemary rising from the steam. I sank deeper into the ornate copper tub, feeling the weeks of grime, sweat and tension slowly melting away. It was the first proper bath I'd had in months, a luxury almost forgotten amidst the ceaseless campaigning and brutal guerrilla warfare in the Kholodian hinterlands.

My new quarters in the castle were a world away from the rough camps and battlefields I had grown accustomed to. The study was a spacious room, paneled in rich, dark wood and lined with bookshelves that reached to the high, vaulted ceiling. A grand fireplace dominated one wall, the elaborately carved mantelpiece depicting scenes of Valtorean military triumphs. Plush armchairs upholstered in deep burgundy velvet were arranged before the hearth, inviting rest and contemplation.

I let my eyes roam over the room, taking in the small details that spoke of comfort and refinement. The heavy drapes were pulled back, letting in the warm afternoon sunlight that dappled the polished floorboards. A crystal decanter of amber liquid sat on a silver tray, accompanied by a set of cut-glass tumblers. Atop the large, ornately carved desk, a vase of fresh flowers added a splash of vibrant color - crimson roses, sunset-hued dahlias, and delicate sprays of lavender.

It all felt surreal like a dream from which I might awaken at any moment to find myself once again huddled in a rain-soaked trench or crouched over a meager campfire. The events of the past hours - the Emperor's proclamations, the restoration of my noble title, the bestowal of the Holy Eagle - seemed too momentous, too overwhelming to comprehend fully.

I lifted my hand from the scented water, watching the droplets trickle down my skin, following the lines of faded scars and fresh calluses. The hands of a soldier, a killer - now adorned with a signet ring bearing the crest of House Kaelitz, the gold glinting softly in the muted light.

Abruptly, a sharp rap at the door jolted me from my reverie. I sat up straighter, sloshing water over the sides of the tub in my haste. "A moment!" I called out, reaching for a towel to preserve some modicum of modesty.

"No need to rush on my account, Lord Marshal," came the reply, the voice instantly recognizable. My eyes widened as I realized who was standing outside.

Emperor Wolfgang himself.

I stood, wrapping the towel around my waist and hastily donning a silk dressing gown that had been left out for me. With a deep breath to compose myself, I strode to the door and pulled it open, dropping into a low bow as he entered, sitting down on a chair.

"Kaelitz. Or rather - Lord Kaelitz." He smirked. Emperor Wolfgang strode into the room, his bearing regal and his expression inscrutable. He was dressed more simply now, the ornate robes of state replaced by a doublet of fine black wool, embroidered with the Imperial crest in silver thread. Yet even in this more casual attire, he exuded an aura of power and authority that filled the space.

I remained bowing, acutely aware of my state of relative undress and the informality of the situation. "Your Majesty," I said, my voice sounding oddly breathless to my own ears. "Forgive me, I was not expecting-"

Wolfgang waved a dismissive hand, his eyes glinting with amusement. "Please, Kaelitz, we are beyond such formalities in private. After all, it is I who have intruded upon your well-deserved respite."

He moved to the armchairs by the hearth, settling himself with an air of relaxed comfort that belied the tension I could sense thrumming beneath the surface. He gestured for me to take the opposite seat, and I complied, perching on the edge of the plush velvet cushion.

For a long moment, the Emperor simply regarded me, his fingers steepled beneath his chin. The firelight played across his features, casting his face into alternating planes of light and shadow. When he finally spoke, his voice was low and measured, weighted with a gravity that sent a shiver down my spine.

"What do you know of politics, Lord Kaelitz?" he asked, his eyes boring into mine with an intensity that made me want to look away. "Not the maneuverings of generals and field marshals, but the delicate dance of power and influence that takes place in the halls of the Imperial Court in Vien?"

I hesitated, choosing my words with care. "I confess, Your Majesty, that my understanding of such matters is limited. As a soldier, my world has been one of battles and strategy, not the intrigues of courtiers and diplomats."

Wolfgang nodded, a faint smile playing about his lips. "As it should be. A military man's first duty is to his troops and his mission. But as Lord Marshal, you will find yourself straddling both worlds - the brutal, straightforward realm of warfare, and the far more treacherous landscape of imperial politics."

He leaned back in his chair, his gaze turning distant and thoughtful. "I have ruled this Empire for two years now, Lord Kaelitz. In that time, I have sought to strengthen the throne, to centralize power and authority in the hands of the monarch. But there are many who oppose this vision, who seek a return to the old ways of feudal autonomy and noble privilege."

I nodded slowly, beginning to see where this conversation was heading.

Emperor Wolfgang leaned forward, his eyes glinting with a mixture of calculation and something almost akin to desperation. His voice dropped to a low, urgent whisper as he spoke, the words pouring forth in a torrent of pent-up frustration and palpable need.

"You must understand, Kaelitz, the precarious nature of my position. When I ascended to the throne after my father's untimely death, I inherited an Empire fractured and weakened by years of misrule and petty squabbling among the nobility. The great houses, each jealously guarding their own privileges and powers, looked upon the Imperial throne as little more than a figurehead, a puppet to dance to their discordant tunes."

He rose abruptly, pacing before the hearth with agitated energy. The flickering firelight cast his shadow large and distorted against the paneled walls, a looming specter of the burdens he carried.

"I saw the rot at the heart of our realm, the slow decay that threatened to crumble the very foundations of Valtorean power. The nobles, secure in their ancient rights and bloated with the spoils of their lands, cared nothing for the greater good of the Empire. They hoarded their wealth, raised their own armies, and plotted endlessly against one another in a ceaseless game of dominance and control."

Wolfgang paused, his shoulders sagging as if under a great weight. When he turned to face me once more, his expression was haggard, the mask of Imperial composure slipping to reveal the man beneath, beset by cares and weighed down by the chains of his station.

"I determined to change this, to drag Valtorea kicking and screaming into a new era of centralized authority and absolute monarchy. The nobles would be brought to heel, their powers curtailed and their loyalty bound unequivocally to the throne. Only then could we hope to stand against the myriad threats that assail us from all sides - the Kholodian wolf, the Arkanthian dragon, the Arlenian fox."

He sank back into his chair, his gaze boring into mine with fierce intensity. "But such sweeping changes cannot be made without resistance, without a bitter struggle against those who stand to lose the most. Already, the great houses murmur and conspire, seeing in my reforms a mortal threat to their ancient prerogatives. They whisper of tyranny, of overreach, even as they plot to unseat me and return Valtorea to the chaos of a weak and fractured realm."

The Emperor leaned forward, his hand coming to rest on my knee with a grip that was almost painful in its urgency. "This is where you come in, my young Lord Marshal. Your victory against the Kholodians, your daring and audacity in striking down the Tsar himself - this is what this Empire needs."

Emperor Wolfgang's grip tightened on my knee, his eyes blazing with a fervor that was at once inspiring and unnerving. "You are a hero of the people now, Lord Kaelitz. A symbol of Valtorean strength and resilience in the face of our gravest peril. The common folk cheer your name in the streets, while the soldiers would follow you into the very jaws of hell itself."

He leaned back, his hand falling away as he fixed me with a gaze that seemed to strip away all pretense and lay bare the very heart of his intent. "I need that loyalty, that unshakable devotion, in service not just to the Empire, but to the Imperial throne itself. To me."

I swallowed hard, the true weight of what he was asking settling like a leaden mantle upon my shoulders. "You wish me to be your agent, Your Majesty?" I asked, my voice sounding thin and strained to my own ears. "To wield my influence and authority in support of your policies, even against the wishes of the nobility?"

"More than that," Wolfgang replied, his tone at once silken and unyielding as tempered steel. "I need you to be my sword and my shield, Lord Marshal. To stand as a bulwark against all those who would seek to undermine the rightful power of the Emperor. Whether they be foreign foes or homegrown traitors, I must know that I can count on you utterly, without reservation or hesitation."

I felt a cold trickle of sweat snake down my spine, a physical manifestation of the trepidation and excitement warring within me. To be so singled out by the Emperor himself, to be granted such trust and such a burden... it was at once exhilarating and terrifying.

The implications of what he was proposing were staggering, the potential for both glory and ruin limitless. To become the Emperor's right hand, his most trusted and feared servant... it was a position of unparalleled power and influence. But it was also a double-edged sword, fraught with peril at every turn.

If I accepted this charge, I would be binding myself irrevocably to Wolfgang's fate, for good or ill. My every action, my every word, would be scrutinized and judged by a court already rife with intrigue and suspicion. The slightest misstep, the merest hint of disloyalty or incompetence, could spell disaster not just for me, but for the Emperor himself.

And yet... how could I refuse? To be offered such trust, such a chance to shape the very course of history itself? It was a heady draught indeed, a siren song that called to the deepest wells of my ambition and my sense of duty.

I met Wolfgang's gaze squarely, my jaw tightening with resolve. "I am yours, Your Majesty," I said, the words ringing with solemn finalness.

Emperor Wolfgang nodded, a slow smile spreading across his face as he rose to his feet. "Then rise, Lord Marshal Kaelitz," he intoned, his voice ringing with solemn formality. "And take your place at my side, as the sword and shield of the Valtorean Empire."

I stood, feeling the weight of my new role settling upon me like a mantle of iron and gold. The Emperor clasped my forearm in a warrior's grip, his eyes shining with a fierce pride and an unwavering resolve. In that moment, I felt the full force of his charisma, the sheer magnetism of his presence that had allowed him to seize and hold the reins of an empire.

Together, we strode from my chambers, out into the vaulted halls of the old venerable Regian castle. Courtiers and servants alike bowed and scraped as we passed, their eyes wide with awe and trepidation. Word of my elevation had already begun to spread, carried on the swift wings of rumor and gossip.

As we walked, Wolfgang spoke in low, urgent tones, outlining the first steps of the great work that lay ahead. There were allies to be gathered, loyal nobles and military commanders who could be counted on to support the Emperor's vision. There were rivals to be watched and neutralized, slippery courtiers and ambitious lords who would seek to undermine us at every turn.

But most importantly, there was an empire to be forged anew, a realm of unparalleled strength and unity rising from the ashes of the old order. It would be a Valtorea reborn, a nation tempered in the fires of adversity and honed to a cutting edge by the will of its Emperor and his faithful Lord Marshal. A new national identity.

I could not have been more thrilled - and more terrified, than the task that laid before us.

Check out my next book, **Wars of the Betrayer! And don't forget to review this book if you enjoyed it!**
For more books, subscribe to my Amazon home page.

Don't miss out!

Visit the website below and you can sign up to receive emails whenever Michael Calloway publishes a new book. There's no charge and no obligation.

https://books2read.com/r/B-A-UWZNB-TWGMD

BOOKS 2 READ

Connecting independent readers to independent writers.

Did you love *Blade of the Betrayer*? Then you should read *Fusiliers of the Betrayer*[1] by Michael Calloway!

Julien Armand knows what it means to lose everything.

A young man who watched the Great Terror strike through Eclairea, Julien stood powerless as revolutionaries executed his family and tore apart the world he once knew. The ideals of liberty and equality, which once promised hope, became a façade for envy and greed. The Republic that rose from the ashes of monarchy now trembles under its own weight, its leaders as corrupt and power-hungry as the nobles they overthrew.

Amidst this turmoil rises General Lucien Beaumont, a man of vision, ambition, and ruthless pragmatism. Once a mere soldier, Beaumont has swept across Eclairea, uniting fractured factions and promising to restore order to the Republic. To many, he is a savior, a self-declared Emperor who will bring stability to a land broken by revolution. To others, he is merely another tyrant cloaked in the rhetoric of liberty.

---

1. https://books2read.com/u/bwxK19

2. https://books2read.com/u/bwxK19

Set between Blade of the Betrayer and Wars of the Betrayer, Fusiliers of the Betrayer is a gripping tale of revolution, war, and forbidden love. Julien's journey through a crumbling Republic and into the resurgent Eclairean Empire pits him against his deepest fears, his darkest desires, and the seductive allure of Beaumont's vision for a new Eclairea. As the lines between savior and tyrant blur, Julien must choose between his duty, and his heart.

Also by Michael Calloway

Shadow of the Betrayer
Blade of the Betrayer
Fusiliers of the Betrayer
Wars of the Betrayer
The Betrayer Chronicles

Standalone
White Against Red

www.ingramcontent.com/pod-product-compliance
Lightning Source LLC
Chambersburg PA
CBHW030347020726
47493CB00003B/726